Praise for C. T. Adams and Cathy Clamp

"I read the book in one sitting. I look forward to the next book in the series, because it has to be the beginning of a series. A world this enjoyable deserves more than one visit. This book has some new twists in the werewolf's tail that are very cool."

—Laurell K. Hamilton on *Hunter's Moon*

"This outstanding duo is unbeatable! Besides captivating plots, it is the rich, dark characterizations that make these books distinctive and mesmerizing. True genre luminaries!"

—*Romantic Times BOOKreviews*

"Adams and Clamp are adept at incorporating riveting plot twists into this fully imagined world, and they don't stint on the romance."

—*Booklist* on *Touch of Evil* (starred review)

"*Touch of Evil* receives The Road to Romance Reviewer's Choice Award for the great writing of the author duo, C. T. Adams and Cathy Clamp. This book has it all and more. Readers don't want to miss this perfect example of fantastically vivid paranormal fiction."

—*The Road to Romance* on *Touch of Evil*

TOR PARANORMAL ROMANCE BOOKS BY
C. T. ADAMS AND CATHY CLAMP

THE SAZI
Hunter's Moon
Moon's Web
Captive Moon
Howling Moon
Moon's Fury
Timeless Moon

THE THRALL
Touch of Evil
Touch of Madness
Touch of Darkness*

*Forthcoming

Timeless Moon

C. T. ADAMS
and CATHY CLAMP

tor paranormal romance

A TOM DOHERTY ASSOCIATES BOOK
NEW YORK

This is a work of fiction. All of the characters, organizations, and events portrayed in this novel are either products of the authors' imagination or are used fictitiously.

TIMELESS MOON

Copyright © 2008 by C. T. Adams and Cathy Clamp

Edited by Anna Genoese

A Tor Book
Published by Tom Doherty Associates, LLC
175 Fifth Avenue
New York, NY 10010

www.tor.com

Tor® is a registered trademark of Tom Doherty Associates, LLC.

ISBN-13: 978-0-7653-5665-9
ISBN-10: 0-7653-5665-1

First Edition: March 2008

Printed in the United States of America

0 9 8 7 6 5 4 3 2 1

DEDICATION and ACKNOWLEDGMENTS

As always, this book is first and foremost dedicated to Don Clamp and James Adams for all the loving support and understanding they've given during good times and bad. Then, with immense gratitude to our families, friends, and the amazing professionals we have the pleasure of working with: we would like to acknowledge our brilliant agent, Merrilee Heifetz, and her able assistant, Claire Reilly-Shapiro, both of Writers House, Anna Genoese at Tor, and all of the other amazing people who help turn a manuscript into a *book*. You're the best, and we're grateful.

AUTHORS' NOTES

To the best of our knowledge neither Grodin nor Pony, New Mexico, exist. Rather than set the action in an existing city we chose to create the locations from scratch so that we could bend the cities to our will. (Insert evil cackle.) It seemed simpler and better than using actual places and significantly altering the landscape. Where actual cities and locations were used we took extensive liberties. This is particularly true of Atlanta/Hartsfield International Airport and Daytona Beach International Airport which have probably been rendered completely unrecognizable.

Bubba's bar does not exist in Denver. The location where Bubba's is listed is the home of a very nice chain drugstore.

Timeless Moon

Chapter One

JOSETTE MONIER STOOD motionless in the faint moonlight beneath the spreading limbs of an ancient hickory. It was spring in Arizona, and the field smelled of moist earth and fresh new growth. But even at night there should be sounds—the fluttering of birds in the trees, or mice moving through the thick tufts of grass. Instead, there was nothing but the rustling of tiny new leaves. The small animals were utterly still and she knew why. They were hoping that remaining quiet would keep them from drawing the attention of the killer in their midst.

It was not *her* they feared right now, although she was frequently a danger to them. No, something else had made them afraid. Josette turned her head, straining as hard as she could to catch any hint of the other predator hunting this night.

There, she heard it. There was no mistaking the soft rasp of scales moving across stone. She was in human form, but her senses were no less keen. Tilting her head back she sniffed the breeze. Even over the scents of soil and wildflowers she could smell the musty, acrid bitterness that was a venomous snake. But this was not just any snake—certainly not one of the native rattlesnakes that made their home in the area. No, there was a subtle difference to the smell that told her this reptile could claim more than one form. He was a shapeshifter like her and probably a Sazi.

It seemed odd that she hadn't known ahead of time she would be attacked out here. Usually, her psychic gifts gave her plenty of warning of such things.

Maybe I've become just as arrogant as my attackers, thinking my visions will tell me everything I need to know. Stupid pride. She was lucky it hadn't gotten her killed before now.

Soft and silent she moved across the sand, deliberately leaving human footprints until she reached a small rock outcropping, where she started removing her clothing.

It would be nice if I could just burn them off with magic like normal, but I can't afford for him to catch the scent of the smoke. She shifted form until, with a whisper of motion, she became a bobcat. She could fight a snake in either form, but it was easier with teeth and claws, and her feline shape was easier to camouflage in the night. Let him look for the human on the other side of the rock. He would find another predator instead.

Moving with graceful economy, she used her claws to climb into the wide lower branches of the tree. She lay in the shadows, nearly undetected from the ground below—even to the cautious tongue of a snake—and planned her attack. A viper was a real threat, because while it took lethal damage to both head and heart to kill an alpha shapeshifter, the venom of most Sazi snakes was potent enough to do just that.

Silvered grass shifted with a rustle of sound below. She felt her pupils widen to pull in light from the moon and watched to see if she could spot the sort of snake she was dealing with. Not that she really needed the light . . . she was a cat, after all. Her night vision was excellent. But the fact that he was in snake form told her he was also an alpha, capable of changing at will using just his own personal magic. And all of the alpha snakes she'd encountered had their own peculiar ways of fighting, depending on the species.

Her enemies always sent their best after her. It was almost flattering. For the assassins, themselves, it was at the same time an honor and a punishment. They knew that, should they succeed, they—or their family if they died in the process—would receive untold wealth. But it was equally well known that no one, thus far, had survived an attempt. She was still alive, despite their regular attempts to kill her over hundreds of years. The prospect had to be daunting.

She stilled, waiting and watching as the movement in the grass stopped. The snake's head lifted slightly, until its blunt nose was barely visible. Oblong pupils, opened to their fullest point, scanned the area as its tongue flicked out, searching for her scent.

Josette stared at the pattern of scales on the visible portion of the snake's head and body. Her ears twitched a bit in surprise. She had expected an asp or a cobra, one of the Middle Eastern snakes that had always hunted her before. But the pattern of dark brown and black splotches on the snake's body was unmistakable, even if she hadn't seen the multiple rattles on its tail. A rattlesnake native to either Central or South America was stalking her.

But I don't have any enemies in either of those places . . . that I know of. She'd never been to the southern continent. But vivid images of the jungles and rain forests there had dominated many of her recent visions, causing her to read up on the region.

Unless . . . There was always the possibility of a killer for hire. Zealots fought with a hot passion to their last breath, almost embracing their chance for martyrdom. A professional, however, would approach the situation very differently. Judging by the one assassin she'd met personally, this contest could be all cold logic and skill. Tony Giodone was an attack victim. He had never planned to be either a werewolf or a seer, but he was dealing with it admirably and she respected his resourcefulness and attention to detail.

She'd best assume the snake below her would have similar traits.

Who sent you? Josette peered down at the reptile sliding in near silence through the tufts of dried grass between the stones. He wasn't big by Sazi standards. But size wasn't everything.

Adrenaline pounded through her veins, leaving a metallic taste in her mouth, making it hard to think. She took a deep breath, gathered her will, and concentrated as she waited for the snake to move forward once again. Her hindquarters began to sway from side to side slightly as she gauged the distance and planned her jump.

The viper's head dropped from sight, and she saw the grass shifting. He was moving away, circling around, hoping to cut her off and meet her face-to-face. He must have caught her scent. She waited until he was just past the tree's trunk, facing away from her. With the power of her mind she froze him in place. He couldn't move, could barely expand his body enough to breathe.

Josette leaped down from the tree, landing just behind the last button rattle. She felt him struggle against her magic, his power flaring with white-hot intensity, as he fought against her with everything he had. It was nearly enough to break her hold. For just an instant she saw the powerful body start to move . . . to turn and strike.

A sharp hiss escaped her lips as she felt a second power join his, emanating from within him. For the first time in many years her power was thrown to the side. Her ears flattened, eyes narrowing in pure instinctive rage. She leaped sideways, out of reach at the same time that she clamped down hard with her mind, using fierce effort.

The snake's body slowed mid-strike. He was suspended in midair, his muscles straining, jaws opened wide to reveal wicked fangs. The enraged red-gold eyes had an almost physical weight to them.

Josette backed carefully around him, always keeping those eyes, those fangs, in sight. He'd been strong, much stronger than she'd expected. Last winter, the leader of *all* the snakes, had not had the power to break free of her grasp the way this man could. This assassin, and whoever was aiding him, was a force to be reckoned with.

She circled slowly until she stood just behind his head. The snake's eyes rolled backward as he tried to watch her, tension singing through his taut muscles as he fought with renewed strength against the mental bonds that pinned him. He smelled both angry and pleased, which confused her.

But then a panicked alto voice sounded in Josette's mind through the connection she'd forged with the male snake. *My love, tell her nothing. You must say nothing, or all will be lost.* The words were in Spanish, but she could understand them as though she spoke the language.

"Who are you working for?" Josette leaned forward, opening her jaws to grasp his spine at a point just behind his head. She closed her jaws slightly, squeezing just hard enough for him to know she *could* sever his head, but not hard enough to actually do so. Still, the bitter taste of blood and flesh filled her mouth, the rough textures of scale and bone grated against her tongue.

The snake winced in pain, but gave a small hissing laugh that told her questioning him further would be useless. And unfortunately, any attempt to pull the information from his brain with her mind would just destroy it. She had no talent for that sort of thing, unlike her younger sister Fiona.

Abruptly, a flood of images filled her mind, rolling from his thoughts to hers like a movie played on fast-forward: a jungle, the air thick enough to drink, the dense foliage passable in human form only with the liberal use of a machete. She could hear birds and animals moving through the dense undergrowth as she followed a guide down a barely visible path—

The snake panicked, and the burst of adrenaline gave him the sudden strength to break the mental bonds that held him. Josette let out a high-pitched, rolling growl, trying to tighten her physical grip, but he pulled strength from outside himself. She saw an image of a tiny woman with dark hair and liquid brown eyes, her body compact, muscular, but with soft curves that camouflaged a cold, calculating mind. The perfect oval of her face was superimposed over the image of Josette's own bedroom—the contents of which were tossed about from a hasty search. The woman looked up, and her face zoomed into sharper focus in front of a scene showing hundreds, even thousands of other snakes converging on an ancient temple in the middle of a jungle.

There was a surge of magic as the snakes somehow added to the power of the one under her. The scent of a hundred bodies, thick sweat, and a powerful metallic chemical filled her nose. He lunged hard against the iron grip of Josette's teeth and slammed his tail into the side of her head, throwing her nearly a yard away. Rattles sizzling angrily, he spun around and shot toward her before she could shake the cobwebs from her head. His scent had moved to confidence, and she had no doubt that the smell of worry had started to fill her own pores.

This time, she really was in over her head.

She barely dodged the flashing fangs and leaped sideways and up, before landing on the snake's broad back to dig in her claws. He hissed and twisted and beat at her with his tail. She lost her grip again and went sailing, but landed on her feet this time, allowing her to jump out of the way of his next strike.

To her left a feline roar vibrated in her ears just as orange stripes flashed by the corner of her vision. A massive tiger grabbed a *second* snake by the neck just before it had sunk its teeth into her hind leg. *Shit! I didn't even realize it was there! What the hell's happening to my foresight?*

Josette didn't dare take her eyes off the attacker in front of her, praying that the new cat was on her side, since she didn't recognize the scent. Sounds and smells erupted around her as natural enemies fought for dominance in the cool night. Minutes slipped by as she parried and slashed with teeth and claws, and threw nets of magic that were shrugged off with annoying ease. She could still see and sense the other snakes in the jungle, and it was difficult to concentrate on what was in front of her. But her opponent had no such difficulty. He moved with a clarity of thought that surprised her. It wasn't until long moments later, when the coppery scent of blood and a tiger's roar of triumph filled the air, that the viper got distracted.

She took the opportunity to attack with every ounce of her strength. With a snarl she threw herself toward the snake, opened her jaws wide and closed them around the back of his neck. The snake frothed and shot venom from its fangs, forcing her to close her eyes to keep them from getting burned. She sunk her teeth deeper, and then twisted sharply. The images in her mind shattered as his back broke and bitter blood flooded her mouth. The snake's eyes went flat and empty, his head hung limp from a narrow strip of scaled flesh.

Josette let the carcass drop from her mouth and spat out the venom-laced blood. The smell wouldn't go away as easily. She'd be smelling traces of the choking acrid scent for the next week.

"Viper blood is awful, isn't it?" She turned her

head toward the new cat and realized she recognized the voice.

"Tasha?" Could this massive Bengal tiger be the lovely redheaded Wolven agent who was her twin sister Yvette's frequent roommate at medical conferences?

The tiger paused from licking her paw and cleaning the red stains from the short orange fur on her nose. As she got closer, Josette realized Tasha smelled like sweet cream and tangy citrus, though it was difficult to smell anything over the venom.

"Aren't you glad I happened to be wandering by? Looks like you had your hands full. Oh, and I found your clothes. I put them over behind the tree."

She shook her head and spat again. "Not right now. I need to get home. I *saw* his mate ransacking my house."

She put a subtle emphasis on the word *saw*, so that Tasha would know it had been a vision. His *mate*. The woman had loved him . . . no doubt of that, and now he was dead. Likely the woman would be, too, from the shock of losing him. Josette's voice was flat, almost emotionless. It made Tasha cock her head slightly and pitch her ears forward curiously.

Josette shrugged and motioned with one paw toward the headless snake. "I was just thinking that this should probably bother me. But it doesn't."

A deep sigh threw mist into the chilling air that enveloped the wide tawny head. "There have been too many attempts on your life for far too long. I wish I knew what to do about it, but I don't even know the cause of it all."

"It's a long story. But if you have time, I could use your help at the house. If this man's mate didn't die with him, maybe we can learn who they worked for. For the first time, I don't think it was Ahmad who sent this killer." Josette took off at a run, leaving the tiger to catch up or not.

Tasha's voice sounded surprised as she easily kept pace with the smaller cat. "Really? Who could it be if not him?"

Josette didn't answer. She just increased her effort, forcing the tiger to speed up. They ran full out, their furred forms blending in the shadows as they moved like the wind over rough scrub grass, sand, and cactus. Josette didn't hesitate. She knew each rock, each plant from long years of experience living here in the desert. It was nice that Tasha trusted her enough to blindly fly through the night at her side.

It was too late, though, as she suspected it might be. The woman was already dead, just outside the front door. But she could smell again. After the cleansing breeze from the run, she knew the woman hadn't been alone. Tasha realized it, too, and, with head high and nostrils flared, the tiger began to slowly circle the tiny cabin.

Josette sighed and stepped onto the covered porch. "You won't find anyone. They always leave after I kill the first one. Cowards." She shifted forms as she walked the few steps to the door, so she was in human form when she walked through the entrance.

The sight that greeted her made her want to both scream and cry. Her pretty home had been ransacked, and obviously by professionals. Lights were on all over the house, revealing furnishings shattered or shredded. Curtains drooped from twisted rods, and even the picture tube of the small black-and-white television had been smashed. Worst of all, her favorite clock—a special gift from her sister that told the time in multiple zones and had the present year—was in pieces.

Tasha walked in behind her and touched her shoulder in sympathy at the sliced upholstery, broken vases, and upended bookcases. "Oh, Aspen! I'm so sorry!"

The name didn't surprise her. Aspen was the name she'd chosen for herself to match her twin's choice—Yvette became Amber, and *Aspen* seemed to fit at the time. But she'd never really thought of herself as Aspen, even after the many years of bearing the name. Changes in identity were common among the longer-lived Sazi, but they didn't always stick.

A growl escaped her while walking through the mess toward the bedroom, skirting glass and nails that could puncture her bare feet. She didn't have many things . . . lived a simple existence here in the desert, but the few things she did have were important to her. Killing her was one thing, but this—

"Damn it! Why would someone *do* this?" She picked up the cracked lid to a painted music box she'd had for over a century and carefully placed it back on the broken dresser top.

"Could they have been looking for something?" Tasha's voice was loud from the next room. It was a logical question for the law enforcement agent to ask. "You were at the council meeting in Chicago before Christmas. Did anyone ask you to keep something for them?"

The question was innocent, with no teasing inflection to it, meaning that not *everybody* in the entire shapeshifter world had heard what happened at that meeting. Thank heavens. It was going to be hard enough to live down within her own family. She shook her head, even though Tasha wouldn't see it. She remembered the meeting of the Sazi council rather . . . *vividly* and that wasn't one of the things that happened.

"I didn't stay long enough. I'd just barely arrived when all hell broke loose. You probably heard about the spider attack, right?" Or did that just happen? She furrowed her brow. "What year is this?"

Tasha told her and she breathed a sigh of relief. Things hadn't gone too far yet. There was still time. She barely noticed when the redhead continued. "Uh, yeah. That's *definitely* been a topic of conversation in the Wolven offices."

No doubt. Spider shifters had been presumed by many Sazi to be a myth—the magical equivalent of a boogeyman. Even Josette had presumed them to be at least extinct. But now they were back—thanks in part, according to Amber's research, to double-recessive genes in human–shifter descendants.

She turned to see Tasha standing naked in the doorway and realized she was still nude as well. She lifted up the chest of drawers from where it was face-down on the floor and pulled a fluffy gray stack of fabric from inside. "Here, I've got some sweats that will fit you if you want. No reason for you to be uncomfortable while I clean up."

Tasha nodded and took the clothes from her grasp. "I'll give you a hand. We can get this place shaped up in no time. Then we can have a drink and I'll tell you why I'm here."

Chapter Two

RICK JOHNSON LOUNGED in cat form on a section of rock that had been warmed by the late afternoon sun. It was a small outcropping on a tall needlelike rock formation. Below him a large white wolf picked his way laboriously upward. He'd recognized Lucas Santiago from a distance even before the scent of buffalo grass and tangy cactus fruit drifted to his nose. Rather than greet the other Sazi, he had decided to wait. After all, Lucas was coming into *his* territory and doing it knowing full well that Rick did not want to be disturbed. Even though bobcats generally interacted well with other Sazi species due to their relative size and nonaggression, when the wolf finally came to a stop a few yards away, sinking onto his haunches, Rick greeted him with a carefully chosen barb. "Took you long enough. You're getting out of shape."

Lucas didn't dignify that with a response. Instead, he used his rear paw to scratch behind his ear, deliberately giving the bobcat a clear view of his backside. It was a subtle invitation among the Sazi to "kiss my ass."

Rick snorted in wry amusement. The old wolf

hadn't changed much in the years since he'd last seen him. Oh, there was probably a little artful graying added to the temples in human form, maybe a tiny paunch—just enough to fool the humans into thinking he was aging. Not that he was. No, Lucas was just the most recent identity of one of the most powerful Sazi Rick had ever met. There was no telling how ancient the old wolf really was, but it was telling that Charles Wingate, Chief Justice of all the Sazi, treated the other man as an absolute equal.

"So, what brings you to the middle of godforsaken nowhere?"

"Looking for you, of course." Lucas lay down, making himself carefully comfortable on the tiny shelf. He didn't meet Rick's eyes, acknowledging that he was in bobcat territory, an uninvited guest. Locking gazes would be a direct challenge. It was a nice gesture, especially since Lucas could wipe the floor with Rick's fuzzy butt.

Rick sighed and smoothed a few hairs on his tawny, spotted hide with his tongue. He'd always known it was too good to last. Sooner or later someone was bound to come after him. The surprising thing was that it hadn't happened before. What he didn't know was whether he was glad or angry, sorry or relieved.

He'd come to the South Dakota wilderness years ago, desperate to escape from a life that had spiraled out of control. When he'd first joined Wolven things had made sense to him, right was right, wrong wasn't. He'd seen everything in crystal clear black and white. But as the years passed, he'd been forced to choose the lesser wrong, to do evil in hope of preventing something even worse. Eventually everything became a uniform shade of gray. There were no easy answers—weren't any answers at all. *Burn out* didn't even begin to describe what he'd felt at the time.

Rather than take an indefinite "medical leave," or early retirement, he'd chosen to fake his own death. He'd rigged an explosion in the mine of a man he'd been investigating, deliberately causing a cave-in when no workers were inside. Only Lucas, Charles, and one other knew he hadn't perished.

Rick forced his mind back to the present. Lucas was here. Judging by the vague answers the old wolf was giving, he was trying to manipulate him by playing into a cat's natural curiosity. He *was* curious, but not curious enough to play along. Instead, he decided to confound the other man by playing host. "There's an old bison down there. She's injured and can't keep up with the herd."

Lucas's ears pricked up. Rick could actually feel the hunger knotting the old man's belly. How long had it been since his last meal?

"I haven't had wild bison in . . ." Lucas let the sentence trail off. It occurred to Rick that perhaps he *couldn't* remember how long it had been. Once upon a time there had been huge herds of the majestic beasts roaming the plains. The ground vibrated under the thunder of thousands of hooves. Rick could remember it as clearly as if it had been yesterday. He suspected Lucas could as well. But the huge herds were gone, disappeared into the mists of history—destroyed mostly in an effort to crush the Native American peoples who relied on them as a staple of their diet. Few buffalo remained, and those that did were nearly as domesticated as cattle.

"Go. Eat."

"You're willing to share? These are your hunting grounds."

"I had a deer earlier. The bison's for you. I can feel how hungry you are. It's making me miserable."

Lucas shook his head, obviously irritated with himself. "I forget sometimes how powerful your gift of empathy is. You really do feel what others are experiencing."

"Yes, I do. And right now your hunger's tying my stomach in knots." Rick tried not to sound too irritable, but it wasn't easy. "When was the last time you ate, anyway?"

"It's been a while." The wolf turned his head to gaze into the distance. He lifted his nose to better catch the scents floating up from the prairie floor on the breeze.

"Then hunt. Whatever dragged you out here can wait until you've had a good meal."

The wolf nodded, rose, and began picking his way carefully down the hill. Rick watched him until he disappeared from sight.

Rising with a sigh, he arched his back and stretched until he felt every muscle loosen. When he was fully stretched out he began the long run back to the cabin to get the guest room ready for company.

It felt good running over the familiar trails. Small animals dived for cover; birds flushed from the trees, taking to flight with startled cries. He ignored the lure of it, keeping his attention on the uneven footing of the rocky trail. The sun was disappearing behind the rocky walls of the canyon, the light painting the sky in shades of crimson and purple as he rounded the last major bend. The scuttling clouds shone with vivid orange highlights. Even from a distance the house looked inviting. Solar lamps lit the stone path, which led to the stairs of the front porch. The scent of wood smoke lingered faintly. By now the fire was mere embers, but it wouldn't take much to bring it back to life.

Rick shifted forms effortlessly, changing from a compact feline with large tufted ears to a man nearly six feet tall, with a slender build and shaggy blond hair. The stones were chilly beneath his bare feet, the breeze cold enough to bring goose bumps to his exposed flesh. He bent to retrieve the spare key from its hiding place beneath a chair made of split pine logs, then let himself inside.

He dressed in the clothes he'd left neatly folded on the coffee table. He pulled his worn blue jeans on over flannel boxer shorts and donned his favorite blue plaid flannel shirt. The clothes were comfortable and practical. There was nothing fancy about them, but there'd been nothing fancy or elegant about his life these past few decades. Quiet and simple had suited him just fine, and he wasn't sure he was ready to give that up, no matter what Lucas had to say.

Still, he was curious. He had a computer. He'd even learned how to use it. He knew the current events of the human world. But the Sazi didn't publicize their news. He couldn't help but wonder what had been going on with his friends . . . and with *her*.

Don't think about it. He moved the fireplace screen aside. Picking up the poker, he jabbed viciously at the remains of his earlier fire. A spark leaped up from the embers to land on his hand. The burn stung his flesh, but then blistered and healed in a matter of seconds.

He set the poker back in its stand, then retrieved dried wood from the holder to stack on the already glowing embers. In short order he had a fresh fire burning. He moved the grate back in place.

It would take time for Lucas to hunt; more time for him to make his way back here. Rick knew it, and yet he still caught himself pacing the floor and looking at the clock every few minutes until he wished to hell he'd just offered to cook something on the stove.

In the end he gathered up some spare clothing that

would fit the other man and settled into his favorite recliner with a good book. Eventually he even managed to doze.

It was well after midnight when he woke with a start to the click of Lucas's claws on the porch. Rick dropped his shields. He didn't feel guilty in the least about using his gift to see how the other man was feeling.

The surface emotion was fairly straightforward—pleasure on a good hunt. But beneath that lay a level of exhaustion and worry that one meal and a few hours' rest wouldn't alleviate.

Things were bad. Rick had suspected as much. Lucas wouldn't have come if he weren't desperate. The operative questions were, what was wrong, and what did he expect Rick to do about it?

The sound of nails on stone changed to the pad of bare feet. There was a light knock on the wood of the front door.

"Come on in. I left it unlocked." Rick picked up the novel that had fallen from his lap and placed it facedown beneath the lamp on the end table. Using the lever on the side of the recliner, he moved the chair into an upright position as the older man came through the door.

Lucas stopped inside the doorway, looking around. As usual, he'd clothed himself in illusion. If Rick didn't know any better, he would swear the older man was wearing jeans and a flannel shirt. He watched

Lucas take everything in, from the fire in the huge stone fireplace that dominated the living room to the bentwood rocker and handmade pine coffee and end tables. The knotty pine he'd used for the interior walls gave off a warm golden glow. Thick Navajo print area rugs were scattered over the stone floor. He'd selected the recliner and drapes to pick up the rich burgundy that appeared in the patterns of the various rugs. Black throw pillows were scattered across a charcoal gray couch.

Above the couch hung a painting, oil on canvas. It was in the Early American style, an autumn landscape of rich russets and golds. It wasn't signed, the artist unknown, but it was a brilliant work. When he'd given up everything else in his life he'd kept this one thing—not only for its beauty, but for the sentiment attached. The painting had been Josette's gift to him when they'd gotten married.

He couldn't bear to leave it when they'd parted ways. It followed him always.

"There are clothes on the chest by the door." Rick gestured to a spot behind where Lucas stood. Illusions might be fine for appearances, but they didn't warm bare skin. "Would you like some coffee? Or would you rather just go to bed?"

Rick felt the wave of longing that passed through the other man at the mention of sleep, but as Lucas began pulling on the sweat pants and flannel shirt Rick had provided he asked for coffee instead.

"You should probably rest."

"No time." Lucas's voice held only the tiniest hint of exhaustion. "Charles will be here in a few minutes and then we can talk."

"*Charles* will be here?" The shock was enough to move him forward in his seat to stare at the other man until the old wolf nodded. Rick couldn't remember the last time he'd seen the Chief Justice. But nothing good had ever come from a visit by him.

"Hell Rick, I shouldn't have taken the time to hunt before he got here, but I haven't eaten in days." Lucas ran his hands through his graying hair with a frustration that pressed against Rick's skin like dull needles. "But Charles insisted on telling you himself, and truthfully, there isn't anyone else to send."

"Fine. Make yourself comfortable." He gestured toward the recliner. "I'll fix us some coffee. When will he arrive?"

"Any minute now. Coffee would be a good thing. Thanks." Lucas took a seat, settling back into the comfortable overstuffed cushions, letting his eyes drift closed. Rick knew the other man would force himself to stay awake as long as it was necessary, but even a small catnap could be a relief. So he moved as silently as he could through the dining area and into the kitchen.

The coffeepot was old-fashioned blue graniteware. Rick filled the metal strainer with coffee grounds and clamped on the lid. It was his favorite blend, and a little hard to come by. He'd gotten used to having chickory mixed in with his coffee back when coffee was a scarce commodity among the tea-loving Londoners, so he went to the bother of having a supply special ordered.

He filled the pot with water from the tap and dropped the strainer and its post in place before putting the lid on the pot and moving it over to the burner on the old gas stove. Giving the knob a deft twist, he listened to the whistle of the gas coming on, smelled the odd, almost sweet scent that the propane company added to it as a safety measure. He used a wooden kitchen match to light the burner, then adjusted the knob until the flames were just right.

"Coffee'll be ready in a couple minutes," he announced.

"Thanks." Lucas's answer was a little muffled. Rick could feel the sleep tugging at the other man's consciousness.

The fragrant aroma slowly began to fill the cabin. Rick took a deep breath, luxuriating in the scent before walking into the living room and taking his seat in the old bentwood rocker next to the fireplace. He'd built the rocker himself. It fit him like a well-worn glove.

"Nice place you've got here." Lucas didn't bother to open his eyes. "The windmill powers the generator?"

"And the well."

"Is that why you chose this site, the water? I understand there's not much of it out here."

He nodded, his gaze locked into the flickering flames. Lucas sounded like he was actually interested. Maybe he was, and Rick couldn't help being proud of it. The cabin wasn't large, but it was *his*—there'd been time to build it just the way he wanted. He'd needed something productive to do, something with results he could see and a product at the end. He'd been a wreck when he left Wolven, not just physically, but emotionally, too. Building this home, living out here beneath the wide skies and endless wind had been his therapy. He was whole now, and he wanted to stay whole. The old wolf might have been his friend once. Hell, he might still be. But he was here for a reason, and it wasn't to admire the damned view.

"Have you been inheriting from yourself again?" There was a hint of laughter in Lucas's voice.

"It's not uncommon for names to stay in the same family for generations." Rick answered calmly. "Isn't Charles his own multiple-great grandson at this point?"

"Yes. And because of the age of his current identity his *actual* great-great-grandson drops the greats from his title when he talks about him. You remember Raven Ramirez, right? Or wasn't he in Wolven yet when you left?"

"Nope. After my time, I guess. He related to Raphael Ramirez? Him, I've heard of. At least by reputation." A curious look passed over the other man's face, and Rick shrugged. "Ivan stops by every decade or so. I'm not really up-to-date, but telling me about that mess—Raphael living with one sister and sleeping with another sister, who just happened to have the head of Wolven mated to her, which drove poor Jack Simpson quite literally insane? Oh yeah, that little soap opera lasted through a whole twelve-pack."

Lucas let out a short guffaw. "Soap opera. Yeah, I suppose it was. Ivan probably gave Raphael more benefit of the doubt than he deserved, for what it's worth." His mood sobered for a moment and he seemed lost in thought. "Jack's dead. In case you didn't know. The warrant finally went through."

"I saw that his helicopter went down on the news. I presumed it wasn't an accident." There wasn't anything else for Rick to say so he continued to stare at the fire. It had been a long time coming. All serial killers are eventually brought down by the council . . . no matter how powerful.

Without missing a beat, the old wolf continued, but Rick could feel the mix of emotions that pushed against his chest. Sadness, relief, anger, and a dozen more subtle ones. "Raven is Raphael's son by Charles's great-granddaughter, Star. Raven's third in command at Wolven right now. He's turned out to be a fine agent, even though he stayed human longer than most before his first change. It was pretty hard for him to face giving up a promising NFL career just because he turned wolf. It wasn't pretty. But Raphael turned him around."

Rick felt his eyebrows raise a fraction and he flicked his gaze toward Lucas's nearly sleeping form. *NFL career*? Wow, he *did* turn late if that was a possibility. Most Sazi turn just before puberty. But there was a good chance it would mean Raven would be one of the longer lived of the current generation. Powerful Sazi lived a long time . . . a *very* long time. Keeping the secret meant that relationships sometimes got tangled. Nearly every Sazi had a will that left their wealth to the next identity they planned to use. Better that than starting over every time.

He fought down his impatience with the polite, social chitchat. It occurred to him that he'd been away from people too long. He'd forgotten how to be social. Was that a good or bad thing? Hard to say. He did know that he enjoyed the quiet, the peace of living out in the open spaces . . . at his own pace, letting his blond hair grow shaggy, and shaving only if he felt like it. Oh, he hadn't become completely uncivilized. A daily shower was a must, and his clothes were always clean and pressed. But if he got gas, he belched, and he didn't have to worry about apologizing for it. If the few knickknacks he had sitting around got dusty, nobody would be stopping by to notice.

The coffee finished percolating and the momentary silence was broken only by the crackling of the fire. The rocking chair squeaked as he rose. Stretching until the bones of his spine popped, he shook out his arms before relaxing into a normal posture and striding to the kitchen. As he was pouring the brew into a matching pair of ceramic mugs, a quiet knock came from the door and he heard Lucas use the lever to recline his chair. His sensitive ears heard Charles greet Lucas. Seconds later he caught the scent of Charles's wife, Amber, Josette's twin sister, and their bodyguard Bruce. He remembered the old bear well from when they worked together. It would be good to see him again.

But what of Amber? Did she even know he was alive? Would she tell Josette or did the reclusive seer already know? Did her foresight tell her everything as it had when they were married? Would it tell her why he'd never contacted her again after walking out on her?

A flood of emotions fought inside him as he removed three more cups from the cabinet and added sugar and a carton of whipping cream from the refrigerator to the tray. He preferred *real* cream in his coffee, and remembered that Amber did, as well.

Charles was already sitting on the couch when Rick walked out of the kitchen. He looked pale and drawn. There were lines of pain at the corners of his eyes, making him look older than Rick had ever seen him.

But in the few seconds he'd been in the kitchen, Lucas had transformed. Gone was the aching weariness.

In its place was an anger just short of rage that hummed through the room and took his breath away.

"What did I just miss? What's happened?"

Bruce turned his head from where he was watching out the window and wiped away a small spot of red at the corner of his mouth that looked suspiciously like blood. "I just killed an assassin outside your cabin who tried to attack Charles. It was a snake, and not one of the friendly ones."

A *snake assassin*? Good God, what were they asking him to get involved with?

"Is there any chance you were followed, Lucas?" Amber's voice was calm, cold, but her own anger blew through the room like an arctic wind as she touched Charles's shoulder. She stood unmoving, but the fiery bobcat was no less terrifying for all that. She reminded Rick so very much of Josette that it made him smile for just a second before he put the tray on the coffee table. But the next words out of her mouth wiped away the smile and raised his brows. "There's nothing funny about this, Richard Cooper. We've been losing agents left and right. People are dying, and I'm not going to have my husband be the next one!"

Ah. So that's why they're here. The agency is starting to reactivate retired agents. He was going to be asked to walk into a pitched battle, rather than avert one. She didn't seem surprised at his presence, but then she'd been married to the Chief Justice for a very long time. There were probably secrets she would take to her grave.

Lucas turned glowing blue eyes to the pretty, petite blonde. "I'm not that incompetent, Amber."

Rick's mind dropped into agent mode before he even realized that there was a switch to be thrown. "Maybe he didn't have to be incompetent."

Lucas gave a low, menacing growl that raised all the hairs on his body at the implication. The heat from his magic rose until Rick raised a hurried hand to forestall an actual attack. "I don't mean that you were involved in any sort of plan against the Chief Justice, Lucas." He waved his hand around to the assembled group. "Haven't any you ever seen the movie *Enemy of the State*? Am I the only person with a DVD player? I do keep up out here, you know. And I remember Jack and Fiona being fascinated with all the latest technology, even when the latest and greatest was the *telegraph*. I bet every single agent is issued a top-of-the-line cell phone and laptop. And I'll also bet that Fiona has them all supplied by the same company. Hell, I've no doubt every one of *you* carries one she ordered." He pointed to Lucas. "You arrived at the top of the mountain in wolf form, but do you have any sort of technology in your *vehicle*? Could someone be using your own technology to track you?"

Lucas stopped mid-stride. He opened his mouth to say something, then stopped himself. His hazel eyes darkened as his expression grew more calculating.

"You mean we might be bugged? The whole *agency*?" He paused, obviously appalled at the thought, and not the least dismissive of the idea. "I've been using the same supplies and suppliers that Fiona used without bothering to check on them." He turned to Charles. "I don't personally know if they're secure or not."

Rick continued. "I don't know who you use as your supplier, and I don't care. But if I were you, I'd strip each one of us down to the skin and use a detector to go through everything. If I found *anything* hinky, I'd crash the system at headquarters."

Lucas stared at him, long and hard. "Do you realize the chaos a complete system crash would cause? *Everything* is routed through the computers."

Rick met his gaze calmly and shrugged. "I'll bet you still have the paper backups on every file. Weren't you the one who used to tell me that you'd never give up paper because people can't stuff a whole file folder down their shorts? Better to crash and start over than be compromised and let our enemies pick our people off at their convenience."

Lucas thought about it in silence for a long moment. The tension in the room mounted with each passing second. "Fine." he growled and then pointed at him. "We'll start with *you*. Strip."

They checked everything and everyone in the room. Rick was clean, as he knew he would be. But when Bruce found that all of the other cell phones had been tampered with, he started in on the luggage they had in the car. The laptops were likewise compromised, as well as several of Charles's suits, Bruce's favorite pair of shoes, and even Amber's stethoscope.

With every bug they found both Lucas's and Amber's rage grew until the heat from their combined power began to scorch the woolen rug by the fireplace. Amber went with Lucas to stand outside until they both cooled down while Bruce went scouting in the predawn chill for more *visitors*.

Charles sat naked on the couch. When he spoke, his voice was calm, belying the fury Rick knew he was feeling. His visage seemed to have aged decades in the few minutes it had taken them to perform their search. He gestured at the discarded pile of clothing and equipment in the middle of the floor.

"Rick, would you be so kind as to throw all that in the fireplace? I feel a bit chilly."

He would have laughed if the situation wasn't so serious. A polar bear shifter . . . feeling a *chill*. Instead, Rick quietly and methodically began crushing the electronic devices they'd gathered, pressing them under the heel of his boot before throwing them into the embers. The cotton suits soon started to smolder and after adding some logs and applying a few puffs of air from the bellows, the cell phones and laptop cases started to melt.

He'd just tossed in the pair of shoes, when Charles spoke. "You know most of the Monier family, don't you?" The voice was deceptively casual. It made the small hairs on the back of Rick's neck stand on end in warning. Still, when he answered, his own voice was easily as casual. Even scent wouldn't give them away to each other. The faint tang of curiosity hung in the air, but that could mean anything, or nothing.

"Who doesn't?" Rick answered as he passed a cup of black coffee across the table. He flicked his eyes toward the door and winked.

Finally, a smile, even though it was weary. "True. They're not exactly unobtrusive."

Rick gave a snort of amusement as he sat once again in his rocker. That was one hell of an understatement: Amber was the quietest of the Monier siblings, but she was well known to anyone who'd ever worked in Wolven. She'd served as the staff physician there since she'd been barely more than a kitten; Antoine was a world-renowned entertainer, as well as the Council Representative for the cats; Fiona had moved through the ranks at Wolven with unheard-of speed, through a combination of raw talent and utter ruthlessness. And then, of course, there was Josette. Her name might be Aspen now to the shifter world, but to him, now and always she would be Josette. Rick didn't want to think too much about her. It always made him wonder what might have been, if he hadn't been too young and too stupid to realize just how special she was.

"You were married to Aspen at one time."

It wasn't a question, so Rick didn't bother to answer. His years with Josette had been the happiest of his life. He'd been a fool, an idiot, and he'd lost her. It was not the kind of thing he wanted to discuss. Emotions clawed at his insides—one of the dangers of being an empath. Not only could he sense feelings in others, but his own supply was overdeveloped to the extreme.

But even over his own feelings of self-loathing, longing, and need came Charles's desperate worry and fear. He raised his eyes to meet those of his old friend and understood with startling clarity that something was truly *wrong*.

"I need your help Rick. I wouldn't have come here if the situation wasn't desperate."

Chapter Three

"NOT ONLY NO, but *hell* no!"

Tasha let out a deep sigh and then took a slow drink of pungent red wine. Josette didn't entertain much—hadn't actually had a person visit in *years*, but she kept a few bottles of good French wine, bottled near where she grew up, in the cellar for special occasions. She was starting to realize she shouldn't have wasted a bottle on *this*. While she appreciated the help with the snakes and cleaning up the house, the Wolven agent was just asking too much.

"I understand how you feel, but—"

Josette snorted and put her glass down on the cracked table hard enough that the remaining red fluid slid up the side and out onto her hand.

"Do you? Do you *really*? You've never been a seer. You *can't* know how I feel. I know you've visited my sister when Charles has had visions, but he has *control* of his foresight. I don't. I see the past, the future, the present . . . all at once, or slathered over the top of one another like some sort of demented Edvard Munch painting. People believe I'm *insane*, Tasha—think I was the *model* for *The Scream*. But I'm not and don't ever plan to be. I'm very careful not to put myself in situations where things could go wrong. No. I won't go to Minnesota and risk losing my sanity. Plus, has it ever occurred to you that what is happening *must* happen? I'm getting so tired of people trying to change the things that have to be and screwing up the future in the process."

The look on the other woman's face was both sad and angry, matching the scent of wet, burned coffee that filled the small room. "Little girls suffered and *died*, Aspen. All because of the leader Josef Isaacson's desperate need for money and complete lack of humanity. They were raped and then turned Sazi against their will. You can't tell me that their pain and their deaths *had to be*. Yes, thankfully, the pack leader in Texas, with the help of the second of Minnesota stopped the trafficking for now. But it was only temporary. We never found out who was running the show. We *have* to make sure it doesn't happen again. You have hindsight—you can see which members of the Minnesota pack were involved in the child slavery ring. Maybe you can see who the contact down south was. It's the only way we can find out who was capturing the girls both here in the States and in South America."

That perked up Josette's ears to the point she could almost feel fur tickle her skin. *South America*? Could what happened tonight be part of something larger, something having to do with both her visions and Minnesota? But she hadn't seen any children that were attack victims in her visions, hadn't seen the deep pine woods of the lake lands. Surely she would have, wouldn't she?

After a few moments of silence, while the tall redhead tapped the side of her wine glass, Josette shook her head. "I'm sorry. You'll have to tell Charles and the council that I won't do it. Not now. It's not only a risk to me, but a real risk to the people in Minnesota. It'll endanger your investigation even worse if whoever is trying to kill me *follows* me there."

Tasha nodded her head and stood up. Her scent told Josette that she had realized arguing was futile, but she was just short of violent. Her words were staccato knives, intended to cut. "Fine. But I hope you can sleep at night if a child *you* know gets captured by these maniacs when you could have stopped them."

The tiger started to step forward aggressively when Josette raised her palm. She might have expended a great deal of magic fighting the snakes, but there was still enough in reserve to handle an angry tiger. The flow of magic extended outward from her hand like a rock wall intended to prevent the other woman from getting closer. "Be very careful, Agent. I'm being careful tonight because you're my sister's dearest friend and you believe what you're doing is right. But there's a *reason* why the council is content to leave me alone out here. Don't make me show you my temper. Please, you have my answer. Now leave my home."

Tasha's eyes narrowed. "Fine. And unlike *you*, I'll remain a professional, I'll bury the snakes on my way back. I wouldn't want you to be *burdened*, after all."

Then, with a snarl that revealed more fear than anger, she stormed out the front door, leaving the loaned clothing in her wake.

Josette sighed. She hated having to say no, but there was nothing to be done about it. She'd made her decision, knowing that Charles and, in turn, her sister, would be furious. Some things have to be, and that tiny part inside of her that felt time in all its forms, told her she'd made the right decision. After taking the glasses to the kitchen and putting them in the sink, she picked up the bag of ruined clothing and broken dishes and stepped out the back door.

It took a second for the smell to hit her, another few seconds for the scent to register. *Dynamite*—and the ozone electricity that could only be a detonator igniting. She tried to turn, to run with supernatural speed to get away from the house, but her momentum made her lose her footing, and she skidded dangerously forward. There was a sound like a gunshot, and the blinding heat and flash of an explosion. Then, enveloping darkness.

EVENTUALLY SHE BEGAN to be vaguely aware of her body, pinned and injured under layers of rubble. She was healing as only a Sazi could, and the pain was distant and dull. She tasted stone dust and stale blood on her tongue. Her eyes, when she opened them, viewed the utter devastation of what had once been her home. Until her mind forced her to see other things entirely.

In a vision so intense she could *smell* things, she saw Rick—*her* Rick, sunning himself on a rock in cat form as a huge white wolf picked his way delicately up to meet him. Josette's heart caught in her chest. No. The vision had to be of the past. Rick was dead. But, oh God how good it felt to see him again! She could even smell wood smoke clinging to his fur and just a hint of the cinnamon toothpaste he used to love.

The image shifted and she saw him riding a motorcycle, the wind blowing back his shirt, baring a muscular chest marred only by old, pale scars where claws had tried to dig his heart from his chest. His face was just the same: square-jawed, with jutting cheekbones that were only accented by a perfectly trimmed VanDyke beard. His blond hair had highlights from time spent outdoors, so that it gleamed with every possible shade from near white to a dark honey gold that matched the color of his eyes. His eyes were honey and amber with flecks of what looked like metallic gold. They were nearly the same in both his human and animal form. Now, however, they were hidden behind sunglasses that reflected the bright afternoon sun.

She'd loved him once, and he her. But it hadn't worked. Try as she might, she had never really gotten over the hurt of his leaving. When she'd learned of his death it had broken something deep inside her.

But he *wasn't* dead. This was real enough to taste. It was a vision of the present, or the very near future. He was riding what appeared to be a classic Indian, but Josette could see the cars as he zoomed past. They were current makes and models, and the license plates had current dates on them.

He's alive! She felt a fierce surge of joy that forced her to wake fully. It was followed instantly by a wave of anger. *Damn that son of a bitch! I grieved for him!* While she understood the need for older Sazi to "kill" an old identity and start a new life, you let people know. You're supposed to say good-bye. You don't just . . . *vanish* from the people who will miss you.

I've missed you—

The thought faded as the scene shifted. She could see it all with perfect clarity, but there was no sound. It was as though she were watching a silent movie, or a television that had been put on mute. Rick again, this time with a large dark-haired man she recognized as Raven Ramirez. The two of them were arguing companionably over a beer. In a flash she saw another image. Her younger brother Antoine, Fiona's twin, looked intolerably smug, as usual, right up until the moment Rick threw him up against the wall with a snarl of utter fury. It took both Raven and Lucas to separate them. Rick . . . and Raven . . . working together. Did they know how they fit into her life in this future time? The man she loved, and the man she had no choice *but* to love?

With each transition the vision that played out behind her eyes seemed to gain momentum and speed. It raced through her mind like a runaway horse. She was losing control. Scene after scene flashed through her mind in an ever changing kaleidoscope of images: Her mother's face, eyes dark with rage, as her younger self tried to tell Maman of a vision she'd seen; then a shift, and a slender blond woman was telling her joyous husband of her pregnancy. It was Raphael, Amber's lover from before she'd met Charles, and he seemed lovingly content with the blonde, who looked enough like Fiona for Josette to do a double take from outside the vision.

A temple appeared next in the same jungle that she'd encountered in the assassin's mind, with snakes converging for a dark ceremony; then feral birds descending on a small pack of desperate red wolves. Then Rick lay dead, his heart's blood leaking out while she was covered in a multitude of snakes just a few feet away, unable to help. Then he was alive again, bouncing an infant boy on one knee.

There were so many images—visions of joy and sorrow, pain and death. She couldn't begin to sort them all.

She felt her grip on her mind start to slip. It was too much.

Josette screamed with rage and frustration. *NO!* She *would* control this! In desperation she turned to the only things that she could count on to bring her back to her body in the present—blood and pain.

She bit down into her lower lip, felt her teeth rip through the skin until red dripped down onto the gray and tan rubble at the edges of her vision. It was barely enough, but she felt her mind slowly clear . . . saw the tendrils of time form a cloudy lace that eventually converged and became the present.

It took several minutes of hard work to clear herself from beneath the rubble. Each breath burned in her lungs from the smoke that boiled up into the azure sky. She could taste the burning chemicals— varnish and plastic, insulation and paint—on her tongue. Very soon the sheriff and others would come to investigate. She didn't want to be here when that happened. There would be too many questions.

The body of the snake's mate still lay near what had been the front porch and she started to drag the burned, bloodied body toward the wall of flames. If she was lucky, the police would believe the woman was her. After all, it wasn't as if the humans had her DNA or fingerprints on file. The Sazi did, but they wouldn't share. No, Aspen Monier needed to die in order for Josette to live.

Raising her chin in defiance she blinked back the

last of the tears from the stinging sooty air, shifted forms, and started to pad her way to the place she'd buried the start of a new life.

It was time to face the future.

Chapter Four

RICK TOOK A long pull of coffee before setting the cup down on the end table next to him. He brushed an unruly shock of hair away from his eyes. "What?" His expression grew guarded, his tone not quite hostile.

"I asked you how much Josette told you about her relationship with her mother?"

He tried to decide what Charles wanted him to say. Josie might not be his wife anymore, but the confidences they'd shared were . . . well, *confidential*.

The older man must have sensed his reluctance. He turned his head slightly and called out. "Amber? Could you come in here for a moment?"

When the door opened, Amber was carrying a stack of clothing that she handed to her husband. "Bruce checked them out. They're all fine. No socks, though. Damned if someone didn't thread in a small wire with a nanotracker."

Charles nodded and stood. "I hope you don't mind Rick, but I'd like to use the bedroom for a few minutes."

"My house is yours." Rick meant every word and was rewarded with a gentle smile from the older man.

"Thank you. I appreciate that. Especially since we

crashed in on you uninvited." He started walking toward the darkened bedroom, each movement heavy with a deep pain that sent ripples of agony through Rick's gift of empathy. Charles paused with his hand on the bedroom door and turned to address Amber. "Tell Rick about Sabine and Josette, please. He might know some of it, or he might not. But he needs to understand what we're dealing with."

Amber sighed and nodded her agreement. Her eyes didn't leave Charles's form until the bedroom door closed behind him. Only then did she pick up a mug and sit down, leaning back into the cushions.

She didn't bother with preliminaries, as though there wasn't time for such frivolity. "My mother hated the fact that Josette was a seer. But more than that, she feared what my sister saw about her. When we were eight years old she paid an ungodly amount to one of the seers in the area to have her block my sister's gift. The woman warned her it should be a temporary thing, that bottling up the magic for more than a day or two would cause problems, but my mother didn't listen. She wanted the gift *gone*."

He'd known part of this. Josie had seldom talked about Sabine, but a few things had slipped out over the years. "What happened?"

Amber shuddered. Turning her head, she stared into the flames. Her voice was deceptively calm as she spoke, but Rick could feel the effort it was taking her to control the emotions brought on by the memory.

"Josette suffered terribly. It started with light sensitivity and a headache; then agitation and irritability, followed by a fever and chills . . ." Amber's voice simply stopped. A wave of panic hit him like a fist to the jaw and tears filled her eyes.

"All of the seers are in terrible danger, Rick." She lowered her voice. "Because of what Maman did, Aspen can't be blocked *but . . .*" She shook her head, causing the first of the tears to slide soundlessly down her cheek.

But what! Rick barely managed to control himself enough to keep from interrupting her.

"She has enemies on the council, and not just Ahmad. They're saying that she's the only one who could be responsible—that she's gone completely insane and is killing the other seers. But I don't believe that. Aspen would *never* do such a thing to another seer. Charles has forestalled them for now, but something has to be done."

Rick froze in mid-motion, his hand hovering in the air above the coffee cup. *Danger . . . Josette's in danger.* He felt a fluttering in his chest and realized it was fear. Josie could handle nearly anything, but if the council turned against her she'd be put down— just like Jack had been.

He opened his mouth to speak, but Amber continued in a rush. "It actually doesn't take that much power to block another person's gift if they're not aware of it or fighting you, and there are several ways of doing it—*if* you share the same gift. And only someone who shares the same gift can break the block."

"It doesn't have to be the same person who blocked it?"

"Not if you find someone more powerful than they are."

"So . . ." Rick started to speak, but Amber interrupted him, in whispered tones so low that even the other Sazi nearby wouldn't be able to hear.

"So, last night Charles collapsed during a vision. Something or *someone* is literally draining his power every time he uses his gift. He shouldn't even be standing, Rick. You see what he looks like." She turned a deeply worried face toward the bedroom door. "I tried to contact the other Sazi seers, to see if one of them was available to come break through what was done to Charles."

"And?"

"I reached everyone but Josette and our most recent seer. He only has hindsight, so he's probably fine. But every seer with foresight has been blocked, and is in the same condition as Charles or worse. It was done so skillfully that they never even noticed until nearly all of their power was drained." There was suppressed rage under those perfectly calm-sounding words. It pounded at Rick's gift, until he had to fight to maintain his own reason.

"Charles told me that, because of what Maman

did, Aspen won't be affected, which means, that if she is alive and sane she can . . . *will* help us."

Rick found himself shaking his head. "Josie's not insane. And I agree that she'd never hurt another seer the way Sabine hurt her."

"She may be our only chance at breaking the block on the others before they die, or before whoever is doing this kills *her* to keep her from doing just that."

Rick's mouth was dry. He had to clear his throat twice before he could manage to speak. "But Josette broke free by herself before. Can't the others?"

Amber shook her head. "Non. Maman murdered the Sazi who set the spell by accident, in one of her fits. Without the spellcaster's power to draw from, the spell began to weaken. Also Josette and I were children." She fought to find the words to explain. "From what I'm told, it's sort of like the measles, or some of the other childhood ailments. Serious, but not necessarily life threatening in children, but possibly fatal in adults, and the older the person, the deadlier it is."

Rick swallowed hard. His stomach tightened with fear. Charles Wingate was one of the truly ancient Sazi. He'd been Rick's mentor, his *friend* for longer than either of them would care to remember. "But . . ."

He hadn't heard the door open, being as engrossed as he was in what Amber was saying, so he jumped a little when Lucas spoke in a low growl. "Our plans just changed. I just got a call on our only noninfected phone. Satellite pictures from earlier today of the house where Aspen lived in the desert show a charred hole." Amber gasped and a buzzing filled Rick's ears.

"I pulled some strings and checked with local authorities. There was an explosion that involved an accelerant. While the fire destroyed most everything, there were traces of human remains. We got lucky that Angelique Calibria, the raptor representative, was nearby on vacation. She found barely enough tissue for Bobby Mbutu to do a DNA match with his tongue." He paused as Rick remembered Bobby, a brilliant chemist with a talented python tongue that could identify anything he tasted. "The dead body wasn't her."

Rick said a silent prayer of thanks, and muscles he hadn't even realized he'd clenched relaxed as he settled deeper into the chair.

"The thing is," Lucas spoke soberly, "she *was* hurt. Somebody had cleaned up the area, but Angelique found faint traces of her blood, and there was a grave containing a dead viper, a South American rattler, not far from the scene. It has all the ear-markings of an assassination attempt gone bad."

Rick sighed audibly. "It's not like it's the first time, Lucas. The snakes have been trying to assassinate Josie since she was a teenager."

The older man nodded. "True. But we're worried. Unfortunately, I don't dare send anyone after her that she doesn't know personally. If she didn't kill them outright, she'd at least damage them, and I don't have any agents to spare." He sighed. "I had sent Tasha to see her on another matter some time ago, but I've lost contact with her." He growled. "I'm *hoping* it's a temporary setback. I can't afford to lose any more of my agents."

This was the second or third time Lucas had referred to Wolven agents in the possessive. Rick had always assumed Fiona had taken over when Jack left to join Congress. "*You* don't have any agents?"

Lucas sighed, but it ended with a light growl, and his scent was filled with annoyance. "I'm in charge, at least temporarily. Jack's dead, as I said. Fiona's unavailable."

Amber spoke up, her voice still a little unsteady. "Fiona and Raven Ramirez, her second before the council added my position over them both are on forced medical leave at the order of the Council."

The council had ordered the two top people in Wolven on *medical leave?* Rick didn't know Ramirez but he could just imagine Fiona's reaction to being benched. He nodded to both Lucas and Amber. "You have my deepest sympathies for dealing with Fiona while she's on forced leave. I wouldn't wish that on my worst enemy." Rick was only half joking. Still, Lucas was a big boy. If anybody could handle an ill-tempered cougar it was him.

Rick had disliked Fiona from the minute she'd walked into the same room with him for the first time. Either she hadn't known he was an empath, or she hadn't cared enough to shield herself. Rick had felt her emotions as clearly as anything he'd sensed in his life: ambition unfettered by anything more than the most rudimentary conscience; ethics that were best described as . . . flexible. It hadn't surprised him at all when he'd heard the rumor that she'd slept with Raphael Ramirez knowing full well that Amber was mated to him and pregnant. Bitch.

One-sided matings in the Sazi world might be the norm, but that didn't make it any easier. To fall in love with a person who might or might not share your devotion . . . it was one of nature's little cruelties in exchange for the dubious blessing of being Sazi. He'd always wondered what might have happened if he had been mated to Josie—if pleasing her had been foremost in his mind, instead of his own selfish interests. Despite what the songs on the radio repeatedly told him, love *doesn't* conquer all. Not even among the supernatural community. Sometimes it just makes things worse.

The bedroom door opened and Charles appeared, looking a little better, but still fairly ill. Charles turned to Amber, his expression grim. "I hate to do this, my love, but I'm ordering an investigation into Fiona's activities."

Her brows shot up and she half-stood—shock plain on her face. "Charles!"

He held up a hand. "I don't believe she's betrayed

us. I can't believe that. But at the very least she's been negligent, and that negligence has cost lives. We can't be certain yet that one of those lives isn't Aspen's. I know she's your only remaining baby sister, but—"

A variety of emotions ran across the woman's face, and every single one of them beat against Rick's mind until he visibly winced. Apparently, she'd forgotten about his empathic ability and when she noticed, she calmed herself quickly. "I'm so very sorry, Rick. I know better than to blast emotions at you. But it's been a somewhat . . . stressful few days." She shook her head and her expression sobered. Rick could feel the stab of anger mingled with regret that passed through her.

When Amber turned to her husband, her face was calm. "Fiona and I haven't spoken more than three words in years. I won't tell her, if that's what you're worried about. But she wouldn't do . . . *this*. Wolven isn't just her job, it's her *life*. She breathes law enforcement. She wouldn't be involved in something so hideous."

"Then she won't have anything to worry about." Charles's words were reassuring, but his tone wasn't. He turned to face Lucas. "You know what you have to do."

The old wolf stank so much like wet, burning coffee that Rick looked to the kitchen to check if he'd forgotten to turn off the stove. But no, it was just anger, laden with regret.

"This is going to be a fucking nightmare." Lucas didn't move from his post, leaning against the far wall. He continued staring out the window, his entire posture rigid with barely controlled fury. Watching him, Rick realized that not all of the wood smoke was coming from the fireplace. The log walls would probably be permanently scorched, and there would be a definite handprint burned into the windowsill.

Still, Lucas managed to keep his voice even when he continued. "But first things first. We need someone Aspen trusts to find her and bring her in to deal with the seers issue. Rick, will you do it?"

This was exactly what he'd been afraid of. This tag team of the most powerful Sazi was intended to use him to manipulate and control Josette. They just expected Rick to play along. That pissed him off enough that he decided to give the other man a little taste of what he was feeling. He let down some of his controls, so the whole room—and probably Bruce beyond them—would know *exactly* what he thought of the idea. Amber began to move uncomfortably in her seat and even Charles took a sharp breath.

"Josette is perfectly capable of taking care of herself, and you know it." Rick felt a high-pitched feline snarl rise into his throat. "And despite what Antoine says, she's *not* insane, and she's absolutely trustworthy." Rick lowered his shields, watching as Lucas fought to control a rage that wasn't his own, though it felt exactly as if it were. "I swear I could *gut* her idiot brother for spreading that rumor! She is absolutely coherent in whatever time she's in. It isn't her fault she's existing in the past, present, and future at the same time. You have no fucking clue the kind of pain she's gone through trying to bring her gifts under control. You want her back—but not because you're worried. Because you want to use her. Like you'll use me. Like you use *everybody*."

Lucas made a low sound deep in his chest that would cause most lesser Sazi to grovel at his feet, and power crackled around him as he stalked forward, enough to make the lamp flicker. Human lips pulled back from his teeth in a very inhuman gesture, and the air suddenly reeked of anger, power, and fear. "You have no concept of what is at stake here. How *dare* you think you can stand in judgment of us when you don't have a goddamn clue what's been going on. You've wrapped yourself up in your warm little cocoon, leaving the dirty work for everybody else and now you think you have the *right* to act superior?"

Rick snarled and swatted at the stinging cloud of magic that Lucas attempted to throw around him. His own power flared with an electric heat as the last of his shields crumbled. The barriers between them melted. Rick felt Lucas's rage, but also his guilt at the truth of the accusation, and the fear of some shadowy, overwhelming . . . *something* he knew was about to descend but couldn't quite put a finger to.

It wasn't until Amber spoke, her voice filled with

wonder and sadness, that everyone began to understand just how powerful Rick's gift of empathy had become, and just how hard it had become to control. "Rick, you weren't just suffering from burnout when you left Wolven, were you?"

He struggled against the pull of emotions like a swimmer fighting a riptide. His voice sounded breathy when he replied, and dizziness overtook him.

"No. I needed to get far, far away from everyone—human and Sazi—until I could get control over my *gift*." He turned to Lucas with panic probably plain on his face. "Do you have any idea what it was like? To know exactly how the victims of my *questioning* felt, because I was feeling it with them? You're asking me to test my hard-won control out among the humans and possibly confront a woman I deserted when she needed me. What happens if I fail? What happens to *everyone* if the emotions overwhelm me or if I start projecting my *own* emotions outward? Do you have any idea of the panic I could cause in a major city? The riots I could start without even realizing it?"

Rick shuddered at the flash of a memory that brought him such pain, such shame. He slammed his shields down, cutting the flow of emotion to the others off an instant too late. The room was awash in pain and guilt, rage and fear.

"*This*," Rick snarled back. "is why I live in the middle of godforsaken nowhere, and why I left Wolven.

It's also why you should probably find somebody else to run your little errand."

Lucas glared at him, his massive hands clenched into fists. But it was Charles who spoke, the words hissed through his clenched teeth from emotions that he recognized weren't his. "There *isn't* anybody else."

Rick scented the lie in the air between them, and gave the other man a look of utter disdain before snorting his disbelief.

"Fine." Charles took a slow, deep breath. He very deliberately sat down, leaned back in the seat, and sighed. "There isn't anybody else I'd expect to *survive*."

That, at least, was the truth. But there was more going on here than anybody was saying.

"You do realize that Josette—" Rick stopped to correct himself, "That is, *Aspen* . . . may have disappeared by choice? What if she saw all this and realized that she was a danger to the rest of the seers? Or that she needed to get here to be with the others? What if she's on her way to *us?*"

Lucas nodded. "We've considered that. It's why we need to send someone to her that she trusts. I'm not certain that the ways things are right now, she'll trust any of the rest of us."

Rick picked up his cup and took a long pull of the nearly cold coffee before setting it back onto the end table. "*If* I agree to do this, and I'm not saying I will,

I'd need to know everything she's liable to be seeing that would spook her enough to make her take off."

Lucas was bleeding suspicion and raised his own shields until Rick couldn't feel him anymore. He'd been careful to put on the Wolven cologne when he went outside earlier to check the SUV with Bruce, so his scent didn't give away his mood, but he'd forgotten just how easy it was for Rick to read him. The old wolf's expression grew flat and impersonal. "You'll be told everything you need to know."

Rick shook his head. "Not good enough."

The two men stared at each other across the room. The silence thickened and magic filled the air. The temperature rose until sweat beaded each man's brow. Rick knew Lucas could beat him. Hell, anyone in the room probably could. But he didn't care. He wouldn't back down. This was too important. *Josie* was too important. If they were going to use his relationship with her as a tool to get her to cooperate, he wanted to be damned sure it was for a good cause. He'd seen too much, done too much to simply trust anyone—especially those in the Sazi hierarchy.

"Mon Dieu!" Amber spat the words out and the air crackled around her. A French accent filled her voice, the same thing that used to happen to Josette when she was too stressed. "Time iz too short for theez. Just tell him, Charles, or I swear to the heavens that *I* will!"

Lucas made a disgusted noise in the back of his

throat, but Charles just sighed with resignation. Apparently, he knew exactly what his wife was capable of. "If we don't find Aspen in five days, every seer in the world will be dead. Within a week after that, the council will fall. After that, the remaining Sazi and humans alike will all be nothing more than cannon fodder, as something unimaginable—and I don't use that word lightly, it's hidden even to the best of us— sweeps over the world like a plague."

Rick stared into the other man's eyes. The intensity of his belief was a thrum like a bass drum that pounded at his temples. "How in the hell did it come to this?"

"Whoever we're dealing with is good. *Very* good. They've exploited every weakness we have to the point where I don't know who to trust." Lucas rubbed the bridge of his nose with his thumb and forefinger. "In fact, it's so fucked up we haven't even got a clue as to the extent of the mess. Worse still, we don't know who we're fighting."

Rick's eyes widened. "I can't believe Fiona let it get this far. I mean, whatever faults she may have, she was one hell of a good agent."

Lucas's flat, cold statement had enough truth inside to chill his blood. "Not good enough. Not *nearly* good enough for this."

Charles sighed. "Someone has apparently been planning this for decades, possibly centuries." He shuddered and was forced to steady himself against the nearest wall. Pain rolled off him in waves, but he fought through it. "Another vision is trying to come, but it can't get through the block. It hurts like a son of a bitch."

It was the pain that did it. Rick probably would have done it for Josie anyway, just to see her again. But Charles had been his mentor and was the closest thing he had to a father. It took a lot to bring the ancient polar bear, once worshipped by the humans as a god, to his knees. He turned his gaze to each of them in turn. "Tell me what I have to do."

Chapter Five

IT WAS STILL painful to move, but Josette did it anyway, digging deep into the packed sand to reveal a plastic Bubble Wrap envelope that was thankfully still buried at the base of the old hickory. Once it was unearthed, she carried it in her teeth and used her nose to follow the path of the snakes back to where they'd hidden their vehicle. Her little Jeep, which had been in the attached garage, was nothing more than a lump of steel by now, but she doubted the snakes would need theirs.

They'd left it a surprisingly long way from the house. She was forced to make a good five-mile trek to find it hidden in the brush just off one of the side roads. A black SUV with tinted windows and all the luxuries a yuppie on vacation could want. The snakes had left it unlocked with the keys in the ignition. There had probably been aversion magic protecting it originally, making humans and Sazi alike unwilling to venture close. But the snakes were dead, and the power for the spell had died with them. So here it sat, ready and waiting for a pair of people who would never return. It was practically a gift.

Still, Josette sniffed around it carefully before she

risked opening the door. There was no scent of explosives; no trap that she could see. Peering through the window she saw a black nylon duffel on the passenger seat. It was unzipped, and she could see it was stuffed with the kind of cheap "one size fits all" clothing Sazi always kept on hand. There were wigs, too, one blond, two dark brown. That was no surprise. Most reptilian women had little or no hair in their human form. They wore wigs to "pass" in normal society.

Josette shifted into human form and pulled open the passenger door. When nothing bad happened she let out the breath she hadn't realized she'd been holding and quickly began rummaging through the duffel. There were clothes for both men and women. She also found a Latina women's wallet. There was a driver's license in the name of Maria Ortega, with a matching credit card. There were no other cards and the picture sleeves had been removed, probably to keep it from looking achingly empty. Most people filled their wallets with photos of loved ones. Not having any would be obviously odd.

There was a little over seven hundred dollars in cash of various denominations tucked in the billfold, some loose change in the coin purse. Documents for the car rental in Maria's name were neatly folded into a side zipper pocket of the bag. The vehicle was due back to the Avis rental agency at 7:00 P.M. the day after tomorrow. That gave Josette more than enough time to get things done. Also in the pocket was a matchbox from the Fontana Bowling Alley in Flagstaff and a key. It looked like it should fit into an old-fashioned pay locker of the type that used to be in bus and train stations before terrorism became an issue. The number on its orange plastic head read 145. She resolved that when she made it to Flagstaff she'd check out the Fontana, see if the key worked at a locker there. There might even be a clue as to who was behind this. Probably not, but it was certainly worth checking out.

She put the items back into their compartment, zipping it closed before choosing an outfit to wear. There was the equivalent of two outfits each in the bag for both the man and the woman. She chose a plain black T-shirt over a pair of black jogging shorts with white stripes running down the size. They were a little baggy, but not too bad, particularly when she tightened the drawstring sewn into the waistband of the pants. The pair of women's running shoes in the bag were about a half-size too large, but she put them on anyway, lacing them as tight as she could so that they wouldn't be any more uncomfortable than necessary.

Josette could hear cars in the distance. They were moving eastbound along the main road, going fast. *Probably the cavalry coming to investigate the smoke*. Not wanting to be spotted leaving the scene of the fire, she decided to look through the envelope, which she'd never opened in the years since she'd paid for the work to be done.

Examining the package, it didn't *look* like it had been opened. Yusef, one of Charles's guards, did identities on the side and did them very well . . . for the right price. He'd sealed it very carefully, even going so far as to sign across the sealed flap after he'd glued it, and then taped the whole thing with two or three layers of the kind of clear shipping tape that had reinforced threads running through it. She couldn't imagine how anyone could have tampered with it without leaving plenty of evidence, and she hadn't noticed the scent of anyone when she'd been digging.

She felt her shoulders relax fractionally, and the knot of terror in her stomach unwound a little. Perhaps things weren't as bad as she'd feared.

She pulled a Louisiana driver's license out of the envelope first and saw a picture of herself smiling at the camera. "Josette LaRue." She said the name softly, getting a feel for it. It wasn't bad; certainly better than some of the names she'd worn and discarded like clothing over the long years of her life.

The first few days were always the hardest. It was difficult answering to a new name, remembering a complicated past you'd never lived. It was like breaking in a new pair of shoes. Also, there were the little things you needed to do to create an individual identity. What was her favorite color? What music did she listen to? Did she have any hobbies? These weren't the kinds of things you find on a driver's license or birth certificate, but they were just as important as good documentation in making a believable identity. A twenty-year-old probably wasn't going to be hooked on Sinatra and Elvis after all.

With nearly unlimited time to work, Yusef's artistry had been given full rein. There was a two-page summary, birth and marriage certificates, death certificates, a driver's license, and a passport in the envelope. There was also a vehicle key, and the address of a storage unit where it was most likely stored. And there was cash; quite a lot of cash by thumbing through the large denomination bills. Most commerce moved electronically now, but there was nothing quite as untraceable as hard currency.

She pulled the summary from the package, scanning it quickly. Josette LaRue had been born Josette Reynard to an American father and French Canadian mother. At age eighteen she'd moved to New Orleans where she met and married Jacques LaRue, a Cajun who had, alas, been a small-time crook. The divorce had been finalized a mere three years later, while Jacques was in the federal penitentiary where he died two years later.

There had been a house in New Orleans, before Katrina. She could have moved there, if she'd chosen to activate the identity earlier. Unfortunately, the map showed that it had been in a neighborhood that was destroyed in the flooding. It was probably too late to make a claim for benefits, but Josette LaRue wasn't wealthy enough to let something like that go. So, sometime in the next few days she'd need to start the paperwork in motion.

Overall Josette LaRue had led a rough life. But she was a survivor, at least that would be how she thought of herself. Josette decided that the story would be that using a little money she'd inherited from her father, she was starting a new life at thirty.

Based on that history she decided on a personality that wouldn't be too much of a stretch, but was definitely different from her normal routine. Josette LaRue would be someone who liked to walk that fine line between flash and trash. Her favorite color would be red. She'd wear dangling earrings and rings on every finger, with bright nail polish on both finger and toenails. Her tops and jeans would be worn a little too tight, shorts and skirts a fraction too short. She wouldn't be caught dead outside the house without her makeup on. As for hobbies, well she'd like to dance and shoot pool, and she could drink a strong man under the table when the occasion called for it.

Looking at the envelope in her lap she felt a wave of sadness and she ran a light finger across the deep indents of his signature into the tape. Yusef was dead and she would miss him. She'd seen his betrayal coming long before he was killed in Boulder the previous winter. She felt a little guilty both that she hadn't warned Charles that his favorite guard would betray him, nor had she warned Yusef that he was making a terrible mistake by siding with Jack Simpson in a war he couldn't win.

It had been a hard decision. She'd *liked* Yusef. She knew how much his betrayal would hurt Charles. But she also knew that if she'd interfered, there would have been other, worse things happen as a consequence.

It was one of the hardest things about foresight— having to choose when to interfere and when *not* to. It hurt her more than she had ever admitted to stand back and do *nothing* when terrible things were about to happen. Tasha's scorn had stung deeply, but there was no way Josette could ever expect her to understand. There were probably harder things in life than looking someone in the eye knowing what would happen and keeping every bit of that knowledge from your expression, even from your scent . . . but she hadn't run into one of them yet.

Her sister Amber wondered why she had chosen to live alone in the middle of the desert. In truth, it was simply easier. Yes, it slowed the visions, helped her control her gift, but it was more than that. Isolation had kept her from having to face people. It was a little lonely sometimes, but for the most part she hadn't minded.

With deft movements Josette stripped Maria's identification and credit card from the wallet, and slid the new ones in their place. Everything else she slid back into the envelope, and then zipped the envelope into the duffel.

The address printed on the key tag matched that of the vehicle title. Pony, New Mexico, wasn't a town she'd heard of before, but she'd have bet that Yusef chose it for its remoteness and relative quiet. Hopefully, it would be the perfect place to get herself together before contacting her family. She knew she had to do that. It was part of the future she'd seen in every vision so far. Flagstaff and the Fontana Bowling Alley would have to wait.

She was as ready as she would ever be. It was time to stop procrastinating. Still, she couldn't help casting one long last look across the fields to where her home had been. Blinking back useless tears, she climbed behind the wheel of the SUV. Moments later, tires spitting gravel, she pulled onto the highway and drove away for the last time.

Josette drove all through the remainder of the night and into the next day, stopping only to gas up. She finally stopped just after dawn to grab some food at a truck stop that advertised "24 Hour Breakfast." It was a buffet, but the meat was fresh and good. Nibbling on a slice of wheat toast, she looked through the newspaper, searching for anything odd about the explosion that might have made it to the national press. An advertisement on one page reminded her of a request she'd made offhand to Yusef that she hoped he'd followed. He'd asked about her car preference and, on impulse, she'd decided on a convertible. It was as close as she'd ever get to the sensation of riding a motorcycle, something that both Rick and Raven adored.

Perhaps it was thinking of him that did it. But the scene in the dining room disappeared. Instead, she was standing in a bathroom filled with steam. She could hear the shower running. Rick was humming a tune she recognized. It was an old folk song, the one that had been playing the first time they'd danced, when he'd just begun courting her. Not from one of the minuets, but a more rowdy tune, perfect for a jig. It was the kind of song that set your toes tapping.

She moved like the mist swirling through the warm air, rising toward the exhaust vent. She stopped, just above the rod holding the shower curtain.

He stood nude, the water pouring over the length of his muscular body, sending soap suds over the muscles of his abdomen to trail down through the coarse hairs that framed his cock. Josette thought she had remembered every inch of that body, but she hadn't. Time had fuzzed the edges in her mind, making her forget the small details, like the mole beside his belly button, or the way the raised scars on his chest pulled his left nipple.

Water beaded in the dark gold of his chest hairs. A part of her ached to be there in truth, to

*join him under the shower's spray, run her hands
over every inch of his body to feel his skin on hers.*

*His head was tilted back to keep the shampoo
from his eyes as his hands worked the soap into a
lather. The humming stopped abruptly. She felt the
flare of his power. His eyes popped open, glowing
bright gold in the dimness of the shower stall. He
stared at the spot where her essence hovered.
"Josie?"*

The shock of finding herself back in the dining
room made her gasp. She blinked repeatedly, trying
to bring the present place and time into focus. It took
a few minutes for the scent of his shampoo to fade
from her consciousness. It took even longer for the
hunger in her body to subside, a hunger that had
nothing to do with the food on the plate.

It wasn't until she was paying her bill at the register
that time solidified in her mind. She still wasn't sure if
the vision of Rick had been of when they were married,
the present, or some time yet to come. But the more often she saw him, the more she was convinced it was the
present . . . and they would meet again. But at least she
was firmly in the here and now, for the moment.

But what was the *here and now?* There were no
newspaper stands in sight—her usual method of keeping track of the day. "Excuse me," she called out to the
woman behind a counter that sold fudge by the pound.
The woman turned her head and raised her brows.

"What's the date today?"

The woman smiled as she cut a block of gooey dark candy from a massive slab and put it on the scale to weigh. "Thursday the eleventh."

She looked around out the window. No snow, but then—would there be any here, regardless of the month? "What month?"

That question got an odd look, but not to the point the woman did more than shrug. "April."

She wished she could ask the year, too, because that could make a large difference in where she went next. She suddenly remembered Pony, but that meant things were splitting in her mind, melding into threads of other possibilities. But if not knowing the month was odd, not knowing the year would seem completely insane. No, she'd have to do this the hard way. She'd managed to find a few coping mechanisms over the years to help in situations like this; by far her favorite was the handy inspection stickers on vehicle windshields. Only in August and September did that method sometimes fail her, when people often replaced their vehicles with the newest model.

"Visine's on aisle two." A male voice in front of her startled her out of her mulling, and she looked up with a quick shake of her head.

"Excuse me?" She turned her head to see who he might be talking to and realized she was the only person in hearing distance.

"Your eyes look pretty red. You been driving all night?"

Did they? That seemed odd, since her eyes should heal as quickly as the rest of her Sazi anatomy. "Um, yes. But I'll be fine."

The man, not much more than a boy really, looked her over again with enough scrutiny that she instinctively sniffed for his scent to see if he were a danger. No, there was nothing but cheap cologne and the lingering smell of stale popcorn and hot dog grease that clung to his pale skin and shaggy auburn hair like glue. "We've got a shower in back . . . for the truckers. I've heard people say it helps wake them up."

A shower. Her breath caught in her throat. Was the vision just a vision, or would she find Rick here, in this stupid interstate gas station? Her heart pounded nervously. She shouldn't still feel things for him—he deserted her, after all. But she did.

The showers weren't unisex, unfortunately, and the stalls were built wrong for the one in her vision. Still, the hot water really helped and being dressed in clothing that fit was even better. One thing Josette had always liked about big truck stops was they carried clothing and toiletries. Everything necessary to keep a trucker—male or female—clean and on the road.

Pressing the button on the keychain, the vehicle's security system gave a reassuring beep. Still, she was feeling antsy. Perhaps it was the vision, but she just didn't feel comfortable. Something was nibbling at the edge of her consciousness, like a mouse at grain. Before she climbed inside, she walked over to the side of the dining room and looked down the length of cars. As she watched, a black SUV much like the one she was driving pulled up to the back of the building. The man from behind the counter where she paid rushed out to greet the pair of suited, olive-skinned men who climbed from the vehicle. She took a tentative whiff. As she suspected, they were snake shifters.

The encounter could mean nothing. But it didn't *look* like nothing. In fact, to her it appeared downright sinister. Was the suggestion of a shower to delay her? If so, it had worked. And what would she have discovered in aisle two if she'd ventured there as the clerk suggested? Josette backed quickly into the shadows, and right into another person. Feminine hands grasped her shoulders and a snarl spilled from her lips as her magic flared.

Adrenaline flooded her system as she turned, expecting to have to fight her way out of the parking lot. But the face that greeted her when she completed her spin was young, probably only sixteen or seventeen, with a panicked expression.

And she smelled of fear and feathers, not scales.

"Please! You've got to help me. They're going to kill my mom if I don't get back there in time." Her words were whispered and hurried and her eyes kept flicking toward the SUV that Josette had been watching.

Time slowed as the girl turned and crouched down behind a pebbled concrete trash can. She'd seen this moment before . . . in a vision years before. The girl was petite, with nearly black hair and dark brown eyes. She had dressed in low-slung jeans and a scooped-neck tank top that clung to her like a second skin, showing off impressive cleavage. Her arms were long, too long to be in complete proportion to her body. One of the birds then; a Sazi almost ready for her first turn. But why on earth was she out in public so close to her first change? Where was her family, her mentor?

"Who are you?" Josette realized her words came out suspicious, but there was certainly cause. "And why do you think I can help you?"

The girl didn't seem to mind the misgiving. She stared at her with near adoration, as though Josette was someone she knew and trusted. "My name's Ellen . . . Ellen Harris. I realize you don't know me, but you're one of *them,* one like me, but with fur. And—" Ellen's face took on an intense, yet somehow helpless expression. "I just . . . *know.* I know things, but I'm not very good at explaining them."

A *seer.* The girl was, or would be, a seer like her. Josette looked at the bright, birdlike eyes, filled with fear and knowledge and felt something in her mind *shift*—enough to nearly make her dizzy, as though the future was rewriting itself as she watched.

She made the decision just as the black SUV's doors slammed and the clerk hurried back into the building. "Stay here. I'll drive over and pick you up. Get in the back passenger door and stay on the floor. We can talk after we're out on the interstate."

Ellen nodded and smiled, a shy turning of lips with tear-filled eyes. "Thank you. I've been waiting for days for you to stop for breakfast—hiding behind the restaurant, stealing food from the Dumpster. I was starting to get afraid that—"

"That you might be wrong?" Josette raised her brows and the girl shrugged with near embarrassment. It nearly made her chuckle. How many times had she done similar things when she was a child, waiting impatiently for a future scene in her mind to arrive? It was like counting days until a birthday or Christmas for a human. She crouched down beside the girl and touched her hand before whispering in her ear. "You weren't. I've seen you, too."

With a quick pat, she pulled away her hand and bolted for the rental, keeping low and moving between parked cars to confuse the men in the SUV. The lingering scent of Ellen's surprise, laced with warm flowery gratitude, stayed in her nose even over the petrochemicals assaulting her from the idling trucks and cars.

It went off like clockwork. A massive tanker truck pulled across the line of sight of the SUV just as she started the car and pulled over to pick up Ellen. Dark smoke rose from the rear tires in the rearview mirror as the men realized she'd escaped onto the frontage road, and they accelerated to start the chase.

The posted speed limit was quickly surpassed as they raced toward Albuquerque to, hopefully, lose the pursuers in the crowd of cars. Ellen seemed to be content to remain on the floor in back while Josette drove with determined intensity. The girl's scent had moved from afraid to pleased relief, despite being thrown around on the floor as the car dodged between slower moving vehicles at an ever-increasing pace.

"Where do you need to go? Where are they holding your mother?"

"We live in a little town to the east of here, called Pony. You've probably never heard of it."

A laugh boiled up out of her chest, nearly causing her to take her eyes off the road to see the girl's face. But that would be a bad thing, considering she was next to a semi and was just crossing a bridge. Instead, she turned the rearview mirror down so she could keep her eyes forward and then pulled out the key tag that Yusef had written, handing it back between the split seats. "Do you recognize this address?"

Ellen took the key and nodded as she read, her short dark hair bobbing in the sunlight just at the edge of Josette's peripheral vision. "Oh, sure. This is old Widow Hunt's place. You mean *you're* the one who bought her husband's Firebird convertible? It's been sitting in her garage since I was born, waiting for the new owner to show up. My cousin goes over every fall to drive it around town a few times to keep the battery charged and then drains the oil for winter." Her laugh was a fluttering screech, the high-pitched sound of a raptor, and she covered her mouth, reeking embarrassment.

Josette saw an opening between the semi and the delivery truck in front of it and pressed down on the accelerator hard to squeeze into the space before slowing. The black SUV started to move into the lane to catch up when a highway patrol car pulled into the median. She was relieved when the SUV backed down its speed and pulled in behind the semi.

"You don't have to be embarrassed about your laugh, Ellen. All Sazi birds make that same sound, or something like it." She did glance down then, just a quick flick of her eyes when fear boiled up out of the girl's pores. "You haven't had your first change yet, have you?"

"Huh-uh. And if my dad has any say about it, I won't, either." Her voice and scent said she truly believed that.

"He *doesn't* have any say about it. If you're meant to turn, you will. Do you have others in your family who turn that can help you through it the first time?"

Again she shook her head. "Gramma was the only one on Mom's side, and Daddy doesn't talk about his family, so I don't know. But Mom said I got it from both sides. I left because I was afraid what he'd do if I did change. I was already weird to him because of the dreams that come true, and he *hates* shifters— hates and fears them, the way people used to hate women healers in Salem. Even mentioning his or Mom's family makes him insane. I just know he's going to use me as some sort of guinea pig for that stuff he's been cooking up with his freaky friends out in the desert. I've heard him talking, like they can cure me, or something."

Josette sighed as she darted the rental between another pair of trucks and slowed to make sure there was no room for their tail to fit. So, there was another group trying to *fix* them. It wasn't the first time. "There's no cure for what we are, Ellen—even though sometimes I wish there was. We are Sazi. It's nothing to be ashamed of. But if you truly feel you and your mother are in danger, I'll give you a phone number to call. A woman named Angelique is the leader of all the birds in the world. She can help you. If you leave—"

"I *did* leave. But then I *saw* what he'd do to Mom if he found out I wasn't coming back, so . . . I have to go back. I can't leave her to—" She grimaced and pressed both her hands to her temples, as if staving off another vision. "Please. I don't want to talk about what might happen."

A wave of pain flashed through Josette, and tension churned her stomach. Talking about bad visions only made them worse; sometimes they triggered a new, darker image just through the speaking of it. "I understand. More than you can know, I understand."

The overhead sign that zipped past revealed the next exit was for one of the main business streets. With careful maneuvering, she managed to make it into the right lane without the SUV noticing, so when she exited along with a flow of other vehicles, their pursuers were caught flat-footed. She ignored the squealing tires and horn honks as the SUV cut through traffic, and across the median . . . as the chase car gave up all pretense of hiding their intent. Josette concentrated instead on moving into the downtown where she might be able to lose them.

That one decision apparently made them more bold and the few horn honks became many as the SUV began to force vehicles off the road in order to get closer. Josette couldn't even bear to look in the rearview to see the images that the sounds hinted at before they disappeared into the distance—squealing tires, yelling, the angry rent of metal twisting and glass breaking. With a hard yank of the wheel, she moved off the main street onto an empty side street. But then Ellen's voice came from behind her, in a whispered singsong that she recognized. The girl was having a vision.

"She can't die. The woman . . . blue sedan . . . must live. Baby . . . future—"

It was a good opportunity to coach the girl on using her visions to help keep an important future on track. "Tell me what you're seeing, Ellen. Look around at the scenery and describe things." She scanned the area ahead. New architecture blended with old on the quiet street. There were a number of sidewalk cafes ahead with a few scattered patrons. She raised her voice and pushed magic into Ellen, causing the girl to gasp and thrash against the door. "I need to know! Where is she?"

Josette passed through a yellow light and cursed under her breath when the SUV zoomed through the cold red in her wake. Glancing down at the speedometer, she realized she was already ten over the limit and was bound to become a danger to people soon.

She needed to end this. She touched Ellen's arm, forced her way into the girl's vision until Josette was standing beside her on the street in a near future time. Yes, a different angle, an altered perspective, but it was this place; this time. The Ellen in the vision turned to her with awe plain on her face. But she was too far inside to separate her mind from that which was happening *to* her mind.

Josette desperately tried to keep her attention on the task of driving while seeing her own car approaching from far down the street. But she couldn't look to the side until Ellen herself did. Not without losing her hold on reality. "Think! Tell me quick. *What's on the street?* What do you *see?* Turn your head and look around." More magic, filled with a subtle persuasion that shouldn't give her too much of a headache.

The girl's head turned and it was enough. Josette saw the location just as Ellen spoke in the car. "Chairs—" The voice was reedy and thin and she started gasping for air. "Green . . . striped awning."

Josette removed her hand, pulled herself away from the image, and looked as far into the distance as she could. *There!* She saw it: a café far up the street and yes, there was a blue sedan parked in front.

Abruptly, anger filled her. She hated this, hated that the people in the SUV cared so little for the humans that they would risk them all just to get her. But she wasn't willing to go down that road easily, nor would she risk killing people that could alter the future.

But maybe she didn't have to do either one.

A slip of movement caught her eye five stoplights ahead, and she focused in with supernatural sight. A utility company was repairing a streetlight with a bucket lift truck, but nobody was in the basket yet. One man in a uniform was pouring coffee from a Thermos into a cup held by the another man.

Yes. Perfect. But the timing would have to be exact.

Another glance in the rearview. They were about half a block back and moving up fast. Josette reached out with her magic, pushed it out through the window of the rental, stretching . . . stretching, until she touched the cool metal of the truck ahead. She began to rock the truck on its wheels, making it seem as though the truck were caught in a strange harsh crosswind. The men on the sidewalk began to back away as the shaking increased.

She gunned the engine to increase the distance between the two vehicles and shot ahead, keeping her hold on the truck as they passed it by. Pulling on every reserve she had to allow herself to continue to drive, she yanked hard on the truck, tightening the noose on it like an errant steer. With a snap of energy that took her breath away and nearly caused her to black out, the truck toppled over into the street—right in front of the SUV.

There was no getting out of the way as the boom extended from the sheer force of the impact against the asphalt, and the SUV slammed headfirst into the basket hard enough to raise the back wheels off the road. She slowed her pace and continued to watch in the rearview as feeling left her fingers, causing a pins-and-needles sensation, and an odd drowsiness threatened to overtake her.

The men on the sidewalk ran toward the SUV. They were safe and whole. As for the snakes in the SUV, they'd heal. Or not. She really didn't care either way.

"Can't die—" Whispered words turned into a shout. "CAN'T DIE!"

Josette felt tears well as they passed by the café,

and a very pregnant woman holding a bagel stopped from getting into her blue sedan to see what the commotion down the street was, just as sirens filled the air. "And she's not going to, sweetie. She's not going to."

Chapter Six

THERE WERE ANY number of things necessary in preparing the cabin for his absence. Rick hoped it wouldn't be a long one, but something told him it might be. A phone call to Lucas just after dawn had been useful. Raven Ramirez had discovered some information in the computers before he'd crashed the system by remote command. It might be a clue to the location where Josie was headed. But, it was far too sensitive to discuss by phone, so Charles had decided Rick should drive to Colorado where they could talk in person.

Unfortunately, there was no telling whether Josette would be at the location, or whether the information would just be the first in a long trail of near misses until he could find her. She was *very* good at hiding her tracks—she'd had plenty of practice over the centuries.

Amber had insisted they all get a few hours sleep, with only Bruce staying awake to guard them. Morning had come too quickly, his dreams filled with snakes and twisted by the emotions of the others in the house.

He didn't know what to think about his shower

earlier. He could *swear* Josette was standing in the room watching him. But when he pulled aside the curtain, the room was empty . . . although it smelled of vanilla, musk, and fur, a combination he'd never been able to erase from his mind, even after all these years. Maybe it was a premonition. Part of him hoped so. Another part of him feared being in easy reach of her formidable anger. A shudder overtook him as he struggled to close the stretched-taut leather saddlebags that fit on the back of his motorcycle. He put them beside the door and stood staring at the wall for a moment, tapping one finger against his hip—trying to remember whether he'd completed his list of tasks.

The others were now safely on their way to wherever they were going to weather out the crisis, and Rick decided it was worth taking the time to shut down the house before leaving. The water and gas were first, then draining the pipes so that he wouldn't come back to splits from a hard freeze. Next, he cleared all the perishable foods from the fridge and cupboards, taking them to the edge of the windmill tank for the animals to feast on. Hopefully, the windmill would still be standing when he returned, but he just couldn't deprive the wildlife of the water they'd come to depend on. For better or worse, they were partners in the life he'd made here, even though they were no substitute for the partner he'd once had.

A sigh eased from his chest and he shook his head.

It would have been easier if he had some clue as to how long he'd be gone, but he really didn't know. It could be anything from a few weeks to years. He did know he wanted to come back here eventually. This was his home in a way few places had been in his life. Only the cabin he'd shared with Josette in what was now Illinois had ever been more dear to him.

While closing up the house took hours from when he started at dawn, packing was accomplished in a matter of a minutes. He didn't want or need much: a couple changes of clothes, a few toiletries. He did pull most of the cash out of his floor safe though, along with his identification and credit cards.

By 10:00 A.M. he was ready to go. After one last lingering look around the cabin, he stepped outside and took a deep breath of cold, clean air, feeling both excited at the adventure and terrified of the prospect of seeing Josette again—or worse, *failing* to see her again. Sunlight gleamed off the polished metal and chrome of his classic Indian motorcycle. He paused to check the contents of his saddlebags one last time. When he was sure he hadn't forgotten anything important, he straddled the machine and kick-started the bike.

The bike started without protest, the engine emitting a rumbling purr that echoed through the nearly empty landscape. He pulled a pair of mirrored sunglasses from the pocket of his coat and slid them on, wrapped a scarf around his neck, and put on gloves.

There was nothing else to do. He was as ready as he'd ever be, so he gunned the engine and was on his way.

The ride to Denver would be a little over eight hours if he went without stops. With breaks for meals and to stretch his legs it would be closer to ten. Rick knew that by the end of it he'd be glad for his healing abilities. A ten-hour ride on a bike when you're out of practice is a painful proposition—just inviting leg cramps, a backache, and an indescribable pain in the backside.

The weather stayed clear, without so much as a single cloud marring the perfect blue of the sky overhead. But even with the warm gear and his Sazi blood, it was a frigid ride through South Dakota and northern Wyoming this early in the year.

He ate an early dinner at a Denny's in Cheyenne, filling up on one of their specials before fueling up the bike at the gas station across the way. The weather had warmed as the day wore on until it was in the seventies. Rick stowed away his cold weather gear in the saddlebags and even left his shirt unbuttoned. He wanted to feel the wind against his skin and blowing through his hair. It was a sensation as close to flying as a cat could get. Oh, it could hurt like a bitch when the bugs hit, and once, a bird smacked into his chest, causing him to wreck. But he didn't care. He'd heal.

Before mounting up he strode over to the pay phone on the wall outside the gas station. Pulling change from his pocket he dropped it in the slot and dialed the number for information. The computerized voice on the line recited the number, offering to connect him for a small additional charge. Since he didn't have a pen handy, he paid it and was rewarded by the almost immediate ringing of the line on the other end.

A voice picked up on the second ring. He sounded young, but businesslike. "Ramirez towing, Pete here. Can I help you?"

"I need to talk to Raven. Tell him it's Rick Johnson."

"Raven isn't in right now. But he told me you might call. He wants you to call him on his cell. Do you have a pen?"

No, he didn't, and as a member of Wolven command, Raven should know damned well that he would *only* talk to the actual contact at the number provided. Good agents didn't leave messages with strangers to pass out like candy. But there wasn't much he could do about it.

"Give me the number," he growled.

Pete recited a series of numbers, Rick read them back from memory. When he had them down pat, he hung up without saying good-bye.

The first call had taken all of his change, so he went inside and bought himself a bottled soda and packet of corn nuts to break a ten. Back at the phone, he dialed the cell phone number he'd memorized.

"Ramirez."

He'd never talked to Raven on the phone and, as annoyed as he was right now, the words came out in a snarl. "Prove it."

The sigh was tired, like the whole world was suddenly too much for him. "God I hate this bullshit. I'm on medical leave. I shouldn't have to put up with this paranoid crap."

When Rick didn't respond to the comment, the other man let out a half-hearted growl. "I'm not sure what you want to hear. My father's got children with your ex-wife's twin sister. Their relationship broke up when he cheated on her with their *other* sister."

"That's common knowledge."

"Not the ex-wife part. Not many people realize Aspen was ever married, and most of them think she's a widow."

He had a point. Rick still didn't like it, but as long as the meet was in a public place, he'd go along with it. "Fine. Where and when?"

"Meet me in Denver at Bubba's Roadhouse at the corner of Speer and Federal at 9:30 tonight." He hung up before Rick could argue or ask directions. With a sigh, he went inside one more time, this time to buy a map of Denver.

Sitting on the curb, he sucked down an energy drink as he studied the map. According to it, Bubba's should be easy enough to find. Both Speer and Federal were major traffic arteries. He just needed to get on I-25, take a straight shot down until he reached the right exit.

Folding up the map, he rose and crossed back to the phone, dumping his trash in the can by the door on his way. Another call to information got him the number of one of the cheap chain motels with a branch on Federal. He reserved a room, guaranteeing it with his credit card since he wasn't sure how late he'd arrive. With that done, there was no other reason to linger. He stowed the map, slid on his sunglasses, and climbed on the bike.

It was an easy drive. He stayed close to the speed limit, enjoying the feeling of the bike under him and marveling in the way the area between Cheyenne and Denver had grown. He couldn't even remember the last time he'd gone on a cross-country ride this direction. It'd been too long ago, that was for damned sure.

He made it to the bar without incident and with time to spare. At nine P.M. the bar was busy, but not packed. More than a dozen motorcycles, all of them Harleys were lined up in the lot outside the front door, paint and chrome gleaming in the yellow-orange glow of the halogen lamps that lit every corner of the parking area.

In the short three blocks since he'd exited I-25 he'd encountered three black-and-white patrol cars. A fourth cruiser drove slowly past as he was dismounting. Feeling impish, he gave the driver a cheery wave and was rewarded with a stern glare.

He heard the snort of laughter coming from one

of the pair of smokers standing by the front door. The scent of tobacco drifted to him on the evening breeze. He turned to follow the scent and saw a bone-thin woman with bleached-blond hair and too much makeup getting a light from a short Mexican man. His leather vest bore the name of a national gang emblazoned across the back with "Las Vegas" embroidered under it in red thread. She didn't love him, barely knew him, in fact. But a desperate need filled her that only the man could satisfy. Whether it was drugs or sex, or something else, Rick didn't know. If the man had any emotion for the woman, he hid it well. But he was pretty sure that there was nothing there, except perhaps lust. They gave him a nod of acknowledgment as he moved past them and pushed through the front door.

Lynyrd Skynyrd was blasting on the jukebox; the click of billiard balls was a sharp counterpoint to the rock beat. Rick's nose was assailed by the mingled scents of cooking meat, beer, emotions, and bodies. No Sazi yet or cigarette smoke, which just seemed odd to him. There was just something *wrong* about a bar that didn't allow smoking. Most likely, a "burn ban" here had forced the smokers to step outside. He'd heard of them, even though they hadn't reached the small towns around his home.

He paused, casually getting his bearings as his eyes adjusted to the dim lighting. Four or five men were bellied up to the bar, drinking beer and arguing about the game playing on the television above their heads. But the arguing was friendly. Nobody felt or smelled of true anger. One or two groups had gathered at tables, downing shots and chatting. A couple was dancing on a floor not much bigger than the average postage stamp, and while she was a good five inches taller and probably weighed thirty or forty pounds more than her partner, it didn't stop her from doing an impressive shimmy that nearly shook her breasts loose from the tight leather vest that was struggling to contain them. She wasn't Rick's type, but she was certainly making an impression on the wiry specimen she was dancing with.

"What'll you have?" The bartender was a woman. Petite and pretty, she reminded him of Josette with her dark blond hair and compact build. He was surprised to see a woman bartender in a place like this. Then again, she had the kind of no-nonsense attitude that let him know trouble wouldn't be tolerated. Tough, she was definitely tough. But when she smiled it lit up a pair of wide greenish hazel eyes and flashed straight white teeth and deep dimples.

"Samuel Adams dark and a menu. I'm starved." Rick took a seat on the nearest wooden bar stool, making himself comfortable as she used a cloth to wipe the bar in front of him before setting down a coaster, bottle, and glass. She pulled a laminated menu from the pocket of the black apron tied around her waist, set it in front of him, and waited.

"I'll have the hamburger platter, rare as I can get it." Rick started to pass the menu back, and then turned at a chorus of cheers and groans from the pool area. Elation and frustration filled the room simultaneously, and he struggled against the strong emotions that threatened to overwhelm him. They pressed against his skin like a raging tide of water, only a thin film of magic held them back. His words came out breathier than he planned, but at least he could talk. "Someone lost a bet."

"Yup, a big one." She took the menu from his hand and waited as he retrieved his wallet with a shaky hand to pay. He wasn't positive he'd be able to do so a second time if the emotional tide kept up.

"Can I run a tab?"

She shook her head no. "Sorry." She pointed to a large handwritten sign taped to the mirror behind the bar. "The boss got burned one too many times. Even *he* pays cash as he goes."

"Fair enough," Rick nodded to let her know he wasn't offended. When she counted out his change he gave her a generous tip.

He watched her walk to the door of the kitchen over the rim of his glass, admiring the movement of her hips as she walked before realizing the admiration wasn't his. One of the drinkers down the way was smitten with her—couldn't take his eyes off the waitress.

Raising his shields a little higher, he took a deep

breath and realized a shifter had come in the bar. His hand tightened on the mug by reflex and his mind focused in on that one smell without giving any outward appearance he noticed. A wolf, by the scent, and powerful enough to tingle his skin. He certainly wasn't up to the level of Lucas, but then, who was?

"Very nice."

The voice was similar to the one on the phone. Rick turned to greet the man who'd joined him at the bar. Yes, this had to be Raven Ramirez. He had a strong resemblance to some in the Alaskan pack, with hair the color of dark chocolate that hung well past his hips. He had it pulled back and held in place with black rubber bands that were nearly invisible against the midnight leather of the biker jacket he wore unzipped. His jeans and boots were black as well. His shirt showed a mouse giving the finger to a striking bald eagle with the caption, "The Last Great Act of Defiance." A casual observer would know at a glance he was dangerous. They wouldn't know he was a werewolf.

"You must be Raven. How's your dad?" Even though he didn't know the man, it never hurt to ask after kin.

"Better now that Jack's gone," Raven said with deadpan seriousness. "He's got a new mate who's keeping him on his toes. I don't know if you heard it from Lucas, but he moved to Albuquerque with her. Denver's not quite the same without him." Raven raised his hand to get the attention of the barmaid. Not that he'd needed to. Rick could tell she'd been aware of the big man from the second he'd walked in the door. He could feel her lust like a living thing, but she was feeling shy and nervous as well. "He told me to give you his best and if you find Aspen, to let her know how much he appreciated the tip."

"Tip?" He noticed his brows raise in the mirror and turned his head just enough to see the other man.

"Yeah. Aspen apparently called the head of the pack in Albuquerque to suggest that Carly call Dad. Like always, she didn't say why. But when that particular seer speaks, people listen. And they jump because she always calls right in the nick of time."

Rick nodded. "She was always like that. Never altering the future, but sort of . . . *steering* it when she could because she was looking at it backward and sideways." A chuckle escaped him. "She was hell to play chess with."

A brilliant smile made a few years lift from Raven's shoulders. "I'll bet. I sure wouldn't want to play a game with her. But let her know there are a lot of people indebted to her. I guess I'm one of them, too. Her name comes up over and over in the files. A sentence here, a cryptic comment there, just enough information to the right people to avert disaster. Speaking as someone who has to clean up the mess, I appreciate her efforts for the agency."

"The weird part is—that would surprise her. She

never thinks about people appreciating her gift. Josie always looked at the negative side . . . who would be *angry* with her for her failures?"

A quick nod before shrugging off his jacket. "Granddad's like that, too. They accept the responsibility that comes with being gifted, but hate it. Anyway, Dad wanted to let you know you're welcome to stop by any time if you make it down that way."

"I may just do that." Rick refilled his glass with beer from the bottle and took a drink, marveling at the taste on his tongue. He didn't get beer up at his cabin often, and he'd forgotten just how rich and complex it was. Sweat dripped down the iced mug to land on the polished bar as he took another drink. While he couldn't get drunk because of his body's ability to heal itself before enough brain cells were killed, he remembered occasionally "cheating" by sitting at a table of happy drinkers. Their euphoria would bleed into him, giving him a close enough approximation that he understood why people sought out bars.

"Is that your Indian out front?" Raven changed the subject easily, and didn't even try to keep the admiration from his voice. "I'd heard you had a nice ride."

He nodded as he swallowed the last bit and set the empty glass on the bar. "Yup. Lucas mentioned yours isn't half bad either."

"Yeah, but I've always wanted one like yours." Ramirez turned his attention to the barmaid, giving her a smile with enough amperage to make the pulse in her throat jump visibly. "I'll have a bottle of MGD and a burger plate."

"Coming right up." She smiled back at him, moving with brisk efficiency to fill his order and prepare another round for the group surrounding the pool tables. Rick breathed a silent gratitude that the losers from the match had left. All that remained in the bar was happy feelings. He allowed them to soak into him until he was feeling a little giddy. Maybe he wouldn't automatically listen to everything Raven told him with immediate, unreasonable distrust if he was a little tipsy. He could feel Raven moving from pleasantries to business. His mood darkened, but it couldn't quite cut through the glow that filled his pores.

After a moment of brooding, Raven spoke—his tone serious. But the words didn't match the mood. "You're not going to want to leave that Indian parked in an open lot at a motel somewhere. What say we take it up to my dad's shop and lock it in the garage 'til you get back from our headquarters in Boulder?" The barmaid appeared from the other end of the long bar, carrying an open bottle and chilled glass. The tall man accepted them with a smile and passed a twenty to her.

"I was hoping not to have to check in with the pack." People and politics, along with all the "visiting dignitary" social crap wolves did sounded like too much of a bother to Rick after a long day's ride. Still, the offer of a locked garage appealed to him. The Indian was special. If he had to play nice with the locals, he would. He'd be damned pissed to get the bike stolen from sheer carelessness.

"Right now there's nobody to check in with." Ignoring the glass in front of him, Raven took a long pull directly from the bottle. "It's absolute chaos around here lately." He swiveled his seat so that his back was to the bar and he could keep an eye on the room. "Nobody's going to know or care if you're here. Trust me."

Rick's sandwich arrived and he decided that discretion would be the better part of valor, so he ate to keep himself from saying the wrong thing. He'd been out of circulation a long time. He didn't have a clue what had been happening in Boulder. But a wolf pack as large as he remembered this one being, without strong leadership, was a disaster waiting to happen.

"Damn that smells good." Raven's nostrils flared and narrowed as he took a long sniff. Almost immediately his stomach started growling and hunger overpowered the other sensations in the bar to push against Rick and make him eat even faster.

The burger was, in fact, surprisingly good—better than he would've expected from a non–Sazi-owned business. Humans had to worry so much about food poisoning that they always seemed to overcook their meat, making it tough and ruining the flavor. But this burger was actually ground steak, cooked rare enough to still have some taste to it. Rick let the combined flavors of rare meat, tangy mustard, and onions sit in his mouth so that he could savor them. When his companion reached a hand across to steal one of the salted potato wedges that had come with the meal, he only gave a half-hearted snarl, not even bothering to swat the offending hand away.

The two men each ordered another beer as the waitress delivered Raven's meal. They ate and drank in companionable silence. It was nice, Rick reflected, to find someone who didn't feel the need to fill every minute with chatter. Ramirez seemed absolutely content to listen to the music playing on the jukebox, watch the barmaid, and relax. When the plates were empty and the beers downed the two men rose in silent accord, heading toward the front door and the business that awaited them.

The man in the vest, and his companions with him, gave Rick and Raven plenty of room to mount up, even though they didn't disguise their admiration of the bikes. One or two of them shook their heads and smiled when the engines roared to life. Rick could still feel their eyes boring into his back as he followed Raven out of the driveway, down Speer to the highway exit.

The drive up to Boulder didn't take long, and Rick didn't begrudge a minute of the time spent. Raven had been right. The Indian would be safer locked in the garage where people or Sazi could guard it, and Rick would have one less thing to think about while he was on assignment. Raven checked in with the night shift, letting them know they were leaving the bike, while Rick unfastened the saddlebags and gathered up his belongings.

"You ready?" Ramirez appeared at the door of the garage, keys in hand.

"Yup." Rick tossed the saddlebags over one shoulder and grabbed his sleeping bag by the belt that he'd used to keep it rolled into a tight bundle. He followed the other man outside, his footsteps echoing in the large open area of the metal garage building. Outside a tow truck was waiting, engine running. Its black paint gleamed, the elaborately painted logo on the doors bright and colorful, even in the pale silver light of the moon. The truck was a large model Ford with an extended cab. There was plenty of room for Rick's saddlebags next to the battered Coleman cooler that took up a section of the backseat.

When Rick was strapped in the passenger seat and they were on their way back down to the hotel in Denver, Raven began his briefing.

"*Spiders?* They really *exist?*" Rick shuddered. Of course, there had been rumors of a race of shapeshifting spiders that preyed on Sazi for his whole long life, but nobody had actually encountered one—save Lucas. But the tale Raven told about his time in Chicago last fall made him absolutely believe.

Raven nodded in frustration and flipped on his turn signal as they neared the hotel. "So far there have only been two of them, but that doesn't mean there aren't others out there. And we know they're actively working with some of the more violent snake separatist groups—the ones who think ruling humanity is some sort of divine right. The snakes were up to something in Germany, but then they always are. Thankfully, Ahmad's been able to keep them in check so far."

Rick didn't *like* Ahmad al-Narmer, the were-cobra who represented the snakes, but he had to admit that the man wasn't nearly as bad as some of the others of his species.

"By the way," continued Raven, "Have you seen the photo of what Aspen did to Ahmad in Chicago?" Curiosity beat at Rick and he shook his head.

Raven pulled into a parking space at the hotel and pulled out his wallet. Rick snickered at the photo of Ahmad and his men pinned to the ceiling—wallets and change raining down onto the heads of the council members and the Chicago pack—as Raven spoke. "She not only did this, she did it with *style*. I can't even *imagine* how much power it must have taken to throw them up there and just leave them there for hours while she casually made the trip home."

Rick thought back to the few meetings he'd encountered between Josie and Ahmad. It was only through outside intervention that they hadn't killed each other. "Well, I know their tempers, and it was probably good that she did it this way. If they'd gotten down while she was still handy, Ahmad would have made a challenge for sure. The cobras are an especially proud bunch. They wouldn't sit still for that type of insult—particularly from a woman." He motioned to the picture and then offered the wallet back. "I'm not surprised that she's been getting more assassination attempts after . . . *this.*"

Shaking his head, Raven put the wallet back into his pocket, then pulled the key from the ignition and opened his door. "But it wasn't a cobra that attacked her at the house. The corpses buried were male rattlesnakes. The DNA was for a female of the same species. And what had the female been doing in her house?"

"Well, explosions are a common enough Sazi tool for getting rid of evidence." There was nothing quite like an explosion and fire to eliminate most of the evidence at a scene. Had she simply gotten careless while setting things up? It was possible, but it didn't seem likely.

"True, but Angelique found tire tracks and footprints for a second set of intruders, with the unmistakable scent of humans—as well as the distinctive scent of a tiger. You remember Natasha Fausek?"

Rick nodded his head. "The redheaded Bengal at Wolven? Oh sure. She was in the service when I was. Good record of captures, and dynamite on a chessboard."

The other man motioned with his head toward the upper balcony of the motel. "She just got into town and is going to tell us exactly what happened with Aspen that night. After that, you might be interested in a little moonlighting job Charles's old guard, Yusef, did for her, including everything there is to know about a little town called Pony, New Mexico."

Chapter Seven

IT WAS A BEAUTIFUL vehicle, a lovingly restored and updated 1969 Firebird convertible. It had a 350 horsepower engine, a glossy black paint job, and lipstick red interior. It had been love at first sight, smell, and sound for Josette. The engine had purred like a very large kitten from the minute she'd turned the key. It might be completely impractical, but it was absolutely perfect. She couldn't help but glance at it again out the window of the tiny motel, the Shooting Star.

Rick would love this car.

She took another sip of coffee and lifted the clean, but worn, drape. The Shooting Star Motel wasn't nearly as well maintained as some of the larger chain motels. It stood on a corner lot at the very outskirts of Pony, directly across the access road from an old-fashioned drive-in theater that had been fully restored. The moment Josette saw the tall neon sign with its five-pointed star she had a sinking sensation of déjà vu. Pulling into the parking lot she'd recognized every detail of the place. The office was a small separate building of tan brick with large tinted windows that sat in front of two long rows of cabins with what should have been a narrow grass courtyard between. From where she parked she could see that the "courtyard" was nothing more than a mass of overgrown weeds. Still, the small tan brick cabins looked as though they were in fairly good condition. Each was separated from the next by a covered parking awning. The corrugated metal of each awning had been given a new coat of dark turquoise to match the window trim and cabin doors.

The place was familiar, but try as she might, Josette couldn't remember the content of the vision. It had been long ago, in a time before motels—before even the cars that had spawned them.

The harder she tried to chase the details, the more they eluded her. But the tightness that wouldn't leave her back and shoulders made her think it was bad.

In fact, everything felt bad lately . . . as though she had walked into a future war zone without knowing when the battle would start or, worse, who the enemies were. When they'd arrived in town the day before, Ellen had taken her to Mrs. Hunt's house to pick up the car. She had the strange feeling that they were being watched, but nothing seemed out of place to her sensitive nose or ears. Even trying to force a present-time vision hadn't been effective like it had so many times in the past.

After picking up the Firebird, they'd made the long trip back to Albuquerque with Ellen, already an accomplished driver at seventeen, driving the SUV.

Leaving the rental in the outskirts of Albuquerque in a nice suburb might not have been the best solution, but at least there was a good chance the snakes or whoever came to claim their bodies wouldn't be able to track them beyond the city limits. The persuasion magic she'd used had kept the humans there from being interested in watching. Nobody should be able to identify them, even if tortured.

Ellen had cocked her head when she'd gotten in the passenger seat of the convertible, as though something was tickling at her memory. "Are you *sure* you haven't met my parents? I could swear I've seen your picture somewhere around the house. In fact, I know I have."

Josette felt herself shrug once more, as she tried again to remember like she did the previous day. "I suppose anything's possible but I'll be honest—the last time I traveled anywhere was fifty or sixty years ago. If your parents are human, I sincerely doubt I've met them, and I never get any visitors at home."

Get . . . used to get. A tiny slip of the tongue. What a difference a few short words made. She had no home anymore.

She needed to call Amber. Her sister might not even be aware of what had happened by now, but if she was, she'd be worrying. Josette was too cautious to call her from the motel phone, or any landline. Calls to and from the residences of the Chief Justice were routinely traced. There'd still been no sign of anyone looking for her thus far, but Josette was going to assume the worst and act accordingly. She'd wait, buy a cell phone at the little grocery store on the other side of town, and call while driving. It wasn't a perfect solution. She'd need to keep the call very short. But to her mind it was better than the alternative. After all, Aspen Monier was gone. Only Josette LaRue remained.

The Josette LaRue who'd picked up the vehicle and checked in yesterday was very different than the person Ellen had met at the truck stop. Gone were her shoulder-length curls that she'd worn for a century. Her blond hair had been cut short before they left Albuquerque, so that it bounced and moved with her. Chandelier earrings graced each ear, giving a soft, musical tinkle if she turned her head quickly. She'd indulged herself with just a single drop of her all-time favorite perfume. It was barely enough for the humans to notice, but she knew.

Her finger and toenails were polished a vivid crimson that exactly matched the tight scooped neck T-shirt she wore over her new black jeans. Strappy sandals with a three-inch wedge heel put a wiggle in her walk, which had drawn admiring glances from more than one man in the grocery store and a sharp elbow in the ribs for one particularly unlucky gent. The only thing that was the least bit out of character was the watch, but she wouldn't have traded it for all the rest combined.

It was, admittedly, ugly. Bulky and black, made of

plastic with Day-Glo numbers it was the kind of sports watch that could tell you more than you wanted to know in several time zones. But it had one feature that made it priceless to Josette. With the push of a button it showed the date, *with the year*. Any time she wanted she could simply look at her wrist and know *when* she was. No more asking embarrassing questions, searching for a newspaper, or scanning the area for clues. She could just hit the button and viola.

And the date was so very critical right now. Visions from two hundred years were all converging on this time and place. Her mind had been worrying at the issue like a terrier with a bone. So many things were about to happen, and some needed to not happen. It was difficult to know what to influence and what to leave alone.

Part of it was the responsibility. Whether they meant to or not, people blamed her when she saw something awful . . . and truthfully, most of the time what she saw *was* awful. But it was more than that. She didn't really trust her foresight completely anymore. There were too many people doing too many important things. Every action affected the whole cloth that was the future in new and unpredictable ways. Sometimes the consequences were good; sometimes bad. But there were always consequences, and it played merry hell with her memory every time Charles and Lucas started mucking about with things. And they both insisted on doing it. They were both so confident that they knew the best course of action. She wished she could be so sure.

It was as if thinking about the vision brought it on. She felt it coming just before it hit. Translucent images superimposed themselves over the rugged rural scenery outside the window. Then the room disappeared, and she found herself in another place and time.

The cave was dark and cool, lit only by the flickering fire of the torch in his trembling hand. The scents of verdant jungle greenery were almost overwhelming. He gathered his courage, forced himself to be strong. The punishment he would receive was well deserved. He should have known better than to delegate such an important project. He should have gone after the cat himself. She was too strong for the ones he had sent to take her out. Now two of their people were dead, and she had vanished.

They would find her. He would find her, and she would die. It was necessary. The Sazi must have no warning of what was about to happen.

A breeze caused the tangled vines that hid the cave exit to sway. He used the snuffer to extinguish the torch, sliding it into the holder with the others. Squaring his shoulders, he brushed the vines aside with one arm and stepped into the blinding daylight.

A knocking sound seemed to come from everywhere at once. It beat against her mind, one moment a booted foot on oak planks, then the hollow tones of iron on stone, and finally settling into light knuckles on a cheap painted door. The last was a tone she recognized. It was the same sound as when Ellen had stopped by the previous evening to deliver towels. Josette gasped for air and fought her way back to the present until she stood blinking in the center of the motel room, the coffee in her cup now ice-cold.

As she walked toward the door, a scent hit her like a blow—warm and musky, tinged with oil and gasoline and just a hint of lemongrass cologne.

Rick! Her brain screamed the name and her heart began to beat frantically. Another knock, this one a little heavier, followed by his voice. "Josie? Are you in there? Are you okay, *mon chere?*"

How long had she waited to hear his voice again—prayed someone would call her and say his death was all a mistake? But he'd even disappeared from her visions of the future. She couldn't seem to move from where she stood, as though she was bolted to the floor by the weight of indecision.

Anger . . . apprehension . . . delight—they all fought for dominance in her heart and she had no doubt he'd be able to feel all of them through the door.

As in times long ago when they'd fought, she heard him rest his head against the door. His voice was soft, because he knew she could hear, and it answered the questions she couldn't seem to get out of her mouth. "I know I hurt you, *mon chere,* my beautiful Josette. I never meant to. But I was too consumed by what was happening to me—to my *gift*—to do anything more than disappear. I swear to you, though, when I heard you were missing, that you might be in danger, all I could think of was finding you. I want to help you face whatever future you're running from. Please, I just want to talk to you, to tell you what I've learned from Charles and the others. And then, if you want me to go, I will."

The last few lines did it. He was lying. She could smell the black pepper so strong that she sneezed. But she couldn't decide why, or what part was the lie. Maybe he wouldn't be willing to leave; or perhaps there was more to his visit than he was saying, but her logic clamped down on her emotions. The annoyance at grieving for him for so long flooded her, so that when she put down her cup and opened the door, she was more than a little suspicious.

Rick looked exactly the same as the day he'd walked out her door, so many decades ago. As in her vision the other day, his hair was sun-streaked with so many shades of yellow that Van Gogh would be impressed. He looked miserably hot in a forest green flannel shirt, which was far too thick for the climate, but the color was the perfect to show off his golden eyes and neatly trimmed beard.

He seemed awestruck at the sight of her, and she fought to retain her annoyance as his eyes raked her body with a need that took her breath away. Apparently, he was even more adept at projecting emotions than in years past, and it was difficult to put any venom behind the first words out of her mouth. "You're lying."

"Probably." He nodded as he reached for her and no matter how hard she fought against it, the burning, desperate desire to be touched by him crushed her willpower. Magic flowed over her skin as their bodies met and when his lips found hers, a nearly anguished yowl rose from her chest.

God, he tasted so good; felt so wonderful wrapped around her again. His grip was like steel around her shoulder, and her own fingers convulsed against his solid back muscles in reflex. When his tongue slipped in her mouth, she nearly giggled at the first flavor to greet her after so long. *Maple syrup and butter. He's still a sucker for waffles and sausage for breakfast.*

How she'd missed the sensation of his rough beard against her face as his jaw moved against hers in the deepening kiss. It was nearly enough for her to forget everything that had happened. It wasn't until his mouth left hers to gently kiss down her neck that he dissolved the illusion of happiness.

"I've missed you so much, Bun."

The words struck her like a blow to the heart.

Bun—the warm endearment went far back in time to the day they were out hunting in animal form and had come upon a young rabbit. Unlike its siblings and parents, it hadn't run from the pair of stalking cats. The little brown rabbit was either too naive or too brave to show fear, and the casual curiosity of the tiny thing as it had hopped *toward* them completely charmed Josette. To Rick's supreme amusement, she'd shifted forms and took the rabbit home to live with them for a short time, until it finally found a mate and moved on. He laughed and called her "bunny-lover," which was eventually shortened to Bunny and then just Bun.

It was that casual reminder of the solid life that they'd had, the warm and loving relationship that had been destroyed when he left . . . and then when he *died*.

She pulled away from him, pushing against his chest. Now the words had venom, and she watched him flinch. "But not enough to call? You didn't miss me so much that you felt compelled to write, or even send a message through my sister? A simple 'I'm alive, but have to stay hidden' would have been enough." He opened his mouth to reply, but she cut him off with a raised hand and a slap of angry magic against his face that pulled a hiss from him. "No, Rick. You *let* me mourn. You knew where I was. I've been in the same house for a century, and never once did you *miss* me enough to seek me out."

He stood there for a long moment, soaking up her

emotions. It wouldn't matter if she tried to hide them from her face, so she didn't bother. Instead, she walked to the small chair at the far corner of the room and sat down, staring at him with all the pain and anger she felt.

Finally, he sighed, crossed his arms against his chest and dropped his head. "You're right. I didn't do any of those things." Tiny little movements of his head now, accompanied by a wave of self-anger were enough to make tears well in her eyes. "I was far too wrapped up in my own life to think about what my decisions would do to other people. I guess I figured—" He looked up and into her eyes. "That it wouldn't matter to you because of how we split." He shrugged before turning to the door and touching it. "I was stupid and immature, and you have every right to tell me to get out and stay out."

He stood there, his hand on the door, waiting for . . . something. She stared at his broad back, felt the rolling tide of emotions he was projecting, and truly didn't know what to do. The part of her that was devastated wanted to slash him to ribbons and throw his bloodied body into the parking lot to heal or not. The part that was still desperately in love with him wanted to forgive all and clutch him to her until the pain went away. But she had no way of knowing whether he wouldn't just do it again—open a second wound that might never heal.

A compromise then.

"I should probably at least hear what Charles asked you to tell me before I make that decision." She watched his shoulders drop a fraction, releasing the tension that had made his muscles twitch.

He was just about to shut the door when a face appeared in the doorway. That's right! She'd forgotten that Ellen was going to drop by for a lesson on meditation. It would help her stabilize her mind when visions were bad.

"Oh! I'm sorry," the girl said when she saw Rick in the room. "I didn't mean to interrupt. Should I come back later, Josette?"

Rick looked back at her with raised brows, waiting for her to decide. Josette nodded. "That would probably be best. I don't know how long this is going to take. Ellen, this is Rick Johnson. He's—" She fumbled in her mind for the right term. Not husband, nor lover, and not really even a friend right now. "Someone I used to know." The words had the desired effect on him. He twitched as though stuck with a sharp needle, and even the girl noticed and bit her lower lip uncomfortably. But Josette continued on calmly. "Rick, this is Ellen Harris. She's a fledgling and a future seer."

He turned his head and nodded to her. "I'm hoping I might be someone Josette is willing to get to know again. But in case I'm wrong, it was nice to meet you."

Ellen cleared her throat and widened her eyes

slightly before raising a nervous hand and backing up a pace. "Um, okay. You too." She turned her face to Josette. "I'll drop by when I get a break at lunch. After that, I'll be on desk duty until dinnertime."

She looked at the girl and realized she hadn't followed up with her since they'd returned. She'd been far too tired to play mediator with Ellen's parents the night before. "Everything okay at home?"

The girl shrugged fluidly, clearly showing the common trait with other raptors whose arms became wings. Her first turn would be soon—quite possibly with this moon. "Not as good as I'd hoped, but not as bad as I'd been afraid of. It's pretty tense, but nothing out in the open."

Josette nodded and waited until she left and Rick closed the door before speaking again. "So, what's so important that my brother-in-law was willing to drag you from the grave long enough for me to put you right back in it?"

The words were tongue-in-cheek, sort of, and Rick knew it. But he took the question with aplomb. He smiled and gave a small chuckle, willing to put the past behind them long enough to carry out his mission. He'd always been a terrific Wolven agent, and this was one of the reasons. He sat down on the corner of the bed so he could face her. Seriousness crept across his features until his expression was grave and all business.

"Charles is in trouble, and so are the other foresight

seers. The spell your mother had placed on you as a child is being used on *them*." He paused as she felt all heat drop from her face, and an icy chill run up her spine. "Amber doesn't think they'll survive the next full moon."

Her hand moved to her mouth. Oh, how she remembered the fever and the pain the spell inflicted on her. To know that Charles, for all his faults, was enduring that—and what of the others?

Nana, the seer for the Boulder pack, who was one of the very few of the original tribe of Sazi. She'd endured the Ravaging, when the humans had systematically committed genocide against their kind. She'd lived a hard life, fought against all odds. But there was no fighting a siphon spell. It was like quicksand—the harder you fought, the quicker you were pulled down to your death.

The Duchess Olga Ivanevna, seer for the Chicago wolves, was the illegitimate child of Ivan the Terrible. She'd survived multiple assassination attempts over the years, much as Josette had, but none had been like this.

And her own brother, Antoine. He'd never forgiven her for Maman's death, yet she knew he someday would. It would be his lovely wife, Tahira, who would change his heart, but not for a number of years yet and only if he survived.

There were others, too—from tribes that didn't walk under the flag of the Sazi council. She hadn't met them, but had seen them in visions; corresponded with them in her mind.

That there was another seer powerful enough to cast a ritual spell to block all of their gifts told her there was something serious indeed happening. "Do they have any idea who's behind it?"

Rick shook his head. "They have suspicions— nothing more." He sighed. He didn't like telling her this next part, but it was better if she knew up front. "There are those on the council who suspect you."

"I would *never!*" She protested.

Rick acknowledged it with a wave. "I know. I know. Apparently, it's been going on for some time. Charles told Amber you wouldn't be affected because of the botched spell from before. I'm glad you weren't. Charles looked awful."

Josette shook her head strongly. "Don't be so certain I haven't been affected, too. I haven't had visions of *any* of this. But I should have . . . these are all critical things to our kind and up until now, I would have known all about this long before you arrived. I should *already be* at Charles's bedside. I should have already eliminated the spell, and yet it remains. Don't you remember the day when I insisted you not go to Lexington?"

He cocked his head slightly and rolled his eyes. "Ah yes, how could I forget *not* becoming legendary, the original victim of the 'shot heard round the world'?"

She barely had time to nod before the vision hit.

It was late in 1773. The weather outside was bitter cold. Iron gray clouds—heavy with snow that had, thus far, refused to fall—blocked the sun. The wind whipped at her long skirt as she hurried down the wooden walkway, the slick soles of her high-button boots making the way treacherous.

There wasn't much time. Nor much chance of success. Still, she had to try. Not just for her freedom and that of her sister, but for all the others. Lives were in the balance. Lives not yet born, but lives nonetheless.

She'd chosen this morning because Maman was with the seamstress. Ridiculous, really, trying to keep up with the height of French fashion here in this new country on the far reaches of the world. But Maman, while deadly dangerous, was frequently ridiculous as well. She felt that the right clothing would make the right impression. And impressions must be made—most particularly on the type of men of means who could make life so much more . . . comfortable for her.

The carved, painted wooden sign swung on chains in the bitter winds: "Charles Wingate, Solicitor."

She reached a gloved hand into the delicately beaded drawstring bag she carried, withdrawing a worn and tattered piece of correspondence. She reread the letter to be sure that yes, this was the correct place. Then, steeling her will, she squared her shoulders and stepped inside.

The room was blissfully warm, heated by a sturdy potbellied stove in the center of the room. Well lit, too. There was an oil lamp for each of the four desks and another on the small wooden table next to the settee.

"May I help you miss?"

The young man who stepped forward was incredibly handsome. His blond hair had been pulled back and tied with a black ribbon. He had the build of an athlete, rather than a scholar, but there was intelligence in those thick-lashed golden eyes, and his clothes were of a quality signifying his status. She would guess him to be a senior apprentice. One who was well thought of and well treated.

It was his scent that made her catch her breath. Even over the smoke of the fire and the scent of the lamp oil she could smell the animal that was his other form, and below that, the personal scent that was just him. He was a bobcat, like her.

It took her a long, embarrassing moment before she could gather her thoughts enough to speak. But even though he had to have noticed, he was too well bred or well trained to react. He simply waited, his expression neutral and utterly calm.

"I am here to see Mr. Wingate."

"Do you have an appointment?"

She blinked, flustered. "What day is it?"

"It is Wednesday, November fourth."

"And the year?"

That unbalanced him, but only for a second. She could hear the sound of quills stopping as the other apprentices reacted. Still, he remained polite. "It is 1773, miss."

"Oh. Then, no, I suppose I do not have an appointment. Allow me to present my card. I have no doubt Mr. Wingate will see me."

He bowed low, seeming more amused than concerned at her state. "Of course, miss."

Charles had seen her, met with her at length. Whether he'd been surprised by her appearance, or her rather radical proposal, was anyone's guess. Then, as now, he was perfectly capable of playing his cards very close to the vest. In the end he had not only agreed to allow her access to the monies her father had put in trust for her, so that she could basically buy her mother off, but also had made the negotiations on her behalf personally. The very next day he and his apprentice, Richard, had met with Maman at their lodgings.

Maman had been furious—beyond furious. How dare Josette bring up family matters to a stranger— even if he was the Chief Justice of the council. And to discuss such matters with a guard in attendance . . . unthinkable! But her mother's hot fury was nothing compared to the cold rage of the messenger from the snake king, when he realized he had traveled across the world only to be outmaneuvered by a mere slip of a girl. The deal was simple. Josette and Yvette got their freedom from their mother and her maneuverings. In exchange, Sabine received passage back to France, and a large lump-sum settlement.

There had been a backroom deal as well, though Charles had been unaware of it. Only Josette, Yvette, and Maman knew its terms. Josette had seen what her mother was capable of. Maman had murdered her own children in the past and would again if she felt it served her best interests. In fact, only the hope of financial gain from the family of her daughters' father had kept them alive and well into their teenage years. In exchange for Josette's silence and a generous monthly stipend from her daughters Sabine had agreed not to have any more children.

That deal had held for a number of years—until the family had approached Sabine about the lack of a male heir; had in fact offered to replace the money her daughters were sending and more if she would breed until she had a male heir. It had been too easy. The girls were in America. They'd never know—particularly if the children didn't live long. So she accepted money from both sides. Bred babies, raised them long enough to keep the lions from being suspicious before having them succumb to accidents, childhood illnesses, or an inability to survive the change.

They might never have known if Josette hadn't

been a seer. But she was; and eventually she managed to break through the magical veils Sabine had erected through a caster-for-hire. She saw the birth of Antoine and Fiona, and of the last little baby. She saw the family watching Sabine closely to protect the youngsters. But when she saw their deaths at Sabine's hands months in advance she interceded to save them from their mother's growing madness.

It had been the right thing to do. She was certain of it. But there had been consequences. The repercussions were still echoing through the years from that decision. Everything Antoine or Fiona did in this life was a consequence. That Richard—her Rick—was still alive was a consequence. And that she hadn't sought out that hired caster right then, might well mean the end of them all now.

She felt a sharp slap against her cheek. "Josie! Come back to this time. Pony, New Mexico. It's the twenty-first century, Bun. C'mon back."

Her eyelids fluttered and bile churned in her stomach. She struggled against the visions that began to flow, as though a pinhole had appeared in the present and future that had been blocked to her. She tasted, smelled a familiar combination that pulled a growl from her. The caster had returned—not the one Sabine had killed when she was a girl, but the one from later, the one who had veiled the deaths of her siblings. She needed to follow the thread back to see the face, to get some sense of the caster.

But the visions wouldn't cooperate. Instead, palm trees with a cool ocean breeze and the frantic feeling of time running out led her to a darkened chamber where her sister knelt, crying. Her husband, her wonderful bear of a man, lay dying and she couldn't help. None of her healing skills could fix what was wrong. More beds with unconscious figures were nearby . . . seers from all over the world who had been brought to this place. Yvette was waiting, praying *it* would arrive in time—but what was it? What was she waiting *for?*

"Josette, you have to come out of this. You know what happens the longer you stay inside!" Yes, she knew. She did know that it became harder to separate herself. But this was important. There were things she had to see that she might not be able to see later if she stopped now. She grabbed onto Rick's hand like a lifeline, prayed that he would be able to keep her grounded. She could feel that her eyes were open from the cool air of his breath hitting them. But she couldn't see the room; there was nothing but blackness and the flashes of images that flickered on a thousand screens.

Her voice was thready, nearly identical to Ellen's as it had been in the car. "I have to finish this. Close my eyes so they don't dry out and keep me here if you can."

Now was the time to show what she had learned over the centuries. She was no longer a girl, to be bullied or buffaloed by cheap parlor tricks. She was a seer, the elite of the Sazi, and she *would* see that which she chose.

She started the flow of magic slowly, leaked it into the vision so the other caster wouldn't recognize it and shut down the spell before she was done.

Again she saw the jungle scene, but this time it was in the present—she was inside the mind of the caster, without the person realizing it. Man or woman, she couldn't yet say, but it *felt* like she was inside a man from the way the person climbed the stairs to the stone temple.

Rick's fingernails dug into her palms enough to make her gasp. But that tiny thing kept her in both places. The many other visions she'd had while they were together had been training for this, and she was pleased that he hadn't run screaming from the room, considering how badly some of the other sessions had gone.

Perhaps he really had grown up.

There. In a darkened chamber inside the cool stone edifice was the casting circle. She studied the symbols with every glance the caster afforded them. It wasn't until she saw the book that panic flooded her. Made of Sazi skin, flayed from a living snake shifter, the splotched leather book was covered with fungus and mold that was drawn to the magic inside.

Josette had seen such a book before. In fact, unbeknownst to every living Sazi save her sister, she *owned* a copy of this same book. She knew the damage it could do to all of their kind. She would have destroyed her own copy except that one of her visions as a child was of her pulling the book from inside a brick building as an adult, and feeling both terrified and relieved that it was there.

Josette started to back away from the caster. She'd learned all she could for the moment. But an instant before she broke free, the other seer happened to pick up the book, and a surge of energy flooded through the joint connection—enough for the caster to recognize that he—yes, it was definitely a *he*—wasn't alone inside his own mind.

Power tore through her mind as the caster tried to track down the intruder. Josette pushed power back, keeping a barrier between their minds. The caster had the combined energy of the greatest minds of their kind—the siphon spell had been drawing power for a very long time. She could feel that the spell had been trickling out for a decade or more.

An idea occurred to her. It was deadly dangerous, but what choice did she have? The power he was using *wasn't his*. Part of it belonged to her, and Charles, Antoine, and the others. If she could summon the strength to connect all the Sazi seers to the caster, their power might, with the right urging, "come home."

Taking a deep breath, she reached down the tenuous connection that bound all of the Sazi seers. They were ill, and so very weak, but she sensed their cooperation and trust. As she dropped the barrier between herself and the caster she prayed she was strong enough to be worthy of it—that what she was doing wouldn't kill them all.

Chapter Eight

RICK STOOD NEXT to the bed, feeling a familiar helplessness. Josie's vision had cost her dearly—as the bad ones always did. He'd had to resort to carrying her to the bathroom and turning on the shower until the cold water revived her. After toweling off her hair and clothing, he'd placed her on top of the bed in a nearly forgotten ritual that was more muscle memory than remembrance. She was bare of emotions, burned to a blank slate from the roller coaster she'd just endured. Even her scent was nearly absent—so faint he could barely smell it, even when she was in his arms.

It would be better if he left before she woke, because he could feel the same old lecture nibbling at his mind—and he no longer had any right to lecture her.

Instead, he decided to check in. If the ferocity of the vision was any indication, things were going to get messy here soon. It would probably be a good idea to stick around for a few days, at least until he could finish filling her in on the situation. He carefully checked all the windows and then locked the door behind him, testing it to make sure she'd be safe until she woke.

A bell tinkled as he pushed open the brass-handled door to the motel office. Stepping inside, he was relieved to find the place both clean and well tended. The small lobby was furnished with either retro furniture from the sixties or the real thing, lovingly cared for. There were newspapers next to a coffeepot on the laminated wood-grained top of a circular coffee table with conical legs with brass rings on their feet. On either side were matching chairs with square orange vinyl cushions. The leaves of a fake rubber tree rustled oddly in the fitful breeze a window air conditioner put out. Everything was neat, clean, but well worn and from a bygone era. It almost felt as though he'd stepped onto a movie set, or into one of Josie's visions.

"Can I help you?" A middle-aged woman moved behind the check-in counter. She was pretty, with dark brown hair and wide, doelike eyes. There wasn't a hint of gray in her hair, but tiny worry lines were starting to form between her brows and at the corners of her mouth. She smelled harried and felt more than a little depressed.

"I need a room for a couple of days. Don't know how many yet, so I'll just keep a tab." Rick stepped up to the counter and pulled his wallet from his back pocket.

"Do you want a roadside view or one of the rooms facing the drive-in? They only show the movies on Friday and Saturday nights, but if you open up the curtains you can watch it for free, and they have a station on the radio that plays the soundtrack."

Rick laughed. He couldn't even remember the last time he'd watched a movie, and watching it on the drive-in screen from the comfort of his own bedroom sounded like a hoot. "I'll take the one with the best view of the movie. What's playing anyway?"

"I hope you're not afraid of snakes. The owner has a preference for action flicks and B movies. Tonight there's a double feature of *Snakes on a Plane* with Samuel L. Jackson and the other one . . . what was it . . . oh yeah, *Anaconda*."

He let out a low chuckle. "No, I think watching movies where a bunch of snakes get killed is just about the perfect entertainment for me tonight."

"Oh good." The woman behind the counter smiled and reached behind her into a set of square wooden boxes, meant to hold messages and mail, and withdrew a orange plastic key chain with an embossed room number and an actual key. "I'll put you in room 104 then." Excellent, just two down from Josie's room. She slid the key across the counter, exchanging it for the cash and driver's license that he offered.

"I'll need to see a credit card, even though you're paying cash. In case of damages."

Rick wasn't happy about it, but there was nothing to be done. He slid the card across the countertop. There was a series of beeping noises as the credit card was processing, followed by a few quick clicks later on a computer, and voila, the paperwork was ready for his signature. The woman photocopied his driver's license, handing it back before she pulled the yellow copy of the receipt from the back of the form and passed it across the counter.

As Rick walked out, the woman called out after him, "If you need anything at all, just call."

"Thanks, I'll do that."

The hotel room was clean. A little gaudy, but then that was in keeping with the whole sixties theme that seemed to have dictated the style of the place. Both the bedspread and curtains had a royal blue, turquoise, and lime green geometric print. It was a mirror image of Josette's room. The carpet was a thick, royal blue shag that would probably last through the next ice age and beyond. There was even a lava lamp, with globs of green goo in constant motion.

Like totally groovy, man.

He walked over to the closet hidden behind slatted doors. Pulling on the knob he found that there were plenty of heavy wooden hangers, more than he'd need for a few days. He would probably need to shop, since he'd just planned for a quick stop. He set his saddlebags on the closet floor, grumbling when they tipped over and fell forward into the room. He heard the crunch of plastic breaking when it impacted. Hopefully, it wasn't anything important. Then, with a sigh and a promise to himself that he'd deal with it later, he kicked it back into the closet, where it promptly fell over again.

Curiosity won. He couldn't help but look to see what had caused it to overbalance. Ah! The floor was uneven because of a trapdoor. That could be handy. He pulled the ring set into the closed lid, and found himself looking down into a darkened crawl space that ran beneath the motel. There was a maze of plumbing, some wiring, and lots and lots of spider webs, more than a few of which were occupied.

He set the door back in place and set the suitcase upright again, making sure this time that it sat on an even portion of the closet's floor before pulling the door closed. Kicking off his shoes, he padded over to the window to check out the drive-in and then flung himself onto a surprisingly comfortable mattress.

A few minutes later, while he was trying to decide what things to tell Josie and what needed to remain confidential in his new capacity as a Wolven agent, there was a series of taps on the window in the bathroom. He ignored it, thinking it was a bird or gravel thrown by a departing car. But then it happened again. He swung his legs off the bed and walked to the bathroom door. A slender silhouette stood on the other side of the thin gingham drapes, and the curves showed it was most definitely female. A quick sniff revealed the fledgling raptor, Ellen, knocking.

He opened the window and she stepped back a pace, being careful to remain mostly hidden behind the massive central air unit for the building. "Yes? Ellen, isn't it?"

She nodded. "I need to talk to you. It's really important. It's about Josette. I think she's in terrible danger."

The short snort of air wasn't quite a laugh and sounded decidedly bitter—even to him. "Why tell me? Josie's perfectly capable of taking care of herself. Just ask her." That was the very lecture he was biting his tongue not to repeat for the thousandth time. She was always at her most vulnerable after a bad vision, but refused to do anything proactive to protect herself in those few twilight moments before she was back in full control of her body. Yes, her animal instincts kicked in if physically attacked. She'd proved that on any number of occasions, but frankly, Rick was a little surprised she wasn't more damaged after years of taking risks. To him, it was the same as putting his keys in the ignition of a motorcycle, starting it up, and then going shopping for the afternoon in a crowded mall. Sure, it *might* not get stolen, but it was a gamble every single time.

He didn't like risks. Too much guard training and then Wolven after that. Josie was so cautious in her animal form, the perfect blend of intelligence and stealth. But slap skin and clothing on her and some days—

He shook his head just as the girl responded.

"I knocked on her door. She must be out. I hope

nothing's already happened." Ellen's voice was low and nearly frantic and the tension beat at him like a snare drum. Whatever was wrong, she believed it was real, and he'd damned well better take it seriously. Especially since someone was actively trying to eliminate the seers.

"Okay, come around and we'll talk inside."

She shook her head and then looked around again, as though expecting to get caught. "I can't let Mom or Dad see me talking to you. They'll know something's up. I told Josette that I'd seen her picture in our house, but I couldn't remember where. She swears she's never met either of them before yesterday. So I did some digging around, and I found it! But I don't dare take it out of the house. Dad'll notice it's missing for sure, even if just for a second."

Josie's picture was in *Ellen's* house? That was odd, all right. Leave it to Bun to wind up right where she needs to be at just the wrong time—smack-dab in the middle of danger. "Okay, what do you suggest?"

"I'll be working the desk until we go to the drive-in tonight. I don't think anything will happen before then, if at all. Dad's out in the desert with his buddies, and Mom will be buying supplies all afternoon. Could you stop by the office around dark? If you hand me out your towels now, you can say you just noticed you were out. Then, if anyone comes in while we're talking, nobody'll get suspicious. Even if Mom carried them to the room for you, you wouldn't be lying."

It seemed a good plan. There might be flaws, but Rick couldn't spot them immediately. He gathered up the towels and handed them out to the girl, who promptly put them in through the window of the neighboring unit.

"Anything else?" he asked as she started to swing her leg through the same window, following the towels.

"Make sure Josette stays out of the office. So far, I don't think Dad has recognized her. Her hair is different and so's her name. But that might not last forever. He can be slow on the uptake, but once he figures something out . . . whoo boy!"

Rick moved his eyes to his watch as the window next door slid closed. It was only two o'clock. At this time of year, it wouldn't be dark for hours.

He stood, leaning on the painted windowpane, looking out at the black clouds rolling in off of the desert. A storm was coming, a bad one. He could smell ozone heavy in the air. In an odd way the weather matched his mood. Something big was happening. The signs were as clear as the clouds darkening the horizon. Amber, a physician who was known for her cool in the face of any crisis was terrified. Lucas had reactivated himself and was pulling old agents out of retirement. Josette was in danger.

And there wasn't a thing he could do about any of it right now. Nobody he could shoot, nothing he could fight for the time being. He shut the window and allowed his training to take over. *Probably a good time to take a short nap.* Especially since he'd driven all night to get here. Staying awake wouldn't solve anything, and he was getting the impression that being alert would soon be critical.

Plus, the comfortable bed was inviting him to make a longer inspection, and it didn't seem right to argue. His eyes were already burning, and his scalp tingled as it always did when he was overtired. It only took a few minutes to set his travel alarm for five P.M. and strip off his jeans.

He was out before his head hit the pillow.

Chapter Nine

THE SUN WAS setting and the moon was rising behind the heavy cloud cover. For the past hour and a half cars had been pouring in to the drive-in theater outside her window, pulling up to the speakers. Some people were setting up lawn chairs. Many more were making a trail to the concession stand. The heady scents of buttered popcorn, nachos, and roasting hot dogs hung on the evening breeze. Josette's stomach began growling, her mouth watering. Finally, she could take no more. She had to have some of that popcorn. Grabbing her purse and key she hurried from the room, hoping to get her snack and get back before the first movie actually started. She had spent most of the day sleeping off her vision. Now she was wide awake and ready to be entertained.

Rick's bike was still in the parking lot, but he'd made himself absent. That was probably best. She remembered how he used to get after a bad vision. Nothing frustrated him so much as thinking her vulnerable—even though she was no such thing.

Well, he knew where she was. If he still wanted to talk, he could stop by. But for just one night, she needed to not think about the Sazi, about the future, and the horrible things that might happen. Just for one night, she wanted to be anonymous, a last respite before the war began.

The cool evening breeze felt good on her skin as she hurried across the parking lot. In the distance she could hear the babble of voices as the first of the ads and the trailers for upcoming movies flickered to life on the huge screen. She could taste the dust on her tongue as it rose up with every step she took across ground that was too well trampled to grow even the hardiest of weeds.

Overhead stars were beginning to twinkle, barely visible because of the light pollution. To the west there was an ominous buildup of clouds. She gave a delicate sniff of the air. The ozone was thick, but the storm probably wouldn't arrive for a few hours yet. Plenty of time for her to watch the movies.

She smiled broadly. It was a circus atmosphere. Everywhere there was movement, excitement. Small children darted wildly through the crowds as exasperated parents tried in vain to keep up with them. A pair of small boys dodged directly in front of her. She sidestepped them, only to run into Ellen. But the girl was with her parents and just gave her a blank stare— as though they'd never met. Soda and popcorn spilled everywhere, and the girl let out an oath that would've been shocking in another place or time.

"Excuse me. I'm so sorry!" Josette grabbed a stack

of napkins that someone ahead of her in line passed her and began dabbing at the worst of the damage. "How very clumsy of me." She took deep breaths, trying to pinpoint a scent that passed by on the wind. It seemed to be fading and becoming more elusive with every second.

"Not your fault," the girl muttered. Her eyes were dark and surly, as though she was annoyed, but as soon as her mother turned her head, she mouthed, "Tell Rick the plans have changed."

Josette smiled, stalling for time. "Can I at least buy you another drink?"

The girl started to respond but was interrupted by her father calling her name. She turned to answer, giving Josette a clear view of the middle-aged human. He was a hard man, with skin weathered by sun and wind. Even from here she could see the muscles in his jaw clenching over and over. The harsh scent of chemicals clung to him and to his clothes. It was strong enough that Josette found her eyes watering. She'd smelled something like it once, back in the town near her home. But she couldn't remember what it had been. She pressed the cup into Ellen's hand and gave her a searching look. But Ellen pulled back from the touch.

"That's my dad. I've got to go." The girl hurried away, moving in a blur of speed that wasn't natural for a full human. The man didn't notice. His eyes were all for Josette. Hatred burned in his hazel eyes and a canny intelligence. If looks could kill, she would be a pile of cinders. But it made no sense. She'd never met the man before in her life; had never even seen him in a vision. Still, Ellen had said something about a picture.

Maybe it was time to talk to Rick, before anything else happened.

Ellen's father grabbed her brutally by the arm and began dragging her away. Josette tried to follow, but he used the crowd and the deepening shadows between the vehicles to his advantage. She didn't dare use Sazi speed to keep up. They were lost from sight in minutes, and she could not follow their scent without being more obvious than she dared.

Frustrated and angry, she made her way back to the hotel, determined to use whatever means necessary to find out just what in the hell was going on. As she was putting the key in the lock, she heard a hiss and light snarl that she recognized. She turned her head to see Rick, in his cat form, peeking around the corner of the building. He motioned with his head for her to follow him and then ducked into the shadows, before a group of teenagers cutting across the parking lot to get to the drive-in noticed him.

Curiosity beat at her and she had a strong suspicion the same was true of Rick. Ellen had apparently planned to meet him, for reasons unknown. She couldn't imagine he would be interested in the girl, nor would Ellen be likely to ask *her* to give him a message about a date. So, clearly, it was business—but what *sort* of business? She entered the room and opened the bathroom window, then stripped off her clothing, shifted into cat form, and sailed through the curtains. As she expected, Rick was waiting for her next to the Dumpster. He still looked great, nearly identical to when they were married. Maybe he had a little more girth around his ribs, but it was all muscle. His gray, mottled fur blended into the dappled shadows until it was like talking to the Cheshire cat. Only his eyes and teeth were visible when he spoke.

"We've got trouble, Josie."

She nodded and slapped a paw at a fly that kept trying to land on her nose. The stench from the Dumpsters was terrible and a variety of bugs seemed intent on bothering her, but *comfort* wasn't very important right now. "I figured as much. Ellen said to tell you that plans changed."

"They sure did, and that's bad news for us. Just to bring you up to date, Ellen dropped by my back window earlier. She said she found where she'd seen your picture in her house and she wanted me to stop by the office tonight, before the movie started, so she could show me. She said you were in danger and she was very obviously worried. Since you were . . . *asleep,* I decided to take a nap, too, in case life went to shit later."

She felt her ears flinch when he said *asleep.* It had cost him a lot not to bring up that same old subject—still sore after all these years. What he felt was foolish risk she considered clinging to normalcy. Even if it was only an illusion, it was important to her to be able to live her life like other Sazi and humans. To barricade herself inside her home 24/7 on the off-chance that she *might* have a vision strong enough for her to get lost inside her own mind would make her feel too much like a prisoner. "Thank you for that."

He didn't have to ask for what. He knew and shrugged one shoulder. "Not my place anymore, if it ever was."

Before she realized she was doing it, she reached over and gave his whiskers a quick lick. "It was. And, for what it's worth, I *did* appreciate your concern. But it's one of the few things I get a choice about, so it's important to me."

He met her eyes and they just stared at each other for a long moment. There were so many things that they'd argued about when they were married that had been born of true caring for the other person. But their own goals and, well, *egos,* sometimes got in the way.

Memories of good times and bad, flitted across her mind, until all that was left was the raw emotion behind the events. She cleared her throat, sounding for all the world like she was about to cough up a hairball. He snorted lightly and it relieved a little of the tension. Looking out past the Dumpster toward the drive-in, she motioned with her head. "So what happened after you woke up?"

He moved closer to her, tipping his head so he could keep watch on one particular area of the parking lot.

She could feel his magic playing over her fur like a cool wind. It gave her shivers.

"I heard Ellen and her father arguing as I was walking toward the office to grab a pop from the machine. Apparently, someone spotted her talking to a guest, but the informant couldn't remember who or where. But she started talking about some cards and how she wasn't going to stand for it anymore."

Josette felt her whiskers twitch ominously. "What kind of *cards?* Do you have any idea?"

"I didn't then, but I do now. Ellen's dad—named Ray, by the way—said he wasn't going to let her out of his sight until *it was time,* whatever that meant. But, after they left for the drive-in, I forced open the window and did a quick search. I found them in her bedroom, under some lingerie. Come over here."

He walked away and she followed, not certain what to think of Rick casually searching through Ellen's undies. But ever the cop, he probably didn't think about it at all.

Rick started digging at the base of a small cactus in the xeriscape garden. He pulled a small plastic bag from the hole and emptied it by holding the bottom in his teeth and shaking it.

"See for yourself. Something big's going on down here."

Reluctantly, she pulled the cards from their box with teeth and claws. The back of the cards had a glossy black background with a stylized pawprint made to look as if it had been printed in blood. But it was the face side that was so shocking. Josette felt the blood drain from her face as she stared at the familiar faces on individual playing cards: Charles Wingate was the ace of clubs, a photo of his face superimposed over the image of a polar bear; a huge bounty was listed beneath his name. The ace of spades was Lucas Santiago. Her own face appeared on the Ace of Hearts, although the name listed was Aspen Monier. With growing dread she moved each card aside, seeing on each a face and the image of an animal along with a . . . *bounty*. Some cards had been printed with a black *X* over the central picture. She recognized the names as Wolven agents who had gone missing recently. It was something Amber had talked about in their last phone call. Josette tried to swallow, her throat suddenly, painfully, dry.

She felt a nudge on her leg and turned wide-eyed to Rick. "C'mon, he's leaving. We need to follow him."

"Who's leaving? Follow him where?"

Rick quickly stepped past her and slid the cards together into a reasonable stack, and then tipped them back into the bag before returning them to the hole and filling it in.

"Ray. He makes my whiskers twitch. There's just something about him that . . . anyway, I think we need to follow him."

She couldn't help but agree. There was definitely something going on. And it was far too big for Ellen's father to be the ringleader. He just didn't seem to be more than a lackey, regardless of his master.

Josette followed Rick into the desert, feeling the darkness envelop her like cool velvet. Ever so slowly she felt the tension begin draining from her body as she concentrated on her breathing and on running in the larger bobcat's wake. It might help them for her to force a vision. Maybe she could get some insight into his plan if she concentrated on Ray personally. She thought back to that brief meeting, remembering the smell of him—harsh with an unknown chemical, along with something pungent, like lingering death.

She'd learned to center herself, control her magic by controlling her mind and body. The old familiar thrill of fear ran up her spine as her mind began slipping through the confines of time and space, but she crushed it with an effort of will. She would control this. She would come back. She would *know* the here and now. The visions had not claimed her yet, and they would not claim her this time.

She closed her eyes, shutting out her surroundings, and forced herself to remember every detail of the man's features. Her magic touched him inside the truck cab just ahead. As she passed Rick to take the lead, he stifled a gasp at the power that pushed past him into the night.

The high beams cut through the darkness, but not well enough. He could see deer moving at the edge of the road. They oughta put some streetlamps out here. He let up on the gas, reminding himself that it was better to arrive a couple of minutes later than to wreck the truck and not get there at all. But damn *it was hard. It was her. He was sure of it. If he was right—well, no more worrying about money. No more listening to the old lady bitch about how hard she was working and how he wasn't "contributing to the household."*

A scowl lowered his brows. He loved Ellen, he really did. But she just didn't get it. She didn't understand that they were animals, monsters. Live and let live my ass. *She hadn't seen what had happened to his brother because of those* things. *But it would be better soon. Once Ellen was made right again, she'd understand just how much her daddy loved her.*

He was so preoccupied that he almost missed his turnoff, a narrow dirt road mostly hidden by the rough brush that grew so plentifully around here. He stomped on the brake pedal, jerking the steering wheel hard to the left. He felt the truck slew sideways, but managed to correct his course well enough to keep control of the pickup as it lurched over the rutted trail that snaked between the prominent "NO TRESPASSING" signs.

Josette felt her speed slow as the truck lost control. It wouldn't do to have him notice the bobcats following. He already knew she was a shifter, and a bobcat.

The card said so, and the look he gave her at the drive-in said he recognized her. Rick slowed along with her, content to let her lead. That *was* one nice thing about him—his pride wasn't wounded by her taking the lead just because she was female.

He slowed even more, shifting into low gear. Almost there now. He could hear the frantic barking of the guard dogs, deep and menacing behind the tall fence topped with razor wire that encircled the area.

A few more feet and the motion sensors picked up the movement of the truck. Spotlights came on, showering the area with light bright enough to damned near blind him. Not that he needed to see the place. God knew he was well acquainted with every inch of it, including the huge metal shed where the actual cooking was done, and the small shabby trailer that had the bathroom and kitchen, which all the men shared.

He heard the trailer door slam and saw Harold appear on the front step. Ray fought down his irritation. Harold was an even bigger pain in the ass than John.

He was a big man, not only tall, but bulky with muscle, so that the camo pants he wore were stretched tight over his thick thigh muscles. His stained sleeveless T-shirt struggled to contain the sheer mass of him. He wore a dog whistle on a chain around his neck, a pair of pistols holstered beneath his arms, and was carrying a rifle in his left hand. His head was shaved completely smooth, without even a hint of stubble to give a clue what color it would be.

Ray sat still and silent behind the wheel, making damned sure that Harold recognized that it was him.

Harold scowled at the sight of him, but pulled the whistle to his lips to call off the dogs. Then he hit the switch for the motor that opened the gate to the property.

After driving through, he pulled the truck to a stop, taking his time. Harold strode toward the door of the vehicle, his expression wary. He stepped close enough to the door that it would be impossible to open it without hitting him and gestured for the other man to roll down the window.

"What're you doing here, mate? I thought you were going to the drive-in with the wife and kiddies." He spoke with a heavy Australian accent that never seemed to sound friendly. But that was okay, he didn't give a shit about whether they were friends.

Josette heard the dogs barking and didn't dare get any closer. Right now, it could be assumed they were barking because of Ray. But if they started to track their scent, the tone would change. No, it would be better to wait until he was safely inside or left before they inspected further. With a flick of her ears to Rick, she explained her thought and how she was connected in a real-time vision, in low enough tones that someone even a foot away would struggle to hear.

"I agree," he said with a quick nod. "You keep relaying what you see. If we need to bust the place up, we can—but I'd rather wait until we're armed. We don't know enough details about the situation there."

She flopped down onto a small tuft of grass and closed her eyes, allowing her breathing to still once more before slipping back into the mind of the man in the truck.

Ray bit his tongue until he was sure his reply would be civil. There was no point in arguing with Harold. You never won, and there was always the off-chance you'd piss him off. And while he wasn't exactly afraid of the other man, he wasn't about to cross him. He suspected that if he pushed Harold too far he'd be pushing up daisies somewhere where no one would ever find the body.

"Yeah, we went. I didn't stay."

"Why not?" The question seemed to harbor some unspoken suspicion—like he wasn't supposed to do nothing except what he said he would. That always pissed him off about Harold.

"I think I saw somebody."

Harold snorted like he was stupid or something.

"You probably saw a lot of somebodies, Raymond. That drive-in's right popular on a Friday night."

Ray fought down his annoyance. He wanted out of the truck, but Harold was still in the way and the damned dogs were prowling around loose. Fucking idiot was playing games with him. He was half-tempted. He reached for the door handle, but then looked into the other man's eyes and stopped mid-motion.

There was death in those eyes. Harold was just looking for an excuse and he wasn't about to give it to him. "I just want to look at the cards. See if I'm right."

"Where are yours? You'd best not say you lost them, either, mate. You know what Damon said would happen if you did."

"He couldn't find the cards. It's why he's out here," Josette breathed the words in a low tone and heard Rick swear. "There's an Australian man who controls the dogs. He seems to be Ray's boss, or at least a supervisor of sorts, but not one Ray likes."

"Can you see anything about how the yard is laid out? Any way to get in there other than the gate?" Rick moved his mouth very close to her face, easing the words into her ear lightly enough to tickle the sensitive hairs inside. Another shiver overcame her, and he noticed and smelled pleased.

The question itself would have made Josette laugh

if it hadn't been such a serious one. How could she forget something so obvious after poking and prodding Ellen to do the same thing just yesterday! "I can't tell the size of the compound. The lights are only around part of it. But from the size of the gate we entered, I'd say it's about fifteen feet wide. There's a building, more of a shack, to the left and what looks like a cabin from a kit to the right." She allowed herself to pull input from Ray's other senses. The effort would probably give him a little headache, but he'd probably assume it was the confrontation with Harold that had done it. "There's a strong chemical smell that I can't place. I've smelled it before, too. When I was at the drive-in. It floated on the breeze, but I couldn't pin it to a source." She stopped speaking as Ray answered the earlier question.

"Hell, no. I just didn't feel like opening up the safe and looking through them with my wife there. She doesn't know about this yet. I want her to see it firsthand before I bring her in."

Apparently that satisfied the other man. Harold gave him a disgusted look but didn't press the point. "Fine, whatever." He stepped away from the door and nodded his bald head toward the trailer. He shook his head in disbelief. "You really think you saw some big muckety-muck Sazi out here in the middle of fuckin' nowhere?"

Ray nodded grimly. His expression soured even

further when Harold guffawed. God how he hated that man. He hated most of the people he was forced to work with. Fucking criminals all of them. But the movement needed money. And there was plenty of money in drugs.

Drugs! That was the smell. Some kind of drugs that she'd heard of in the news, but never encountered. "They're making drugs out there. They're raising money for some sort of project that Ray calls 'the movement'."

He opened the door and climbed down from the cab of the truck. He forced himself to move casually. The damned dogs made him even more nervous than Harold. But showing it would be a sign of weakness the other man would lord over him. So he pretended not to notice the burly furred forms with their wicked teeth; pretended not to see how they moved as a unit, as if they were hunting prey.

Without warning the vision shifted. She barely had time to hiss a warning to Rick before she was sucked inside. "I'm being pulled out to . . . somewhere else. Keep watch on the truck for me."

If he responded, she didn't hear.

She was in a cave, watching as a dark-haired woman stood reading harsh-sounding syllables from an ancient book she held in her hands. The cover was whitish green, the color of mold—or of the lighter scales that sometimes appeared on the underbelly of a snake. The naked woman bound to the stone with silver chains was her new sister-in-law, Tahira. And Giselle—Grandmere, her voice clear and cold—was taunting her captor.

Josette felt a pang of regret. Grandmere was dead. This was the past then. The scene was one that had been described in Antoine and Ahmad's reports. Amber had sent them as a way to notify her of Grandmere's death. But why was she seeing it now? What did it have to do with the current problem?

Again and again her eyes were drawn to the book. Was this the same one she'd seen in the previous vision—the one the caster was using? She needed to see more, but the information eluded her. It was incredibly frustrating. There was no pushing into this vision. It had already happened. With a thought, she stopped it as though it were a movie on a screen, and then backed it up several times, searching the narrow view for anything that might give her a clue as to why she was seeing it. But the focus was narrow—on Tahira and the book. The cave looked like any other.

Her muscles tensed, causing a cramp that made the posture she'd taken too painful to hold. Her body rebelled, dragging her mind forcibly back to the present. Rick was there, patiently watching the distant compound, but close by, guarding.

She was lying on her side, panting heavily and while she shouldn't be able to sweat while in cat form, her fur was nonetheless soaked and rank with fear and anger.

"Did anything happen while I . . . well, *while?*" While she was unconscious; comatose; out of her mind in a strange part of the desert with no way to protect herself? To Rick's credit, he didn't comment for the second time. He just shook his head and kept watching the compound.

His voice was barely loud enough to be called a whisper. "They've gone inside briefly, but then they're leaving. I got a little closer before the dogs quieted down completely from Ray arriving and overheard that the cards are at the other man's house. They're both going to go there in a minute. Oh, and the dogs are only Dobermans—so no big deal. But it would be better overall if we didn't raise an alarm by killing them."

She agreed. No sense in harming the creatures, even if they were *dogs*. "If one of us can hold them with magic, we should be able to climb the tree by the shack and drop onto the roof."

He smirked as well as a bobcat was able. "Seems of the two of us you're the expert on *holding*. I saw a picture of your handiwork in Chicago while I was in Denver."

Oh God! There were *pictures*? She let out a small frustrated snarl. "There was a good reason for—"

A quick bump of his head against her shoulder stopped her explanation. "There's no need to justify yourself, Josie. I know how Ahmad provokes you. He intentionally pushes your buttons. I'm surprised you left him alive."

Her chuckle was tired. It was so hard having to plan her every movement by possible futures. At least this time, she'd chosen correctly. "I had no choice. If I'd killed him, Sargon would have lived. He had to be in Germany to bring down his father."

Rick's jaw dropped and his eyes went wide. "*Sargon?* That insane son of a snake was still alive?! I thought Ahmad had put him down centuries ago."

A truck started up in the distance and Josette twisted her ears. They were leaving. It was time to make their move. "No time. More later. If we're going in it has to be now."

There wasn't much to see, and getting inside was ridiculously simple—almost as though nobody cared if they wandered around. They'd left the gate wide open and the dogs penned. It felt for all the world like a trap, but nothing happened. The shed looked like a chemistry classroom. Beakers of noxious smelling fluid bubbled over low flames, while white smoke swirled through coiled glass tubes. Small packets of nearly clear crystals were stacked on a table, and there was a cash counting machine against the opposite wall.

AS THEY RAN back toward the hotel, Rick mulled out loud. "I need to get someone from Wolven out here. I'm way out of practice for this sort of thing."

She shook her head as she dug her claws into the pea gravel of a dried creek bed halfway back. "Why involve them? It's a human matter. Just make an anonymous call to the police."

"Not so human, Bun. What about Ellen?"

The cool breeze was turning into a wind as the storm approached. It was hard to talk without coughing. "What about her?"

"She's underage," he said, as they slowed down near the edge of the drive-in lot. "What happens if both her folks go to jail on drug charges? I don't know about New Mexico, but up in South Dakota, Social Services would be all over this case. I could smell her feathers, but she still smells mostly human. We can't afford for that to happen. We have no idea when she'll turn the first time."

That had never occurred to her! Her mind just didn't think in that mode. "Oh. Yes, I suppose that's an issue. But what will happen to her folks if Wolven comes in?" Wolven didn't deal well with felonies committed by Sazis. Usually, the involved parties were simply put down and the bodies removed.

Josette remembered well what it felt like to have a parent put down by Wolven. Even though Maman had been insane, and Josette already an adult, it had been . . . difficult.

From the sounds they heard as they passed behind the massive screen, she could tell they were well into the second movie of the double feature. While the trip to the shack and the visions had felt like they took only a few minutes, it had obviously been otherwise. It was often like that. Time just seemed to warp, running too fast, or too slow to mesh properly with reality. It was one of the many things that made the gift so disconcerting. Another was the fact that the visions were often so very vivid, so *real* that actual reality seemed to pale in comparison. She suspected that only someone who'd actually experienced it could understand just how confusing it could be.

"How about we concentrate on getting back to our rooms and getting cleaned up. Then we can talk about where to go from here." It seemed like Rick had already made his decision and had raised valid points, but maybe he'd listen to reason. Ellen was distraught enough without losing her parents to the very thing they hated and warned her about.

It was only a few minutes before she leaped back inside her room and changed back to a human. She carefully sniffed around, but didn't notice anything out of place that would say anyone searched her room or had even been inside. She decided to take the few minutes for a shower. Heaven only knew when the next time she'd get the chance would be. Although it probably wasn't necessary, she even put on some makeup, choosing the shade of blue eye shadow that matched the flowers that used to grow at their Illinois cabin. Even her teeth felt filthy, although she'd cleaned them just before she decided to go out for popcorn.

After getting dressed and gathering up her key to go to Rick's room, she paused to lift the glass of soda she'd poured for herself earlier. It was probably flat, but better than the water from the tap. One glass of that stuff had been plenty. She'd stick with bottled from here out.

The glass was halfway to her lips when she heard the slamming of a truck door and the angry stomping of a man's heavy boots as he passed the door to her room. Through the wall she heard soft swearing, and the sound of a window being opened frantically as the man in front pounded on the hotel room door.

She set the glass silently onto the back of the toilet tank and moved to the bathroom window. She pulled aside the blinds to get a better look. There, in the tall weeds, stood a handsome man of about thirty. He was buck naked, and smelled of equal parts anger, embarrassment, and fear. Still, he held himself with confidence, and while his dark blond hair needed a trim, the rings on his hands spoke of money.

"Ma'am." He stepped toward the window, speaking

to her through the screen. He was using one hand to cover his crotch, the other brushed his hair out of eyes the color of new grass. A small tattoo adorned his neck, barely visible at the hairline.

His voice was an urgent whisper. "I know you don't know me, and y'all have no reason to trust me, but I swear to God, if Greg actually finds me back here like this he'll kill Dawn and I both. I need help real bad. Even if you just let me use your cell phone."

A man's voice began shouting obscenities, and there was the sound of something being thrown into a wall.

"*Please,* ma'am. I'm begging you!"

Josette sighed. He was an idiot. He'd known the woman was married—apparently even knew the husband. It was certainly none of her business. But he smelled all right, and she *didn't* want to see him get killed.

"Go hide next to my car. It's the black Firebird. I'll be there in a minute with some clothes and a phone."

"Thank you, ma'am. God bless you."

Josette sighed again. She'd been that young once and easily as stupid. It wouldn't hurt anything for her to give the Lothario one of the inexpensive T-shirts and a pair of sweatpants she'd bought, and by now the cell phone would be fully charged and ready for use.

The argument next door was rising in volume. The woman appeared to be giving as good as she was getting. The drama and noise would probably have already drawn the police if the movie hadn't been running so loud right next door. As it was, murder and mayhem could probably be taking place with no one the wiser. Certainly nobody noticed when she slipped out of her room on her errand of mercy.

"You just saved my life. I can't thank you enough, ma'am. I really can't. If there is ever anything I can do for you—" He repeated the words over and over as he started to dress.

"I doubt that there will be. I'm only in town for a few days." The scent of his gratitude and relief was nearly overwhelming. She leaned against the fender of the car, keeping him in her peripheral vision while at the same time giving him a semblance of privacy.

"Just the same. You can count on me if you need anything, anything at all." He pulled the drawstring tight around his waist and knotted it. He grabbed the T-shirt from where she'd set it on the hood of the car, pulling it on over his head. It was a little small for him: tight across his chest and back, but at least he was now decently covered.

"My name's John Simmons. I've got a farm just a few miles to the west of town. You need anything, you give me a call. The number's in the book."

He sounded desperate to save face, not that she blamed him. So she said the words he needed to hear. "If I need anything I'll call."

"Good. You do that." Now that he was dressed he seemed more confident, less nervous. But he still kept casting glances over his shoulder at the next unit. It spoke well of him that he was worried about Dawn, but he needn't have been. Josette could hear that the argument was over and had, in fact, transitioned into a particularly energetic bout of sex.

"I wouldn't worry about her." Josette reassured him. "I'm pretty sure you'd be able to hear if there was anything wrong. The walls really aren't that thick."

"I s'pose." He didn't sound certain.

"Trust me." She passed him the cell phone and waited as he dialed a number from memory. She was only half-listening to him arguing with a man on the other end of the line. Her mind was elsewhere. It had almost been too easy keeping track of real-time, where her body actually was. Something had been different about today. She took her time, reviewing each of the visions that had passed through her mind. The man was nearly done with his call when it finally hit her.

She was seeing the present just fine, and the past; but as for the future, she wasn't in it.

Chapter Ten

RICK SAT ON the chair in his room, one boot in his lap ready to slide his foot inside, tapping the cell phone Raven had given him before he left to come here. It would be a simple matter to call him and ask him to send someone down to handle this. But he understood Josie's reluctance. She identified with Ellen, despite the girl being a raptor rather than a cat. The girl was still young to be developing seer talents. Most didn't develop them until *after* their first change. That she was seeing visions before—she might well end up with multiple gifts, like Josie.

In the current atmosphere, with the system crashed and everybody suspect as being a traitor, could any Wolven agent come down here and react to this threat without going to extremes?

But, Rick had met Ray briefly when he'd first arrived here. The man had been working on his truck in the parking lot as he rode the bike in. The way he'd snarled at Ellen said that he wouldn't be very supportive of the girl's gifts getting *worse*.

"Not yet," Rick said the words out loud and tucked the phone into the holster on his belt, laced his boots, and then made his way down to Josette's door. He felt slightly more refreshed after a brief shower and the mouthwash that had taken the scent of doberman from his nose and tongue. There was just something about dobermans; the scent just stuck with him.

It only took one knock for her to answer. The room smelled of another man, one in a panic and strongly laced with recent sex. His head moved around, trying to find the source, and she noticed.

Her snort was close to a laugh but more frustrated. "Some idiot was messing around with another man's wife next door. He had to go out the bathroom window naked and asked if he could please use my cell phone to call someone to pick him up."

Rick shot her an amused look. "And you *let him?*"

She shrugged. "Why not? He wasn't exactly a threat to me and—" The indifference on her face turned to a smirk and she crossed her arms over her chest. "Where would you be today if *you* hadn't snuck out my back window at Maman's house?"

Her eyes were twinkling merrily, and he realized he missed that look on her face. He remembered the incident well and couldn't help but grin. It wasn't that premarital sex didn't happen in Colonial America, but one had to be . . . discreet. He still remembered Josette, bearing a lovely French accent and an even lovelier set of curves, arriving at his master's offices that cold winter morning. (There was no embarrassment in calling your employer your master in those times, and Charles had always treated him well—even after he'd actively, and shamelessly, wooed the young woman.) Perhaps Charles had seen that an innocent flirtation would lead to something much deeper and that Josette would be made honorable again a few years later when the two married.

"That was a rather . . . *exciting* night, if I remember. We wouldn't have cut it nearly so close if not for that damned corset. Those laces were murder."

She shook her head and chuckled, then walked over and sat down on the bed near him. "I hated those things. So did Yvette. But Maman insisted they were *all the fashion* and had our dresses sewn so they were required. I couldn't even get into my petticoats without the contraption on." She paused for a moment and then looked a little uncomfortable. "So, what should we do from here?"

He'd been thinking about just that the whole time he'd been getting dressed. "I think we need to stay in a different town tonight."

"That seems like a good idea. I'll get packed." She started to stand, but he touched her shoulder and shook his head.

"I don't mean we should *leave*. We just need to be elsewhere for tonight. We still need to get more information, but on our terms. They'll change their plans if they know you've checked out, or even if you got in the car and ran. No, we need them off balance—not sure what to do, but not yet panicked."

That seemed to make sense to her and she nodded, smelling of ozone relief and understanding. "Then you should probably leave openly, and I'll sneak out and meet you somewhere. Right now, only a few people can probably connect us. I don't think Ellen will say anything. She would have already if she was going to."

"Right. Then your car will still be here. By the way, I like the car. It's very *you*." Josette smiled broadly and glanced toward the window. "But they won't know where you are or when you'll be back."

A HALF HOUR later, Josette was waiting behind a large tree, listening as the rumble of Rick's motorcycle neared. She'd packed a few toiletries, most of her paperwork—leaving only the passport to prove the room was hers—and a change of clothing into a book tote she'd purchased in Albuquerque. She then slipped out the back window, trusting Rick to lock up both of their rooms and pick up the deck of cards before meeting her at the edge of town.

Their destination was an even smaller town nearby called Nelson that had a bed-and-breakfast overlooking a small natural pond. It had looked so charming when she drove through the previous day that she'd nearly checked in, but Ellen wouldn't have had a way to get home. It might be something the girl would remember if she needed to find them in a crisis.

She ran toward him and slipped onto the motorcycle as he slowed to make the corner. That way, nobody would remember the bike stopping if asked. It was a stretch to turn and bend enough to put her items in the saddlebags, but she managed it by tightening her leg muscles around Rick's hips.

He didn't seem to mind. In fact, he grabbed her knee to steady her when he dodged around a dead rabbit and never seemed to get around to removing his hand.

A tall, padded bar that rose from the back of the bike kept her pressed against his back for the trip, and the scent of him naturally flowed into her nose as the wind blew around them. She'd forgotten how well their bodies fit together. How could she forget something so important, even after a century?

He turned his head slightly, while still keeping his eyes on the road, lit only by the broad high beam from the single headlamp. "Do you want to try to talk while we drive, or just enjoy the night?"

"We'll talk when we get there." He nodded and smiled slightly, and then cranked on the accelerator enough that she gasped when her body hit the padding behind her. It wasn't a long trip, and a part of her wished it would have lasted longer. She understood now why he drove a motorcycle—the scents and sounds on the night wind were incredible. Maybe when this was all over, she'd—

But no. Over would be *over*. Josette abruptly realized

that she was shaken to the core at the thought of her own death. Yes, people had been making attempts on her life for as long as she could remember. But after all these years, she never really expected them to succeed. Perhaps she had gotten inexcusably cocky, but alpha Sazi were notoriously difficult to kill. "Head and Heart" was the mantra in Wolven, because if the brain could still send signals then the heart would heal, and if the heart was pumping blood, then the brain would. Damn few, even among the Sazi themselves, knew that.

If the lack of foresight was any indication, she wasn't going to survive these events, unless something drastic changed.

Of course she could be wrong. Perhaps she hadn't "starred" in her visions because she was out of the loop and not currently doing anything that would affect the future. She told herself that it was possible, and it was . . . barely. But the truth was, she didn't believe it. And thus, for the first time in a very long time she was well and truly frightened. If there was any chance at all that she would die soon, she wanted to hear her twin sister's voice on the phone. She needed to tell Amber how much she loved her, Charles, and the children.

But what about Rick? Feeling him pressed against her so intimately made her realize that she still had feelings for him. Yet, not all of them were *good* feelings. Did the bad ones matter anymore? Should she just let go of the hurt and grab whatever little bit of happiness she could while she *still* could?

She just didn't know.

RICK SEEMED CONFUSED at the change in her mood as they knocked on the door of the darkened building. As they suspected, the owner lived on the premises and was happy to take their cash for a single night's stay—after a little magical persuasion on Rick's part.

There was only one room available on the second floor, and they quietly mounted the stairs to avoid waking the other few guests. A balcony overlooked the pond, and she immediately opened the French doors to stand out in the night and listen to the crickets and frogs and smell the rich, thick scent of decaying vegetation and fish.

Rick didn't approach. As an empath, he probably realized her feelings were in an uproar. Instead, he unloaded the items from the saddlebags, carefully separating her items on one side of the dresser, with his on the other.

"You feel melancholy," he said softly, and she nodded. "Thinking about times gone by?"

"Thinking about what might have been and what might never be." She turned then, leaning on the railing with the wind making the copper earrings tinkle, and stared at him. "I'm not seeing myself in the future, Rick. I don't think I survive this."

She swallowed hard and felt tears well in her eyes. She watched him take the emotional tide like a blow to the chest, visibly moving on the bed. "And for some reason, I feel like it's my own fault. Something I did or didn't do. Who did I let die that should have lived, or didn't kill that I should have?"

He stood then and walked over to her. She let him pull her into his arms and for the first time in a very long while, she cried. Mostly it was frustration at the current situation. She knew it, but allowed herself to finally grieve for Giselle, strong proud Giselle, who had turned the burden of putting down Maman as a Wolven agent into a lifelong role as a substitute mother for the young twins, Antoine and Fiona. In a way, she'd been very much a mother figure, even to her, helping her train her gifts as Maman never could. Like Rick, she'd been an empath and a skilled one. Her death had been for a noble cause, helping to bring down Sargon's evil plan, but it was a death nonetheless.

When she finally finished sobbing quietly against his chest, he released her and walked to the nightstand to retrieve a box of tissues. "Better?"

She nodded and accepted the slip of soft paper. After blowing her nose, she asked the obvious question. "So, did you find what you were looking for?"

If the question surprised him, he didn't show it. Their last argument had been a long-standing one in their relationship, and thinking about Giselle and Maman reminded her. Rick had wanted children, but she didn't. It was bearing children that had driven Maman insane, and she never wanted to risk becoming Sabine. Her siblings were all born *special,* whether healers or seers or magically powerful. Whether it was as Giselle believed, and Maman had what was currently known as postpartum depression, or whether the sheer power literally affected her brain, the truth was that she had been sane until she bore the twins a few years younger than she and Yvette. Money and power hungry, yes—but sane and rational. Josette just wasn't willing to risk bringing a child into the world that she would later intentionally kill.

Rick wanted a family, wanted a stable life, and she just couldn't give it to him, even after he pleaded and argued for over a century. So, he left. And try as she might, she couldn't blame him for wanting what he wanted. For wanting what *most* people wanted. "Did you have your houseful of children with someone else?" Tears threatened again, but she held them back through sheer will.

He shook his head, then sat down on the bed and leaned against the carved mahogany headboard. "Nope. At least, not that I'm aware of. There might be a few out there through sheer accident, but none intentionally."

"But—" Now she was really confused. "It was the *reason* you left. Wasn't it? Or was there more to it that I haven't been aware of for all these years?"

He started to kick off his boots, using the toe of one to pull at the heel of the other, before letting it drop to the floor. His voice remained soft, and she could hear the emotion play through it. But his scent was reflective of her own scent. She couldn't sort who was feeling what, and possibly he couldn't either.

"It was the reason, alright—or at least it's what I told myself was the reason. And I married again, twice. But they didn't last for more than a decade and suddenly, *I* was the one who didn't want children." He looked up at her with a sad smile. "I think it's that I just didn't want children with *them*. No, I've been living alone, building my house, for close to a century now, ever since I left Wolven."

She felt her eyebrows raise and she stepped back inside the room, silently closing the glassed doors against the worsening wind and continued to keep her voice low. "You've been building a house for a *century?* That must be one hell of a house!"

The shrug was accompanied by a small smile. "Not as much as you'd think. But when you're carving each stone with chisels right out of the mountainside, it takes a little while. I started with just one room and then added on. It's close to two thousand square feet now. And I hand-dug the well for water, *and* ran the electricity when it was discovered and brought west."

Now she sat down at the foot of the bed and wrapped her arms around her knees as rain began to splatter against the glass. "You always did like to try out new toys. You've probably gone solar by now, or have wind generators."

A chuckle escaped him. "Solar yes, but they make you get permits for the big wind turbines, and I haven't felt like bothering. I do have a wood-fired hot water heater, though. Staying off the grid suits me." His smile lessened and a tiny line of worry creased his brow. "I heard your house is gone. Were you there at the time?"

She nodded and sighed. "Just outside. I don't miss the house so much as I miss the things in it. I lost *everything*. Papa's pocket watch; Maman's pearl earrings; the quilt Grandmere Giselle gave us as a wedding gift . . . even the ring you gave me."

A variety of emotions flashed across his face and roiled in his scent as she admitted that she'd kept it this whole time. But she wasn't trying to accuse, she was just saying she'd miss them. None of the things she'd wept for had any great monetary value, but each had been priceless to her. Losing them hurt like losing a part of herself. "What I'm going to miss the most is the hand-carved toy cradle from Charles."

Rick laughed. "Oh yeah, I remember that. He put that note inside: 'The reason it's empty is because I robbed it.'"

It had been given to her as a joke gift after she very pointedly gave Charles permission to court her sister. While Amber was easily seventy when she first met

Charles, the Chief Justice of the council was *ancient*—even by Sazi standards. Josette's hindsight had allowed her to see just how long ago he was born. There were fur garments and stone tools involved.

Another chuckle moved his chest and he crossed his arms over it. "I've always wondered if he never mentioned me wooing you because he had it in mind to do the same thing. I mean, you were a pretty . . . *mature* woman when I met you, and I was just a lad of twenty-five."

Her skeptical look was enough to elicit another shrug. "I seem to remember you being plenty *mature* enough to convince me to sneak you into Maman's house. In fact, if memory serves, you were exceptionally skilled at certain tasks, even as a *lad*."

Now his smile turned lecherous, but there was a warmth to his eyes that added weight and made her shift nervously. "Still am." He moved his arm and patted the other pillow, while still keeping his eyes locked on hers. "If the future's in question, how about we make the present something worth remembering?"

Once again, indecision flooded her, locking her into an almost frozen position at the end of the bed. Rather than cajole or convince her, he simply stood up, walked around the bed, and slid his arms under her bent knees. She didn't stop him, didn't do anything as he carried her the two steps to the pillow and laid her back down. It wasn't until he cupped her chin with his fingers and pulled open her jaw as he pressed his mouth against hers that she realized just how much she wanted this. She'd wanted him to make the first move, just like he'd made the first move to leave.

Her arms slid up around his neck as he deepened the kiss, using his tongue to massage hers as he used to. There were no corsets this time, and their clothing disappeared with alarming speed.

Rick's palms bore calluses now, thick and rough, probably from the years of carving stone. There was only so much that Sazi healing could heal, especially when it was repeated day after day. Calluses weren't injuries, per se, just a thickening that prevented damage. But they raised the hairs on her skin as they glided over her naked body, making her squirm. When his hand reached her knee and moved inward, his lips moved to her neck. A light growl escaped her. Her animal remembered long, playful nights under the full moon where teeth and claws struggled for dominance. She had more magic, but he more muscle, so he usually won and would clamp his teeth into her neck while he mounted her.

Those hands still retained the memory of what would make her moan and scream and climax, and he didn't hesitate to use that remembered skill. Already she could feel wetness between her legs. Her body felt swollen and tight. She let go of past hurts, just for tonight, and let him suckle her breasts while his fingers slid deep inside her. Again and again he rubbed his rough thumb against her swollen nub, until she was forced to hold a pillow over her own face as the combination of sensations took her over the edge. No sense waking up the neighbors if the storm already hadn't.

"Time for the main event." His voice was deep and edged with growls. His scent was so deeply musky that she could smell it through the feather pillow. Her body was still squirming from the intense climax when he spread her legs and slid his thick, pulsing cock inside her. Another sharp gasp, which was close to a scream, escaped her before he ripped the pillow out of her grasp and claimed her mouth with his.

Her hands clutched at his hips as he moved in and out of her while his tongue probed her without mercy. She could feel his lust like a living thing; she wanted to drink it in, let it fill her until she could take no more. He let magic play over her body like a thousand fingers—tickling her toes and nibbling at her ears.

Her nipples were so hard they hurt from the pleasure of his body rubbing against them and she felt another orgasm building inside her. She tried to slow it, to slow him, but he would have none of it.

"Oh, no, little bobcat," he hissed into her ear after releasing her mouth. "I promised you a night to be remembered." He lifted her hips suddenly and began to push and pull harder, using magic to increase his own size inside her until she couldn't even speak. Lowering his head to her chest, he bit at the mounds of her breasts lightly ... then harder as he sensed she was close. His skin was glistening now, a combination of sweat and magic that was intoxicating. His scent was enough to remove the last vestiges of civility from her.

As the rain poured down and the wind howled outside, she grabbed at his hair, his back, his neck. He rode her until they were both growling openly and desperate for release. "Oh, God!" she whispered. "God, Rick! Yes, please."

He chuckled deeply and lifted her hips even higher. "And just wait until I flip you over later." The memory of some of their bedroom adventures long ago was too much in her current state and with a cry that was quickly stifled with his mouth and tongue, another climax raised her shoulders from the bed.

Rick's control was lost when her muscles seized his erection hard enough to pull a moan from him. He gave himself over to the sensation and pounded her body with his while frantically kissing her neck, mouth, and cheeks. His climax was just as intense, and his entire face distorted and reddened from the power of it.

He collapsed onto her and they held each other as their heartbeats returned to a semblance of normal. But his whispered words in her ear sped up her heart again, for a different reason.

"I've never stopped loving you, Josie."

Chapter Eleven

IT WASN'T UNTIL the next morning, over breakfast in bed, that she decided it was time to check in with her family. She hadn't had any visions at all this morning, and it concerned her. It was probably the first time in a century that she wasn't getting hourly visions of *something*. It could mean nothing, but it worried her nonetheless. They decided, after a truly delightful romp that still had her glowing, that Rick should call Raven. While Josette hated that particular choice, he was the most logical person to come down. He'd been human far longer than most Sazi, not turning until he was a junior in high school, so he would be able to understand Ellen's plight. And, if things grew difficult, he'd be able to draw power from her. She was going to eventually have to tell Rick about the mating. She knew that. But not quite yet.

She took a short walk around the pond and tossed bread crumbs to the fat orange koi, who didn't seem to fear her at all, using the time to sniff carefully for signs of any other shifters. There were none, even in the deeper grass, so she sat down on a stone bench far from the house and dialed her sister's number into the cell phone.

Amber picked up on the first ring. "Hello?"

"Bon matin, ma soeur. Comment vas-tu?" Greeting her in French would help in case anyone happened to be listening, which seemed unlikely.

"Aspen! Thank God you're alive." There was desperate relief in Amber's voice. It carried over the line clearly, despite the poor connection. The storm had passed, but the morning was cloudy and smelled of more rain. "Where *are you?*"

She opened her mouth to answer, but her sister interrupted. "No! Wait. Don't say anything. You need to call me back at a different number. We're in a full system crash."

"What?" Josette nearly dropped the phone. Surely she hadn't heard correctly. A full crash was an utter disaster—the kind of thing she *should* have seen coming. She hadn't had a clue. None.

"Do you have a pen to write down this number?"

"Give me a second." Propping the phone between her shoulder and her ear, she began rummaging through the tote bag she was carrying with her everywhere. It only took a second to find a pen, which had the logo of the Shooting Star Motel, along with a small pad. "Go ahead. I've got it."

"Okay, the number I'm giving you is a sterile phone. We're only going to use it for the one call. You'll need to get rid of your phone after you use it. Use top security protocol. Remember that plan? We talked about the details in Monte Carlo during the regatta."

Josette forced herself to remain calm despite the adrenaline that was racing through her veins with each beat of her heart. So much code, so many worst-case scenario plans they'd made long ago, when Amber married Charles. There was no Monte Carlo, no regatta races that they'd attended. They were just codes to confuse the enemy—whoever that might be during any given crisis.

There was a bitter taste on her tongue, and her mouth had gone dry with the same fear she could hear in her twin's voice. Amber recited the series of numbers that formed the cell phone number she was to use, and Josette repeated them back.

When Amber confirmed she had the numbers right she disconnected the line. With trembling fingers Josette tapped in the numbers and waited for the call to go through.

"Bonjour? La soeur, cela vous est? S'il vous plaît confirmer avec le nom de notre grandmère."

That seemed a logical enough question—asking for their grandmother's name. People trying to impersonate her might know one of them, but not Giselle. She wasn't a true relative, after all. *"Oui, c'est moi. Grandmère Giselle ou Grandmère Helene?"*

Josette switched to English. "Both, apparently. Now tell me what's wrong."

"What isn't?"

She heard the panic in her twin's voice and was surprised that she couldn't feel any sort of emotional bleed from their twin connection. It didn't happen often, as they were fraternal rather than identical twins, but sometimes when things were especially bad—

"Calm down. Take a deep breath. Then tell me what's going on."

Amber took a steadying breath. When she spoke, her voice was still a little higher and breathier than usual, but there wasn't the edge of panic that had been so apparent a moment before.

"I have to make this brief. Rick probably already told you if you've seen him, but in case not, we found electronic bugging devices on all of the standard-issue equipment for agents while we were visiting his cabin. Lucas ordered the entire system to be crashed and rebuilt from scratch."

Josette nearly fell off the bench. The immensity of the problem was staggering. A full crash meant that every agent was effectively cut off, completely on their own. There were protocols for checking in, but that in itself would be perilously dangerous for the agents currently on deep cover assignments.

"I do understand that this is very bad, but what does that have to do with me?"

"Nothing. Lucas is handling it. But there's the other crisis going on. Have you seen Rick? Do you know anything at all?"

She hesitated. How much should she say over the line? Yes, she bought this little prepaid phone off the shelf, but who could say that it wasn't tampered with before she arrived. It had been the *only* phone in the tiny convenience store. "Yes. We've . . . met."

Amber paused for a long moment, and then a hint of something briefly playful, and immensely pleased came over the wire. "Are you two—?" She didn't have to complete the sentence. They'd talked on too many occasions about the situation.

Josette shook her head. "Yes . . . no. I don't know. But he did tell me about the seers. I think I saw the caster in a vision, but I couldn't see a face or get a location."

"We need you here. Now."

That widened her eyes and she glanced around her carefully to make certain nobody was in sight or scent range. "Can you explain?"

"Not over the phone." Amber's frustration was evident. "No, wait. I have an idea." She paused, her voice very careful as she asked the next question. "Do you remember what mother did to you when you were eight."

She shuddered at the memory and began rubbing her arms from a chill that had nothing to do with the weather. "It's not the kind of thing one would forget. Yes, Rick explained it."

"Only Charles, Antoine, Nana, Duchess Olga from the Chicago pack are involved. Tony Giodone is fine. Does that make sense?"

Amber had just named all of the seers besides herself with *foresight*. For an instant she wondered if . . . but no, she had been having future visions. She just hadn't been *in* the visions. Besides, Charles himself had told her that her powers were too erratic as a result of what Maman had done. They would have to kill her, because never again would her powers be bound.

Silence stretched along the line for so long that Amber began to panic.

"Are you there? Did you hear me? We need you here, need you to break the spell. They're dying, Josette. All of them. We'll be *blind*."

Josette wondered if her sister realized the danger of what she was asking. If Josette wasn't strong enough, if even the smallest thing went wrong in a breaking ritual. But no, in reality, it didn't matter. Even if it killed her, she had to try. Maybe that was why she wasn't in the visions. Perhaps she would be forced to give her life to the spell. The others were the true eyes of the Sazi. They watched the future, planned events, kept the entire world, both human and shifter, safe. Josette knew in her heart that she was expendable, while the others weren't.

"I heard. We're in the middle of nowhere. I'll leave for the city immediately. Just tell me where you are and I'll take the next plane out."

"No, we'll send Bruce and Lucas with the jet. It will be faster and safer. They know where we are going, so I won't say it on the line. But can you make sure the weather is clear enough for them to land at either end?"

She shook her head. "That's a bad idea. We have no idea how strong whoever did this is. I don't want to waste strength that I may need for the working. There's an airport in Grodin, New Mexico. I can meet them there." She thought for a moment, considering everything she might need to break the magic that bound her friends, for while most of what she did would simply use her own innate power, there were words and rituals that might help. "And when I get wherever you are I'll need a white pillar candle for each of the seers affected, some church incense, and the book."

"*What* book?"

"The book *Grandmère* Helene gave me, the one that had been in her family for generations. Surely, you remember."

"Oh! *That* book." Amber didn't quite manage to keep the disgust from her voice. Not that Josette blamed her. The book had been a gift to Josette from their paternal grandmother when she had discovered that Josette was a seer. It was ancient, with different sections written in various ancient languages, but was, she'd been assured, a mystical volume exploring the seers' gifts. The cover was made of snakeskin identical to the ones in the jungle cave and the German cave—which would not have been nearly as disturbing if Josette hadn't had a vision where she was inside the mind of the Sazi snake who had been flayed for his skin to make the bindings. It had only been a matter of sheer luck that the volume hadn't been in the house at the time of the explosion.

Could that have been what the snakes were looking for? But they already had a book. She'd seen it. If they needed more than one . . . Oh, this was bad.

Thankfully, a year or so ago Charles had asked to borrow it. He'd wanted it available for Tahira's research on power wells when she finally appeared in the canvas of the future, which was now the past.

"Do you still have it?"

"Of course. It's at the house in Germany. I can get everything you require and have it all waiting when you get here. We're in Charles's old hometown." There was no hesitation in her voice. "We're having all the others brought here as well, so you'll only need to do the ceremony once."

Josette understood the logic of her sister's plan, but it couldn't happen in New York, where she'd first appeared at his offices so long ago. Too many powerful Sazi in one place would affect the weather patterns. More to the point, security would be a nightmare. How tempting would it be to their enemies to strike when all the seers were in one central spot. And New York was a major hub. People could arrive from anywhere.

"Amber . . ." she began to argue, but her sister cut her off.

"We have to risk it. There's not enough time to do anything else." Her voice dropped to a mere breath of sound that only her sister could hear. "They're not doing well Josette. Please hur—"

With an annoyed yowl that would probably be heard inside, she snarled, "*Arrêt, Yvette!* Stop! Listen to me, *petite souer*—" She didn't often call Amber *little sister*, especially since she was technically the younger born, so it stopped her cold. "You *must* listen. *Not* New York. This must be south, much farther south. I *saw* this event once, long ago."

That did it. Amber stilled completely and her voice regained its usual calm. "I see. Very well then. I must rely on your judgment in this. Where must we go?"

How could she tell her the location without anyone overhearing? She fumbled in her memory just as Rick started to walk down the railroad tie steps to where she sat.

"Do you remember when we visited the grasslands together, down at the tip of the country?"

A pause and then a slow answer. "Vaguely."

She prompted more, without directly saying anything. "Surely you remember that austere British gentleman, Matthias . . . oh what was his last name? Morning? Evening? Night? He built that lovely hotel."

Amber's voice brightened. "Oh. *Oh!* Yes, I do remember him. He was quite the flirt. Yes, I think we can manage that. It's too early in the season for anything horrible. Good pick."

It wasn't without reason. The vision she'd seen so

long ago said that the book wouldn't be the one they needed. No, she would need the *other* book—the one from *Grandmère* Giselle. Even Amber didn't know about that one. Nobody did, except Giselle herself. There were four ancient magic books originally, and three were needed for any great ritual working. Most believed that there *were* only three, which is why one was kept secret. At any given time, those who sought to do evil with them might have all three. But the one Josette possessed, and which was safely hidden in Daytona Beach, Florida, could undo them all. It wasn't a power book by itself. It was strictly an eraser. With one power book and the canceling spell, anything could be corrected.

She folded the cell phone closed and removed the small battery pack. Then, with casual strength she crushed the phone in her hand, ignoring the pain as the sharp plastic shards dug into the flesh of her palm. She needed to get out of here, now. They needed to get to Florida before the others arrived.

She turned in time to see Rick hurrying toward her.

He stopped a few feet from where she sat. "What's happening? You're upset." Rick's voice rumbled with the panic that she felt. She wished she could explain it better.

"I haven't foreseen this, Rick. Haven't seen *any* of it, and I should have." That was alarming, terrifying even. Because her friends, her family, needed her. She would *not* let them down. Not so long as there was breath left in her body. There might be frictions between them, old grudges that would never heal, but none of that mattered now.

He seemed taken aback. "But I thought I just heard you tell Amber that you did *see* this."

She pulled back her arm and tossed the crushed cell phone into the center of the pond and pocketed the battery to dispose of in the trash inside.

"Pfft. You just weren't close enough to smell the lie. I just needed to get them to the town where we need to go next. You know Amber. Without the comfort of a vision, she won't risk anything. There were visions, old ones, but without form, just impressions about potential events. But we need to get back, deal with whatever's happening here quickly, and then leave to meet the others. Tell me about your conversation on the road."

He nodded and put an arm around her waist as they walked back toward the house. They were a team again, at least for a time. At this point, she trusted him, and she couldn't trust many people.

Once they were back on the motorcycle and riding back toward Pony, he told her about his conversation with Raven. He had to speak loud to be heard over the rushing wind, but she was enjoying holding him close and resting her chin on his shoulder so she could hear. It felt familiar and safe.

"Okay, here's the scoop. Lucas, Amber, Charles, and Bruce came up to my house in South Dakota and told me about the problem with the seers. You already know that. But as they were arriving, someone attacked Charles. It was an assassin, a snake."

Oh! That changed a lot of things. "But how would the snakes know where you live and—" She didn't complete the thought because he nodded and continued.

"Precisely! They shouldn't know, unless someone was being tracked on the way up there. And, in fact, everyone was being tracked. All except for me. We found bugs in the cell phones, the laptop, and even the clothing and Amber's stethoscope."

"*Merde!* No wonder they shut down the whole network. Who could have done such a thing?" But before the words even finished leaving her mouth, she knew and could kick herself. "Yusef. He must have done it. I knew he had betrayed Charles, but didn't warn either one."

But, to her surprise, Rick shook his head. "Stop blaming yourself for the failings of others, Bun. For as many visions as you've had over the centuries, you can't see *everything*. It's a bad habit and one that Charles shares. He blamed himself, too, but Amber swears she bought the stethoscope *after* Yusef died, and it's only been out of her sight a few times—one of them while she was visiting Wolven headquarters. He might have been involved, but he's not the *only* person. Unfortunately, we're not certain who else might be involved. I know it's not me, and I'm pretty sure it's not you—"

A semi passed them, and the rush of air forced them nearly onto the shoulder before Rick could correct the bike back onto the two lane road. "That's stating the obvious. And I can't imagine Lucas, Amber, or Charles are involved. But frankly, I've never trusted Bruce completely. I know Charles does, but Bruce has always troubled me. I'm certain he's in league with the snakes," Josette said.

Rick shrugged. "Anything's possible, I suppose. But the snakes aren't who worry me. I don't think they're behind it." The words sounded loud in the sudden silence; they were coming to a stop at the light near the edge of town.

She could hear the incredulous tone in her own voice. "What do you mean? The snakes are *always* involved in plots to overthrow the world! They've been trying ever since Sargon sat on the council."

He turned his head and gave her a serious, nearly offended expression. "Your prejudice is showing, Bun. You might as well say that all lion shifters are insane because Sabine was. That was another nasty habit of yours even when we were married. I know it's with good cause, but it's not fair. I happen to like a lot of the American snakes. I'd trust any number of them to guard my back."

He was dead serious, and she reared back in surprise. Her temper began to rise. "I am *not* prejudiced! I killed *snakes* at my house. Somebody set an explosive that blew up my home, and the only scents were *snakes,* plus me and Tasha. There were *snakes* in the SUV that tried to kill Ellen and me in Albuquerque. It was a *snake* seer whose mind I entered in the vision in the hotel, and who had a fucking *casting circle* painted on the cavern floor in the jungle. Those are *facts,* Rick. How do you figure I'm blindly throwing suspicion their way?"

"I didn't say it was blind suspicion. But just because they're after *you,* doesn't mean they're after all the seers, or involved in every evil plot in existence."

She couldn't even decide how to respond to that, and knew her anger was soaking into him. It would make it nearly impossible for him to drive, but he had no right to call her a bigot! She'd told him everything last night, after they made love. Brought him up-to-date on what had happened in her life for nearly a century, and he did the same. There wasn't much to tell, up until the past several days. But snakes were definitely in the picture. She just didn't know what they were planning.

She watched as he battled the emotions, trying to stay calm—and finally, he pulled the bike over under the metal shelter of an old, closed gas station, then straddle-walked it through a gap in the corrugated fencing so they were hidden from traffic. The twin pumps standing in the old repair yard were tall and rounded with real dials, instead of a digital ones. There were skeletons of vehicles that seemed to be from the fifties and sixties. She doubted anyone would be wandering nearby while they talked.

He got off the bike, stepped away from it, and leaned against the wall near a faded logo so he could face her. The wind was rising again, and she was a little afraid that the dark clouds appearing on the horizon were her fault.

"I'm not disputing the things that have happened to you. But do you *seriously* believe that the snakes would work with someone like Ray? You know Ahmad. He's one of the more tolerant of them about full humans, and he'd squish that man like a bug."

She thought about it for a moment—thought back to the various encounters with him. Her words came out slow and thoughtful. "Actually, no. Ray's from a raptor lineage. Ellen said she got her feathers from both sides of the family. They will work together if they must, but I can't imagine *Ray* would have survived more than a week. He's just not bright enough not to say something stupid—and I saw that he detests shifters. All of us."

Rick's head dipped an acknowledgment. "So, then, what about the cards? There were pictures of seers on them, including you. If Ray and his buddy aren't working for the snakes, then who *are* they working for? Is there some sort of raptor group starting up? I can see birds calling a working plot a "movement." Could Ray's family ties be bullying him, even while he detests the family members who turn?"

Josette pursed her lips and looked down while she tapped one finger on her jeans. The polish was chipping badly. Either she was going to need to remove the glossy red or smooth over the missing bits.

"I suppose it's *possible,* but he didn't really seem the type. He's more of the passive aggressive sort. He'd tell them he'd help and then just never get around to it. No, I was inside his head. Whatever this "movement" is, he's in for the long haul. He's working with people, like Harold, despite disliking them, for the greater cause. I could sense a fanaticism in him—he's a true believer in whatever's going on."

"In other words, we've got *two* problems. The snakes are casting some sort of spell on the seers, and The Movement is trying to eliminate them. Does that sound about right?"

Josette noticed he'd turned Ray's term into a title of sorts. And now that she was thinking along the lines of two distinct threats, more of the things in her recent visions and conversations were making sense.

Rick opened his mouth to say something when she interrupted. "Something that just occurred to me might be important." He closed his jaw and raised his brows for her to continue. He always was good at letting her speak when a thought possessed her. He seemed to instinctively know that she might lose track of the thread if he interrupted. "When I first met Ellen, she said Ray didn't intend to let her take her bird form on the moon." After Rick snorted his opinion on that and rolled his eyes, she continued. "But then I saw in Ray's mind during my vision that as soon as he *made Ellen right again*, she'd know how much he loved her."

Now she had his full attention and he pushed off from the wall to walk closer to where she still sat on the back of the motorcycle. "So what are you saying?"

"Ellen mentioned that she was afraid her father was going to use her as a guinea pig for some stuff he and his buddies were brewing in the desert. Could it be that what we saw isn't a drug lab?" She amended quickly, "That is to say, it *is* a drug lab, but not recreational drugs for the humans?"

He was quiet for a long time, staring blankly at one of the gas pumps while tapping his foot, like he always did when he was working out a big problem. Finally, he shook his head.

"Well, I don't think either of us will have any way of knowing, even if we went back. Plus, we'll just be inviting someone to connect the two of us. For the moment, I think we need to proceed like we planned. Get Raven out here and turn this aspect over to him. Even with the network shut down, there are still untraceable ways for agents to contact one another. He can sneak out there, take a sample of whatever the stuff in the test tubes is and get it to Bobby Mbutu, the chemist at Wolven. I imagine he's still there, even after all these years. What *we* need to do is get you to wherever it is you need to go to meet Charles and the others."

"And, in the meantime, make sure that The Movement doesn't find me. I didn't notice your picture on those cards, so you're still unknown to them. That could be useful. But I'm just not willing to walk away and leave Ellen to some sort of horrible fate, either. Maybe what I need to do is track down that caster in my mind again and try to eliminate him. If the caster's gone then, like when Maman killed the one blocking my gifts, the spell will dissipate on its own. Then we can stay and concentrate on things here until they're resolved."

He shook his head. "That's a huge risk, Bun. What happens if something happens to you? Are you willing to—"

Rick's voice disappeared as the world abruptly shifted. She felt herself slump and fall from the motorcycle but couldn't feel anything beyond that, like whether or not she slashed open her head on the discarded, jagged metal fence that had been next to her in the yard.

Rich soil and decaying vegetation filled her nose as she walked through the verdant jungle. The recent rain had coated every leaf, so that as she walked, wetness splattered on her skin and clothing. She paused to dip her hands into a massive fern frond where fresh water had collected. The hands that came into view were definitely male— slender and hairless with a dark, nutty pigment to the skin. The water tasted cool, but her nose detected the bitter overtones of a viper over the scent of the greenery.

She walked a familiar path toward an ancient stone temple. So, she was with the caster again. While she had understood Rick's warning, she felt confident from her last meeting that she could turn the caster's own power back on him. All she had to do was draw on the siphoned power and force-feed it into the caster's system. Rather than storing it in reserve through the spell, he would literally drown on the power. As the caster stepped up toward the circle of power, she readied herself.

But then the scene shifted again. She was in a new place, where it was hot and dry and dark. It felt like where her body was in New Mexico, but the air smelled different. There were oddly scented animals, too, and now her body moved differently. There was a swing to her walk and when she looked down, there were ample breasts—to the point that she couldn't see her sandaled feet until they individually stepped out past the shadow of the chest. Was this the present time, or the future? Or even a past event? No, this didn't feel like the past, at least not one Josette had experienced herself. So, the present or future then.

She tried to get some sense of where and when she was, but the woman whom she inhabited kept her eyes downcast. Only feet and moonlit sand were visible. The feet were small and tanned, with ragged *overgrown nails and thick calluses on the toes. That led her to concentrate on the body. It was tired—a bone-aching weariness that filled every muscle to burning. The spirit was likewise weak and dejected. Hopelessness and depression had set in, and she could feel herself wondering if this would be her entire life? Was she just to be used and thrown away like the others? A voice to her left finally raised her head. "It's time. We have the sacrifice ready." The words had a distinct accent she'd heard recently, but she couldn't place it immediately.*

A single massive tree stood in the center of a vast, flat landscape. The sky was clear of clouds, and the woman looked up briefly, appealing to God to let this end tonight. Let this be the last time she would have to watch another die so she could live. Josette watched as she walked closer to the tree and realized that she was looking at a different *casting circle—nearly identical to the one in the jungle, but with different symbols around the outside of the central ring.*

What in the hell was going on?

The woman closed her eyes as she stepped into the circle. Josette felt her flinch as the screams of another rose into the night and then ended with a gurgle that chilled her blood. An object was handed to the woman and she fondled it without opening her eyes. It felt like leather, but it was smooth in one direction and rough when the hand moved the other direction. The woman liked the feel of it—it amused her. She reached for the edge and Josette realized it was a book. It was another power book! She could feel the energy that surged through the woman's fingers as the pages opened.

A headache suddenly began to throb in Josette's own head, distant and apart from where her mind was. She tried desperately to listen to the words, tried to remember them so she could find them when the time came, so she could remove this spell—because it was absolutely a spell that was affecting her real body.

But then she was sucked away again, pulled forcibly from the mind of the woman, and back into the snake caster's mind. The shift from desert to jungle made her gasp for breath, and she could feel Rick's frantic hands on her, trying to revive her. At the moment, though, she needed to be here. She knew it. This was important. This time, the snake caster knew she was there and spoke to her consciousness directly. Josette could both feel the mouth and feel the words appear in her mind.

"Welcome, Sazi seer. Your power will be my greatest prize for my master. Know that your life force will bring a great new age and finally return the world to its rightful state."

She pulled on her own power to reply. "I think you're mistaken. Because this meeting will be *your* undoing, not mine."

A chuckle was the only reply before the power of the casting circle rose and filled the small rock room. She gasped as power began to pull out of her and into the circle. But the caster apparently didn't realize who he was dealing with. She hadn't lived this long without having a few tricks of her own. She allowed her power to flow into the circle until it was full to bursting, and then called it all back to her again like a growing storm. Energy swirled around her real body, raising her earrings into the air and pulling at the hairs of Rick's beard. Rain began to fall on them as storm clouds filled the sky over Pony. Lightning flashed dangerously close as she felt outward for the other seers. She pulled power from them, and they gave it willingly—feeling her presence and adding their will and fury.

With murderous intent she turned all the power on the caster, forced it to fill his veins, his limbs, his mind. He was taken by surprise and had no way of knowing what she was doing was even possible. His blood began to boil from the heat of the surge until he screamed and screamed and then . . . stopped.

She came back into her body just as the caster died and felt her own power kick back to her so hard and fast that she turned over on Rick's lap and vomited her breakfast onto the nearby junk. She heaved on hands and knees until she was empty, leaving her dizzy and with a migraine that seared her eyes every time she tried to open them.

Rick's voice was shaken and rough when the air bubble in her head finally popped, so that she could hear. "What in the hell just happened."

"He tried to kill me from the inside out." The words were tiny little gasps and her voice was hoarse. "My throat hurts."

"Uh yeah. No doubt. You were screaming bloody murder. But fortunately, every time you did, thunder boomed from the storm you brewed up, so nobody would have heard it."

After three tries, she finally got her eyes open in a squint, but wide enough to see that his leather jacket was covered in blood. Most likely it was hers from the way her right temple and shoulder were pounding. "Did I cut myself?"

He nodded and took another shaky breath. "Big time. But it's healed now. You've been out for nearly half an hour. Are you okay?"

She chuckled lightly, and even that made her stomach hurt. "Hardly. But I will be now. I was right. There was a spell, and it was a snake. But it wasn't the only one. This one was a siphon spell. There's another one, too—a different caster who's a woman. *That's* the blocking ritual."

* * *

"I DON'T UNDERSTAND the difference. You mean there are different kinds of spells that can be used against Sazi, outside of simple power? There's ritual magic, too?" Rick hated sounding like an idiot, but he needed to know what she was talking about if he was going to be of any use.

Josette nodded and moved to a slightly different position, so she could lean her back against a rusted tractor wheel. "Pretty much. We Sazi don't use it much. Mostly we rely on our personal magic—our 'gifts.' But while it is slower, and takes a lot of delicate, uninterrupted work, ritual magic can be immensely powerful. A lot of it predates Christianity. I think it was partly the spread of Christianity and the witch hunts that curtailed most of the use."

"But these snakes used it."

"Yes, they did. And apparently, they've been using it for some time—pulling power from all of the seers without our knowledge. I don't know why yet, but Charles might know. He should be starting to feel better any time now."

Once again, Josie had gone her own way, without thinking of the consequences. He didn't try to fight when the frustrated noise rose and exited his mouth. He stood up to put the motorcycle back on its tires, where the wind from the storm had knocked it over. "So, you just killed him. Without finding out what he was up to?"

Her voice was calm, the sort of stillness that

challenged him to argue. "He was trying to kill *me,* Rick. I didn't have much choice."

He offered her a hand up, but she used the massive wheel to get to her feet instead. "You know that's not going to be the end of it, right?"

She gave him a look like he was stupid. "Of course. There'll be other plans, and probably other seers who can do ritual magic. All the council has *ever* been able to do with the snakes is beat them back. If you think them safe or trustworthy, you're a fool. They rise up and you beat them back. They plan and plot and we foil it. It's a never-ending game. Short of killing them all to extinction, there's nothing to be done except keep fighting them, one battle at a time." She must have noticed his expression and sighed. "You think I did the wrong thing, don't you?"

He threw up his hands before straddling the bike once more and wheeling it around to make sure everything functioned. He hated when it tipped over. "Hell, I don't know, Josie! Everything with you is just so damned black and white. But as much as I hate it, I learned in Wolven that there are a million shades of gray. I trust my instincts with people, where you look for traps and plots. Maybe some of the snakes are inherently evil. Perhaps I'm wrong and you're right, and they're *all* evil. Maybe you *did* do the right thing this time. It just frustrates me that you don't stop to think about *whether* it is the right thing before you start. You just do it and then worry about it later. One of these days, that's going to bite you in the ass."

He turned to see her face, fully expecting it to be livid. Instead, she was close to tears and the wave of pain hit him in the chest hard enough to make him flinch. The words were whispered and filled with hurt. "Do you really believe that? That I just go off half-cocked and do things without thinking—*kill* people without considering the consequences?"

"Do you?" The question was serious and his voice flat and cold. He needed to know. The Josie he used to know couldn't kill as easily as this new version that Lucas and Raven had told him about—the one who casually talked about all the assassins she'd disposed of over the years last night, the dozens of *people* that were dead by her hand. "Do you even think about them being *people* anymore? Or are they just *the snakes* . . . the villains, the enemy to be destroyed? Who are you, Josie? Who have you become?"

This is why he left Wolven, because he was getting the same way, killing without thought because there was no other choice. At the end, he didn't much like himself anymore.

A thousand emotions pierced his chest as quickly as they fluttered across her face, making his heart race. The scents of sorrow and fear blended with the ozone still in the air and he fought to breathe through it, to think through the tide. He watched her arms wrap around herself, as though she were freezing cold. She was still so pale from the vision, and he nearly pulled her against him to warm her and make her feel better. But he just couldn't. Last night, she'd seemed like the old Josie—proud and strong, a warrior with a heart, the woman he'd loved with everything he was. Today, though . . . this was a new person, colder, with sharp edges. No, right now he couldn't hold her—not until he knew who, or *what*, he would be holding.

She lowered her eyes to the ground, where foamy bile still dripped from the edge of a rusted sign. "I . . . I need to think. We probably shouldn't arrive back at the motel together. Maybe you should—"

He nodded, understanding that she was tap-dancing around. "I'll go drive around for awhile. I'll be back around dark and then we can drive to the nearest airport. I'll still get you where you need to go safely. On my honor, I swear that to you."

She looked up then, her face still stricken, but she nodded. Her face and scent showed that she understood what lay beneath his very formal vow. He would travel with her and keep her safe, but there was no future for . . . *them* if she'd really changed so drastically from who she used to be.

"Grodin. Lucas and Bruce will be flying into Grodin to meet us."

Rick dipped his head in acknowledgment, then kick-started the bike and eased it back through the broken fence, heading not toward the hotel, but back to Nelson. He should pick up a new phone and get hold of Raven again, and then keep watch on the compound to see if anything developed. Or maybe he'd just wander at the little pond and think. Perhaps it was *time* to do a little reflection about life and ... things.

Chapter Twelve

JOSETTE EASED HER legs to a straight position. She'd been sitting on the bed for so long with them tucked against her chest that they'd cramped. *Standing up and stretching would probably be a good idea.*

She swung her legs off the bed and began a series of exercises, side-to-side stretches with hands on hips, and then palms flat on the floor. Her mind had been wandering back and forth in time—not visions, but memories. Had she changed so much? She remembered the numbness that had settled over her mind when she decided to kill the caster, and before, when she realized she *didn't* feel for the rattlesnake and his mate. Was she still the same woman who could be charmed enough by a tiny bunny to ignore her own stomach?

And if she'd changed was it because she didn't *want* to be that woman anymore? Or was it Rick who had changed? He used to be harder than her; more matter of fact, the eternal cop. Who had changed, and could they go back and become people they'd perhaps outgrown?

Yet, it had felt so good being with him again. It wasn't just the sex, but the total release, allowing her to be herself. She'd let down all her barriers for one night, barriers she'd built up over a century while being alone. He took her at face value, and she let him. A part of her she'd nearly forgotten had leaped at the closeness, at the honesty, and didn't want to lose it.

Soon it was going to be time to leave and he was going to want an answer. Her heart had pounded almost painfully at the thought that he might be interested in more than a simple one-night stand—a frolic for old times sake. But was there still enough inside her that she could bend to fit herself back into a relationship, if a future even existed for her? And did she want to?

The blinds were rattling, beating against the tile wall with each gust of wind that blew through the open window. Another storm, but she wasn't surprised. The energy over this town had increased tenfold with the killing of the seer. She walked to the bathroom and reached beneath the blinds, intending to pull the window closed when a flash of lightning illuminated the area behind the building. The weeds, where John Simmons had hidden, were crawling with snakes. The largest had a wedge-shaped head the size of a dinner plate—much too large to be anything native to the area. Josette concentrated, trying to listen beneath the sounds of the storm. Yes, there was movement on the roof overhead, or perhaps between the roof and ceiling.

This was *so* not good. Moving as quickly and

silently as she could she crossed into the main part of the room to peek out the window. With the flashing of the neon sign she could made out snakes hidden in the grassy verge that edged the parking lot. Lots of them.

Shit, shit, shit.

She needed out of here, *now.* There were too many of them to fight. Too many to hold if it came to that. Whoever had orchestrated this knew her reputation, and had decided to counteract any magic she might raise with sheer, overwhelming numbers. If surprise didn't work, they'd wear her down by making her overextend her magical abilities.

Another glance at the parking lot showed that Rick's bike was still gone. And she'd crushed the cell phone this morning. Not surprisingly, when she picked up the room phone, it was dead.

The front door was out. The back window was out.

Her attention was caught by the rattle of metal coming from the bathroom ceiling. Looking up, she noticed the entire fan unit moving slightly. There was no *time*. She needed to do something. She glanced furiously around the room, looking for anything that might help. Her eyes lit on the perfume bottle on the nightstand and then she remembered something Rick had told her last night—a humorous piece of trivia about his saddlebags continually falling over and breaking a bottle of aftershave inside.

There was a trapdoor.

She grabbed the bottle from the nightstand and began spraying it vigorously, filling the air with a fine, potent mist of scent that she hoped would confuse the snakes' senses of smell. She threw open the door to the closet she hadn't even bothered to open before, found the ring, and lifted the trapdoor lid, identical to the one Rick had described.

Ignoring the spiders on webs, shooing away several small scorpions crawling along the ground, she wormed her way inside, flattening onto her back so she could reach up to pull the closet door shut, pull in her purse, and lower the lid to the crawl space. Unfortunately, there was no room at that point to roll over, so she was forced to slide across the raw concrete on her back, her nose nearly grazing exposed pipes and beams. To free her hands she set her purse on her belly. Then, using her hands and feet she began to pull her way through the confined space. The thin fabric of her T-shirt hiked up almost immediately, leaving her bare back to scrape across the rough concrete.

More than once she felt sticky webbing drag against her skin, and the crawling of legs across the exposed flesh of her stomach. She ignored everything, concentrating on using the dim light that came through the ventilation grates to navigate her way to freedom.

She'd gone only a few feet when she heard the sound of footsteps moving above her, followed by sneezing and the sound of vicious cursing. The footsteps moved in the direction of the bathroom, and Josette put on a burst of speed. She heard voices arguing in rapid-fire Spanish, followed by the sound of a door not far from her head swinging open.

She froze, stilling even her breath as booted feet ran past the grate beside her head. It wouldn't take them more than a minute to search the room and find the trapdoor. Here, in this enclosed space, the snakes would have the advantage of mobility. She had to get out of here, into the open where she stood a fighting chance.

Josette set aside her purse, then, concentrating, shifted into her familiar furred form. With a deft twist of her body, she was on her feet, running toward the grate at the far side of the crawl space. A voice called out behind and above her. The creak of hinges drove her on. She put on a burst of speed. At the last second she turned, taking the impact on her shoulder as she burst through the grate to slam into the corrugated metal side of a sunken window well.

The pain of her dislocated shoulder was intense. Tears mixed with the pouring rain, blurring her vision. Her left front paw hung useless at an unnatural angle. Behind her, in the dark of the crawl space she heard the slithering of scales across concrete.

Desperate, she gathered her power and threw it behind her, hoping to buy a few minutes by freezing the snakes in place as she had done so many times before.

The magic flew out—she even felt it impact against the strength of the combined force of snakes. Then a draining sensation began. Even without their caster, they were managing a rudimentary siphon spell that was pulling her own power to use against her.

She struggled to cut off the energy drain as she forced her body up onto the grass and into an awkward run.

Voices called out in Spanish from locations around the parking lot. They were converging on her in human forms as the snakes moved with breathtaking speed to catch up with her.

Her body struggled to heal the damage to it even as she ran. Her shoulder moved back into place with an audible pop, and she used that new mobility to put on a burst of speed. She ran in a zigzag pattern, avoiding her pursuers. They herded her toward the wide gulley that served as a storm sewer, moving in a pincher movement. She hissed, glaring at the approaching attackers before turning and gathering herself for a massive leap.

She nearly didn't make it. The muddy bank on the far side gave way beneath her back paws, the water pulling inexorably at her. She struggled, digging her front claws deep into the roots of the weeds that lined the embankment. With a massive effort that tore at her injured shoulder she dragged herself out of the sucking current.

Still they pursued, the humans running awkwardly

over pavement made slick by rain mixed with oily tar. She didn't wait to watch. Instead, she chose to dash onto the road, dodging between the oncoming cars before disappearing in the tall weeds of the empty lot across from the hotel.

Flashes of lightning lit her way, followed by the ominous boom of thunder. She paused, listening for the sounds of pursuit. She could hear them in the distance. The rain, while cold and miserable, was serving her well, washing her scent and tracks away, so there was little for them to follow. Still, she was exhausted and injured. She needed to lose them entirely and find a place to rest and heal. The adrenaline pumping through her system kept her moving, but she wasn't sure how much longer she could keep on. Even powerful Sazi had their limits, and she was rapidly reaching hers.

To her left she heard the clang of metal in the distance, followed by the chug of engines and clang of the crossing alarm. A freight train was out there if she could only get to it. She couldn't see the lights, so it had to be some ways away. But it was a chance, possibly her only chance, of escaping her pursuers.

She turned and ran toward the distant sounds. Her muscles burned from the effort she was expending, her breathing grew ragged. She was nearly ready to give up hope when she saw the glimmer of flashing red lights reflecting off of wet pavement, heard the rattle and clank of a train moving slowly on its tracks.

It was a freight train and a long one. Battered boxcars alternated with tank cars and the occasional flat car loaded with stacks of huge metal shipping crates, all emblazoned with identifying information, many decorated with graffiti. The air stank of oil, exhaust, and rusty metal. As Josette eased herself out of the weeds and onto the gravel next to the tracks she was convinced it was the sweet smell of freedom. She cast her gaze up and down the line of cars, looking for the shelter of an open boxcar. Instead, she caught a glimpse of her pursuers closing in. She ran, matching her speed to the nearest loaded flat car. Gathering all her strength, she jumped.

She misjudged the jump badly. Her body skittered across the smooth metal top of the shipping container, hydroplaning on a thin film of water. Claws scrabbled against metal with a sound like nails on a blackboard. Still, she slid ever closer to the edge. She was actually falling, the rear half of her body dangling in midair, when her front claws caught purchase on the metal rim of the container.

It took every last ounce of her strength to pull herself up to safety. She collapsed, panting and weary. It was cold, wet, and uncomfortable, but she was alive. Eventually exhaustion and the rocking motion of the cars lulled her into an uneasy sleep.

She dreamed of Rick. It was summertime, and the warm sunshine caught all the colors in his long blond hair. His beard was a little darker, with just a hint of red. His skin was bronzed from the time spent outdoors working in the fields or on their cabin during the day without his shirt on. It was hard work, and his body was rock solid, every muscle well defined.

The humans who were their nearest neighbors were several miles away. French settlers, they farmed the land using plow animals that the Sazi couldn't. Horses and cattle were wild-eyed with terror even if they approached at a distance. Naturally, they didn't socialize much, which was just as well. It would be hard to explain why she and Rick never went hungry, no matter how harsh the weather.

The nights were filled with hunting and making love in the moonlit meadows or in the still pool where the two of them would bathe and fish. The French Territory of America was an amazing place. The rich black earth would grow nearly anything. Deer and rabbits were plentiful, as were nearly every other kind of prey. Oh, the winters were cold and wet with snow, but she'd loved the changing of the seasons, the bright reds and golds of autumn ceding to the glittering diamond white of winter.

She remembered this particular morning with great joy. It had been one of the happiest of her life. At last their home was finished. The sun had barely cleared the horizon when she and Rick had carried the bedding and the belongings they'd brought west in from the leaky lean-to they'd been living in.

She was so proud of him. The house was small, but

perfect. He'd worked hard, never cutting corners. Every chink in the logs had been carefully filled, every stone of the large fireplace laid to fit together. The chimney drew perfectly. Not a bit of smoke entered the house when the fire was burning.

She'd been carrying in the last bundle of clothes when he'd come up behind her. Laughing, he scooped her into his arms, carrying her up the steps and through the doorway. He'd stopped her half-hearted protest with a kiss, his warm tongue parting her lips, exploring her mouth as his hands explored her body through her coarse woolen dress.

His skin was so warm beneath his homespun shirt. She slid her hands over the muscled flesh and coarse hairs, tracing the fingers of her right hand lightly over the raised scars until they found the hard flesh of his nipple. He groaned then, pulling away from her mouth to press a trail of kisses along the line of her jaw to her throat as his hands struggled with the fastenings of her dress. She, meanwhile, had used her left hand to unknot the tie at the waist of his trousers so that she could reach inside and stroke the long, hard, length of him, feel his throbbing need as his breathing grew ragged.

"Je t'aime, mon couer. Je t'aime," he whispered the words in French. It wasn't his language, but he was struggling to learn it—in part because many of the locals used it, but more as a gift to her. It was a small thing, but it and dozens of other small things were in part why she loved him so very much.

He slid the cloth away from her body, leaving her lying bare atop the homemade quilt, warm sunshine playing with the dark gold curls of her mound. He tossed her clothing aside without so much as a glance. His gaze was all for her, golden eyes gone dark and knowing as they explored every inch of her body. His callused hands were both rough and gentle as they cupped her breasts. He teased her nipples with his thumb and forefinger as he moved his head slowly downward. Warm wet kisses and the rough scrape of his beard over her tender flesh made her ache with the need to be touched. She whimpered, writhing, her hands clutching at the quilt, her back arching as his tongue traced lazy circles around the core of her, never quite touching what she wanted, needed, most.

Over and over he brought her to the edge, pulling back at the last, breathless instant until she screamed with frustrated need. Only then did he part her lips with his fingers, slowly sliding the long hard length of him inside her, so that each glorious inch dragged against her inflamed clitoris.

The pleasure built and built, their combined powers building with it until the room swam with warm, flowing energy. Rick's shields vanished, so that as he moved within her she could not only feel his flesh in hers, but her flesh squeezing his, welcoming each thrust. They climbed together, each feeling and feeding the other's need in a breathless spiral until a single massive orgasm exploded through the two of them leaving them breathless, exhausted, and shaken.

She woke when her head slammed against the metal crate. She almost lost her balance. Only instinct and the reflexes of her cat form kept her from sliding off the edge to fall beneath the wheels of the train. It was slowing, preparing to stop. At the slower speed the rocking seemed even more pronounced. Josette shook her head, trying to clear it of the cobwebs that seemed to have formed between her ears.

Her mind lingered over the dream, unwilling to let the moment go in favor of harsh reality. But like all dreams, it faded. With a sigh, she took a look around.

It wasn't particularly encouraging. The rain, at least, seemed to have stopped, although the sky overhead was uniformly overcast and gray, giving her no clue what time it might be. She didn't panic. Not knowing when, or where, she was had become an all-too-familiar sensation after years of dealing with her gifts. She stretched, arching her back to ease her sore muscles before jumping nimbly onto the gravel area between one set of tracks and the next.

She'd have given a good deal for a cup of steaming coffee right now. She was cold, tired, and her body ached. That was just . . . wrong. She had been resting for hours, granted, not under the best of conditions, but resting. Her body should have healed itself to the point where she felt fine. Instead, exhaustion dragged at her, making it hard to focus her mind and keep moving.

Picking her way across the railroad yard she avoided all of the workers with ease. They were bustling about, doing their jobs, calling to one another on handheld radios as they dealt with their usual routines. A few yards away she could see an Amtrak train, stopped in front of the station house, its passengers already loading. Signs near the red-roofed station house told her she was in Albuquerque. She began wending her way inexorably toward the station house, using what little energy she could muster to cast the illusion of a kitten. If she was lucky, someone would slip her food. If not, she would be forced to resort to digging in the garbage. Because if she didn't eat soon, she was going to collapse. She couldn't afford that. Lives were at stake. Somehow she had to meet up with Rick and get to Grodin. She just didn't know how.

With fierce determination, she stumbled forward, but walking was harder than it should be. Every time she raised up a paw, it felt like lead. By the time she reached the back door of the station, her head was swimming and her movements were wobbly. Even inhaling was difficult. She'd just stepped behind a tall bush to catch her breath for a moment when without warning, the ground suddenly raced toward her head and darkness enveloped her mind.

Chapter Thirteen

RICK PACED OUTSIDE the small white building that served as the terminal for the Grodin Municipal Airport. Back and forth, until Bruce made an exasperated noise in the back of his throat and went inside rather than watch and feel the unending, panicked guilt that rolled from him in waves.

She wasn't here. She hadn't been here. They'd checked every inch of the airport grounds, including sniffing around the various private hangars. Nothing.

When he'd returned to the motel and discovered the struggle that had occurred—her room broken into through the bathroom ducts, the scent of a dozen vipers that had touched every surface, and another dozen scenting the grass outside, he'd gone nearly insane.

How could he have doubted her? If this was what her life had become, no wonder she'd hardened. What sort of person would he have become if every dawn brought a new battle, and it was the same people over and over?

Something was obviously wrong. The drive from Pony to Grodin should have taken only a little over an hour. Her car had been gone when he arrived, so she must be driving. She should have arrived here long before he did, considering that the snakes had gone long before he arrived back. But neither the secretary, nor the airport manager had seen any sign of her. Nor had the man working on the engine of a plane in one of the private hangars.

It wasn't like there was anywhere she could hide here. The airport was a small affair: single 5,005-foot asphalt runway with a parallel taxiway, a few private hangars, and the terminal. They were lucky that the management had fuel available for private jets.

Still, he couldn't fault the place or the people. The little white terminal building was only the size of a one-bedroom house, but it was clean, well-kept, and had modern equipment. The scent of fresh coffee filled a lounge area packed with vending machines and comfortable furniture.

Rick checked his wristwatch again. It told him that precisely two minutes had passed since the last time he'd looked—ten minutes since he'd arrived.

Where the hell is she?

"She hasn't been here." Bruce reappeared in the doorway carrying a pair of Styrofoam cups filled with hot black coffee. He passed one over to Rick, who accepted it with a nod of thanks. For just a moment Rick wished Lucas had been able to come with Bruce as originally planned. Unfortunately, something had come up. Which left Rick in charge.

"I know." Rick resisted the urge to take out his

aggression on the nearest wall. It wouldn't do any good. Still, it was getting harder and harder to control his aggression. They were only a few days out from the full moon, and he was feeling the effects.

"So." Bruce dug in the pocket of his jacket and pulled out a plastic packet of trail mix he'd bought from the vending machine inside. "You're the boss. I'm just the wheel man. What do you want to do?" Setting his coffee cup carefully on a nearby porch railing he pulled the packet open.

Rick took a sip of hot coffee as he pondered his options. Lucas had been unable to come down. Raven wouldn't be here until tomorrow. He and Bruce could stay here and wait, but there wasn't much point to it. If Josette only hadn't destroyed her cell phone this morning. Rick stopped himself right there. Indulging in "if only" scenarios was an exercise in futility that would only frustrate him further. Whether Josette had car trouble or something more sinister had happened didn't really matter. She wasn't here and the clock was ticking.

Rick drummed his fingers on the side of his cup. "All right. This is what we'll do. You stay here, keep an eye out for her. I'm going to head back to the motel in Pony. If she gets here while I'm gone, call me on the cell to let me know and then take off. We want to get out of here before the weather system hits tomorrow."

"And if she doesn't?" Bruce tore open the bag and

tilted it upward, dropping the fruit and nut mix into his mouth.

"I'll call you with status reports every half hour to let you know what I've found."

Bruce nodded and swallowed the bite in his mouth. "Sounds good. I'll wait outside so I can keep an eye on the plane."

"Good idea." Rick moved past him and grabbed the handle of the terminal door.

Bruce didn't say another word, simply waved the hand holding the snack bag. Rick watched him stroll across the parking lot to where they'd left the plane before and mounted up. It was a straight one-hour drive down the highway. Simple enough that it would almost take effort to get lost. Yet another reason to worry about Josette. He drummed his fingers on the handlebars. The wind tugged at his leather jacket, still a little damp from scrubbing off blood and bile. It was still warm, too warm for the heavy jacket really, but it hid the gun and holster he had tucked into the small of his back without making it clumsy and slow to draw. After he saw the condition of her room, he decided it was time to arm himself. Glancing up he saw that clouds were moving in. Apparently the weather forecast was going astray again—unless it was Josette brewing it up. In either case, it was the kind of thing that would make flying damned tricky, particularly in a small craft. According to Amber, Josette was afraid of flying at the best of times. She'd be a wreck if they wound up going through heavy weather. He'd try to calm her as much as he could, but there was only so much he could do in the face of a full-blown phobia.

It was a slower drive than he would have liked. Major sections of the highway had been designated "safety zones" and were under construction. Traffic moved at a painful crawl. Still, the slow speed allowed him more than enough of an opportunity to scan the gas stations, rest stops, and road shoulders for stalled or wrecked vehicles.

Nothing. There was no sign of anyone having had any trouble, and he couldn't smell her on the breeze. Rick drummed his hands against the brake lever in an uneven rhythm. Shit, shit, *shit*. Where *was she?* He wished he could drive faster, but it was impossible. With every mile he grew more irritable.

By the time he reached the motel, it was all he could do to pretend the calm he wasn't feeling.

He pulled into the lot of the Shooting Star Motel and looked around. The air was still heavy with mist, not rain yet, although that would probably start soon. Dark clouds hung low and ominous in the sky. He took a deep breath, trying to gather what information he could through his nose. Very few smells remained. The driving rain of the storm, which had apparently already blown through, had washed away nearly everything.

He made a show of stretching slowly and taking a

good look around, then deliberately dropped his keys so that he could squat down close to the ground. He needed a better look to see if what he thought he was seeing in the mud at the edge of the parking lot was actually there.

Those were paw prints on this side of the gully alright, and they were just the right size and shape for a bobcat. And on the far side was clawed ground and loose soil where the bank had given way beneath her.

But more worrisome by far were the other tracks. The prints of male boots, sunk deep into the muck, half-filled with water, didn't cover or erase the obvious tracks of multiple large snakes. They'd been *chasing* her. She'd left on foot, not by car!

His stomach in knots, he forced himself to stroll casually across the parking lot to the office. The feel of the Glock in its holster at the small of his back was a comfort. He didn't want to have to use it, but it felt good having a clip full of silver bullets with him.

Pulling open the office door he was greeted by the ringing of a bell. The cloying sweet smell of roses overwhelmed his nose so that he could scent nothing else. Two dozen long-stemmed red roses in a large crystal vase took up most of the counter space. He had to peer over them to see Ellen. He could smell the older woman who'd checked him in just beyond the next wall, so he kept his voice light and pretended not to know her.

"Good afternoon. The flowers are lovely." He gave

her his best smile, but he could feel her nervousness. Combined with his own nerves, it made him feel as though his skin might start twitching at any moment. But he kept up the charm, even pushing a little emotion the girl's way so she could relax.

"They're not mine. They're for Ms. LaRue. We left a message for her, but she hasn't come to get them yet." She said the words very pointedly and motioned with her eyes. He nodded and moved his fingers as though writing. She got the hint and handed him a pad and pencil without making it obvious. A door in the next room closed, but he couldn't tell if someone had arrived or left.

Rick felt a sudden stab of irrational jealousy over the flowers, even though he knew it was probably the method the snakes had used to find her room number. It took effort to school his expression and voice to sound charming. "Looks like you get to enjoy them for awhile."

In plain block letters, he wrote: "Did Josette leave in her car?"

"Oh, and I will." The girl's eyes widened and she struggled to keep the fear from her voice. She did a fine job of making it sound light and friendly. She wrote on the pad in frantic cursive, "No. Men, Mexican accents, hot-wired and stole it. I'm worried."

He nodded as he read but kept up the act. "I'm in Room 104. I'll be checking out. Do I need to sign anything if I pay cash?"

Rick pulled the wallet from his pocket and withdrew a wad of bills. At that very moment the back door to the office opened and Ray Harris stalked in. He smelled of chemicals, greed, and rage.

The girl's panic hit Rick like a blow, so hard that he had to put his hand on the door to steady himself. Her eyes pleaded with him to say nothing. Not hard, he wasn't positive he could speak around the lump her terror had formed in *his* throat.

"Where's your mother?" The man loomed over the girl, his expression thunderous.

"I think she just went to go clean a room, Dad. She'll be right back." Her voice took on an irritating whining quality Rick had only ever heard from teenagers who weren't quite bold enough for open defiance.

The man glowered. Rick could see the muscles in his jaw clench, his hands ball into fists.

"What're you starin' at buddy? Does this look like it's any of your business?"

No. It didn't. But Rick didn't like the thought of leaving Ellen here. Josie had been right. This was only going to get worse. He hoped that Raven arrived soon, because the man was obviously eager for a fight. Once Rick was out the door, there would be nothing stopping him from taking his emotions out on the girl cowering behind the desk.

"Daddy, please! He's a guest. He's just checking out of 104."

The man's lips pressed into a thin line, but his hands

relaxed, and his scent and emotions both calmed marginally. "Fine. What room is your mom in? I need to talk to her."

"Probably 107. They called earlier asking for more towels."

Rick watched the man turn on his heel and leave the way he had come. When he heard the door slam behind the other man, he turned to the girl, hoping to finish the conversation they'd started. But she stopped him.

"You'd better go quick."

He nodded, but then pulled the deck of cards from his pocket. He'd taken the time at the airport to make copies of them. He hadn't planned on giving them back, but Ellen didn't need any excuse to get hurt before Raven arrived. "Here. I took these from your room the other night. When you didn't show up here—" He let the rest drop off when he noticed the nearly dizzying relief from Ellen.

"Oh, thank God! I was afraid I'd lost them and you wouldn't get to see them. I'll put them somewhere so Dad can *find* them. He'll just think he was drunk and was playing with them." Her face hardened. "He's drunk most of the time any way. I can't wait until I get my wings. I can feel them, just under my skin. And then I'll be gone—I'll leave here and never come back. But I'll be fine for the moment. Please, go. Find Josette and keep her safe. She's been so nice to me. You might check the train stations. One came by right about the time they were taking her car. I didn't call the police, because I wasn't sure if you guys wanted that."

"Thank you. We *are* sending some people down. They're not the police, but they can help. The first one that will probably arrive is named Raven. He's bigger than me with long dark hair. He rides a motorcycle, too. Talk to him. You can trust him." There was no time to say any more. He left, but he felt like a heel doing it. Something was definitely up here, but he was pretty sure it didn't have anything to do with Josette's disappearance. She'd been right—the snakes were after her.

As he walked out of the office he heard muffled shouting. It seemed to be coming from room 107. *Big surprise,* Rick thought sourly. He tried to ignore the voices as he crossed the parking lot to his bike, but it was impossible. There were too many emotions beating at him from the people inside that room, all of them powerful and so mixed together that it was impossible to tell where one started and another left off.

"I *told* you not to leave her alone. Not for a minute. The full moon's in a couple of days, damn it! They've sent the stuff via Albuquerque, but if you let her run off somewhere we're liable not to find her until it's too late."

"She's right there in the front office, Ray. It's not like she's going anywhere! Even if you're right—and I don't think you are—it's going to be fine."

"Oh, so I'm just being stupid. Stupid ole Ray, can't tell his ass from a hole in the ground."

"I didn't *say* that!" The woman sounded frightened, but had the same streak of defiance as Ellen.

"No, but you're thinkin' it."

"I was not! God you are so . . ."

"So *what?*"

"Paranoid. You're so damned *paranoid*. You see problems coming at you from every shadow. It's those damned drugs. I hate what they do to you. I hate it!"

"You mean you hate me. That's what you're really saying."

She let out an inarticulate shout of rage and frustration before saying. "Will you just *stop!* I can't stand this anymore. Just . . . go . . . get away from me. Go hang out with Ron and the rest of them down at that goddamned meth lab and stay away from me and Ellen until you have control of yourself. None of us want to deal with you when you're like this."

A semi passed by on the road, the noise covering the sound of the argument. A moment later Ray burst from the room. Slamming the door, he stormed across the parking lot and climbed into a dirty four-wheel-drive truck. The engine roared to life. He threw the truck into gear and, tires squealing in protest, the vehicle zoomed out of the parking lot and was gone.

Rick stood still for a long moment, taking slow

breaths, letting the man's rage, which had flooded into him, flow slowly outward to ground itself in the muddy earth surrounding the parking lot. When he was back in control, feeling only his own emotions, he went to work following Josette's trail.

He crossed the road, prowling the edge of the open field until he found a partial paw print nearly obscured by boot prints and snake markings. Heart in his throat, he kept at it. There were few traces of Josette. It was easier by far to follow the trail of her pursuers, who hadn't even attempted to hide their passing.

Across the way, he could see a woman standing outside a small restaurant next to a wheeled bin with cleaning supplies. She was smoking a cigarette and watching him, her eyes avid with curiosity. Just what he needed. Not that he blamed her. Strangers to town generally didn't just start wandering through wet fields for no good reason. He began calling out the first name that came to mind, acting for all the world as if his beloved pet had run off. "Pierre," he shouted. "Here boy. Where are you? Pierre, come!"

He turned to look at the woman, calling out. "Have you seen my dog? He's a Doberman pinscher, about so tall . . ." He gestured with his hand, making sure he made the size suitably imposing. He didn't want to risk her offering to help with the search.

"No," she called back. "Sorry. Good luck finding him." She gave a friendly wave before dropping the cigarette butt onto the pavement and grinding it out with her toe. He watched long enough to see her walk into the restaurant's back door, waiting to resume his search until she was safely inside.

He continued calling the dog's name sporadically as he followed the trail in a nearly straight line across the field. It was miserable work. The ground was rocky and uneven. It was sandy in some places, in other spots the mud sucked at his boots like an eager mouth. Scattered around was the kind of litter and junk that always seems to accumulate in empty lots.

The rain had brought out biting insects, too. They buzzed annoyingly around his head. He didn't know, or care, what they were, just wished they'd go the hell away. Of course they didn't. They buzzed right along with him as he followed the trail to the top of a small rise. The soil here was more what he had expected, sandy enough that it was firm and already starting to dry. The tracks changed, too. Instead of the deep impression of her toes digging deep as she shoved off of the ground there were lighter treads. She'd stopped here. There weren't many of her paw prints that hadn't been spoiled by her followers, but there were enough to give him hope. She'd been far enough ahead of them to stop for a second to rest and take a look around. He straightened up, turning in a slow circle, searching for anything that might have caught her eye. There, in the distance he saw the unmistakable pole with crossed boards that indicated a railroad crossing. Ellen had said a train passed.

In Josie's place, he'd have made a run for a moving train if the car wasn't available. He bent down, examining the grass. Sure enough, the trail led that way.

Attagirl Josie. He hurried forward, following the trail. Sure enough, it ended at the gravel. And no matter how far up or down the line he went, he found no further bobcat tracks on either side of the rails.

Chapter Fourteen

JOSETTE WOKE TO the scent of rare steak and freshly brewing coffee. Eyes still closed, she took a deep whiff. Beneath the mouthwatering scents of breakfast she could smell a Sazi presence, and the trace of another one lingering on everything. The latter was a cat, perhaps a jaguar. The former was a wolf she knew very well indeed.

"Raphael Ramirez." She spoke the name out loud as she opened her eyes.

In some ways he looked just as she remembered him, a handsome, well-built Latino with softly curling hair and deep dimples when he smiled. But there were differences as well. Laugh lines were beginning to form at the corners of his eyes, and his scent was deeply content. Marriage obviously agreed with him, as did his new pack.

"Aspen Monier," he replied with a grin that lit up his handsome features and dissipated the heavy pall of worry that was thick in the air. "You're awake." He sounded relieved and utterly weary.

"I'm going by Josette LaRue now." She kept her tone light so he would know she was joking when she continued. "And don't sound so surprised. I'm tougher than I look."

"I don't doubt it for a minute." He put a laden plate and huge thermal coffee mug onto the wooden coffee table in front of the sofa she'd been resting on. It actually smelled good enough that she found the energy to sit upright.

"Not that I'm complaining, but how did you find me?" She began cutting the meat into delicate bite-size chunks as she spoke.

"You got lucky. When Wolven crashed the system they notified the alphas of every wolf pack that stranded agents might need aid. I posted some of my people at the airports, bus and train terminals—just in case." His expression sobered, and worry once again rose in the air. "You were unconscious and fading fast. At one point, your heart actually stopped. Fortunately, Betty Perdue joined our pack recently. She's one hell of a healer. She recognized what was happening to you, started doing CPR and contacted me."

Josette blinked with shock. Raphael was, very delicately, telling her that she'd died. It shouldn't have been possible. "What happened?"

Raphael ran a palm over his scalp, smoothing his hair. It was a nervous gesture she remembered from when he'd been with Amber, and from her visions of him. It made her smile. Some things might change, but others just didn't.

He spoke slowly, as though he was having to search for the right words to describe what he wanted. "When I kill by touch I create a magical bond with a person—

or use an existing bond, and pull the magic out of their bodies, letting it drain out onto the ground. It's not a common gift, and it's not easy. I have to be touching them *and* have some sort of bond with them to do it. Somebody was able to do the same thing to you at a distance." The look he gave her showed just how much that worried him. "I've never even heard of that. If you'd asked me, I'd have said it wasn't possible." He shook his head. "I was able to break the connection and you revived. But it was a damned near thing."

Lucky indeed. She'd survived, when even her own lack of visions had predicted otherwise. Moments like this made her seriously wonder if there really was a higher power. She hoped so, and hoped that he or she was on her side. Because she was going to need all the help she could get to connect back up with Rick and get to Charles and the other seers in time to save them—if it wasn't already too late.

"How long was I unconscious?"

"Honestly, I'm not sure. We brought you here a little over an hour ago. Betty stayed long enough to make sure you'd be all right, then left. She had to get to work. She's opening a new practice down here, and they're moving her furniture down from Denver." He admitted. "But if it helps, it's 10:00 A.M. on Saturday, and tonight is the first night of the full moon."

"Oh, thank God!" She started to leap to her feet and wound up right back on her fanny as her vision dimmed and a wave of dizziness hit her.

"Sit. Eat," he ordered. "You're not going anywhere until you do. You came damned close to dying. Your body will heal, but you need food and rest. You won't be any good to anyone if you don't."

"I don't have *time*," she snarled, but her heart wasn't in it. He was right, damn it. She felt weak as a newly birthed kitten, and ravenous as a half-starved lion—which made sense, since she *was* half lion. Closing her eyes, she forced herself to calm down. "I'm sorry. I really do appreciate everything you're doing, but I'm in the middle of a crisis. If I don't meet Rick Johnson and go find Bruce Levin at the Grodin airport, they're going to go to where I was—and walk right into a trap." She closed her eyes, trying to bring her talent to bear, force it to show her what she wanted to see. Nothing. It was as if she were completely head blind. "Can you get me a phone and the number for the airport while I finish this food?"

"Of course." Raphael pulled a cell phone from the back pocket of his jeans, punched in the number for directory assistance, and requested the information she wanted. When the recording offered the option of connecting the call, he took it, and passed the phone to her waiting hands. "I'd heard Johnson was dead."

Josette gave a little growl between bites. "So did I. Believe me, I've been giving him hell about it."

Raphael gave a snort of laughter. The scent of his amusement rose off him in a visible mist. "I'm sorry

I missed it." He gave her a wicked grin. "I've got a picture of the last man you 'gave hell' to."

Josette sighed. Lucas had been a very busy man indeed. If she'd known he'd take and distribute photos of Ahmad and his men plastered to the ceiling to every shifter she knew, she might have reconsidered doing it. Or not. Ahmad had, after all, been even more snide and condescending than usual. God, but he could be an *ass!*

Raphael was chortling as he walked out of the room. She heard him open a door down the hall. It sounded like he was rummaging through a dresser, but she couldn't be sure. Still, when he returned a moment later he was carrying a bundle of clothing topped with a pair of flip-flops. Bending over, he set them onto the coffee table next to her plate.

"I don't hear any talking." He observed.

"I'm on hold."

"Ah, in that case . . ." He plucked the phone from her hand and put it to his ear. "Eat." He glared at her. "Your food is getting cold."

"Yes sir." She cut a large chunk of rare meat away from the bone and put it in her mouth. She took a minute to savor the flavor. It was perfect, absolutely marvelous: rare enough to be bloody, but warm, with just the hint of mesquite smoke. He must have cooked it on the grill. It was a thoughtful thing to do. But Raphael had always been exceptionally kind to her. She knew she made him nervous, especially since he'd managed to single-handedly turn the entire Monier family against one another. But he was nice to her anyway. She appreciated that more than he probably realized.

She was busy chewing when Raphael got through to an actual person. She listened as he explained that he urgently needed to speak with a pilot that was probably waiting around the airport. "He flew in on a private commuter jet registered to Wingate Enterprises. Short burly man with thinning hair, goes by the name of Bruce Levin." There was a long pause as he listened to the woman on the other end of the line. A small muscle tic started at the corner of his left eye, and she could see the pulse pounding in his neck. "That's odd. He *left?* Did he happen to go with a large blond man named Rick Johnson?" He paused again. "Hm, well, if either of them come by, could you have them call this number right away? It's urgent." Raphael recited the number.

"What's wrong?" Josette asked between bites.

"I'm not sure. I was just talking to the secretary at the airport. She said that she overheard Rick saying he was headed back to Pony. Bruce said he'd stay at the airport in case the person they were supposed to meet came by. But Rick hasn't gotten back and Bruce seems to have disappeared. The airport isn't that big. If he was there, they'd know it. He's just gone."

She frowned and forgot to chew for a moment, but then did so quickly and swallowed. "Bruce wouldn't just take off like that." Or would he? There was just something about him—

"Not when he's under direct orders from Charles and Lucas."

Josette set her fork back onto the plate. Suddenly she just wasn't hungry. "I've got to get back to Pony."

"Josette—" Raphael began, but she interrupted him.

She waved it off with her hand and drank down the glass of milk that was on the tray of food. It was thick and nearly warm, and richer than she remembered tasting in a long time. But then she remembered that Raphael was mated to a cat, and a rich one to boot. Small surprise there would be quality whole milk with extra butterfat in the house. After the last swallow, she spoke. "I know. I can't explain it. It doesn't make logical sense. It's probably a trap. But I have no choice. I *have* to get Rick. He needs to come with me to Florida. I—" She struggled to find the right words, but they wouldn't come. It wasn't just that she wanted Rick safe, he was necessary to this. She was sure of it, even though the future was still just a muddy haze in her head. Since she couldn't explain the feeling she used logic instead.

"Finding Rick and getting to Florida may be the only chance we've got to save Charles and the others. I can't fly commercial. I don't have any identification. And Bruce was the only one with the specifics as to where they're staying. I know the general area. I don't have an address."

Raphael paled. "*Charles* and the others?" He raised his hand before she could say anything more. "Never mind. I don't need to know. I don't even *want* to know."

"I wouldn't tell you details even if you wanted me to. But we're in the middle of something important enough that I'll do whatever it takes." She knew she sounded grim. She couldn't help it. The situation just kept going from bad to worse. But she wouldn't give up.

"All right." Raphael was suddenly all business. The joking exterior simply vanished, leaving him looking very hard, and very, very, dangerous. "Tell me what you need." Raphael pulled a pen out of his pocket. Grabbing an envelope from a stack of mail on one of the end tables, he flipped it over and got ready to make a list.

She thought about it for a moment before ticking items off on her fingers. "I'll need a gun and silver ammunition, a sterile cell phone, a car, some cash. I want you to stay here. Rick has at least heard of you. He mentioned your name once, and I know he's met Raven. If he calls in, you can contact me. Just give me a code word so I know it's you. In the meantime, try to find a way to get hold of Amber and call me with the number. Maybe Lucas has been in touch with his wife, Tatya. I don't know. But I need to find out where the hell I'm supposed to be going. If she won't tell you have *her* call me. But everything is going to shit here, and I am *not* going into this blind."

She cut another bite from the meat. Hungry or not, she needed her strength. Pausing with the bite halfway to her mouth, another thought occurred to her. "Oh, and if you can get me one of those sports watches that have the date with the year I'd appreciate it."

Raphael glanced up from the list. He met her eyes without hesitation or flinching. His voice held the unmistakable note of command. "Take the car outside. It's the pack vehicle. If you wreck it, don't worry. I'll just put in to the council for another. Now go freshen up. Cat keeps the guest bath fully stocked. Use whatever you want. I've got work to do."

She gathered up the clothing he'd left on the coffee table and followed his directions down the hall to the guest bathroom.

It was a beautiful room, not large, but airy, with cream-colored tile and cream-on-cream-striped wallpaper. A skylight with frosted safety glass let in light that was both bright and softly diffused. The plants scattered around the room seemed to love it. They flourished, giving the room color and warmth. The towels and floor mat were a warm shade of gold. They perfectly matched the color in the floral pattern curtains and were luxurious enough to sink into. Opening the linen closet, she found that Raphael hadn't exaggerated. There was a wide variety of soaps, toothbrushes, bath oils, and lotions; really everything she could possibly want, including her favorite mouthwash and toothpaste.

She started with her teeth. She brushed thoroughly before using mouthwash. Next came a shower, setting the water as hot as she could stand it with the shower massage set to high. It was handheld, giving her the ability to put the spray directly on the spots that were aching the most. It felt utterly wonderful—right up until the vision hit.

She was inside an aircraft hangar. It was mostly a large open space, made smaller by the plane that had been backed in through the open door. Metal trusses painted primer brown supported an insulation board, which was intended to keep the heat from being unbearable. Thus far it wasn't too bad, but judging from the angle of the light pouring through the windows it was still early morning. On a sunny afternoon it would probably be miserable.

The concrete floor was mostly bare, although a large tarp had been spread on the floor beneath the engine area of an old twin-prop plane. The "hood" was propped open, and Bruce stood chatting amiably with a slender Latino man wearing stained gold overalls. His skin bore the mark of old acne scars, but his smile was warm, his eyes large and dark. The two men were in the middle of an animated conversation, discussing the pros and cons of various aircraft models, complaining about the cost of flight insurance.

The far right wall of the building was used for

*storage. Ready-to-assemble shelving held boxes of
spare parts, paint cans, and various miscellany. A
large wheeled toolbox stood behind a "mule" utility vehicle that could be used for towing a small
plane if need be.*

*Josette focused her gaze on the bottom shelf.
She wasn't sure, but she thought she'd seen movement. Yes, there. She exerted an effort, managing to
freeze the image in place, adjust the focus as though
she were using the zoom on a VCR.*

*It was a snake. Not a large one, though it
wouldn't matter. It was a horned viper. Since they
weren't even remotely native to New Mexico and
were generally even smaller than the specimen in
hiding, she had no doubt he was a Sazi. Was this
scene before or after she was attacked at the motel? She couldn't judge by anything she could see.*

*She pulled back inside the vision, watching the
scene again from a distance.*

*A shadow crossed the floor near the doorway.
Both fell silent, turning to see . . . Josette, standing
there, weary and filthy! But she hadn't been there
yet. Was this a future yet to be, or an alternative
present where she hadn't boarded the train? The
alternative threads of time were the most frustrating. It might happen, or not. The future was often
like that, too, but the present far worse.*

"Bruce? They told me I could find you here."

Bruce turned. "Josette, thank God!" The relief

in his voice was palpable. The part of her mind that was still in the present cringed, because she knew, or thought she knew, what would happen next. This wasn't her. It was an impersonator. Would the woman be able to fool Rick, too?

He started to take a step, hurrying toward her. "You look terrible, are you all right?"

It was a consummate job of acting. She knew now the woman was acting. She was swaying, almost gray with exhaustion. Bruce hurried forward, grabbing her in his arms so that she wouldn't fall.

But it was her arms that held him, *held him tight, so that even when the garage door began to close, and the snake darted out from hiding, he couldn't escape.*

"Josette . . . *Aspen!*" She heard her name, felt the crack of a palm against her cheek. The pain gave her something to center on, brought her, gasping, back into her own body. She was lying nude and soaking wet, on the floor of Raphael's guest bath. She had a headache and a lump the size of a goose egg on the back of her head. Raphael was kneeling in a puddle on the floor beside her, wide, wet stains spreading on the legs of his jeans. She blinked twice, slowly trying to acclimate to the time. So, Bruce had been loyal and faithful, as Charles had believed. And now he was dead, and she was indirectly to blame.

"It is a damned good thing my wife isn't here.

Otherwise, I'd have a lot of explaining to do." He tried to make a joke of it, but his eyes were dark. She could scent the worry thick in the air.

Josette clutched at his arms, her nails digging into his skin through the thin fabric of his shirt in her excitement. "I'm an idiot! You're wife's a *telepath*. She can contact Amber and—" She let the sentence trail off as she watched him shaking his head sadly.

"I'm sorry, Aspen, but ever since Cat got pregnant . . . it's not working. Betty thinks it's just the baby hormones wreaking havoc, but we can't be sure, and the only person who would've known is dead."

"Shit!" Josette swore with feeling. She turned onto her side, grabbing the edge of the vanity to haul herself upward.

"That's exactly what Lucas said when he asked. Believe me, Cat's miserable over it."

"Tell her not to be. It's not her fault. We'll manage. We always have before." Once she was steadily on her feet Josette grabbed the nearest towel and began patting at her hair. The towel came away stained with blood. She winced. Her head really did hurt. "How did you know I was in trouble?"

"I heard you fall." He sighed. "I was still a little worried, so I was listening."

"Ah."

He stood and stepped close, placing his hand gently on the lump on her head. Josette felt the warmth of healing magic pouring over her. The pain receded immediately, fading slowly. It didn't disappear entirely, but she felt much clearer headed. He might not be a full healer, but it was a damned sight better than driving around with a concussion.

"Thank you." She went up on tiptoe to kiss him on the cheek. "For everything."

He turned, giving her a gentle kiss on the forehead. "I just wish I could do more. I owe you more than I can say for setting me and Cat up down here."

"It was nothing," she protested.

"The hell you say." Raphael tapped her on the nose with his index finger. "Using the information from your gift to put me in touch with a pack that needed an alpha and would accept his jaguar mate is hardly 'nothing.' Now if you're okay, I'll head into the other room and get back to work."

"I'm fine." She wasn't, but it didn't matter. They had too much to do for him to be in here fussing over her. He scented the lie, she could see it in the look he cast over his shoulder as he went out the door. Still, he went, leaving her to turn off the still-running shower and finish getting ready.

When she emerged from the bathroom five minutes later she was clean, dry, and dressed. She realized with a small laugh that she looked like a teenager in the clothing he'd provided: black cotton running shorts with a black sports bra under a black T-shirt that read "Don't get even. Get ODD." Even the flip-flops he provided matched. They were made of simple black rubber and made that odd flapping sound when she walked that no other type of shoe would.

She turned right, moving toward the sound of voices in the living room. Raphael was talking with Carly, the alpha female wolf for the Albuquerque pack. She'd never met her, just heard about her from Amber. Still, she seemed very nice.

"I brought what you wanted, Raphael, but are you sure this laminator will be heavy-duty enough for what you're planning?"

"It'll be fine. Plug it in over there by the end table so it can start heating up."

"What are you going to be laminating?" Josette asked. She stepped out of the hallway into a scene of intense activity. Carly was petite and delicate with the face of a model. Wide dark eyes were framed by the longest lashes Josette had ever seen. Her light brown hair had been expensively styled and frosted. Wearing a lavender business suit, she looked every inch the executive woman even as she crawled around on the floor to plug the laminating machine into the wall socket. A large plastic sack with the logo of an office supplies store and another from a twenty-four-hour chain grocery and drugstore lay on the floor next to her

Both of them looked up and smiled when they heard Josette walk in.

Raphael answered her with calm professionalism. "If you can't find Bruce and his plane, and wind up taking a commercial flight, you'll need identification. I don't have time to work from scratch, so I'm going to adapt the identity documents that my wife used recently. What do you think of the name Cerise Boudreaux?"

She shrugged. She'd heard worse. He sighed and shook his head as he turned on a bright magnifying light. "I don't like doing it, but we're in a time crunch and we don't have a lot of options." Working with a single-edged razor blade, he began to cut a photograph to fit on what Josette assumed was going to be her driver's license.

"If you do wind up having to use this ID—" He didn't look up when he spoke, his eyes were focused intently on his work. "Be sure to use a little push of illusion or persuasion. I'm doing the best that I can, but—" He let the sentence drag off.

"It'll be fine." Josette assured him. She looked around the room, trying to decide where she'd be of most benefit. "So, what should I be doing?"

"There's a prepaid phone in that bag over there." Raphael gave a slight nod in the direction of the plastic sacks. "There should be directions on the box on how you can go online to activate it. Computer's in the office upstairs. Try not to be intimidated by it. Catherine's a bit of a techno-junkie."

"Right." She crossed the room and picked up the

bag. The phone was there, along with a card for airtime, a package of underpants, a women's wallet, and a sports watch. She pulled the timepiece from its packaging and strapped it onto her wrist. It was 10:27. It had only been twenty-seven minutes since she'd woken up on Raphael's couch. Amazing.

"It's the first door on the right at the top of the stairs, across from the bathroom. You're welcome to use the phone to do it, but I don't recommend it." He still didn't look up. He was holding a pair of tweezers with the cut photo in his hands and was getting ready to affix it to the old license. It would need to line up perfectly, or the fake would be obvious and the attempt ruined.

"It's always faster to activate those prepaid phones online around here. They must be short staffed at the local number. It takes forever." Carly agreed.

"All right." She followed his directions and found herself in a very nice office. Decorated in pale blues and gold, the furniture and built-in bookcases were made from solid oak polished to a golden gleam. Three top-of-the-line computers graced the desktop, attached together by an impressive set of what she presumed were servers and routers and other things she'd only heard about on the Internet, while a row of office machines was lined up on the credenza behind.

Taking a seat in the leather desk chair, she turned on the machine in the center. It started up with amazing speed and before a half minute was out, according to her new watch, the desktop was loaded and the Internet launched. She began the series of steps that would activate the telephone for her use. In the other room she heard the phone ring. While she punched the keys on the phone according to the directions on the computer screen she half-listened to Raphael's side of a conversation with Tatyana Santiago, Lucas's wife.

"Tatya, have you heard from Lucas? Can you get in touch with him? I need Lucas to call me *immediately*. It's a Wolven matter. Top security clearance."

There was a pause. Josette couldn't hear Tatya's response, but she could deduce the gist of it from Raphael's half of the conversation. She'd only met Lucas's wife once, during a stopover visit to see Charles and Amber at her home. The woman was lovely and sophisticated, but a little too aggressive for Josette's taste. She had no doubt the alpha wolf could be formidable in a crisis—regardless of which side she was on.

"Do what you can, as fast as you can. The matter is time sensitive." He paused. "And thank you."

He laughed at whatever she said, and answered, "I may just do that."

The phone in her hand beeped, indicating that it was ready. It would need to charge some more. The instructions suggested plugging it into a wall outlet for twenty-four hours. That wasn't practical. Hopefully a couple of hours plugged into the cigarette lighter of the car would be good enough for their purposes. They only needed it for a few calls after all.

"You about ready in there?" Raphael called.

"All done." Josette hit the series of buttons to turn off the computer. As she walked into the living room to join Raphael and his pack mate it occurred to her just how much she owed him. In a very short time they had managed an amazing amount. She hadn't believed his time estimate earlier. She'd been wrong. Raphael may not have been a Wolven field agent in years, but he hadn't lost his touch. Josette was intensely grateful to have him on her side. With his help she began to hope that she might just manage to rescue the others in time.

Chapter Fifteen

THE CELL PHONE rang for the fourth time before the voice messaging picked up. Rick pressed the End button with frustration. Where could Bruce have gone? It had only been a couple of hours since he left, and the other man had promised to wait. Rick knew he would've called in if Josie had arrived. Could something have happened to him?

Things were getting out of hand. He was getting more frantic about Josie by the second. He'd been driving up and down each side of the railroad tracks, searching for some sign that she'd gotten off. But there was nothing. It was all he could do not to scream. Finally, in desperation, he pulled out his wallet. On the back of a dollar bill, written in ballpoint ink, was a number Lucas had given him to use in case of a complete disaster. Of course to Rick's mind the entire damned mission thus far had been hovering about a half-step away from disaster.

"Screw it," Rick muttered to himself. "If the old man gets pissed that I called he can *take* a strip of hide. There's just too damned much going on here that I don't understand."

Taking a deep breath, he dialed in the number. A male voice answered on the first ring.

"Ramirez." Could this be Raphael? It didn't sound like Raven.

"Rick Johnson. I got your number from Lucas Santiago. Identify yourself fully."

"Better yet, how about you tell *me* the password?"

Password? Lucas didn't give him any password. Of course maybe that was the point. Maybe it was a trick question. Hadn't Lucas done this one other time to him? He struggled to remember and then steeled himself to say the words, hoping it wouldn't cause the other man to hang up. "There isn't one."

"Got it in one." The voice on the other end of the line sounded relieved, almost cheerful. "I was hoping you'd call. Before you get started, there are some things I need to brief you on."

Rick blinked a few times. It was almost as if Ramirez had expected to hear from him. That just seemed . . . wrong. Unless, of course, Josette—didn't someone tell him recently that Raphael had taken over as Alpha of . . . *Albuquerque!* Thank God!

His thoughts were interrupted by Ramirez's rapid-fire delivery of his briefing. "Here's where we stand. The person you came to pick up is alive and well and headed back your way. You can't go back to the airport in Grodin. It's been compromised. We were lucky that there was a *second* private plane going down your way already. The pilot is someone you'll recognize. You had a beer with him a few days ago. Do you know who I mean?"

He breathed a sigh of relief. He was fairly confident

he could trust Raven. But then, he'd thought that about Bruce. "Yes, I remember. Does your pilot know that we're moving from here? He'd planned to stay."

"We got the information from Amber. I'd have had him come here first, but the passenger was already on the road to you. I made a few calls and found out that there's a private airstrip on a farm outside Pony. It's not much, but it'll do. We faxed the owner government credentials and he agreed to let us use it, no questions asked. The guy's name is John Simmons. Do you have a pen? I'll give you directions."

Rick rummaged in his saddlebag and came up with one. He scribbled directions on his palm, as the other man dictated them, and then read them back for accuracy.

"Oh, and if you haven't already been there, stay away from the Shooting Star." Ramirez directed. "Our friend was attacked there last night and barely made it out. It could be being watched."

"Too late." Rick's tone was rueful. "But it seems clear at the moment."

"Yeah, well, be careful. I'm going to call and tell our girl not to stop for you. You'll need to get to the plane on your own. But be damned careful not to pick up a tail. We don't need any trouble."

"You mean any *more* trouble." Rick corrected him. As quickly as he could he explained what he'd stumbled onto, including the situation at the meth lab.

Before he was even finished, Ramirez was swearing a blue streak.

Eventually Raphael calmed down enough to stop swearing, but there was still no question he was unhappy when he said, "We're going to need those cards and the girl. I don't know who in the hell we can get to deal with the felony. But at least the fledgling's not involved."

"She's a minor, and her father's running it."

"*Shit!* Can this get any better?" Ramirez's voice was frustrated and disgusted. "I suppose we should be grateful. If it wasn't for her teenage rebellion we wouldn't have a fucking clue about any of this." He gave a gusty sigh. "Talk to her, get the name of any relatives she has that change, and call me back. I'll see if we can get some help dealing with her parents at least. I don't want to send our girl to pick you up unless I absolutely have to."

"I understand. Let me get some names from the kid. I'll call you back in fifteen minutes."

"Do that."

The line went dead in Rick's ear. He flipped the cell phone closed and slipped it and his wallet back into the side pockets of his jacket along with his keys.

Josette was alive. Rick felt a surge of joy mixed with pride. She'd jumped onto a freight train— exactly what he'd expected. He just hadn't expected her to ride it all the way to the city. Still, she was on her way to meet Raven and together they'd go rescue Charles and the others.

God willing, the two of them would make it out of this situation in one piece. If they did, Rick promised himself he'd tell her how he felt, how he'd *always* felt, and he'd apologize for having been an idiot. And, he'd make certain he never left her side again. If he was lucky she'd take him back, give him another chance. But first, they had to get through the next few days. He wouldn't let her die, wouldn't let her visions of a future without her come true.

He sank down on the motorcycle seat and dialed the number of the motel. As expected, the line connected him to the office and Ellen picked up the line.

"Hello?" She spoke softly. Her voice was breathy with suppressed excitement.

"I found her. She's okay. But I need the name and telephone numbers of people in your family affected by the moon."

"Omagawd! I don't know if I can find out that without them figuring out something's up. I'd have to ask Mom or dig through her stuff." She started to object.

"Look, you said you wanted my help. If you do, then you have to cooperate. Give me names and numbers."

She lowered her voice to a whisper. "There's an address book in her purse. I know Grandma's number is in there. She's the only one I know who turns, but

I'm certain she'll know the others. I can make a photocopy and bring it to you. Will that do?"

"Fine. Do that." Rick ended the call without saying good-bye.

Trying to get Ellen out of here was going to be a disaster. But those cards made it impossible to ignore her and her father. And if she had more information about The Movement, it was well worth the risk.

He closed his eyes for a moment, gathering his strength for the next push. His emotional highs and lows of the last few days, coupled with the constant wear of being around others, had wearied him. He was tired, wet, and muddy from his trek along the tracks.

He forced himself to fire up the engine once more. He had to get moving; needed to be awake and alert. Mostly, he needed to get gas for the bike. Still, after a couple swigs of an energy drink, which he had purchased from the machine after he left the motel office, he felt a little better and definitely more alert than he had been. He wondered if Bobby Mbutu had ever managed to finish his research on creating a drug to keep Wolven agents going in bad situations. He'd definitely have to check into that . . . if he survived this.

Rick stared into space for a long moment, lost in thought. If Ramirez could be trusted, Josette was safe and long gone from here. And, the information tallied with what he himself had seen while tracking her. It would make sense for Lucas to have given him Raphael Ramirez as an emergency contact. Lucas had said that the two men had worked together as Alpha and Second for decades. Lucas would have to trust him implicitly, because he wouldn't put up with anything less. Too, Raphael was former Wolven. Aside from the idiocy in getting involved with Fiona, he had a good reputation. Even knowing all that, Rick worried.

The drive back to the Shooting Star didn't take long. He parked the bike, originally intending to go into the office, but he heard women's voices raised in a loud argument.

As he rounded the corner, he caught sight of Ellen and her mother. They looked equal parts angry and terrified. Ellen shrieked, the sound of fear and the need to fight that only birds of prey could make. No owl, this one. She was going to wind up a hawk or a falcon. Rick winced, the sound hurt his sensitive ears.

A blur of movement from where the girl's eyes were pointed, and a rustle of grass caused him to whirl around—his hand automatically going for the weapon at his back.

"You don't want to be doin' that, mate." It was Harold. He held a .357 Glock that was nearly identical to the one in Rick's holster. But this one had a very professional looking silencer attached to the end. Rick's eyes moved from the barrel of the weapon to the man holding it. He was full human, but big and burly. And he wasn't slow. He'd proven that coming out of the weeds. His natural scent was lost beneath the reek of the skunk oil he'd used to camouflage his scent. The choice of cologne wasn't lost on Rick. The man had been expecting Sazi, which meant the ammo in the Glock was probably covered in high-grade silver.

"What do you want?"

"Well, now isn't that just the question." The Aussie smiled, showing crooked teeth. He looked perfectly comfortable with the gun. Then again, he was holding the "good" end.

"See poor ole Ray, he told me he'd found himself a big old bounty, said she was staying right here at the hotel. Fool that I am, I figured he was bonkers—'least until he showed me the photocopy of her driver's license." The smile broadened, becoming more of a leer. "Pity Ray was too damned dumb to know when to keep his mouth shut or who to trust."

Rick was getting the distinct impression that "poor ole Ray" was no longer among the living. After a few glances around and forcing his nose to work past the skunk scent, he finally spotted the lifeless body in the tall brush at the edge of the parking lot. Just a few pale fingers poked out of the weeds.

Unfortunately, it looked like Rick was about to join him. He strained every sense without appearing to, looking . . . scenting . . . feeling, for anything that could be of use.

Ellen's mother glared and shifted, trying to put herself between her daughter and the gun. Poor Ellen was too frightened to move.

Harold didn't even turn his eyes in their direction. They were far enough away that he didn't consider them a threat. *Damn it.* No, he kept the gun nice and steady, pointed at Rick's chest. "Now don't you go doing something stupid like shouting for help. You'd just get these nice ladies killed along with you."

Ah. "So you *do* plan on killing me."

He snorted, like it should have been obvious. "Bloody right. But I'm hoping to *coax* a bit of information out of you first."

"What makes you think I'll give it to you?" Rick kept his voice pleasant. He was stalling for time, searching for anything that could distract the man so he could relieve him of the gun. Without the threat against the women, he could easily handle the man.

"Oh, you'll give it to me all right. By the time I'm done you'll tell me everything you know and then some. I've had loads of experience in getting information from you Sazis. You're not so tough once you're trussed up with silver chains, and you'd be surprised how effective some of the industrial acids are."

Rick gave an involuntary shudder. There was actual delight in the man's wide hazel eyes. It was obvious he was looking forward to this, which meant it was liable to be very bad indeed. He needed to rethink his options. Yes, there was no doubt he was faster than the man. He might get winged, but he doubted he'd be killed. Ellen and her mother were the only wildcards. If he turned and attacked, they might get in the way. Or worse, might interfere.

A moment later it didn't matter. Ellen shrieked, "Daddy!" her voice hitting a pitch high enough to hurt Rick's eardrums. Apparently, she had finally spotted Ray's lifeless body. She jerked away from her mother, turned, and began to sprint across the grass.

Time seemed to slow. Rick let his fur take him, felt the clothing rip from his body as Harold turned and fired three shots in rapid succession. Ellen dropped in a silent heap after the first shot and then bounced lifelessly after the second two. The beginnings of her mother's scream were cut off by three more.

Rage blew through him, creating a primal snarl more vicious than he'd ever heard himself utter. Blood filled his vision and the world hazed over in pink. Ellen had wanted nothing more than to be happy. But she was forced to live in fear for her life, just as Josie had for so long. It was too much for him and Harold couldn't even comprehend the ferocity with which he was attacked. The gun was nothing against claws and teeth. He wanted the Australian to *hurt* for everything he'd done—for everything The Movement was planning. The first bite snapped the man's wrist and the Glock fell to the ground uselessly as the screaming began.

He heard feet running and dimly heard a police siren through the carnage that he inflicted on the man. Claws tore through skin like paper and the taste of blood, the scent of fear, only increased his fury. Legs and arms were carved to ribbons before he finally went for the jugular, ignoring the kicks and one good arm that tried to pull him away. Rick hissed with bloody fangs over Harold's limp, dead body when people arrived and started yelling and throwing rocks.

Then he ran off between the buildings, across the parking lot, and through the empty fields.

Chapter Sixteen

JOSETTE STARED SILENTLY out the windshield. There was an austere beauty to the scenery she passed, but she didn't really notice. Her attention was all for the weather. Clouds were building up on the western horizon in a menacing black mass. The wind had started gusting. It pushed against the car hard enough that she had to hold tight to the wheel to keep the vehicle from being pushed off course. She wouldn't want to fly an airplane in the weather as it was now, and it was only supposed to get worse. She hated flying in the best of weather, and this afternoon she'd be airborne in the middle of a storm. She'd risk that and more—for Charles, for Antoine, and the others. But, oh, how she was dreading it.

It was just one more worry in a tall pile. Raphael had called on the cell phone just a few minutes ago with an update. As usual, there was both good and bad news.

Rick had checked in. He'd gone looking for her at the Shooting Star. Things had gone to hell in a hand basket. She needed to pick him up at a bar in Pony. He was alive, but there were bodies on the ground. One of them was a teenaged girl.

Ellen was dead.

Tears filled Josette's eyes when she heard, and she'd had to pull over for a moment after hanging up with Raphael. She was suddenly thrown back to the day when Maman had killed her siblings—the sweet children who had done nothing more than be born into the wrong family. Hot, angry tears flowed down her face as she remembered the few moments she'd shared with Ellen. Ellen had wanted her wings so badly, and not just because she wanted to escape. She'd instinctively felt the inherent joy of her animal and while she'd considered her gift a minor burden, it was one she'd been willing to bear. She'd deserved so much better from life.

The cold joy Josette had felt when she learned that Rick had eviscerated the Australian said that maybe she wasn't completely dead inside. Wanting revenge said she still cared about people.

Without even thinking it all the way through, she picked up the phone again. Her hand was trembling and it was all she could do to dial. Whether the telephone number showed up on the caller ID, or their "twin connection" broadcast Josette's state of mind, Amber knew to pick up on the first ring and knew who was calling.

"Tell me," were the only words she said, but it was enough.

Through choking sobs, Josette told her sister about the pretty fledgling. Amber listened without complaint or comment as she went on and on, babbling for long minutes that were interrupted only when she had to blow her nose on an oily rag she'd dug from under the seat, or to catch her breath. Maybe she just wanted *someone* to know about Ellen, in case she didn't make it. Perhaps she just needed to, at last, talk about all the deaths of the innocents she'd had to watch over and over in her mind, century after century. There were so few she could save. It hurt so very badly, and no one seemed to understand. Instead they blamed *her.*

She realized after a moment that her sister was crying as well. "I'm so sorry for your loss, dear Josette. I hadn't even thought to imagine what it must have been like for you to see such things all these years." A long pause and then a shaking breath. "I wish I could find something to say to make it better. And I'm so sorry."—Amber took another breath that ended with a sob—"so *very* sorry, that I have to add to your pain. But . . . Charles and Antoine are still in serious condition. Nana is worsening badly with every hour that draws closer to the moon, and the same is true of the Duchess.

The news stemmed her tears and furrowed her brow. "But *why?* They shouldn't be getting worse. They should be getting better!"

Worry replaced the sadness in Amber's voice, but it was still thick with her recent tears, even over the static. "I know, which is why I'm so worried. I hate to impose this on you, hate that the lives of so many people keep falling on your shoulders. But please, *ma souer, please* find a way to save my beloved Charles."

A knot formed in Josette's stomach. Time was running out, and even her best efforts so far hadn't been enough. What was she going to do? "Is the plane still on the way?"

"It is. And what are you going to do about that, anyway? Does Rick even *know* about you and Raven?"

Another problem that she'd been neatly avoiding. She sighed heavily. "Even *Raven* doesn't know about me and Raven. He barely even knows I exist and I've tried to keep it that way. I don't love Raven. I never have. But I also can't help *but* love him."

It was her sister's turn to sigh. "It would be wonderful if we were like true wolves and mated for life every time. But those blasted human genes give us a semblance of free choice, which screws everything up. No, I think you're going to have to tell him when he arrives with the plane. If it is a one-sided mating, you may be safe enough. He could draw from you, but not you from him. But if it's a mutual mating you'll pull power from him instinctively and he'll become involved in the ritual whether he likes it or not. In your altered state, you won't be able to control it. You haven't slept with him have you—unless something's happened that you haven't told me about?"

"No. We've never even touched."

"Good. Every touch, intimate or not, makes *any*

mating bond tighter. It is why we put mates with the gravely injured. The bond helps them, even in a one-sided mating."

"I know. I know. I just wish I knew what to do."

"I'm so sorry, Josette. It's going to be hard for you until this is done, but not as bad as it could be. It's so very difficult when you love another that isn't your true mate. I would know."

Josette gave a sad smile. Her sister *would* know, better than most. She was mated to Raphael Ramirez, even bore him twins. But when that relationship ended, she found another, even stronger, relationship with Charles Wingate. That love might not have the "magic" of a mating bond, but it was no less strong or real for the lack.

Josette shook her head. "It may not be a mutual mating. I can't be sure. And I don't know if Rick and I—"

Amber made a rude noise that translated just fine over the wires. "Oh, don't even try to deny it. I know you're still in love with Rick, and he with you." She paused and the tone of her voice made Josette realize just how difficult the next words were to say. "And . . . I . . . I have to apologize to you, *grande souer*. I *knew* Rick was alive. But I was sworn to secrecy. That's no excuse, I know, and I wouldn't have kept the secret if you'd still been married. But—"

She *knew?* All these years and she knew Rick was alive? Josette opened her mouth to spit out a curse, to blister the air with pent-up anger, but then stopped.

Was she guilty of any less? How many secrets had she withheld that later caused pain?

It was easier to just let it go. There was already so much hurt and pain in the air; there was no need to add to it needlessly. "I forgive you, Yvette. I know it must have been hard. Now, the phone is beeping at me, so I'm going to hang up. Tell everyone I'll be there soon."

"*Merci*, Josette. *Bon chance.*"

She pressed the End button and leaned back into the seat. There were so many details, so many things to consider. Raven and Rick had already met, but she had no idea how they were going to respond. And what *of* Rick? If only she could see clearly what was going to happen, know that he wasn't going to share Ellen's or Bruce's sad fate. She didn't know if she could stand that. It seemed odd to her that she accepted that her mate, Raven, might die. But the thought of Rick dying when she'd just found him again—

Whether because she was thinking of him, or for other reasons entirely, the scene outside the window dimmed and a vision played out in her mind—one that filled her with the first feeling of joy she'd felt since learning of Ellen's death.

Rick bellied up to the bar. He was wearing a plain white T-shirt tucked into a pair of faded jeans. No gun. No cell phone. No notes. He'd had to leave everything when he ran. It sucked, but he could re-

place them later. His wallet was in his saddlebags with the motorcycle back at the motel. He could go back for it, eventually. He was a registered guest after all, and no one could connect a wild animal attack with him. They'd either figure Rick's gun was another one of Harold's, or that he'd stolen it from the room. But right now the scene was crawling with cops.

It had been damned difficult sneaking back into the hotel without being noticed. But he couldn't leave the cards behind, and he'd needed clothes and shoes. So he'd broken in, used an aversion spell, and taken what he needed as quickly as he could.

It was a fucking nightmare. Without the police and emergency services, he'd have set up a gas explosion to get rid of the evidence. As it was, everything was going to be gone over by the human cops. He was tired, angry, and the jeans he was wearing were too damned tight. They made the deck of cards tucked into his back pocket dig painfully into his backside.

Thinking of the hotel made him wince inwardly. Ellen was dead. Her mom was dead. Hell, even poor ole Ray was dead. That, at least, hadn't been his fault.

The jukebox blared to life, Toby Keith bellowing the words "How do you like me now?" The bartender finished wiping a glass dry, setting it in place next to the others as he walked over to greet the customer.

"What can I get you?"

"I'll have a Sam Adams if you have it, Bud Light, if you don't."

He dug into the front pocket of the jeans to pull out the cash he'd stolen along with the cards. Peeling a five off of the stack, he set it on the bar before stuffing the rest back and taking his seat on the nearest of the battered vinyl bar stools.

He spun the stool so that he could watch the couple of good ol' boys shooting eight ball at one of the two bar boxes at the back of the bar. They were arguing good-naturedly, making bets as to who would win the game.

The bartender set the beer and a glass onto a coaster, setting the change on the bar next to it. Reaching behind him he turned the radio to the local station just in time to hear a news flash about a multiple homicide and animal attack at the Shooting Star.

"What the hell?" Everyone in the bar hurried to the windows, straining to see what they could of the action down the street. Rick went right along with them, acting just as surprised and worried as the other men—straining to see what was going on. In the distance ambulance sirens wailed. Rick felt a flicker of worry, but set it aside. No, they were all definitely dead. The ambulances would just be a formality.

"You wanna head down and see what's goin' on?" The blond asked his buddy.

"Yeah, maybe we should." He turned, resting his cue against the wall. "We'll be back in a couple of minutes to let you know what's up, Ben."

"Do that," the barman replied.

They loped off, leaving him to stick around, listen to the news. Sooner or later Rick knew his ride would show up. They'd go to Daytona where he'd get to explain how the entire mission had gone to hell.

Josette jerked her attention back to the present. Apparently, sometime during her vision she'd gotten the car back on the road and had blindly driven toward Pony. A sign indicated that the exit from highway 40 for Pony was one half mile ahead.

The Shooting Star would probably be crawling with officials for hours. The investigation could go on indefinitely. As motel guests she and Rick would eventually have to check in and be questioned, but they couldn't take the time now. They had urgent business elsewhere. They would alibi each other and be fine, unlike Ellen and her mother.

She sighed, the tears finally gone. If she had gone somewhere else, stayed at another hotel, would things have turned out differently? There was no way of knowing and no possibility of going back. She would have saved them if she could. But like so many things right now, she hadn't seen it coming. Was this what it was like for the rest of humanity? To feel so incredibly helpless, without any reprieve or hope?

She took the exit, and was caught in slow-moving traffic a uniformed police officer was hand-directing. Looking down the road she saw the dimly lit gravel parking lot of a restaurant and bar. The sign outside read "The Roadhouse," and there were neon lights advertising brands of beer in each of the small rectangular windows.

The view from those windows would be exactly what she was passing now, and would match what she'd seen in her vision. She'd found her destination.

RICK ORDERED ANOTHER beer and a hamburger plate. The pool players hadn't come back. Most of the other patrons had left as well. It was just him and the bartender. They'd listened to the reports for a few minutes, but when it was announced that there were no survivors, the barman had switched off the station. The echoing silence was deeply disturbing to Rick. He found himself wanting noise, a distraction from the morbid turn of his thoughts. He walked over to the jukebox, slid in a few dollar bills, and began making his selections. Johnny Cash's version of "Hurt" had just started playing when he heard the crunch of gravel in the parking lot. Seconds later the door opened.

The scent hit him first as he was turning to see who

was coming in. It was her. He froze in mid-motion, unable to move or think. She was okay! Even the ill-fitting shorts and T-shirt she wore couldn't disguise her.

She stood in the doorway, waiting for her eyes to adjust to the dim light. He knew he should greet her, say *something*, but his mouth was too dry to form words. He'd been waiting for this moment, practicing the phrases he would use to win her back. But looking at her he was simply tongue-tied with the fear of rejection.

Their eyes met across the room, and even through his best shields he felt her sympathy for his pain, and her own deep sorrow. But underlying both emotions was something he hadn't dared allow himself to hope for. Love.

She crossed the room in a few rapid steps and pulled him into a fierce embrace. The purse hanging from her left wrist dug into his back, but he didn't care. His arms closed around her and he buried his face in the soft silk of her hair, breathing in the scent that was uniquely Josette. A shudder passed through him as their combined emotions slammed into him, sweeping away his shielding in their intensity. In that moment the rest of the world ceased to exist. There was no failure, no peril, only the two of them together again.

She raised her lips to his. The kiss was sweet and gentle, a bare brush of skin, but it burned through his body like a sudden wildfire. He had to fight himself not to crush her to him.

"I missed you."

He ran his nose through her curls and then led her to a table to sit near the window. "I missed you, too. When I saw the tracks, and couldn't find you—"

It should have been a little embarrassing, looking like a moonstruck teenager while he stared at her. But the embarrassment faded after a moment. Who the hell cared what the bartender, or anyone else, thought?

"I heard what happened. I know about Ellen."

He flinched as though she'd slapped him. He'd almost rather she had. The pain of his failure at the hotel stung him far worse than any blow.

She touched his cheek gently. "It wasn't your fault, Rick. There's nothing you could have done."

He shook his head. He leaned back so that he could look down into her eyes. "You're wrong."

Shaking her head, she sighed. "Sacrificing yourself wouldn't have saved them. The Movement wouldn't have left them alive, even if you'd stopped Harold tonight. They were witnesses."

His body stiffened. The warm moment of reunion was ruined. She'd meant well, but she didn't understand. Not really. How could she? His stupidity hadn't just cost them a witness that could shed light on a threat to their entire race. No, a young Sazi would never turn; would never have children or fly under the moon.

She stared at him with tears brimming in her eyes and a wounded look on her face, as though she could sense his thoughts. In that moment, he realized she *did* understand. He could feel it like a fluid wave that lapped against his pores. Her sorrow and pain, for the hundredth, or the thousandth time over the last century. This one tiny death was just *one* to her. She'd endured many such senseless deaths, while he'd hidden himself away from everything, including the burden she bore without complaint.

"Are *you* okay?"

"I'm fine," Josette said hollowly and he knew it was a lie. But then, seemingly on impulse, she changed her mind. Turning away from the window she shifted in her seat so that she could face him. "Actually, I'm not." She took a long moment to organize her thoughts. "I'm trying to hold it together, to keep everything under control, but I can't, Rick. Too much is happening. People keep *doing* things. The future is changing so fast and I can't see any of it. People I love are in danger. I need to help them. But how can I when I don't even know what the hell is going on?"

"Welcome to what the rest of us live with every day." Rick's voice combined dry amusement with honest sympathy. "You're not Wonder Woman, Bun. You're doing everything in your power. That's all you can do. It's all any of us can do."

Now her lip started to tremble. "But . . . what if it's not enough?"

Rick touched her hand, then pulled her arm a little closer. "We're not gods, Josette. We're people. We live. We die. We make mistakes. Sometimes those mistakes have dire consequences. That's life. The best we can do is try to honor her death by preventing more of them."

"You're not being very reassuring."

"Would you prefer it if I lied to you?"

Josette gave a wry smile. "Yes, I think maybe I would."

They laughed together, and while it didn't solve anything Rick had to admit he was feeling a little better afterward. It *wasn't* his fault Ellen had died. It was Harold's.

Josette stood up and walked off without another word, heading down the small back hall that led to the bathrooms. He didn't bother watching. Instead, when the bartender raised his hand to catch Rick's attention he went up to the bar to get his food.

The food smelled good enough to make his mouth water. He hadn't really been all that hungry when he'd ordered, just figured he needed fuel. But now that it was actually in front of him he realized just how long it had been since he'd had a decent meal.

Taking his seat again, he started in on the big burger, enjoying the amazing combination of tastes as his teeth crunched into rare meat, lettuce, onion, and the sharp tang of mustard.

When Josette returned, he gave her a stern glare. "You need to eat to keep your strength up." He pointed a finger meaningfully at the top entry of the menu still lying on the bartop. "Protein. *Lots* of protein."

Josette rolled her eyes but put a small Gucci bag onto the counter. When she opened the purse Rick saw a brand-new wallet and cell phone. "Yes, sir." He could smell that she was pleased he was taking an interest, so he just gave a small grunt that always used to make her laugh.

It did this time, too.

The bartender came up, wiping down the counter in front of her. "What can I get you?"

"I'll have the double cheeseburger plate and a tequila sunrise." She opened the wallet to display an impressive amount of cash. Rick's eyebrows rose in surprise.

Josette caught the look and laughed. "Catherine called while Raphael was getting everything ready for me. She agreed with him that they should give me everything I needed including enough cash for any contingency." She grinned and her eyes sparkled with mischief. "I'm fairly sure Raphael was planning to do all that anyway. But he seemed grateful that she agreed."

It was a pleasant interlude, and while they knew it couldn't last, they were determined to enjoy the moment. Rick was almost sorry when it was time to go.

They stepped out of the bar into a fierce wind that nearly blew the door from Rick's grasp. The scent of rain was on the air.

Putting up his shields like a knight donning armor, he began preparing himself for the trouble ahead. "Let's get out of here. We'll have to come back to the hotel later." His voice was suddenly harsh, cold, and he wasn't quite sure why.

He followed her across the lot to a newer model white Volvo. She hit the button for the lock. When the beep sounded, he opened the passenger door and climbed inside. "We've got business to take care of."

Josette stood behind the open driver's door and looked up at the sky, her brow creasing with worry and . . . something else. He couldn't put his finger on it, but it was something between guilt and fear. The wind tore at her hair like claws as she leaned her arms against the roof of the car. "Do you think he'll be able to fly in this? It's getting pretty bad. The only way I could make it rain was to make the storm worse."

"But I thought you could—" Rick cringed at a particularly loud crack of lightning overhead. "You know . . . fix it."

She snorted. "Make nice weather come and go? No, I can't *control* the weather. I just sort of *steer* it. And I have to be very, very careful. One wrong move could make things worse, cause wind shears, or a tornado in a different place. People could die just because I wanted a sunny day."

"Oh. Yeah, I can see your point. But it sure would be nice."

"No, it wouldn't be nice. I don't want to bring down

any more bad luck on this adventure that I already have. I can't see the future right now. I just can't risk it. We're just going to have to wing it."

He gave a small, sad smile. "And hope for the best. Can't forget about the hope."

Chapter Seventeen

THEY'D SWITCHED POSITIONS in the car so that Rick was driving. Josette kept getting flashes like there was going to be a vision, but then it would fade. Still to be safe, she turned over the wheel position and was staring out into the storm, trying to relax her mind and grab onto any vision that happened by. When it came, it sucked her inside completely.

Amber buried her head on the crook of her elbow where it rested on the white tile surface of the kitchen table. Warm late-afternoon sunshine streamed through the sheer white curtains on the windows, but her mood was bleak as midwinter.

Nana was dead. She'd done everything she could, poured every ounce of her strength into the old woman. It hadn't been enough. The old woman's body simply hadn't been strong enough. Her magic had shredded itself against the walls that had been erected around it, and when the power grew too great and her body tried to change . . . Amber's body shuddered. She was a physician and a healer. She had never thought she would see anything so terrible.

Josette felt another wave of sorrow, but then wondered if this was a real future, or even the present. This was Amber's house in New York, not a hotel in Florida. But rather than constantly analyzing the vision, she just let it run to try to get some hint of what the import of this vision might be. She seldom dropped inside her sister, and the thoughts seemed important.

Amber dreaded Lucas finding out. Nana had been his kinswoman, the last of their line other than Lucas's own children. But more than that she dreaded what would happen to Charles, Antoine, and the others if Josette didn't get here soon.

She turned her head at the sound of someone coming in the room. Tatiana Santiago appeared in the kitchen doorway. She was dressed in jeans and a cerulean blue polo shirt, her silver-blond hair pulled out of her way by a pair of silver combs. She looked utterly weary except for her eyes. Those vivid blue eyes burned with an intense rage.

"So help me God, if I find the people who are responsible for this—"

Amber didn't argue with the threat. She felt exactly the same way. "I heard the phone ring. Was it Lucas? Has there been any word?"

Tatya walked over to the refrigerator and grabbed a can of soda for each of them. She came and sat in the chair directly across from Amber. Shoving one drink across the tile surface, she opened the other.

Only after she had taken a long, slow drink did she answer.

"Tahira found the book you sent her after and is on her way back now."

Amber sighed. "That's good news at least."

"Yes." The tired blonde made a similar sound and rubbed the bridge of her nose with two fingers. "The raid at the Grodin airport wasn't as successful. We didn't have any casualties, but they were unable to capture any of the snakes for questioning."

Amber popped the top on her soda, but didn't answer. She stared down at her hands, not trusting herself to speak. Yes, the raid had been important. She knew that. And she knew how worried Tatya had been for Lucas's safety. But to her nothing, nothing mattered as much as the old bear lying ill in the other room. She'd do anything to save him, but there was nothing she could do but sit here and wait. Charles had always been the strong one—so very strong . . .

Tatiana reached across the table to grasp Amber's shaking hand. "He's holding on. We still have some time. Even the duchess seems to have stabilized for now."

The words were meant as a comfort, but Amber noticed the other woman wasn't meeting her eyes and she smelled faintly of a lie. Not an actual one, but a sin of omission.

"What aren't you telling me?" She pulled her

hand from Tatya's grasp, glaring across the table at her, daring her to lie.

Tatya's features took on an expression Amber had both seen and used before: the calm, professional face that a physician used to give a patient bad news. Amber fought not to scream in pure rage and frustration. "Just tell me."

"A storm front moved in over New Mexico suddenly, just as Aspen and the others were taking off. The plane went down. Nobody's heard from them. But they're hoping when the weather clears in a few hours—"

"A few hours." The words sounded hollow, defeated. "The full moon will have risen."

Tatya touched her hand. "You mustn't give up hope, Amber. There's still a chance—"

Josette found herself rather abruptly back in her body as Rick slammed on the brakes and she was thrown hard enough against her seatbelt for the shoulder harness to choke her.

It had stopped raining, but the pavement was still wet. The car skidded a few feet along the narrow two-lane road, but Rick managed to remain in control. "Sorry. I nearly missed the turnoff."

Discreetly as she could she wiped the tears from her face.

"What did you see?" His voice was gentle as he reached a hand over to touch her cheek.

She shook her head, not trusting herself to talk about it. It simply hurt too much. Nana was her friend: one of few people who had earned that title. The old woman had taught her, listened to her, encouraged her to try things like yoga and the kind of weather workings that hadn't been done by anyone in millennia. A woman of wisdom, power, and humor. Was her life going to be snuffed out like a candle? Was this even a real vision or a "might be?" Would the plane crash? Would she Raven and Rick all be just lonely deaths, sucked away from a future that looked increasingly unsure?

Josette sat bolt upright in her seat. Sucked. Siphoned. A thought occurred to her. The theory was sound, but there was no way of *knowing* if it would work. "Where's my cell phone?"

"You plugged it into the cigarette lighter." Rick pointed with a thumb, but kept his eyes on the pockmarked road. "I think it fell between the seats."

Josette began digging frantically in the small open space. Her body vibrated with contained energy.

"You've thought of something." Rick's curiosity filled the car as he turned the Volvo onto a gravel road with no name. He had to slow the car dramatically as it jerked and bounced on the rough surface.

Josette punched the speed dial with a trembling finger. Holding up one hand she signaled for silence as she held the cell phone to her ear. "Amber, it's Josette. Is Nana still alive?"

"*Oui*, yes. Just barely. We're still in New York, but

were just about to get everyone ready to go to the airport."

A wave of relief passed through her. There might still be time. "I think I may know how to keep them alive until we get there. I just hope I'm right."

Her sister's voice was harsh with excitement. "What have you got?"

Josette took a deep breath, trying to steady herself so that the words didn't come tumbling out too fast to make sense. "The problem is that Nana and the others are *too* powerful. As the moon starts approaching, they're going to start to change. But their power is going to hit the caster's shield, so their power will turn on itself and chew them apart. That's why they're growing weaker! The snakes were actually doing us a favor, but I didn't know it."

She heard Amber suck in a breath. "So what do we do about it?"

Josette heard the triumph in her own voice. "Tahira is a *power well*. Her very nature is to pull magical energy from other Sazi. If she pulls power *from* them, makes them weaker—"

"Snakes? Shields? What are you talking about?" *Mon Dieu!* That's right, Amber didn't know about anything that had happened! She'd spent all that time on the phone earlier telling her about things that didn't really matter to the present situation.

Rick's jaw dropped as she slowed down and explained the situation to her sister.

After multiple questions that were quite medically

technical, Amber responded, "It *sounds* good, *grande soeur,* but what if you're wrong? Weakening the seers when they're already under attack—it sounds like an awful risk . . ." She let the sentence trail off to silence.

"I know. I know." Josette was frantic. "But we have to try it. If we do nothing Nana is going to die. I *think* I just saw it. But things are changing so fast I'm not sure if it's real."

"I'll call. I don't know if Tahira and Tatya will go along with this, but I'll ask. Tahira will be willing. I have no doubt. She's a very giving person, and she's terribly worried about Antoine. And if Tatya won't agree to store the magic in her, then I'll take it instead."

"Thank you."

"Let's just hope it works, *chère* Josette."

She ended the call, letting the phone drop back onto the seat.

"That was a good thought. It never would have occurred to me." Rick was nodding his head and smelled of pride.

"I just hope I'm right." Josette picked at the seam of her shorts with a fingernail. "I remember how it *felt*. Based on what I went through in the vision—" She gave Rick a desperate look. "But what if I'm wrong? What if it's what I just *suggested* that winds up killing them?"

He deliberately projected as much calm as he

could when he met her gaze. "You're doing the best you can. You said yourself that the others gave their power to you to kill the caster. That says they wanted a say in their own fate. That's all we can do. Don't be so hard on yourself."

Her eyes narrowed slightly. Her voice held more than a trace of wry amusement when she answered. "Talk about your pot calling the kettle."

Rick snickered and winked at her. Their destination was only a couple hundred yards away and a little to the right of the road. It was accessible by a small gravel drive that led up to a large metal building one side of which proudly proclaimed "Sim Peanuts." From the blown over paint cans on the ground and the distance between the *m* and *P* she'd have to say the name wasn't complete yet. And if the storm got any worse, the building might not be here in the morning for them to finish the job.

THE BUILDING COULD have been used for storage of farm equipment, or anything really, but the orange wind sleeve attached to the roof, which was flapping in the breeze, and the concrete runway suggested that it probably served as the hangar for a private plane.

Across the fields he could see a farmhouse and barn, along with animal pens and various outbuildings.

Everything was neat, prosperous, and well tended.

Even the smells were just as they should be. The air coming through the car vents was rich with the scent of crops growing, humans, farm animals, and fresh-cut grass.

Despite the almost idyllic setting, Rick began twitching uneasily in his seat.

Josette cocked her head. She could probably scent his frustration. "What's the matter?"

"I had to leave my gun at the motel. I don't like being unarmed."

She nodded. "Raphael sent weapons. They're in a bag in the trunk."

"In the *trunk?*" He couldn't keep the disgust from his voice.

She rolled her eyes. "We couldn't exactly have had you arming yourself in the middle of the roadhouse parking lot, now could we?"

He growled. "You should have kept them inside the car in case of trouble."

"And if we got pulled over?"

Rick grunted with displeasure, but didn't argue. He felt exposed out here in the middle of nowhere. The landing strip was a narrow ribbon of concrete stretched between two large fields. The first blush of green peeked up through the tilled earth. It was impossible to tell what the mature plants would be, but she'd wager they were peanuts. She could see for miles in every direction.

Gravel crunched beneath the Volvo's wheels as

Rick pulled to a stop. Whether by chance or design, he'd put the hangar between the car and the farmhouse, giving them at least some semblance of privacy. He leaped out the door the minute the car was no longer in motion and circled to the rear of the vehicle, key in hand.

It was obvious which bag held their munitions. It was big, bulged oddly in several spots, and smelled of gun oil and silver. He pulled it from the trunk and set it gently on the ground. Squatting down beside it, he pulled open the zipper.

The average pack leader didn't have much need for armament, but no doubt Rick would find something useful, since Raphael Ramirez was not the average pack leader. The bag held a variety of handguns in holsters, with silver and regular ammunition available for each. Every weapon was clean, oiled, and appeared to be in perfect working condition. A low whistle and the light scent of citrus told her Rick definitely approved.

He chose a Ruger with an inner pants holster as his main weapon. He pulled it out, admiring the four-inch barrel before opening it up to check the chamber. Sure enough, it was fully loaded with silver-plated rounds. Rising to his feet he untucked his T-shirt and put on the holster. "It'll be uncomfortable with these jeans as tight as they are, but I'll feel better knowing we'll be going into whatever we're facing armed. Pick something for yourself, and then we'll let Raven choose when he gets here."

She shook her head no. "I've never handled a modern pistol. I'd probably wind up shooting myself in the foot."

Rick growled viciously under his breath. "You've spent your entire life being stalked by assassins and you couldn't be bothered to learn how to shoot? How in the hell have you managed to stay alive, being that stupid?" It was an invitation for an argument. He knew it the minute the words left his mouth and he tried to close his mouth before he said anything else. But apparently she could sense how keyed up he was feeling. She looked at him with curiosity rather than anger.

"Um . . . should you be feeling this aggressive, Rick? It doesn't really match the situation. You know I've never needed to shoot."

He stopped cold and stared at her like she'd grown a second head. "It . . . um . . . no, you're right." His eyes went blank for a moment as he slipped inside his own head. "This emotion isn't mine. In fact, most of it is coming from outside."

Armed with that knowledge, he lowered his shields and focused. He could probably block what was coming, but it might be better if he could track its source. Just identifying that it wasn't his emotion helped cleared his head. It allowed him to look at it in the abstract instead of letting it overwhelm him. But apparently, his tone of voice had been more accusatory than the'd intended, and Josette got the wrong impression. Her head dropped into a defensive position and a small snarl rose into her chest.

"So now it's all *my* fault?" Josette growled.

Rick put a finger to his lips, sending a small tendril of magic. "I'm tense, but someone else is projecting, too. It isn't you, but it's *affecting* you through me. Can't you feel the difference now that I've started to block it?"

Her expression grew thoughtful but then she shrugged. "We're both wound pretty tight. It's been a rough couple of days."

"Yeah," he agreed. "Maybe." And yet somehow that didn't feel quite right. What he was sensing felt more . . . well, *male* than anything he'd ever gotten from Josette.

"Maybe I'm picking up something from Raven up there in the plane," Rick suggested. "God knows *he* probably has enough to be nervous and angry about."

"*That* I can believe." She looked up at the sky and shuddered. She could control her expression, but she couldn't hide the hint of terror in her scent. Rick could clearly feel the fear pumping through her body with every adrenaline-laced beat of her heart. He wished there was something he could say to ease her mind, but flying was a full-blown phobia for her. Nothing he said or did would make any difference. "I'm *really* not looking forward to Raven arriving."

Rick reached over to give her shoulder a reassuring squeeze. "Don't worry. It'll be fine. I'm going to patrol the area. Something's bothering me."

"Fine. Patrol." There was a tense edge to her voice that he didn't like. For a second he considered just flat out asking her what was the matter. He decided against it because right now he didn't want to know. It would only be a distraction.

Rick started his patrol by walking around the hangar, paying particular attention to the dirt and grass at the gravel's verge. There was no sign of snakes having been here. If there was any scent trail, it was far too faint for him to catch under the overpowering scent of chemical fertilizer coming from the building and the remaining ozone in the air. The smell of the chemical bothered him, even though it only made sense. They were, after all, on a farm. The plane was probably used to spray the crops. But fertilizer was a major ingredient in ANFO, a high explosive that was used by terrorists worldwide because it was both effective and easy to make.

He paced restlessly to the front doors of the building. They were secured with a large, impressive-looking padlock that probably wouldn't prove much of a challenge to a professional thief, but should at least keep out the riff-raff. If he had a set of picks . . . but of course he didn't.

As he strode down the runway he looked carefully across the fields in the direction of the farmhouse. There was a clear line of sight between the buildings and the strip. Again he felt a shiver of . . . not nerves exactly . . . more like anticipation. Whatever the emotion was, it wasn't his. He shook his head to clear the unwelcome intrusion and headed back to the car.

The closer he got, the more his frustration grew until he was nearly livid with anger and hate as he reached the car.

"What is the matter with you?" Josette snarled. He didn't blame her.

"Wish I could tell you." Rick shrugged, then stretched, feeling the bones of his spine move back into place and then shivered. The thin white fabric of his T-shirt wasn't doing much to keep him warm. Normally he could control his body temperature better than this. But the full moon was near, and he was tired and stressed.

She gave an irritable little growl and might have said more, but the cell phone rang inside the car. The noise startled Josette. She jumped, making one of those silly, squeaking noises that used to embarrass her. It broke the tension a little and Rick was grateful for it.

She brushed past him and opened the car door. Grabbing the phone from between the seats she managed to answer just before it would have gone into voicemail. "Hello?"

There was a long pause as she listened to the person on the other end of the line. In the distance, faintly, Rick heard the sound of an aircraft engine. They both turned and looked upward to the northeast, following the direction of the sound.

"Raphael, he's arriving now. Yes, yes, I'll give him the message. Not that he's liable to listen . . . okay, fine, I'll tell him that, too."

Rick was only half-listening. He could see the darker speck of the plane against the leaden skies. It was being badly buffeted by the winds. He felt his stomach tie itself in knots from nerves. It was going to be a very rough landing.

The blue-and-white twin-engine plane looked tiny against the towering clouds. It grew larger as it came closer, and Rick could see that the pilot was fighting hard to hold it steady against the wind. It came down fast and hard, bouncing against the concrete runway. Rick cringed as the machine rocked, one wing nearly touching the ground as it slewed hard to the left.

"Come on, come on," he muttered under his breath. "Hang on. You can do it."

The plane skidded sideways across the wet pavement, with the smell of burning rubber coming from its brakes. It came to a shuddering stop after it fell off of the edge of the concrete and into the muddy grass partway down the runway.

Rick and Josette ran to the plane. The machine was listing to the left, its weight forcing the landing gear deep into the viscous mud. Off-balance, it shifted uneasily as the door to the cockpit swung open.

Raven stood in the opening. He was a big man, and had to hunch over to fit through the door. But his knuckles were white where he gripped the edge of the doorframe, as he vomited noisily into the grass. The black clothing he wore made the grayish pallor of his skin all the more noticeable. He was obviously shaken. He stepped carefully onto the metal step and down to the ground. There was no mistaking the wave of relief flowing off of him as his boots touched the earth.

"Are you all right?" Josette was at his side almost instantly, and Rick felt a strange twinge of jealousy in the way she treated him. Did she know Raven better than he'd thought?

"Fine." Ramirez's voice was hoarse, so he cleared his throat and tried again. He didn't react to Josette like anyone he knew, but didn't object to her touch, either. "I'm fine. Glad as hell to be on land again. If I never set foot on a plane again it wouldn't bother me."

"But how—" Josette started to protest, but Raven cut her off with a wave of his hand.

"Oh, I'll do it, but you can't make me happy about it." She stepped back from him, but it was obvious she was still concerned.

"Will we even be able to?" Rick gestured toward the plane that was listing more and more as it sank into the soft mud. He didn't know anything about airplane mechanics, but it didn't look good. Aside from having run off the runway and getting stuck in the mud, it looked like there was damage to the wheels and landing gear that would need work before they could take off.

Raven turned around and began swearing. He

motioned to Rick and grabbed onto the wing. "Here, give me a hand getting this back onto the runway."

It took all three of them to fight the wind and lift the plane high enough to scoot it back onto the concrete. Without their Sazi strength, there's no way they could have done it.

Raven bent down to inspect the damage. "Well, I can fix it, but I'll need some tools." He glanced over his shoulder at the locked shed. "We'll have to ask Mr. Simmons if we can borrow his."

"Simmons?" Josette had stopped several feet short of the rest of them, keeping her distance. "John Simmons?"

"That's the name Lucas gave me. Why?"

She laughed, and it made her eyes sparkle. "I've met him. In fact, he owes me a rather large favor."

Rick suddenly remembered the naked man who'd dallied with the wrong woman and laughed. "You sure you're going to recognize him again with his clothes on?"

Raven's eyebrows raised just as Josette's jaw dropped. She put her hands on her hips.

"Richard Aleric Cooper! Get your mind out of the gutter!" Josette's toe started tapping an impatient rhythm against the concrete as she mock-glared at Rick.

Cooper. It's a surname he hadn't heard in a century. It was his given name, and the one he'd given to Josette when they'd married. But how stressed was she that she'd forgotten they'd changed it even as early as when they moved to Illinois?

"If the two of you are done?" Raven was obviously tired and irritable, he glared at each of them in turn. "Aspen, since you already know Simmons, you should probably be the one to talk to him."

"Fine." She turned and started to leave.

"I'm coming with you," Rick announced.

She rolled her eyes. "Fine. But hurry up." Turning on her heel she started across the pavement in the direction of the farmhouse. The wind whipped her hair around her face.

Ah. The scent of his jealousy had finally caught up to her. Rick went after her at a half-trot. He had the sense not to touch her. Just matched his pace to hers. "I'm sorry. I'm having a hard time today. I'm not sure why. Please ignore me. You're too important to me to upset."

When she spoke, her voice was soft, barely audible. He knew Raven wouldn't catch the words, even with his keen hearing. "Then why didn't you come back? If I'm so important, why did you let me mourn for a century?"

He sighed. "Pride mostly, and fear. You can be damned hard-headed. That you didn't come after me told me a lot. I didn't figure you'd want me back, and I didn't exactly fancy dragging in with my tail between my legs."

"What changed your mind now?" She'd started

walking again, but more slowly, giving him the chance to come up beside her.

Rick wanted to say something clever, to protect himself from revealing too much of what he felt. But he could hear the vulnerability in her voice. Lying now, making light of the question, might cost him his chance. So he steeled himself to tell the truth. "Charles said you were in trouble, and it occurred to me that if you got yourself killed I'd *never* get the chance to work things out with you."

"So you came riding to my rescue?" She arched an eyebrow at him. He didn't miss the irony in the look.

"Would it help if I told you that Lucas figured you'd kill anybody else on sight? And neither of us was *positive* that you wouldn't do even worse to me." Rick made his tone light. He knew better than anyone how much this particular lady hated the "helpless little woman" stereotype. Yes, he'd come to rescue her. Not because he thought she was incapable but because he loved her. Damn it. There it was. He was still in love with Josette Monier Cooper and it was time to stop playing around. And everybody needs help now and again, whether they admit it or not.

She gave a full-throated laugh that tilted her head back showing a long expanse of pale throat, lighting up her entire face. "You certainly do know how to turn a girl's head."

"We aim to please, ma'am." He pretended to tilt an imaginary hat.

She laughed again, her annoyance forgotten. She picked her way delicately around yet another deep puddle in the gravel drive. "Why do I have such a hard time staying angry with you?"

"My irresistible charm?" he suggested. The two of them had started walking again. They'd almost reached the last bend in the driveway.

"Maybe." The smile she gave him made his heartbeat speed up, making him warm in spite of the wretched weather. The sight of her nipples pressed hard against the thin fabric of her top dragged a reaction from his body that was almost frightening in its intensity. He wanted her. Here, now . . . hell, *any* time, *any* place. But here and now would definitely be good. The reaction was ridiculously impractical, but that didn't change a thing.

She saw his reaction, or smelled the lust pouring off of him, and her smile grew mischievous. "We'll talk more later. We're almost there."

Rick stopped long enough to convince his unruly body to behave. They were rounding the last bend.

The house was a large two-story affair with a wide front porch. It gleamed from a fresh coat of white paint, the trim a bright, fire-engine red that matched the barn a few yards away. Four trucks were parked in a straight row along the white metal livestock fence, which formed a pen next to the barn. All of the vehicles were large, four-wheel-drive monsters meant for heavy work and rough terrain.

A man stood alone on the porch, lounging casually against one of the support columns at the top of the stairs. He wore jeans, which had been professionally pressed to have a perfect crease, under a heavy blue work shirt. His blond hair had been recently cut very short, a mark showed fresh skin against tan. Rick caught a glimpse of a red tattoo, half-hidden under the man's collar. He was a good-looking fellow, with a strong build and open features. But something about him felt . . . wrong. Rick lowered his shields, using his gift to take a read of the other man.

"Good afternoon! Did you get the flowers I sent?"

"They were lovely, thank you." She gave him a smile that could have melted the polar icecaps. Rick wasn't jealous. In fact, he barely noticed. *This* was the source of the aggression he'd felt earlier. Simmons was a consummate actor. His face practically glowed with bonhomie, but that wasn't what he was feeling. Instead, he was triumphant, eager, and angry.

Rick reached out to touch Josette's arm, to warn her, when he saw the play of light reflecting off glass from the hayloft of the barn. Instinct took over. He tackled her just as the shot rang out. Rolling off of her, he drew the gun from the small of his back.

Time seemed to slow. Rick saw everything with painful clarity: the rifleman; Simmons drawing his own weapon as he darted for cover; two more men were moving, the barrels of their guns propped on the bed wall of the largest of the trucks.

There was no way he could shoot them all. He knew it even as he pointed his weapon at Simmons and pulled the trigger.

"No!" Josette's scream was as much from rage as fear. He felt a flash of heat as she gathered her power, followed in an instant by the crawl of electricity across his skin.

Blinding light brought tears to his eyes as heat followed the screech of metal and an explosion of sound shook the ground beneath him. Dirt sprayed up into his face, deafening him to the screams of their attackers. A bomb. There *was* a bomb in that barn! Potholes littered the long strip of concrete and one wing of the plane was hanging by bits of wire. Simmons and his men had intended to murder them. The bomb had been placed near enough to the runway that if they'd taken off immediately as planned, they would be dead now. But *why?* Were they part of The Movement, or a *brand-new* threat?

Josette leaped to her feet and started running in a zigzag pattern across the field, passing Raven, who had changed to wolf form. He was an impressive wolf, nearly the same height at the shoulder as Rick's chest. He streaked by and leaped on one of the men, pulling him down with a scream that was followed closely by another rifle shot.

Dirt sprayed inches away from his feet. Simmons was injured, but not down. He raised his weapon, aiming for Rick, but he was too slow. Before he could fire, his body jerked and blood sprayed the snow-white paint as Rick sent two more shots into his chest. It was quicker than changing.

He was looking where he was firing, but he heard the blare of a car horn. Turning his head he saw the Volvo speeding up the lane, the front passenger door swinging open wide. He couldn't spare more than a cursory glance. The men in the truck bed were stirring, shaking off their shock. With Josette out of range the rifleman turned his attention to Rick. His first shot hit the exact spot where he'd had been standing an instant before. Rick was gone. Running at Sazi speed he joined Raven in a mad dash across the muddy field to catch the car.

The car had reached the gravel road and was fighting for traction. Josette was shouting for them to hurry. Raven reached the vehicle first. He jumped in the front door, entering as a wolf, but landing as a human before diving into the backseat. A moment later he was sitting on the windowsill he had guns in each hand, steadied on the roof of the car, firing continuously. Rick doubted he was hitting anything, but the gunfire would discourage his pursuers.

Putting on a burst of speed he dived, face first, into the car. The door slammed closed behind him. Josette shouted, "Got him."

Rick felt the car lurch beneath him as gravel transitioned to pavement. Josette took a hard left and floored the accelerator.

"Are you hurt?" Raven was back inside the vehicle, reloading his weapons from the bag on the floor as Rick climbed into the backseat. He dropped the spent clips onto the floor, his eyes on the road behind them.

"I'm fine."

"Trucks coming, fast," Josette announced and jerked the steering wheel hard to the left.

"Shit!" Rick struggled to get to his hands and knees in the confined space. Neither he nor Raven were small men. Having both of them in the backseat made things damned crowded. There seemed to be arms and legs everywhere, all of them in his way.

"I either need a different gun or more ammo for this one. I'm out." He honestly didn't remember firing that many shots, but he must have because the clip was empty.

"In the bag," was Raven's curt response. His attention was on the vehicles behind them. He climbed back through the window, firing backward.

Josette took a hard right that nearly threw Raven out of the car. He was only holding on by tucking his bare feet under the seat back and bracing his back against the window pillar. Fortunately, Rick had just enough room to maneuver himself up and over the seat to sit next to her. It would be better not to have them both hanging out. Dropping into a sitting position, he pulled a handgun and holster from the bag,

"Left turn ahead," she announced. It was good she'd warned them. She hit the brakes and steered sharply to the left, forcing Raven to brace himself, so he wouldn't slide across the slick leather seats.

Rick heard a crack, and the glass of the rear window exploded, sending small square chunks of glass raining through the backseat. Unspent, the bullet from the rifle continued through the windshield. More by chance than design, the glass missed Rick's eyes. Raven, too, had been spared, except for a few minor cuts across his bare chest. But they healed almost faster than Rick could blink. Josette was huddled low in her seat, trying to keep her head out of firing range, while still peering over the dash to drive.

Turning, Rick knelt on the seat, aiming his gun through the frame of the window, firing shot after shot behind them. He wasn't aiming for the passengers. The trucks were moving too fast, and he was too out of practice. So he left that for Raven. His goal was to put enough holes in the radiators and engines of the trucks to stop them, because they weren't going to be able to outrun them. The Volvo was a great car, and Josie was doing a damn fine job of driving, but they were on unfamiliar roads in bad weather.

"Right," Josette shouted to be heard over the wind and rain whistling through the vehicle. She slowed only marginally before taking the turn, and Rick felt the vehicle shudder as the electronic brake distribution and traction control kicked in.

As Rick watched one of the trucks missed the turn, driving hard and fast into the middle of a muddy field, the vehicle lurched to a stop, the gunman in the bed being tossed in the air like a rag doll.

The second truck was bearing down.

"Hang on!" Josette yelled.

Rick braced himself as the Volvo sped up an incline and over a railroad crossing, becoming airborne for a brief moment before slamming with jarring impact against the pavement on the other side.

"Gun." Raven reached down, exchanging his spent weapon for the one Rick had pulled from the bag.

"Right!"

Rick continued to fire into the grill of the remaining truck, not even noticing the shifting vehicle anymore.

But the driver of the truck had apparently been waiting for just this turn. He gunned the engine, closing the distance between them until there were only inches between them.

Raven and Rick were firing almost continuously. The truck was now too close to fire at the grill. Rick aimed at the eyes above the rifle steadied on the roof of the truck as Raven fired at the driver. Blood exploded from the driver's chest. The truck lurched to the right as the dying man fell sideways. The vehicles impacted with the scream and grinding of twisting metal. Rick and the others were thrown into a tangled heap as the Volvo swerved out of control off the pavement and started to roll.

Chapter Eighteen

"HOW BAD IS it?"

Rick could hear Josette's voice as if from a distance. He wanted to open his eyes, but couldn't seem to manage it. It was as if they were leaden, too heavy to move. He knew his body was in pain, but shock had set in, so it was more of an esoteric realization than an immediate agony. The knowledge that he was probably dying didn't panic him. In fact, he wasn't capable of feeling much of anything.

"Bad enough." Raven's voice was thick with exhaustion. "It was silver ammo. Then there's the damage from the wreck. I don't have the strength—"

"You can use mine." Josette's voice was wet with tears, but there was an underlying steel to the words, a demand that would not be denied.

"From . . . *you?* No, we can't share energy. We'd have to have some sort of . . . bond."

She didn't say a thing, but something must have passed between them because he heard Raven say, "Does Rick know?"

"It doesn't matter. Just do it. Take whatever strength you need. I don't care. Just heal him." The desperation in her voice cut Rick like a knife. He wanted to say something, but he couldn't seem to make his body cooperate. Nothing seemed to be working right.

The first sensation started in his spine. It began as a warm electric feeling that flowed in a long line from his skull to his tailbone. Only then did he feel pain. It was excruciating. Each breath he drew into his damaged lungs brought stabbing agony. His hips, pelvis, *everything* hurt. He felt his mouth open and ragged screams split the air. Again and again his body reacted to the damage. It wasn't until long minutes later that strength began to build slowly, as blood vessels healed, bones reknit, and muscle and skin tissues repaired themselves. He forced his eyelids open and saw Raven kneeling on the ground beside him. The air around the healer's hands glowed with the power that he was pouring into Rick's chest.

Josette stood behind Raven. Her hair was matted with blood that covered one half of her face, running and thinning in the rain that soaked all of them to their skins. She was steadying herself with her hands on the big man's shoulders, and he abruptly knew why. He'd seen this before in other Sazi. The magic that was pouring into him came from her, filtered through the man who was . . . *her mate*.

No wonder she'd rushed to him, was willing to wait until he arrived.

Seized with a fit of coughing, Rick rolled onto his side, choking out the blood that had been trapped inside his windpipe as he healed. He spit it out on the ground as he forced himself to his knees.

"Josette?" His voice sounded ragged. It hurt to speak after all the screaming he'd done. They'd healed the gravest wounds only and from the exhaustion plain on both their faces, he knew why. His body would have to take care of the minor injuries. "The bad guys?"

"Dead." That, at least, was good news. Because right now, none of the good guys were in any condition to fight.

Rick shifted positions until he was sitting upright. He was sitting in a puddle, not that it made any difference. He was soaked to the skin anyway. Lucas would throw a fit about him letting the playing cards in his rear pocket get wet, but it was too late now, and Rick honestly didn't care. He'd done his best every step of the way. His best just simply hadn't been good enough.

"I got the cell phone. It doesn't seem to be damaged." Josette lowered herself onto the ground beside him. Her body made a squelching sound as it sank into the mud, but he could see she was too sad and weary to care. "We'll need to report in."

"I'll do it." Raven took the phone from her hand and rose slowly to his feet. His expression was deceptively calm, his voice controlled, but there was a deep burning rage in those dark eyes. Rick could feel its searing heat. It was the type of anger that had led more than one agent to cross the fine line between justice and vengeance. Rick watched the other man stalk off, phone in hand. Staring at Ramirez's retreating back he wanted to hate him. He couldn't. Raven was a good man. If he had to lose Josette to someone else, at least it was someone he could respect. But damn it hurt. He almost wished they'd let him die. Almost.

Gathering his courage and strength he turned to face the woman he loved with as blank an expression as he could manage.

"Rick, we need to talk." Her voice was barely above a whisper, pitched so that Ramirez wouldn't be able to hear. She was giving him that courtesy at least, telling him directly and privately instead of in front of the man who'd be taking his place in her heart and her bed.

He turned to meet her gaze, saw the sadness and regret in her eyes. He watched her struggle to find the right words. It was too much. He couldn't bear to hear it. So he broke the tension instead. "What's to talk about?" He fought to hide the pain that threatened to tear him apart. "You're mated. Congratulations. He seems to be a great guy."

He watched in shock as tears filled her eyes. She stared at him for an eternal second, then rose in a blur of motion. Before he could do anything, before he could even *think* of what to do, she was gone.

"Josette—" he called, but she didn't answer. He

struggled to his feet, only to find Raven standing in front of him, blocking his way.

"You are such a fucking idiot, Johnson."

JOSETTE RACED AWAY from the wreckage, tears coming to her eyes. Well, now he knew, and there wasn't a thing she could do to turn his heart back to her. Either he would be angry or he'd walk away, as most Sazi did when a mating occurred. Yes, there were cases of love overcoming a mating bond, but it didn't happen often.

Trouble was, she didn't want Raven—had never really loved him. Oh, she had *hoped* for the longest time, and she watched every vision that had him in it. She'd waited for the day they'd meet and happily showed up in Chicago, just on the chance. But the timing hadn't been right. In Chicago, he'd been too torn up over the loss of a beautiful owl shifter named Emma, who had been killed by one of the spiders, in just as senseless a death as Ellen had endured.

The bond was there. The *potential* for a future was there. She knew from her visions that they *could* be happy. It wouldn't be perfect, but what is? But that had been before she knew Rick was still alive. That she hadn't seen him, had been given no sense of his presence, still astounded her.

Even from here, she could feel Raven's anger beat at Rick like blows from a baseball bat as he spoke. His every word dripped scorn to her sensitive ears. It was sweet that he'd realized so quickly what was happening, but then, he was Charles's ever-so-great grandson. He understood that things happened strangely sometimes. "That is one of the most amazing women I've ever met. She is crazy in love with you, was ready to *die* for you, but you're just throwing her away."

"What in the hell are you talking about?" Rick's frustrated fury threatened to boil over. He lurched to his feet, his power flaring until steam rose from the wet ground. Anger and hate roiled into the air until even the rain stank of it. "It's not my fault she's mated to you!"

Frantic to get away from what could erupt into a full-fledged war between them, she turned to cat form and crawled among the roots of a massive tree. She needed to think and part of her wanted to just run away. If they fought, she honestly didn't know what would happen. Would the mating ties overcome her heart? Would she spring to Raven's defense, instead of the man she loved?

"It's not her fault either, asshole." Raven leaned forward until his face was a bare inch away from Rick's. Rick jerked back from the electric power of the other man's magic. "She may be mated to me, but you're the one she's in love with. It's obvious from the way she looks at you, the way she says your name. And you're ready to just walk away. Doesn't she mean *anything* to you?"

"She means *everything* to me, damn it! Why in the hell do you think I'm willing to go?" Rick clenched his fists at his sides.

"Then *tell her!* Just because she's mated doesn't mean she's going to choose me. Open your eyes. Amber's mated to my father, but she married Charles. Tatya chose Lucas. If you want the woman, then fight for her damn it! Don't just roll over and give up. She deserves better than that." Raven's eyes blazed, but his voice was controlled. "If you don't love her, don't want her, *fine*. Tell me now. But know that this is your only chance. If you don't go after her . . . right here, right now . . . I will. I will happily claim her and I will do everything in my power to make her happy."

There was a long pause, and she could feel Rick's eyes boring into her fur. His voice was cold and harsh when he spoke to the taller man. "Get out of my way."

Rick strode toward her haven with purpose, only slowing to a stop when he was a few feet away. The rain was starting again. Not heavy yet, but steady, individual drops plopping against her body as he stared down at her makeshift shelter. The rain and wind swept away scents before he could even notice them, but there was no mistaking the misery in his posture. She turned her body so she didn't have to look as he said whatever he was going to.

"I'm sorry." He squatted down so that he could look her in the eyes, but she turned her head away, unable to believe him after the anger she'd smelled and felt. "I just assumed." He sighed. "I mean, he's your *mate*, Josette."

"Don't care." Her words were muffled by dirt and fur as she desperately faced away from him.

"I love you," Rick said the words softly, but it felt like he put every ounce of feeling and intensity he possessed into those three words, pushing the emotions at her to break through the barrier of power she had raised in defense. "I always have. I don't want to lose you again."

"Could've fooled me." She turned to face him then, her eyes tear-filled even though cats weren't supposed to be able to cry. She could feel her whiskers drooping with the misery she was feeling.

Rick seemed unsure what to say. His face moved through a variety of expressions and his scent along with them. Finally, he said the only thing that mattered. "I love you and I'm so incredibly sorry. I just couldn't believe you'd give up a true mating for someone who deserted you and made you suffer every day for a century."

He crept forward on muddy knees until he was inches away. Slowly, gently, he reached forward, stroking the soft fur of her head and back with his left hand as he scratched the sensitive skin of her jawline with his right. "I love you, Josette. *Ma chère*," he whispered the words again into the soft fur of her ears. Closing her eyes, she reveled in the scent of his skin, in the emotions that washed over her.

"I love you, too," she whispered the words. "Even if you are an idiot." She nipped at the soft skin of his wrist and he jerked back his hand quickly.

"Gee thanks." He gave a dry chuckle as he rubbed the tiny bleeding marks. "I have to say you do wonders for my self-esteem."

She raised her chin with what little pride she could muster. "You'll get over it. Besides, you deserved it."

There was no arguing with that, so he just shrugged. Then, he changed the subject. "We'd better get back."

He reached inside the root ball and pulled her out into the cool night. She expected him to put her down, but he didn't. Instead, he carried her back to the scene of the wreck. It felt right, good, to purr against his chest, to scrape fur and whiskers against his jaw.

Rick picked his way carefully across the wet, uneven ground, making sure of his footing. Raven sat waiting, tired and bedraggled. Josette's purse sat at his feet. He looked up, face drawn, eyes hollow. "How do you feel about another train trip?" he asked Josette. "There's no other chance to get you to Florida on time."

"If it's the fastest way to get there, I'm all for it," Rick answered.

"It is. Nobody else is stupid enough to try to fly in this weather, and we're not even sure exactly where we are." He stood. "But we passed railroad tracks running east–west not too far back. You can catch the next freight train in to Albuquerque. I'm supposed to stay here and do a basic cleanup, then head back to the Simmons place to do a thorough investigation." He bent down to pick up Josette's purse, which he passed over to Rick. When he spoke his tone was polite and utterly neutral. There was no hint of the warmth or friendship that had marked their relationship earlier. Rick understood. If their positions had been reversed he wasn't sure he could be even that calm.

"The phone's in the bag, along with her identification. As soon as two of you hit Albuquerque you're to call my father. He's arranging a commercial flight to Daytona Beach."

"How are the other seers holding up?" Josette asked the question hesitantly. He could feel the tension vibrating in her body. Her mate was in pain and she might well be putting him in more. A part of her wanted, needed, to go comfort him. But she couldn't, and she knew it. She'd made her choice.

"They've stabilized." It wasn't an answer, but it was information she needed. Then Raven actually looked at her. Until that moment he'd refused to meet her eyes. "Amber called, too. She told me to pass on the word when she couldn't reach your cell. Your idea bought us until the moon rises tomorrow night. She explained the rest of it, too." He paused for a long moment and then sighed heavily. "I don't know if the mating's mutual. But if it is—I understand what will happen. I'm okay with it, I suppose. It's not like either of us have a choice. I just wish I had more to offer you. With the situation down here, I don't know how good of care I'll be taking of myself for the next day."

RICK STARED AT the other man for a long moment. If things were different, this was a man who he'd have had a real friendship with. But things were what they were. Josie would always come between them, whether they liked it or not. It was just a fact. But that didn't keep him from asking. "Are you sure you'll be all right dealing with *this?*" He gestured at the scattered wreckage and the dead bodies that littered the ground.

"I've handled worse." There was a hint of steel in the words. "I'll call in a few people. My mom lives just south of here. Some of her tribe from Alaska are visiting. They can be very discreet."

"It's not that, it's just—" Rick tried to find a way to say what he was thinking without insulting the other man. Unfortunately diplomacy wasn't his best thing— as he'd proven so admirably with Josette moments before. Still, he had to try. He'd been burned out before. He remembered how it felt. It had taken him decades of peace, quiet, and solitude to recover. Even now he wasn't the same. If it wasn't for Josette he'd still be retired. He could feel Raven's weariness, his rage. The job hadn't broken him, but he was only a hair's breadth away from it. "Will anyone on the council get on your case for jumping off medical leave?"

Perhaps Rick was projecting, because Raven seemed to understand what he was trying to convey. "I'll manage. I always do." He brushed a stray hair back from his forehead with a weary hand. "But do me a favor. Get her to Daytona safely. Save my grandfather."

Chapter Nineteen

WAITING WAS HARD. They sat in a makeshift shelter of rocks and scrub oak a few yards from the railroad tracks. A westbound Amtrak had sped by not more than a half hour before, but so far there had been nothing going east.

Josette was back in human form. This time she wore a black jogging suit over a black sports bra. She liked the T-shirts with their clever sayings, but she was getting damned tired of being cold. She was too exhausted to expend energy to keep herself warm when a simple change of clothes could do the trick. It seemed odd to her that the wreck that had destroyed the Volvo hadn't put so much as a scratch on the luggage. She nearly laughed when the first thought that popped into her mind was a stock report: *sell Volvo, buy Samsonite*.

Rick was pacing again, in part to keep warm, but mostly because he couldn't stand not to. She didn't remember him being this keyed up all the time before. On the other hand, there hadn't been people trying to kill them back when the two of them had been living in Illinois. That sort of thing did tend to make one a little nervous.

"So, Ahmad and the snakes want you dead—" he started, but she interrupted him.

"I'm not sure Ahmad is working with these snakes." He raised his brows, so she amended. "Don't get me wrong. He *does* want me dead. But I don't think I can assume anymore that they're in this together. Wrong kind of snakes."

"He *is* the council representative for the reptiles, Josette. *All* the reptiles, not just the cobras. Wouldn't he at least know about all this?"

"He is their representative, yes. But I've noticed he has a certain . . . *prejudice*. All of his *personal* guard, everyone in his immediate circle, is not only a snake, but a snake of Middle Eastern descent. The snakes that attacked me at my house and the hotel were either Central or South American. They spoke Spanish, and they were all breeds native to the new world."

He felt his brow furrow and he squatted down beside her. "So you're saying that you think two *separate* groups of snakes are trying to kill you?"

"Yes. I think the Central or South American snakes are one group. The humans are a separate group."

"And Ahmad?"

"Who knows." Josette raised her hands in a gesture of utter defeat. "I gave up trying to figure him out centuries ago. I deal with him when and how I must, but I can't say I trust him or enjoy his company."

Rick started to say something more about it, but stopped suddenly. Excitement filled his scent until the area bloomed in her nose like a citrus orchard. Eyes nearly glowing, he leaped to his fee. "Do you hear that?"

As she listened, a smile lit up her face. "It's a train, and it's heading east."

"Thank God!" Rick reached down to help her to her feet.

Staring in the distance, she could see it heading around a curve. It was a freight train and a long one. It was moving at a steady clip, the various cars swaying rhythmically along the rails. There were probably a dozen flat cars behind the engine, each piled with a double high stacking container like the one she'd ridden on to Albuquerque—was it only yesterday? Next came three or four tank cars and several boxcars.

"The fourth boxcar is empty."

"How can you tell?"

"There's less weight in it, so it's moving differently." He sounded absolutely certain, but she couldn't tell the difference.

"I'll jump on first and get the door open. Then you can toss in your purse and jump in after."

"I just hope the conductor doesn't catch us."

Rick's face sobered. "Good point." He looked up and down the line. "There are some trees up there, right before the curve. If we hurry, we can get in position."

They'd have to hurry all right. The train was moving toward them faster than she'd originally thought. But, if they timed it right, the engine would be around the corner and out of sight when they climbed on board. Of course, that assumed nothing went wrong. Josette slid off her flip-flops, stuffing them into the bag and forcing it closed. She'd rather risk cutting her feet than have the silly things slow her down. They were worse than useless for running.

They made it, but it wasn't easy. Sprinting full out with a purse on her arm was awkward, and made her feel both girly and foolish. But there was no help for it. She needed the phone and her ID, and there were no pockets in her outfit.

Rick wasn't in much better shape. His too-tight jeans and too-small sneakers made it hard for him to move as well as he normally would. Still, he managed to get there ahead of her. He ran next to the train, gravel crunching beneath his feet. With a perfectly timed jump, he grabbed on to the ladder. Moving along the narrow metal rim had been an exercise in dexterity that had Josette's heart in her throat. But he managed to reach the heavy latch, open the sliding door, and swing himself inside.

It was her turn. There was no time to waste, no time to think. She ran. When she was parallel to the open door she tossed the bag in. Rick appeared at the door. Holding on to something inside with his left arm, he leaned out with his right arm extended.

"Come on. Jump! I've got you."

She jumped, grabbing onto his arm with both of hers. He caught her, swinging her inside to safety.

She collapsed onto the floor, breathing hard from both exertion and nervousness. Her feet were bruised and cut. A nasty shard of brown glass from what had once been a beer bottle had embedded itself in her heel. Hissing in pain, she pulled it free and tossed it out the open door.

The cut bled for a moment or two, but then healed with faster than normal speed. She could actually watch the wound close. She sat on the wood and steel floor, her back pressed against the metal wall, not bothering to gather up her purse or put the shoes back on. There was no point. She'd just have to take them off again when they disembarked. And right now she was just too damned weary to bother with much of anything.

It wasn't physical weariness as much as pure mental exhaustion. Oh, the past couple of days had been physically trying, no doubt about it. But it was the constant upheaval that was wearing her out. One crisis after another, year after year—never feeling safe for even a moment. It was just too much. Still, they probably had at least an hour-long ride on this train, maybe more. For that long, at least, she could relax. She refused to think about Raven or Ahmad, or even those waiting in Daytona. For the space of a train ride she wanted to just exist in the moment.

"It must be handy being able to pull on his healing abilities." Rick lowered himself onto the floor next to her, giving a nod at her foot.

She shook her head. "I can't. It's a one-sided mating. He can pull from me. I can't pull from him."

Rick's expression grew serious. "Are you sure?" He sighed. "What I sensed when you were helping him heal me didn't seem all that one-sided." Rick's voice was ever-so-carefully empty of emotion. In fact, he was shielding so hard he was practically vibrating with the effort not to let her sense what he was feeling.

"It doesn't change anything either way." Josette met his gaze. He would have turned his head, but she reached up, holding his face in the cup of her hand. "I love *you*. I chose *you*."

"But—"

"No buts. And no arguments. I've made my choice, so unless you intend to dump me . . ." The lilt in her voice made it a question.

"Not a chance in hell."

"Then you're stuck with me for the duration." She closed her eyes. "Now can we please just sit? I'm utterly exhausted."

He wrapped his arm around her, pulling her close. "I can relate to that. It's been a rough couple of days." He paused for a moment. "I'm really sorry about Ellen. She thought you were wonderful. I could feel this deep sense of admiration emanate from her, as though you were a lifelong mentor."

"And it's odd, but I don't really know why." But that wasn't quite true. She *did* know why, because

Ellen had said so herself. "No, that's not right. She told me when we met that she'd been waiting for me to arrive for days, hiding behind the truck stop. She'd probably had visions about me for years . . . had built up the relationship in her mind. Maybe I *was* a life-long mentor to her, and just never knew it."

"I know all about admiring someone for years." His voice was warm and rich. It felt so good to be snuggled up against his warm chest. In fact, his *really* warm chest.

"Do you need to change? You feel warm." She pressed her fingertips against his forehead, which was unnaturally hot, as though the moon was trying to pull his fur from beneath his skin.

"No." He smiled. "I'm intentionally raising my temperature, trying to make you comfortable. You're not wearing much, after all." His warm, knowing chuckle tightened things low in her body. Josette was suddenly very aware that the two of them were alone together. No one would likely be interrupting them until Albuquerque. He seemed to sense it, too. She heard his breath catch, felt his heartbeat speed beneath the hand she'd unwittingly laid on his chest.

She looked up, meeting his gaze. He had stubble on his chin, dark circles under his eyes, but she'd never wanted or loved him more than she did at this moment. "Let's move away from the door." Her voice was a hoarse whisper.

They stood and staggered clumsily against the

rocking toward the dark recesses of the boxcar. It should have been funny, but Josette wasn't amused. The scent of Rick's lust was filling her nostrils, his hunger pouring out in an empathic wave that washed over her until every inch of her body throbbed and ached with the need to be touched. The train jerked as she started to kneel, costing her some balance. Rick tried to save her. Instead, he fell, too, their bodies ending in a tangle atop a small pile of hay, left over from the last cargo.

"Are you all right?" Rick propped himself onto his hands in a half-push-up. It gave Josette just enough room to roll onto her back. The lust had faded slightly, but not vanished. Still, overlying it she could scent his concern.

"Ouch. That hurt." Splinters had been driven into the flesh of her palms. She turned her hands over so that Rick could see.

"Ouch indeed." His head moved forward, and he kissed her palms gently.

Power flared between them in a flash that was erotic, but walked the fine line between pleasure and pain. It stole her breath in a gasp as it tightened muscles deep within her until she ached with the need to be touched again.

He bent his elbows, lowering himself slowly toward her until their lips met. The kiss was tentative at first, a bare brush of warmth against her lips until Josette leaned into his mouth, her tongue teasing against his lips as her hands moved down his chest to slide beneath the thin fabric of his shirt.

The kiss deepened, his tongue delving into her mouth, teasing and tangling with hers as her hands skimmed gently across the warm muscled flesh of his abdomen. Gentle fingers teased the scars that marked his chest before moving to his hardened nipples.

His heartbeat pounded against the sensitive skin of her aching palms. Groaning he pulled back and shifted positions until he lay on his side on the floor beside her. Propping his head onto one hand, he stared down at her. "You are so beautiful."

He meant it. She could hear it in his voice, scent it in the air. Despite the ill-fitting sweatsuit, lack of makeup, and weather-tangled hair, he truly believed she was beautiful. Love must certainly be blind.

"I love you Richard Aleric Cooper." He might be Johnson now, but before . . . she would always be Josette Cooper in her heart.

"Yeah?"

"Yeah." Her smile was so broad it pulled at the corners of her mouth and increased the twinkle in her eyes.

"Prove it. Or are you too *tired?*" She could hear the teasing challenge in his voice.

"Hmnnn." She was grinning, she couldn't help it. "I'm pretty pooped, but somehow I think I can manage something."

"I have some suggestions." He offered hopefully.

"I just bet you do." She shoved him gently, until he was lying on his back. "But let's see what I can think up on my own. Shall we?"

"It'd better be good."

"Oh, I will be." Her voice was a throaty purr, filled with promise. Rising to her knees she moved to straddle him, one knee on either side of his body so that her crotch hovered just above his. As she leaned forward onto her hands and knees she felt the brush of him, hard and ready against her. The knowledge sent a shiver of anticipation through her body that hardened her nipples and made her back arch.

Rick's hands reached up to grasp the bottom of her sweatshirt. In one deft movement he pulled it over her head and off. He tossed it quickly aside, his hands moving to take her bare breasts in his hands. He squeezed them gently, his thumbs working to tease her sensitive nipples until she found herself whimpering, eyes closed.

Her hands seemed to move of their own accord, working at the buttoned waistband of his trousers, struggling to unfasten a zipper straining to contain his erection. She leaned her head forward to nibble his earlobe and kiss a delicate trail down his neck to the warm hollow of his throat.

She could feel his pulse beating a frantic rhythm against her lips and tongue as her hands finally mastered the unruly zipper, freeing his cock to her touch. She stroked him slowly, gently moving her hand downward to cup his balls and trace a finger in a feather-soft touch along the delicate skin that stretched between them.

His hands caressed her back, moving down her body to slide beneath the elastic waistband of her trousers, pulling them down with one hand, he used his other to support her weight as he rolled her over so that now she was on her back. In one deft moved he tugged both pants and underwear from her body and tossed them aside so that she lay naked on the floor beneath him.

Their eyes met, and Josette's breath caught in her throat. There was need in his look, but there was so much more. A world of emotions, held back by his shields, was there, naked and vulnerable in his gaze.

"Drop your shields."

"Josette—" His tone was of both warning and panic.

She did understand, but she needed this, especially tonight. "Please, Rick. I want to feel what you're feeling. I want you to know what's in my heart."

He closed his eyes, and she felt the walls that separated them crumble to so much dust.

She rose up on her elbows to kiss him, claiming his mouth as the two of them were caught together in a tide of emotions that roared over them, leaving them both breathless and elated. She felt his love, and gave him her pain at his leaving, and, in the same moment her love and forgiveness. He cupped her face with one hand, as the other moved slowly, gently, treasuring every curve, fingers dancing gently downward before tracing a slow, lazy path upward to tease at the lips between her thighs.

She whimpered then, body arching to urge him onward. Still, he teased her opening until she was ready to scream with frustration.

"Please," she begged him breathlessly. "Please."

"I was going to wait. I know I won't last."

"It'll be long enough." She gasped as his finger found her clit and moved across it. "Oh God, *please.*" Her orgasm was building with each touch. The air around them sparkled with magic, dust motes becoming like tiny stars that were almost blindingly bright.

His member throbbed and jerked in her hand. She heard Rick as though from a distance. "Yes. *Now.*"

Strong hands grasped her thighs, spreading them wide, tilting her until she was fully exposed. He thrust inside and it was almost too much. She thought she was ready, and she was, but she was still tight. It was an exquisite pain that brought a scream from her lips, made her claw at his back as she rose to meet each powerful stroke.

His breathing grew ragged, his rhythm speeding. Over and over again, his body moving in and out with almost bruising force in a rhythmic slap of skin on skin.

She couldn't think. Her awareness narrowed until all that was left was the two of them and the rapidly building pressure of her pleasure and his, rising in a tightening spiral. When the dam burst in an explosion of pleasure, shouts of joy erupted from their throats as their bodies convulsed together again and again, until they collapsed to the floor in a sated, exhausted heap.

RICK DIDN'T DARE sleep. He just held Josette and stared out the open door as the miles rolled by. She smelled of sex and contentment, and he could feel her deep happiness and love for him. He stared at her in amazement. She was an incredible woman. What an idiot he'd been to leave. He wouldn't be making that mistake again, that was for damned sure. All he had to do now was keep her alive long enough to prove it to her.

He kissed her lightly, and she shifted positions, snuggling in closer. He hated making her move, but they needed to get dressed. They were starting to pass houses and intersections with flashing railroad crossing signs. It would only be a few minutes before they needed to jump off of the train.

"Josie, sweetheart. We need to get dressed. We're almost in Albuquerque."

Her eyes opened a slit, just enough to glare at him as he slapped his hand playfully against her rump.

"C'mon, we've got to get dressed and out of here before the railroad workers catch us and arrest us for indecent exposure or something."

That got her at least to sit in an upright position. When he started tossing her the clothes she'd discarded earlier, she managed to pull them on.

"How are your palms?" He asked as he pulled on his jeans and zipped them. The wood wasn't much of an issue, but these boards smelled of creosote, which could quickly get infected, even with healing abilities. The gun and holster came next, a project made more difficult by the increasing rocking of the train as the conductor applied the brakes.

"Fine. The splinters all worked their way out." She grabbed her purse from the floor. "We'd better hurry. The train's slowing down."

She was right. The rocking of the cars seemed even more pronounced now that the train was braking. "I'm ready when you are." Rick finished pulling on his boots and rose to his feet. He moved to stand next to the open doorway.

There was a certain trick to dismounting. He managed it, but was damned glad the train had slowed, otherwise he probably would have twisted a knee or worse. As it was, he had to put up with being slapped and scraped by tree branches that had grown too near the track area. Josette, being smaller, seemed to have less trouble altogether, even though she was barefoot and carrying her purse. She came up limping beside him where he stood at the edge of the graveled area just a few steps away from a steep drop off.

"Why didn't you put on your shoes?"

"Have you ever tried to run in thongs? On gravel? I'd have broken my neck."

"Oh." The thought hadn't occurred to him. Of course there was no reason why it should. He'd never worn a pair of thongs in his life. They seemed a little silly to him. There wasn't enough to them to really protect your feet, so why bother. Either wear shoes or boots, or go barefoot. Still, he kept his mouth shut and waited as patiently as he could while she sat down, opened her bag, pulled out the sandals, and slid them onto her feet.

"What time is it anyway?" he asked.

"How would I know? I'm not even positive of the year right now."

"Doesn't it say on your cell phone?"

"Oh." She pulled the phone from the bag and hit a button. "Seven o'clock."

It was earlier than he would've expected. So much had happened during the course of the day that time seemed *off*. It hadn't helped that the rain and the clouds had kept him from seeing the movement of the sun. What would it be like to feel this disoriented all the time? He'd never really thought about it. He'd just dealt with the result.

"Do you want to call Raphael or should I?" she asked.

"You do it."

Nodding, she hit the button for Raphael's number. He must have answered on the first ring, because she began speaking almost immediately.

"We're here." She put a hand over the speaker and turned to Rick. "Are you sure we're in Albuquerque? He says he was expecting us a half hour ago."

Rick turned to look at the train rumbling slowly behind them. There were still more than a dozen cars to go before it ended. "It must be Albuquerque. There weren't any stops before this one."

"Could we have slept through it?"

"I didn't sleep. Besides, the railroad workers would have found us."

Josette moved her hand. "Maybe the train was delayed? We're in a residential area, but I think I see gas station lights in the distance. We'll head that way." She sighed. "Well, it'll take that long to get identification for Rick anyway. Do you want me to just get us a cab to a hotel near the airport?"

Rick shifted impatiently from foot to foot. Now that they were up, he wanted to be moving. A restroom would be nice, too. He just hoped that the gas station Josette had spotted was open, because this didn't appear to be one of the city's better neighborhoods. He could see what looked like gang graffiti decorating the privacy fence guarding a yard at the foot of the hill. Many of the houses were ramshackle, with rusted or burned out vehicles in the yards. They were Sazi, and he was armed, but they didn't need the kind of trouble they might find here.

He heard her end the conversation, watched as she turned off the phone and tucked it back into her purse. "Well?"

"We'll go to the gas station and call a cab. Raphael's got his hands full right now." She accepted the hand he held out to her, letting him pull her to her feet. "It's a small pack and someone is having a difficult birth."

"No problem." Rick lied. It was a problem. He could sympathize with Raphael, caught between his responsibilities to his pack and the help he was trying to give them. He'd already done more for Josette than anyone had a right to expect. It was not his fault that things had gone wrong in nearly every way they possibly could.

"We'll be fine." Josette assured him. "Any bad guy with an ounce of sense is getting showered and cleaned up for his Saturday night out." She made her voice light, breezy, but it was a lie, too.

"You're probably right." Rick played along, but he kept all his senses fully alert as he edged sideways down the drop-off. The two of them moved like shadows among the trees, picking their way over the uneven ground, careful of the half-buried junk and broken glass that littered the way.

The barking and growls started almost immediately as the dogs in the neighborhood caught the scent of the two cats moving under the trees. They strained at their leads, their barks filled with rage, and their scents filled with anal pheromones as they fought to protect their territory and the humans in the homes they guarded.

Rick winced. The racket hurt his sensitive ears,

and it made him even more irritable and nervous. There was no chance of them passing unnoticed now. They'd be lucky if someone didn't come out to investigate armed with a shotgun. He started to move more quickly, and was startled when, instead of following Josette came to a complete stop. Tilting her head back she gave voice to the deep throated roar of an angry lion.

Silence descended as abruptly as if someone had flicked a switch. Rick turned to face her, eyes wide with surprise. "What in the hell?"

"Just a little something I learned from my mother. Works really well. I haven't used it in years." She grinned. "They were giving me a headache."

He stared at her for a long moment. "Woman, you never cease to amaze me." He shook his head as he turned to continue their walk.

Chapter Twenty

THE GAS STATION was open. It sat at the corner of a major intersection, across the street from an adult video store on one side and a paint and body shop on the other. It was close enough to dark that they'd turned on not only their sign but every light they had, so that every inch of the lot was illuminated as brightly as if it were midday.

Rick followed Josette through a glass door that had been modified by adding heavy security bars. Inside, the tiny convenience store four or five other customers were walking its narrow aisles, picking up junk food and various sundries while they stopped for gas.

Rick made his way quickly to the toiletries. As long as he was here he would pick up a few things. He particularly wanted a toothbrush, toothpaste, razors, and a comb. He hadn't missed the worried look the old man behind the counter had given him. He didn't blame the man. He knew he looked both scruffy and dangerous. He just hoped that nobody noticed the gun. If that happened things would get ugly quick.

Concentrating slightly, he used the slightest touch of illusion to hide the weapon. He kicked himself for not having thought of it sooner. It was the kind of stupid, rookie mistake he had no business making.

He moved from the toiletries to the far end of the store where the high ticket travel items were displayed: there were stuffed toys, souvenir T-shirts and tote bags, travel pillows, inexpensive nylon duffels, and more. He half-listened as Josette charmed the man behind the counter into letting her use his phone book, while he selected a clean T-shirt in his size and one of the duffels in navy blue.

Josette turned to Rick and smiled. "The cab will be here in about ten minutes. I want a hotel room."

"A room?" Rick moved to take his spot in the line and pay for his purchases.

"Absolutely. I don't know about you, but I'm ready to drop. I need to eat, clean up, and change clothes before I go anywhere or do anything else." She passed the telephone book across the counter, nodding her thanks to the cashier.

"Are we going to have time for that?"

"Sadly, yes. Raphael said the plane doesn't leave until this evening." She sighed. "Did you get me a toothbrush?"

He wasn't used to thinking for two anymore. "Sorry. I didn't think about it."

She grabbed a small plastic basket from a stack next to the door. Keeping the phone to her ear she moved away, gathering items from the various aisles as she arranged for their lodging.

They paid for their purchases just as their cab pulled up at the front door. Thanking the cashier again for his help, Josette hurried outside. When she gave the cabbie the address of an elegant chain hotel, just across the street from the convention center, the man's raised his eyebrows, but didn't argue once she handed a hundred over the seat. They might as well make use of the money they had, and they'd certainly paid the price to earn a little pampering.

It wasn't that long a drive in terms of distance, but the change in setting was startling. Gone were the security bars and boarded-up windows; they were replaced with tasteful landscaping. The cars parked and driving on the streets transitioned from aging and rusted vehicles to brand-new shiny luxury cars and SUVs.

A doorman stepped up to greet them as the cab pulled to a stop in front of the hotel. He opened the car door for Josette, who stepped gracefully out and opened her purse. Taking a look around, she nodded in satisfaction before pulling out a pair of tens for a generous tip. She strode confidently through the glass doors leading into a well-lit lobby, deliberately ignoring the scandalized looks they drew at their appearance.

"May I help you?" The uniformed attendant behind the reception desk greeted them. The words were polite, but his tone was cold as he very deliberately looked down his beakish nose at them. Rick's eyes narrowed, and irritation flooded him. But Josette spoke quickly and pushed magic at him gently, very obviously hoping to avert a scene that would do them no good at all.

"It has been a very long and difficult day." Her smile was a baring of teeth that was meant to intimidate. "Our private plane had engine trouble and our bags were sent ahead of us. We're stranded here for the next few hours." She set her bag on the counter, noting with satisfaction the attendant's raised eyebrow when he recognized the brand. "I know it's short notice, but we need a room." She opened the purse and withdrew her wallet. Pulling her driver's license and credit card from their plastic sleeves she pushed them across the dark marble countertop.

"One moment please." As the attendant walked over to the computer, carrying the small squares of plastic, Rick added his own brand of persuasive magic to hers ever so delicately. He watched the muscles in the clerk's shoulders relax beneath the stiff navy blue blazer he wore. When the approval for the credit card went through he returned, carrying their paperwork and wearing his best professional smile.

"We have a room with a king-size bed available if that would be suitable? Or would you prefer a larger suite?"

"The king room will do nicely. We're hoping to freshen up a bit while they make the necessary repairs."

"Of course." He tapped a manicured finger next to

the line for her signature. "Basic toiletries are provided. There is a coffeemaker in the room as well. The restaurant opens for breakfast at 6:00. Room service will be available at that time as well." He glanced a second time at their clothing, but this time with sympathy, rather than prejudice. "Our clothing store might be able to replace your . . . garments. Anything can be charged to your room if that's more convenient." He gathered up the papers she signed, deftly separating the various copies before passing the pink carbon, along with her credit card and identification back to her.

"Your room number." He pointed to the number on the page. "It's on the twelfth floor. When you get off the elevator, take a left. It will be the fourth door on your left side." He passed one of the two plastic room keys to Josette and held the second out for Rick. "If there is anything you need, please feel free to call us here at the desk."

"Thank you very much. We'll keep that in mind." Rick took the proffered card from the man's hand, barely managing not to sound surly. It was unfortunate that magic should have been necessary. It was annoying how some people responded to such useless trappings as proper clothing. They strode across the lobby to the elevator, the flip-flopping of Josette's sandals on the marble floor echoing oddly through the empty space.

The silence in the elevator as they rode up was

broken only by the irritable tapping of his toe, and the whir of the motor. When the bell dinged, and the doors whooshed smoothly open he finally confided in a harsh whisper. "I hate snobs."

Josette sighed. "I can't blame him for wondering whether we could pay for the room. I mean, *look* at us." She gestured at the mirror that hung on the hallway wall.

Rick winced. His ill-fitting clothes were filthy from the floor of the rail car, he had a two-day stubble, and while the untucked T-shirt partially obscured the holster and gun, it was still fairly visible when he moved.

"You have a point."

"Thank you." She turned and walked down the corridor to their left, her rubber sandals sinking soundlessly into thick plush of the tan and turquoise patterned carpet. It was too thick to even allow the flips to flop. When she reached the fourth door she slid the card key into its slot. When the light flashed green, Rick opened the door, holding it open for her.

It was a nice room, not elaborate, but definitely comfortable. The walls were papered in textured linen, the carpet and drapes a deep tan. The furnishings were of heavy dark wood, polished to a warm sheen. The king-size bed took up most of the room. It's bedspread was tan, off white, and brown stripes that exactly matched the fabric of the chairs that flanked a circular table in the corner beneath the window. Josette crossed the room to look at the view. Rick, meanwhile, made his way to the bathroom.

"DO YOU NEED in here? I'm going to take a shower?"

"Go ahead, I can wait." Josette sprawled out on top of the king-size bed listening to Rick hum to himself as the water began running in the shower. There was a folder on top of the nightstand. She supposed it probably had the room service menu. She needed to eat. Rick needed to eat. The sun was going down on the first night of the full moon. She didn't doubt that as powerful alphas, she and Rick could control their beasts. But eating a meal heavy in protein would help. Unfortunately, she wasn't the least bit hungry. In fact, the thought of food was a little bit nauseating.

It was nerves. All the time and effort she'd spent, and here she was, back where she started. They were no closer to saving her friends, and they'd lost Ellen in the process. People could use every platitude they wished about it not being her fault, but she knew better. She should have removed Ellen from the home as soon as she met Ray. One call to Angelique, the head of the raptors, would have been all it would have taken. But instead, she worried about *appearances* and relied on the judgment of others.

Tears stung her eyes once more. She closed them, fighting not to cry because once she started she wouldn't be able to stop. She was so afraid, and so unutterably weary. But from now on, she was going to rely on her own instincts . . . her own reaction to—

—reaction to the news.

He was standing in a greenhouse, hat in hand. Shifting nervously from foot to foot as his brother entered and spoke. "What do you mean, she escaped and cannot be found?" The words were spoken in Spanish, but Josette translated them in her mind. She couldn't see the face of the speaker, he had his back to the man whose mind she was in. He appeared to be busy tending an exotic plant of some sort. "You had the Sazi's bruja in the palm of your hand in the motel, you and how many of my men? And yet still, somehow, she survives. And she managed to kill Maja in the process!"

The body began to tremble, when he spoke, his voice was unsteady, "Paolo, brother . . . I—"

"Do not call me brother, Ernesto." The man refused to turn and look at his sibling, and spat on the floor. It was as though he considered the other man beneath his contempt. "I will not have the shame you have brought on yourself spread to the rest of our family. We have a calling to serve her. To protect her is our sole purpose for living."

"I will go back—"

"No. That job is for others now."

Ernesto felt the rush of power behind and above

him, heard the gentle rustle of leaves. He spun around, and might have cried out, but the giant anaconda had wrapped him in its coils quicker than the eye could see.

He tried to fight, but the coils tightened inexorably, crushing the bones and breath from his body. His vision narrowed, darkened. The last thing he saw was his brother casually trimming dead leaves from his favorite plant with a pair of garden shears.

Josette sat upright in the bed, gasping for air. Her lungs burned as though starved for oxygen. It took a long moment before she fully recognized that she was in an elegantly appointed hotel room. She stared at the textured wallpaper and striped satin chairs, deliberately reminding herself that it had only been a vision. Another real-time one, it felt like. But she was in Albuquerque, not in the Colombian jungle. Yes, it was Colombia. She knew that now.

But *this* was reality. She was alive in this hotel, with Rick. She reached over to grab the television remote from the bedside table. With the press of a button she turned on the flat-screened television in its dark wood armoire. She entered the number for the weather channel, seeing for herself the date and time. But still the tears came. So many deaths, and all because of her damned *gift*.

Rick stepped out of the bathroom, wearing only a

towel around his waist, using another to rub his hair dry. He stopped just inside the main room. Nostrils flaring, he turned to Josette.

"Josie, are you all right?" He crossed over to the bed in two quick steps, letting the towels drop to the floor in his haste.

"A vision." She gasped out the words. "It was just a stupid vision." She looked up at him through tears. *Stupid, so stupid.* Ernesto had been her enemy—had come in force to the hotel with the express purpose of killing her. She had killed so many snakes just like him just as casually as Roberto had in the name of self-preservation. It made no sense to be this upset by his death. And yet, she was. Rick had reminded her of what she'd lost.

"*Mon Dieu* . . . I *have* become a monster."

"What?" He touched her face gently. "You're not a monster."

She shook her head. "You asked at the gas station what I'd become . . . *who* I'd become. That's my answer. I've become a monster. But I'm not willing to stay one."

Rick sat down on the bed beside her. Gently, he pulled her into his arms. She rested her head against his chest, small rough chest hairs, tickling her cheek as she breathed in the mingled scents of soap and skin as he held her close, stroking her hair with one hand.

She felt him lean down and kiss the top of her head. "Better?"

She nodded, still not trusting her voice.

"Do you want to talk about it?"

"No."

He nodded once, without pushing. "Okay."

Josette wrapped her arms around him in a fierce hug. His complete acceptance and kindness was exactly what she needed right now. She knew of no one else in her life capable of allowing her to talk, or not talk about the things she saw in her visions. Rick alone seemed to accept that for the space of the visions she *lived* that reality, the perceptions and emotions she experienced were just as intense and real as any she had in the here and now.

"Do you have any idea how much I love you?" She breathed the words against his drying skin.

"Oh, about half as much as I love you." He reached down to take her chin in his hand. Ever so gently he tilted her head up so that he could claim a kiss. "Let's order some food and rent a movie on pay-per-view. It'll take your mind off things."

"All right." She agreed. "But first I have to call Raphael and let him know where we are."

She used the hotel phone to dial the number. When no one answered after the third ring she left a message for him, just Cerise's name and the name of the hotel.

They chose a cartoon from Pixar and were cuddled up together naked under the covers laughing when the food arrived. Giggling, Josette ducked into the bathroom, leaving Rick to wrap himself in the sheets and deal with the room service attendant.

The almond trout was heavenly. It had been cooked to perfection, and the tastes melted on her tongue. She was savoring a large bite, her mouth full, when the phone rang.

Rick reached across her to pick up the receiver. "Hello? Oh hi, Raphael."

Josette set down her fork and moved her tray to the table. Coming up behind Rick, she snuggled against his back. She could hear his heartbeat speed at her touch. She could also hear every word of the telephone conversation.

"I've got someone dealing with your paperwork issue right now, Rick, but it's going to take a few hours. We've arranged for your tickets on Delta, leaving at 9:00 A.M. tomorrow. I know I said this evening, but we couldn't nail down the connecting flight. You'll have a short layover in Atlanta. You should get to Daytona Beach at around 5:30."

"5:30 *tomorrow?*" She couldn't keep her voice from cracking. They would be cutting it so terribly close. Especially since they had to find the fourth book, buried a hundred years ago beneath the bricks of a lighthouse.

Raphael sighed. "I know. I know. It's later than I'd like, too, but I swear it's the best we can do. You wouldn't believe the hell I had to go through just to manage that."

"I'm sorry." Josette spoke up, knowing he'd be able to hear. "I don't mean to criticize. It's just that—" She stopped, unsure what to say. She didn't need to worry people any further. They'd just have to get the book quickly.

"I know. I'm worried about them, too. Cat even offered to *buy* a frigging jet if it would help, but Tatya swears that they've got everything under control for now, that we just need to get you there before sunset tomorrow." He continued. "Amber says to thank you—the siphoning worked perfectly. They've been able to maintain an acceptable level of power by constantly pulling and then feeding it back to them. Antoine's wife is a little tired, but is hanging in there. The main thing is to make sure that you're rested up and at full strength when you arrive. So, stay at the hotel tonight. Get a good night's sleep. I'll send Carly over in the morning."

"Raphael," Josette spoke softly. "I can't thank you enough for everything you've done."

"You'd do the same for me. Hell, you practically *did* by putting me in touch with Carly. I figure we're even."

"Not even close. But thank you."

"No problem. Now you two get to bed, and try to get at least a little sleep. Otherwise Amber will have my head."

He hung up while they were laughing.

Josette and Rick finished their meals and left the

trays in the hall for pick up along with their completed breakfast selections. Unfortunately, the clothing shop closed before they could buy anything, so they'd have to rely on Raphael coming through in a pinch. Rick decided to watch one of the many CSI shows on the television. Josette took a shower. The two of them were cuddled together in bed by nine and asleep by ten with a wake-up call scheduled for 6:00 A.M.

Chapter Twenty-one

JOSETTE WOKE AT 5:00, spooned tightly in Rick's arms. His breath tickled where it ruffled the hair by her ear. His heart beat slow and strong against her back. Moving carefully so as not to wake him, she shifted out from beneath his grasp. He made grumbly noises in his sleep, but settled down deeper beneath the covers.

Stifling a chuckle, she padded over to the bathroom. She made use of the facilities, then started running herself a hot bubble bath using the bottle provided by the hotel. She did it not because she needed to get clean, just because she wanted one. The past few days had been incredibly long and stressful. The day ahead promised more of the same. While she had the luxury of time and unlimited hot water, she wanted to do something nice for herself.

She'd settled in nicely, submerged up to the neck in bubbles, when she heard Rick climb out of bed.

"Josie?"

"I'm in the tub."

"Shit." She heard him mutter under his breath.

"It's all right. You can come in if you need to. The door's unlocked." She pulled the shower curtain closed to give them each a bit of privacy. Yes, they'd been married. She had seen Rick going to the bathroom before. But still, they were just starting to get reacquainted. She wasn't in any hurry to have the "newness" wear off.

He pushed open the door with an apology and took a deep breath of the steam-filled air. "Wow. That actually smells like . . . mango and grapefruit instead of chemicals."

"I know. It's one of those aromatherapy blends that's supposed to be energizing and invigorating." She ducked under the water to get her hair wet, and also so she wouldn't hear what he was doing. When she emerged a moment later she heard him turning off the taps of the sink.

He pulled the edge of the shower curtain aside to peek through. "I don't suppose you'd like some company in there?" He wiggled his eyebrows lasciviously. "I could use some invigorating."

"The tub's not that big." She observed. "And I'm sensing a certain amount of vigor from you even without the bubbles."

"Ah." He pulled the curtain fully open and sat down on the edge of the tub. "Can I at least scrub your back for you?" He reached over to pluck a washcloth from the rack mounted on the wall. He tried for an expression of helpful innocence, but she wasn't buying it. Not with the way his eyes were dancing, and the muscle at the corner of his mouth twitching.

"Sure. Why not?"

He reached down, dunking the cloth in the water. He pulled it out, squeezing it over her shoulders, so that the warm water ran in rivulets between her shoulder blades and down her spine. Slow and easy he moved the cloth in his left hand over her skin, first down, and then up. His right hand trailed down his own body until it held his hardening cock. When the cloth was clear of the water he "accidentally" dropped it. It disappeared beneath the bubbles.

"Oops. Guess I'll have to look for it, hunh?" He let go of his swollen member and began "searching" for the cloth with his right hand, a search that had his fingers trailing gently along her shin, then between her thighs, as he bent forward to kiss her. It was everything a kiss can be, slow and deep, the muscles of his mouth working hers open, his tongue exploring, savoring the warmth and taste of her. She gasped when his fingers found her opening beneath the water. He stroked and teased her, the water making her body even more sensitive by washing away her natural lubrication.

Her hands traced down his chest, fingernails scraping against the raised smoothness of scars before moving slowly downward to stroke more delicate flesh.

Moaning, he pulled back from the kiss. His mouth moved to her throat. As he took the skin of her neck between his teeth, he bit down, hard enough to bruise but with not quite enough force to draw blood. He kissed her again, shifting position so that he was kneeling on the floor. Gently, carefully, he slid his hands beneath her ass. She slid her arms around his neck, letting him lift her from the tub.

She expected him to take her on the floor or carry her to the bed. Instead he lifted her until her rear was barely perched on the edge of the countertop. She leaned back, putting her hands flat on the cold tile surface for balance as she bent both knees to wrap her legs around his hips. He stepped forward, hands guiding his erection into her opening as his mouth pressed burning kisses onto the flesh of her breasts.

Josette whimpered, her body writhing at his touch. She opened her mouth to tell him she was ready, but he was already there. With exquisite control he slid the whole length of him over her sensitized clit, then pulled out. Again and again, his rhythm sped with every cry from her lips, every movement of her body against his.

Faster and harder, he drove himself into her, his balls slapping against her opening at the end of each thrust. She felt a great tension building inside her. She was close, so close. Her magic flared against his, and his shields crumbled so that she felt what he felt. She felt him slide in her, but at the same time, felt her body closing on her member, squeezing every ounce of pleasure from his body, which was her body, too. It was as though they were one person, one body, caught in an almost unbearable loop of physical ecstasy.

The orgasm hit them both at the same moment, drawing cries that were not quite screams from their lips.

He pulled himself out of her reluctantly, physically, and psychically, until they were once again two separate people. Breathless and sated, but definitely separate.

The bathroom was a mess. They hadn't broken anything, but things had definitely been knocked around a bit. There was water everywhere, and even a bit of blood. She didn't know or care if it was hers or his. It had to have been a minor injury, and it would certainly heal, as would the sore and stiff muscles.

"Wow." The word came out a little breathy. She was still having a bit of a hard time pulling herself together. "Remind me to have you scrub my back more often."

Rick laughed. He stumbled over to take a seat on the toilet stool. She could tell he was still a little breathless himself. "Any time, any place. Just say the word."

The phone started ringing. The two of them looked at each other. Neither seemed particularly inclined to move. Josette wasn't even sure her legs would hold her yet. She was still having little mini-orgasms.

"Oh hell. That must be our wake-up call," Rick complained.

"You get it."

"Why me?" He grumbled, but staggered to his feet. He managed to stumble out of the bathroom and dive across the bed for the phone.

"What time did you put down that we wanted breakfast?" The bedsprings squeaked in protest as he rolled over.

"Six-thirty. I figured that would give us a half hour to get cleaned up." Slowly, carefully, she lowered herself until she stood on the bathroom floor. "Carly is supposed to get here about seven."

"We'd better get moving then." He said it, but she didn't hear him actually *doing* anything. She, on the other hand, was taking a minute to climb back into the tub. She needed to rewet her hair, because it was starting to dry badly. Besides, it would be rude to greet the Alpha Female of Albuquerque smelling of fresh sex.

She didn't linger over the bath this time. The water was cooling rapidly, the bubbles were nearly gone, and Rick needed time to take his shower. Grabbing one of the least-damp towels from the pile that had fallen to the floor she dried herself vigorously and walked out into the bedroom carrying the hairbrush she'd picked up at the convenience store the night before.

"Next." She gestured to the bathroom door on her way to stand in front of the mirror hanging above the dresser.

Groaning, Rick rolled off of the bed and padded

into the bathroom. A moment later she heard the shower running.

Carly arrived at the hotel room door at 6:45 juggling two suitcases, a garment bag, and her purse. Apparently, she believed in coming prepared. She looked lovely as always, impeccably dressed in a suit in a shade of coral that complemented her complexion. The skirt was short enough to show a long expanse of shapely leg. The high heels she was wearing made her legs look even longer.

Josette stepped aside, allowing the other woman to enter. "Good morning. Breakfast arrived with a pot of coffee. Would you like some?"

"Coffee would be lovely," Carly admitted, looking at them dressed and ready with a little surprise. "I got in very late last night, I haven't even had the chance to go to bed. Is Rick in the bathroom?"

Josette nodded her affirmative as she poured coffee into one of the hotel mugs for her guest.

"Yes. He'll be out in a second."

Carly hefted each bag onto the bed in turn. "The blue one is for you, the black one is Rick's." She accepted the mug, taking a long, slow drink before continuing. "Nothing's open yet this morning, so I had to make do with clothes from my son's closet."

"I'm sure it'll be fine." Josette answered.

Carly gave her a meaningful look over the rim of her coffee mug. "You haven't seen the way my son dresses. Colt is fifteen, and he has a very . . . distinctive style." She reached over to unzip the bag. "Take a look."

Josette reached into the bag. The three T-shirts were pretty much what she would've expected a modern teenage boy to wear. They were black and emblazoned with colorfully violent images and the logos of bands she'd never heard of. There was one long-sleeved black thermal shirt with olive green topstitching and an olive green skull and crossbones that didn't seem too bad. It even went well with the pants she had laid out on the bed: black jeans with huge wide legs, attached metal chains, and more buckles than a belt factory.

"You see what I mean."

Josette was spared having to comment as Rick chose that moment to emerge from the bathroom.

He looked at the pants for a long, silent moment. Looking inside the bag, he found a pair of black satin boxers. It took real effort not to laugh when he pulled them out and discovered the crotch was emblazoned with a bright yellow smiley face.

"Look on the bright side. At least they won't bind like the ones yesterday did." She managed to keep a straight face as she said it, but she couldn't conceal the amusement in her scent. It overrode everything else in the room, the coffee, his irritation, Carly's embarrassment.

"I'm really sorry!" Carly began apologizing again.

"It's no problem." Rick picked the clothes up from

the bed and headed back into the bathroom to dress. "I'm fine."

He emerged, fully dressed, a few minutes later. Josette expected him to look silly, but he didn't. Young, it definitely took years off of his appearance, but the shirt clung in a way that emphasized just how broad his shoulders were, how muscular his chest. The pants hung loose, allowing him freedom of movement, showing just a hint of the satin boxers at the waist.

The look in his eyes dared Josette to say anything untoward, but she wasn't even tempted. "All you need is a pair of sunglasses and we'll be getting mobbed for autographs."

"Josie." There was a growl of warning in his voice.

"Am I wrong?" She turned to Carly, who was staring wide-eyed. Her scent was changing, getting more than a hint of musk. Josette didn't blame her a bit. Rick might feel like a fool, but he looked *hot*. "You've got rock star written all over you."

She cleared her throat. "My son does *not* look like that in those clothes."

"Be grateful," Josette suggested. "Otherwise you'd already be a grandmother."

"You're so right." She agreed.

Rick relaxed fractionally, mollified more by the scents in the air than their words. "What did you bring for Josette?"

Carly gestured toward the second bag on the bed.

"We're close to the same size, so I brought some things I had in the closet that I haven't had the chance to wear yet."

Josette unzipped the garment bag. Inside were a pair of designer suits. The first was tomato red, the second, daffodil yellow. Both had been cut in such a way that Josette knew they would hug every curve of her body, making the most of her compact figure. The jackets were meant to be worn either with or without a blouse. With would be more professional. Without, more sexy. Catching a glimpse of Rick's expression she knew which look he would prefer.

"There are hose, underwear, and shoes that match in the other bag."

"Red or yellow?" She asked Rick his opinion.

He smiled and wiggled his eyebrows. "Oh, red. Definitely the red."

"Red it is." It was her turn to gather up the clothes and go dress. Yes, she could've changed in front of Carly and Rick. But she didn't want to. She wanted to step out that door like he had, making an impression. It was silly and vain, but true nonetheless. It was also worth every bit of trouble when she saw the look on Rick's face, smelled his scent on the air.

Carly looked from one to the other, her expression indulgent. "You two! Put your eyes back in their sockets and settle down your scents. We've got to get you to the airport. You've got a plane to catch." She took one final gulp of her coffee before setting it onto the table. Reaching down, she began zipping up the luggage.

Rick reached across the bed and under the pillow. He withdrew Raphael's gun and holster from its hiding place and held it out to Carly. "I can't take this to the airport. Be sure to tell Raphael thanks for letting me use it. It's a sweet weapon and it came in damned useful."

"I'll let him know." Carly reached down to where she'd let her purse drop on the floor. Opening it up she put the gun inside. She managed to close it, but it wasn't easy, and the bag bulged oddly.

"Is my identification in there?" Rick asked.

"Oh, my mistake." She opened the bag again, withdrew a large brown envelope and placed it in his waiting hand.

Slitting it open with a fingernail, he tilted the contents out onto the table next to Carly's empty cup. There was a well-worn passport, a battered brown leather wallet, and two typewritten pages. All bore the name Richard Atwood and listed a date of birth of May 21, 1983, and a New Orleans address. Flipping through the wallet Rick found everything from a library card to family photos. It was an absolutely brilliant bit of work, particularly considering the short timeline. Rick slid the passport and wallet into the back pocket of his jeans. The pages he folded in fourths and stuck in his front pocket. He'd study them on the way to the airport then destroy them.

"Everybody ready?" Carly glanced at the delicate gold watch adorning her wrist. "We really do need to get moving."

"We're ready when you are." Rick threw the envelope in the trash and picked up his duffel from the night before and the suitcase Carly had given him. "Josette, do you want me to get your luggage, too?"

"No, I've got it." She stood, smoothing the wrinkles from her skirt in an automatic gesture. She put her left arm through the straps of her purse, draped the garment bag over the top, and picked up the suitcase with her right hand. "Let's go."

It was a quiet drive to the airport. Rick was memorizing his identity in the backseat. Josette was trying hard not to think about the day ahead. She hated flying. She truly believed that if God had wanted her in the air, he would've had her born into a raptor family. He hadn't, so she didn't believe she had any business flying anywhere. Whenever there was any chance at all of traveling by any other means, she would. But this was an emergency. She had to fly if she was going to save her friends and family. That didn't mean she had to be happy about it. She sat in the front seat of Carly's Camry doing the breathing exercises she'd learned in her yoga classes, telling herself that she was not going to be sitting in a glorified tin can floating God knew how many miles above the ground.

When Carly pulled to a stop at the curb in the passenger loading zone, Josette leaned across the seat to give the other woman a hug. "Thank you so much."

"You're welcome." Carly hugged her fiercely.

Josette would have pulled back, but Carly held on. "I need to ask you a favor." The words were a bare whisper of air. There was no way Rick could hear it from where he was standing by the trunk. She loosened her grip, and Josette leaned back enough to look in the other woman's eyes. They were dark and wet with tears that threatened to spill over.

"What do you need?"

"If Raphael finds out I asked—" She swallowed hard.

"He won't find out from me." Josette assured her.

"We need a healer. Even if only for a little while. Raphael's got some talent, and God knows he's trying his best, but Betty was badly injured during the birthing yesterday. I'm one of only two other alphas in Albuquerque. Our people don't even have enough power to heal themselves, and they don't dare go to a regular doctor. Raphael's helping you because it's the right thing to do, and he'd be furious with me if he thought I was trying to use what he's done to blackmail you into helping us, but Josette—I don't know what else to do." The tears were falling now, streaming unheeded down her perfect features. Her voice was tight with strain as she pleaded.

She patted Carly's thin back. "I'll talk to Amber. She'll know what to do."

Carly pulled back and then grasped both of her hands in a trembling grip, squeezing hard. "Thank you! You have no idea how much that means to me . . . to our whole pack."

"I can't make any promises," Josette warned. "You do realize that."

"Just try. Please."

"I will." Reaching over, she gave Carly's hand a reassuring pat. Then she climbed out to join Rick. He'd removed their luggage from the trunk. Josette gathered up her bags from the ground in front of him, watching as Carly pulled away from the curb to drive quickly away.

"What was that all about?"

"They need a healer. Raphael won't ask and didn't want her to, but they're in trouble since Betty hurt herself last night."

"Shit."

"Rick." She met his eyes. "I want you to promise me that if something happens to me, that you'll see to it Amber gets them their healer. They've helped us so much during this."

"Nothing is going to happen to you." He answered gruffly.

"You don't know that." She sighed. "Neither one of us knows that."

"Well, if it does I still won't be able to help her. They'll have to have gone through me to get to you."

She answered that the only way she knew how, by

going on tiptoe and kissing him. It was just a tender brush of the lips, but she tried to let him know with that small touch how much he meant to her. She loved him. God how she loved him. He was an empath. Surely he knew, could sense what she felt for him.

"The look on your face," he whispered the words softly. "There aren't words to say how I feel when you look at me like that."

"I love you, Rick."

"Yeah, me too."

They both had their hands full of baggage, so they really couldn't do anything more, and there were no other words that needed saying. So the two of them went into the airport to face the lines, the bother, and the flight to Atlanta.

THE RECYCLED AIR humming through the airplane vents was filled with the ammonia scent of panic. Rick knew not all of it was Josette's, although he supposed she accounted for a good portion. She held onto the armrests with a death grip and very determinedly kept her eyes averted from the windows, with their view of floating clouds and the ground oh so very far below. He heard the crunch of plastic cracking and glanced over. She was damaging the armrests. Slowly, deliberately she forced each individual finger to let loose of the plastic.

"I'm sorry." Rick shifted in his seat so he was facing

her once he had her hand firmly resting in her lap. His expression was serious. "I knew you didn't like flying, but I didn't think it would be this bad."

She gave him a *look,* and he chuckled. "Here, hold my hand."

She shook her head as she once again closed her eyes. She was quite possibly too terrified to move. But then she spoke. "I'll break it."

"It'll help you feel better." He intentionally changed his voice so that it hinted at a hidden meaning behind the words. "The right touch can be wonderfully reassuring."

Her eyes flew open as he began to push some very intoxicating emotions her way. He was an *empath,* after all. He could project emotions. He was surprised he hadn't thought of it earlier. Of course, normally he wasn't dealing with a full-blown phobia. But he needed skin contact to take the edge off of this terror.

SHE HELD OUT her hand, trying as hard as she could to keep it from shaking. The minute his skin touched hers she felt the warmth of magic flowing over her, wrapping around her like a warm fluffy blanket. Instead of panic she smelled bread baking. The knotted muscles in her back and shoulders began to unclench, and she felt herself sinking back into the seat. Her frantic heartbeat slowed and steadied until it matched his.

"Better?" He brought her hand up to his lips and kissed her knuckles.

"Much."

"Good. I don't like seeing you so miserable."

She met his gaze easily now. So long as she kept her eyes away from the window and concentrated on the man next to her she would be okay, maybe . . . she hoped. Taking a slow, deep breath she made herself look him directly and felt the warmth and reassurance pour over her again.

"Thank you."

"Does that make up for making fun of you earlier?" He moved until he could whisper directly in her ear, his warm breath tickling the sensitive hairs there.

She thought about it for a minute. "If you can manage this all the way to Daytona, I'll forgive you anything you've *ever* done wrong."

"What a deal." His smile was practically heart-stopping, and now that she could sense things beyond her own panic she noticed that the stewardess and more than one of the female passengers were reeking with lust and glaring daggers at her.

"You're making quite an impression." She spoke softly, so that only he would hear.

"There's only one woman on this plane whose opinion matters to me, and she's sitting right next to me."

It was the perfect thing to say. The type of line she'd expect to hear from a cad—what was the term now? Ah yes, a *player*. He certainly looked like a player in that outfit, and while he'd been a little self-conscious at first, he seemed to have settled into it comfortably.

"Sit back and try to relax," he suggested. "We've got about another half hour before we arrive."

A half hour sounded like forever, but she tried to relax, to not fight the emotions he was pouring into her. She had just refused the flight attendant's offer of a drink when her perceptions shifted.

The sign above the doorway read Atlanta-Hartsfield International Airport. People were moving purposefully past with their luggage in tow, most looking annoyed and frustrated. Her host stood between the doors to the restroom and the shoeshine stand. "What the hell is taking her so long?" He turned his arm to pull back the sleeve of his suit jacket, showing a starched white shirt cuff and elegant Rolex. 2:14 P.M. She'd been in there more than ten minutes already. How long did it take to go to the toilet and "freshen up" for Christ's sake—particularly when she knew he was out here waiting?

He was just about to walk over there and call through the doorway when she emerged. There was no mistaking her—not many statuesque brunettes were strolling around the airport in a tomato red silk dress and three-inch heels. But rather than come over to meet him at the agreed spot she started walking purposefully in the opposite direction, the heels of her shoes clicking sharply against the tiled floor.

"Janice! Janice!" What in the hell? He was gathering up their bags to go after her when he saw something move. There was a flash of agony in his ankle. He tried to cry out, but couldn't seem to get any sound past the frantic pounding of his heart. He fell to the floor, but he didn't feel the impact. His senses were dimming, but he heard a woman's shrieks coming from the bathroom and thought he saw a snake slither into hiding behind the shoeshine stand.

"Josette . . . honey?" She could hear Rick's voice, as though from a distance. He whispered to the flight attendant that his companion was prone to petit mal seizures, that it was nothing to worry about, she'd be all right in a few minutes.

"Are you sure?"

"I—" Josette blinked her eyes as dramatically as she could. "Oh! I had another one didn't I?"

"Yes, you did." Rick looked relieved that she'd heard, understood, and was back in the present. "But it's okay, sweetheart. Are you all right?"

"I . . . I think so. But I do think I'll have that drink. Do you have any orange juice?"

The attendant, who smelled strangely of fresh white glue, poured the beverage. As she passed the clear plastic cup over to Josette she asked, "Are you *sure* you're all right?"

"I'll be fine. Thank you. This is so embarrassing." Josette didn't have to force herself to blush. People all over the cabin were staring. It was humiliating. Thank God Rick had managed to come up with a reasonable excuse for her odd behavior.

The pilot announced they were ready to land not long after. The attendant had other things to deal with, so she scurried off, leaving Josette and Rick to fend for themselves.

"What did you see?" His words were a mere breath in her ear.

"Snakes, at the airport," she answered. "I *think* it all happens a few minutes from now, but I'm not sure. I didn't see anything that showed the date.

Rick had stopped in mid-step, his eyes wide. "You're seeing the future again . . . and you're in it?"

She smiled and nodded. "I wasn't sure before, so I didn't want to say anything, but Rick! Think of what that could mean!"

RICK WOULD HAVE been ecstatic if it weren't for one little problem. Snakes. "It's wonderful, *ma chère*. But how in the *hell* did they track us here already?" He kept his voice too low for human ears, keeping his face hidden while fumbling with the seatbelt at his waist.

"Who knows? Maybe they've got people at every hub with flights to Daytona. We can't be certain that they didn't get the information out of Bruce before they—"

He nodded grimly. "Maybe. But that's a lot of manpower."

"Somebody wants me dead *very* badly."

"Well they're just going to have to live with the disappointment."

Funny thing, thinking of the snakes waiting in the terminal seemed to make Josie a lot less nervous about staying airborne.

It was nearly two o'clock when the plane touched ground. It took another five or so minutes for everyone to gather up their luggage and disembark. Rick and Josette hurried down the tunnel connecting the plane to Concourse A. They'd come in at gate A-30. Their flight to Daytona was leaving at 4:07 from gate A-15. Unfortunately that information was posted on every one of the departure screens for anyone and everyone to read.

"Describe it to me in detail—everything you can remember." Rick pulled her aside to stand by one of the telephone kiosks in the main corridor.

She closed her eyes, apparently trying to shut out the noise and distractions of the busy terminal. Step-by-step she went through every second of the vision, pulling every detail she could from the images. There wasn't much, but it was better than nothing.

"All right. We're going to see if we can find one of

those maps of the building they sometimes have. We'll look for all of the places where a shoeshine stand is next to the bathrooms. In the meantime, keep your eyes and your nose open and stay close."

They were standing in line at a Delta information desk when Josette grabbed his arm. "Psst! That's her! Look, there's the shoeshine stand, and the bathroom. What time is it?"

"Two-ten."

"*Shit!*" Her eyes moved frantically back and forth several times, and then she smiled grimly. "I have an idea. It's crazy, but I think it might work."

Rick opened his mouth to protest, but Josette pulled away from him. She walked with faked casualness in the direction of the shoeshine stand. When she was less than six feet away she started to shriek.

"*Oh my God!* It's a snake! Richard, I saw a snake crawl under *that* stand! *Oh my God!*"

She dropped her bags and threw herself into his arms. He could feel her put every ounce of fear she had for flying into portraying a full-blown case of ophidiophobia. All the while she screamed, cried, and generally raised the kind of commotion that was guaranteed to bring security, the police, and more unwanted attention than you could shake a stick at.

The man in the navy suit who'd been standing there waiting stared at Josette as though she were a madwoman, but grabbed his bags and started putting his distance between himself and the shoeshine stand.

Drawn by the commotion, the statuesque brunette in her red dress hurried out of the bathroom to join the man. "Clifford, what's going on?"

"This woman swears she saw a snake crawl under the shoeshine stand."

"Oh my *God*. I hate snakes. Get me out of here!"

"Fine. As you like." From the corner of his eye Rick saw the two of them leaving. There was no point in stopping them, and Josette's performance apparently wasn't nearly over.

"Ma'am." A uniformed security officer came on the scene. He came up to her slowly, and worked hard to be polite and reassuring, while at the same time trying to minimize the commotion. He shouldn't have bothered. A crowd had gathered, all staring avidly at the raised wooden shoeshine platform with its black leather seats. "You need to calm down. There's no reason to think—"

She turned her panic into anger with the flick of an expression. "Excuse me? Are you calling me a liar? I know what I saw. There's a *snake* under there! You need to get animal control out here. Who *knows* what kind it is. It could be poisonous!"

"I'm sure it's not, ma'am. Now if you'll just come with me."

Rick answered for her, drawing a sharp glance from her. "Of course, officer." They gathered up their bags, but before either of them could take a step a teenage boy with more curiosity than sense kicked the platform with a booted foot. As it scooted away from the wall, there were gasps and screams from the bystanders.

"There *is* a snake in there. *Damn,* that's a big one. Would you look at that!" The boy seemed fascinated, he kept trying to get a better look at the squirming, hissing reptile he'd revealed.

Josette whimpered in mock fear, leaning into Rick's body. "Oh my God—he'll get bitten!"

Damned if it hadn't worked. At least to keep the humans out of the way. "It's all right, baby. Don't worry." Rick's arm tightened around her waist. The two of them started backing away, moving into the bulk of the crowd.

"Everybody move back!" The cop ordered. "Move away!" Now that an actual snake had been sighted the officer had stopped treating Josette like a crazy nuisance. Grabbing the walkie-talkie attached to his uniform shirt he called for backup and requested that animal control be summoned to the scene. Security people began to converge on the stand, keeping the snake from bolting after them.

Rick was only half-listening. Most of his attention was on the crowd. Her scheme might have trapped one snake, but he hadn't been working alone. Somewhere in the airport was a shapeshifter capable of changing his or her appearance to look like anybody. He was betting that the same person who'd impersonated *Josette* to kill Bruce was here now. He doubted the man would abort the mission just because his partner was captured. Far more likely that he'd try to finish the job, and then eliminate the partner. Lucas would want to do a thorough interrogation of the snake that was about to be in custody. He just hoped he'd get to.

She nearly read his mind with her next whispered statement. "We need to call Raphael, have him get in touch with Lucas. He's going to want to question that snake."

"Fine. Call. *I'm* more worried about the one that got away." Rick was taking deep breaths through his nose, searching for the unmistakable scent of a snake shifter. There were things he wanted to say about this reckless tactic, but he held his tongue.

JOSETTE REACHED INTO her handbag and pulled out the cell phone. A quick press of a button and the call went through. She listened to the line ringing as she watched Rick turn in a slow circle, his nostrils flaring as he sought his prey.

"Ramirez." Raphael sounded dead tired and worried.

"It's Josette, we have a situation."

"*Oh for the love of God!* Now what?" She could almost imagine him throwing his hands in the air, as he used to when he lived with Amber—and usually when her name was invoked in the conversation. She flinched at his tone. It wasn't that she blamed him, but it did hurt her to hear such bitterness directed her way.

"Well? What's gone wrong now?"

Looking around she saw several people from the earlier crowd passing by. They seemed to recognize her. Worse, they were eavesdropping. She needed to be very, very careful and choose her words wisely.

"There was a welcoming committee waiting for us in Atlanta. Oh, and the most incredible thing happened! They found this huge snake in the building. Animal control is capturing it now. I bet it will make the national news. You should have Lucas watch. You know how interested he is in those kinds of things."

Raphael started swearing loudly enough that she had to hold the phone away from her ear. When the volume decreased enough for her not to fear going deaf she put the receiver back in position.

"I'll tell Lucas," He growled low in his throat. "You said a welcoming *committee*. I take it there was more than one?"

"Yes. We're working on that. It's a little tricky."

She could actually hear his fingers drumming. "*Tricky*. Yeah, I can see where it would be." He took a deep breath, letting it out in a sigh. "Just be careful, and for God's sake, don't miss your flight. We need both of you in Daytona."

"I do know that."

"I know. I'm sorry. I'm just tired."

"Did you get any sleep at all last night?"

"Sleep? What is this 'sleep' you speak of?" He was joking, but the weariness in his voice wasn't funny.

"Raphael—"

He chuckled tiredly. "You sound just like Cat when you say my name like that. I'll tell you what I told her. I'll sleep when I hear that you and Rick have landed safely in Daytona. Until then, I'm on duty. And check back in thirty minutes from now. Lucas is going to want a status report."

"Right. I'll do that—Raphael." She blurted out his name before he could hang up.

"What?"

"I'm sorry. I didn't mean to drag you into the middle of this."

"It's all right. I know that none of this is your fault."

RICK FOUGHT THE urge to throttle her. At the moment he almost agreed with Antoine. She was insane. Once again, there had been no "plan" to what she'd done. She couldn't possibly have planned to draw the attention of the enemy, the local police—in fact, everyone in the entire fucking airport. Yes, it had worked. They'd gotten away, but that was more by luck than design. Relying on luck would get them both killed.

She was a loaded gun, always half-cocked, ready to use the weather, the police, anything handy. He couldn't *work* like that. How in the hell had she managed to stay alive all these years? He felt as if he was partnered with Riggs from the *Lethal Weapon* movies. He'd enjoyed the films immensely, even as he thought them ridiculously unrealistic. But he had never, ever, sympathized more with the Danny Glover role than he did right now.

He looked away from her, forcing himself to calm down. His rage and frustration weren't just his. There were too many panicked people around him, and he was amplifying those emotions and was starting to bleed them out onto the other travelers. He could hear arguments breaking out as people approached, intensifying as they drew near, only to fizzle out when the group was a few feet past him. Worse, people were watching him, their eyes nervously flicking away as soon as they thought he might notice. It was too close to the moon for this sort of aggravation. The anger and fear were bringing out the beast in him, and the humans were beginning to act like prey. It was a recipe for absolute disaster if he didn't get control of himself right now. Just another reason why he hated crowds.

"Have you caught his scent?" She moved until she stood just in front of him. He loved her, but at this precise moment he didn't like her much.

He blew out a slow breath and struggled not to yell. "A hint. What did Raphael say?"

"Mostly he swore." She admitted. "But when he finished that he said he'd let Lucas know so they can do the interrogation. I'm supposed to check back in a half hour so he knows there haven't been any more disasters."

"Wouldn't that be lovely?"

"Ah. You're pissed."

"Me? Why would I be pissed? It was a logical, well-planned, perfectly executed—" His voice sounded just like he planned, sarcasm like a poisoned whip to lash out at her.

She didn't back down. If anything, his tone just set her off worse. A rolling yowl was coiled around her harsh whisper. "It worked, didn't it? Or is that what's bothering you? You weren't making the decisions. *You* weren't in control, and yet somehow it still worked. All these years away, and I'm still miraculously alive through stupid, thoughtless plans." Her hands were on her hips, that ridiculous purse swinging from her wrist as she glared at him, green eyes blazing.

Distantly he was aware that the other travelers were watching. Some smiled, others were moving to give them a wide berth.

"We don't have time for this now." Rick closed his eyes and growled.

"No. We don't. But let me tell you one thing Mr. *Atwood*." She spit out his new name like a curse and with the practiced ease of a Wolven pro. "I have been taking care of myself for a very long time without your help. Believe me when I tell you I can manage *just fine*. So don't you worry about me one little bit. You just take care of your end."

She stalked off, her suitcase squeaking as it rolled along the floor at a fast clip. A big part of him was tempted to let her go, but no. He'd regret it, and sooner rather than later. He just wished he could figure out why love and anger were so closely married in their relationship. But, they were scheduled on the same flight in a couple of hours so he'd better go after her.

Too, if anything happened to her—if the snakes got to her because he wasn't there—he'd never forgive himself. He'd never forgive himself for losing her a second time, annoying as she might be right now. So he adjusted the strap on his duffel, moved it up on his shoulder and started following at a distance.

She backtracked until she wasn't more than thirty or forty feet from the shoeshine stand. The crowd seemed to have dispersed for the most part, but the area from the restroom to the shop just past the stand had been cordoned off. A pair of uniformed security guards were keeping passengers at a distance while the animal control officers struggled with the problem of safely capturing a huge, venomous reptile.

He only allowed himself to be distracted by the spectacle of it for a moment. Turning his attention back to Josette he watched in sudden admiration as she stopped, pretended annoyance that the bathrooms were cordoned off, and turned away.

Rick moved to where she had been. Yes, there it was, the scent of a male snake, musty, but without the acrid overtones of most of the venomous breeds. That didn't mean he wouldn't be dangerous. In fact, he might be more so, particularly now that they had the upper hand.

With his long legs, it didn't take long for Rick to catch up with her. "*Do* you have a plan?" He felt like biting his tongue the minute the words slipped out of his mouth. The question hadn't been a bad one, but he hadn't meant to sound so sarcastic.

"Yes, but it requires your cooperation." The look she gave him said plainly that she wasn't sure he'd give it. She continued walking, and kept her voice pitched softly enough that no one could easily overhear. "The last group of snakes I ran into had done their homework. They knew I could hold them motionless. In fact, they were counting on it. They'd done something, probably some ritual magic, that was like Raphael's death touch. When I used my personal magic to hold them it triggered the trap and started draining me." She sighed, then shook her head.

"I'm thinking it's an amulet of some sort; probably something small enough to swallow, so that it stays with them in either form."

"That would make sense. I just wish I knew more about the kind of magic we're up against."

"I'm surprised you didn't run across it having worked with Charles for so long."

"This isn't his kind of thing." Rick knew he sounded defensive. He couldn't help it.

"No. I suppose it isn't." She reached out to touch his arm. "I meant no insult. I was just surprised, that's all."

"Fine." Rick let go of his irritation, forced it into a tight ball and threw it out into the crowd. It was something he learned while he was in Wolven, and it served him well here. He might start one fight with one group of people, but it wasn't such a broad brush that it would affect everyone in the concourse. "None taken. So what is the plan?"

"Can you use your empathy to literally scare someone stiff, so that they're caught like a deer in the headlights?"

"Um . . . probably. But won't that trigger the trap?"

"It shouldn't. The trap is for power imposed from the outside. The emotions will be immobilizing our victim from the inside."

"Okay, I hold him still. Then what?"

"I touch him, and see if I can trigger a real-time vision." Rick felt his eyebrows rise to disappear beneath his bangs.

"Don't look at me like that. I have a lot more control than I used to."

Rick didn't mention the vision in the plane, or the hotel or car. She hadn't seemed to have much control over those. But the look on his face must have been eloquent, because he could feel her annoyance rising.

Raising his hands in a placating gesture, he held off the impending tirade. "Fine, you trigger a vision if you can. If you can't?"

"I fake it." She smiled so sweetly it was positively poisonous.

"Excuse me?"

"Their big fear is my abilities as a seer. It's why they want me dead. So I give them a seer and you shake him until we see what falls out." She grinned. "Not literally, of course. There are too many surveillance cameras."

"You're actually looking forward to this." The accusation popped out of his mouth and he could hear the surprise in his voice.

"Why yes, I am." Her smile faded, her eyes going very dark until she looked, and smelled, dangerous. "I am getting very, *very* tired of these people. They've tried to kill me. They destroyed my house, my car, my *life*. They've killed Ellen and her mother, and God knows how many others. I'm going to find out *why*. And then they are going to go away."

Chapter Twenty-two

THEY FOLLOWED THE scent through the main intersection, to a glossy black door with a silver handle. The door had been forced open, the simple lock in the knob no match for Sazi strength. Josette pushed the door open with Rick at her heels and found herself in a narrow service hallway with plain white walls that stretched up to the high ceiling, the expanse of painted drywall broken periodically by black doors similar to the one she'd just walked through. Each door had been painted with a gray stenciled code number.

This area of the building was for employees only and apparently didn't get much use. The scent of humans was here, but faint. The scent of snake was not. He was here. Behind one of those doors. And he was afraid.

She shoved her suitcase against the far wall. It would only get in her way. Her purse she kept with her. It was smaller, and had their tickets and her identification. On the off-chance someone did come down the hallway, she didn't want to lose it.

Rick set his duffel on the floor next to her suitcase. Moving in front of her, he took the lead. Slowly, silently, they followed the trail to one of the doors.

With a hand signal, he directed her to stand against the wall on one side of the door while he took the other. Turning the knob, he yanked the door open.

Josette felt more than saw the movement as the snake's head dropped down into the doorway. She heard Rick's gasp of pain as its fangs sank into his left arm and muscular scaled coils started to wrap around his chest. Using his free right hand he grabbed the snake behind the head and began to squeeze, blood and meat spurting as his fingers dug through the scaly flesh.

She felt the electric heat of magic as Rick sent his power into the reptile. Its red eyes widened, the slit pupil dilating until there was only a faint ring of color showing. She could hear his heartbeat racing, smell ammonia panic as the creature froze in place, too terrified to move.

Josette followed Rick as he walked awkwardly through the doorway, his body overbalanced and top heavy from the weight of the constrictor's body. She pulled the door closed behind them.

The room they were in was large, but not spacious. Most of the area was occupied by a maze of pipes of various sizes that snaked around one another like a nest of vipers. Information was painted on the sides of the larger pipes, or posted on the metal brackets that connected them to each other and the supporting walls. A black metal staircase led up to two levels of catwalks that provided maintenance access to the higher pipes. The room was lit by large electric bulbs protected by metal caging that cast eerie shadows onto the bare concrete floor.

"He's fighting me hard, you'd better do this quick." Rick's voice sounded strangled and breathy.

"Are you all right?"

"Just, *do* it."

She reached out to lay her right hand on the body of the snake. Its tan and brown mottled scales were cool and smooth beneath her skin. Her hand slid over the muscled body as easily as her mind slid into the vision.

She was rushing down a hallway in the body of a young man, walking fast, not quite running. Anger bubbled through her veins. They had failed. She was not dead, the book of knowledge had not been recovered. The priests needed all three volumes— The Book of Faith, The Book of Power, and The Book of Knowledge, to bring on the days of renewal and the new era. Without the books, all of the sacrifices in the world would not allow her to be born and rise to the Goddess she was meant to be.

Word of the failure had been sent in the form of a messenger from Paolo Rivera, the secular jefe of their people. The messenger had been snide, the words from his mouth might be suitably humble in addressing the high priests, his tone had certainly not been. It reflected the attitude of the jefe him-

self. He believed that the priests had grown soft over the centuries of her hibernation, but it was his arrogance that was the real threat.

Paolo had always underestimated the Sazi and their allies, believing them to be fools addicted to luxury and soft living—never noticing that he himself lived in just as much luxury as any. How many of his people had the little cat killed over the years? And the Prince who led the Sazi snakes— Paolo considered him a child and a weakling. He would not risk including him in their plans. But Ahmad had killed Sargon. And while Sargon may have been a madman, killing him was not the act of a weakling.

The snake writhed beneath her hand, and magic poured from his body in an electric wave that blistered the skin of her hand where she touched him, bringing her abruptly back to her body.

Rick's eyes narrowed, blazing gold with his magic and anger. He began unwrapping the snake from his torso as if uncoiling a rope, blood pouring in wet rivulets down the snake's body from the wounds Rick's fingers were digging in its neck.

The reptile gave a massive shudder, then his body stilled once more.

She was in a private library. Books of all shapes and sizes lined every wall. Many were bound in leather with gold foil. Others had more esoteric coverings. A set of modern paperbacks were stacked crookedly on the desktop. She recognized the cover and titles. These were the Sazi training manuals that had been printed in the guise of fantasy novels.

But it was not one of these that was open on the desk. No, this was a far older volume, its parchment pages were yellowed and brittle with age. The ink with which it had been written had discolored until it was no longer a rich purple, but more of a reddish brown. Still, the words were legible enough, and they described just the ceremony they would need to create amulets that would counter the little cat's abilities. Always assuming, of course, that the translation was correct. It was not a certainty. Only half of the spells they had tried using this particular copy had been effective.

He hissed in irritation. Sargon had insisted on keeping the book in his personal possession. He had been right not to trust Paolo. But his death had thrown everything into disarray. The book was missing—missing. So that now they only had the corrupted translation to work from.

"No!" A voice intruded on the vision. It was a boy's voice. It belonged to the snake in Rick's hands. The vision wavered, becoming transparent as his magic fought hers.

Their powers wrestled. The vision of the library wavered and was gone, replaced by shattered images: temples built on temples like Russian nesting dolls. Visions of priests and rulers with different faces, different garb, but serving one purpose throughout the long generations. Together they served and protected the great creature gestating below ground. She, the goddess who would be born, and with her birth would renew the fortunes of their people. They were almost ready. The temple built, the sacrifices gathered—

A purely mental scream of rage and terror shredded the vision. The connection between her and the boy broke

"Shit!" Rick collapsed to his knees. Josette couldn't seem to move. A white-hot needle of pain lanced through her left eye drawing tears that poured unheeded down her cheeks. The room around her was a complete blur. Only Rick seemed to be in focus.

He stayed on the floor for long moments. He was deathly pale, his breathing was as ragged as if he'd run a marathon. Circles of blood darkened the sleeve of his shirt where the snake had bitten him.

"Are you all right?" It seemed to take all of his effort to speak.

"Are you?"

"He gave me one hell of a squeeze that last time. But it'll heal. You?"

"My head feels like it's going to explode." She took a few unsteady steps over to the staircase. Sinking gratefully onto one of the lower rungs she sat with her head between her knees. If she was lucky, in a few minutes her body would heal whatever damage had been inflicted. If not, well, she didn't want to think about that.

The phone in her purse rang. The sound was so loud that she whimpered in pain. Rick crawled across the floor until he was at the foot of the stairs. Turning, he sat with his back propped against the metal.

Josette fumbled with the clasp of her purse, but finally managed to withdraw the phone. She flipped it open and hit the button to answer.

"Hello."

"Who am I speaking to?" Raphael's voice was heavy with suspicion.

"This is Cerise."

"Prove it."

"Oh for God's sake Raphael! Give me a fucking break." She gasped in pain. Shouting made the headache excruciating. "Fine, I have a twin sister who is mated to you. Your daughter with her is getting married this summer to a man neither one of you likes very much. You will be giving the bride away, but Charles is going to get the first dance. I helped come up with the compromise because you have both been fathers to the girl."

"Good enough. Why the hell didn't you check in? What's gone wrong now? Do you need help or backup?"

Rick reached over to take the phone from her hand. "We caught the other snake. Josette used her gift to get some information from him. It got a little messy, but we'll heal."

"Are you going to be make your flight? It leaves in ten minutes."

"Yeah, but somebody will have to clean up the mess—unless you want to leave it to the humans?"

"I'll make the arrangements. Just catch the damned flight." He hung up without saying another word. Rick snapped the phone shut and dropped it into Josette's bag.

Josette rose, groaning, to her feet. She extended her arm down in an offer to help Rick up as well.

They strapped Rick's duffel onto Josette's suitcase using the strap that had been built into the bag's handle. Then they draped the garment bag on top. With the wheeled bag acting almost as a walker Rick and Josette made their way as fast as they could manage through the concourse to their gate as the last of the passengers were lining up to board.

"Are you all right sir?" The pretty blond attendant who took his ticket looked him over carefully, her blue eyes lingering on the fresh, dark red stain on his sleeve.

"I'm a bit tired is all. It's been a long day." He very deliberately let go of the bag to shove the sleeves of his shirt up enough to reveal his forearms. Seeing that there were no marks or injuries, she relented, giving him back his ticket with only a slightly strained smile.

He followed Josette through the square tube and around the accordioned corner. When they reached the plane itself he detached his duffel from her suitcase and collapsed the handle so that he could carry both bags into the plane.

It took a few minutes to board. They had to wait as passengers crammed luggage into the overhead compartments. He desperately wanted to get to his seat. His ribs were healing, as were the organs that had been damaged in the scrap with the snake, but he still hurt, and the healing was taking all of his energy.

The smell of panic assaulted his nostrils as he passed a woman seated near the center of the plane. Her eyes were closed, her mouth moving silently as she fingered the beads of a rosary. He expected his beast to rise to the bait, but apparently he was too injured to react. He supposed that every cloud had a silver lining. At least he wouldn't be having to work not to change and hunt while in flight. Wouldn't that just be a nightmare?

Still, the woman's fear reminded him forcibly of Josette's reaction earlier. Reaching out a hand, he touched her shoulder so that she turned to face him. "Are you going to be all right?"

She gave him a weary smile. "So far so good." One corner of her mouth twitched slightly, and she gave him a wry look. "I think I'm too damned tired to be really afraid at the moment." His eyes sought her. "Here's hoping that lasts until we land."

"I hope so." He stopped as she started to scoot into her assigned seat. Reaching up he started to load their bags in the overhead compartment. It hurt. A lot. Apparently the snake had managed to screw up the alignment of his spine when he'd broken the ribs. Rick grimaced in pain, but managed to get the luggage stowed safely away. He settled gratefully into his seat before continuing. "I'm afraid I'm not going to be much use to you on this flight." When he twisted at the waist to fasten his seatbelt pain shot through his body in a way that made his breath catch in his throat.

Josette didn't say a word. Instead, she reached over to lay her hand on his bare forearm. The touch was gentle, tentative and kind. But when he raised his head to meet her eyes he felt a surge of power that pushed him back into the seat. Electric heat made every hair on his body stand on end. He locked his jaw so as not to cry out.

He saw the stewardess moving in the front of the plane, heard the pre-flight safety instructions were playing, but he couldn't move, couldn't take his eyes from Josette's face. Her eyes glowed green and gold, and looking into their depths he felt the pain melt from his body like ice cream in a sunbeam. He almost expected to feel himself dripping onto the worn carpet.

The magic faded, and her eyes were just eyes once again. The scents of baking bread and homemade cookies filled him with the warmth of a different magic altogether. He took a deep gasping breath and felt the air fill his lungs without the stabbing pain of broken ribs. He leaned down to brush her lips with his in the tenderest of possible kisses, noting as he did that he could bend and turn without the shooting pain that had plagued him moments before. "I thought you weren't a healer." He breathed the words across her mouth.

"I'm not," she whispered back, "which is why it hurt. All I could do was push my power into you and let your body do the work. I didn't take much, which is why you still probably hurt a little. I have to save most of my strength."

He kissed her again, nibbling a little at her lips. "Have I told you today how much I love you?"

"Maybe, but feel free to show me."

"Right here?" He deliberately raised one eyebrow as if shocked. "In front of everybody?"

She punched him in the arm where the snake had bit him. It didn't even hurt . . . much.

THEY'D BEEN IN the air for an hour and twenty minutes. It was as smooth a flight as any pilot could hope for. No doubt if she looked out the window she'd probably see fluffy white clouds as the plane approached the vast blue-green expanse of water that was the Atlantic Ocean. She didn't look.

Rick was asleep. With his eyes closed and his hair tousled like it was he looked very young, and more innocent than he'd been in two hundred years. A soft smile touched her lips. Stubborn fool. That snake had damned near killed him, but he hadn't complained, had even insisted on putting the luggage into the overhead bins. Of all the idiotic—"I'll heal," he'd said. Yes, he probably would've, but after days, even weeks of pain.

Not that she was in much better shape. This late in the afternoon on the day of the full moon she should be restless and irritable, not listless and exhausted. They were scheduled to land in just a few minutes. The pilot had instructed the passengers to raise their seats into the upright position. Three hours remained until sunset and what was probably going to be one of the most elaborate and complex bits of ritual magic she'd ever worked in her life. She couldn't even work up any adrenaline over flying.

She closed her eyes, trying to ignore the sinking sensation as the plane began its descent. On the theory that it could only help if she thought about something, anything, else she tried to recall the details of the visions she'd dragged from the mind of the snake.

He'd said that they needed all three volumes. Destroying one might stop them from raising this goddess of theirs. Or not. And how much knowledge would be lost in the process? What if they destroyed the very information they needed to protect themselves. Ritual magic was different from natural magic. And at the moment the Sazi didn't have a single practitioner familiar with ritual powers and limitations, save her—and she'd never read all of the books. Just the ones she possessed. God only knew what might be in the other two.

That was going to have to change. If nobody else was willing, she'd take the books they had into the middle of nowhere, where there were less likely to be accidental casualties, and start educating herself. Because so long as their enemies knew they had this weakness they were bound to try to exploit it.

Enemies. Plural. The more she thought about the events of the past few days, the more she believed that they were the actions of two separate groups, with different goals and ambitions. The snakes were working for the return of their goddess. The Movement that Ray had been part of . . . Josette couldn't imagine what humans might be up to. But the humans had played no part in any of her visions of the jungle, nor had she seen them in her contact with the snake's mind. But what about the sacrifice in the desert night, under the tree? Could that have been humans? Were there ritual practitioners who *weren't* Sazi?

Whatever they were planning, it was big. They were well organized and, judging from the bounties on the cards, obscenely well funded. In a world filled with billions of others just like them, they'd be damned near untraceable.

The plane touched down with a soft thump that made her clutch the armrest in a panic. Josette reached over and gave Rick's shoulder a quick shake. "We're here."

He blinked a few times, trying to make the transition from sleep to wakefulness. His nose twitched, and she knew he could scent her fear.

"You should've woken me sooner." He reached over to brush a stray hair back behind her ear. "I would've tried to help."

"It's all right. I was fine." She didn't tell him that it wasn't the flying that had frightened her, but rather the thought of another human purge of the Sazi. It could happen so very easily.

She shuddered at the thought, and Rick unfastened his seatbelt so he could take her in his arms. "When this is over, I'm going to rent us a car and we will *drive* back to Pony to get my bike—provided it's still there. From there we can either go to my place in South Dakota, or wherever it is you want to live. But we are not setting foot into another airport for anything short of the apocalypse for the next decade."

"What an utterly *wonderful* idea."

It took some time to disembark. The flight had been nearly full, their seats at the very back of the plane, and Daytona was the final eastern destination for this plane. While they were waiting for people to wrestle their luggage out of the overhead bins Josette pulled her purse from beneath the seat in front of her and retrieved her cell phone.

The readout said that she was "roaming," but it didn't really matter to her how many minutes she used. With any luck at all, this would be her last call to Raphael for a *very* long time.

He picked up on the first ring. "Ramirez."

"We just landed."

"Good. Lucas and Ahmad are waiting for you in the passenger loading area."

"Lucas?" Josette couldn't keep the surprise from her voice. "I thought he'd be heading to Atlanta to deal with the . . . situation there."

Rick had taken down their bags and was waiting for the aisle to clear in front of them. He pretended he couldn't hear, but she could tell he was listening intently.

"There was no point. It's all over the news. A sniper took out a pair of animal control workers. The snake escaped."

"Oh." Josette wasn't sure what to say. It hadn't even occurred to her that there might have been a *third* snake with a sniper rifle. *That* was liable to haunt her dreams for quite a while.

Rick coughed, getting her attention. The plane was nearly empty now. It was time to go.

"Raphael, again—" Josette hesitated, not knowing

the right words to say. He'd done so much for her, for *them* over the past few days. Thanks just didn't seem adequate.

"You're welcome. It was my pleasure. Now get moving. You're burning daylight."

He said it to make her smile, and it did. "Yes *sir*." She laughed and hung up the phone. Dropping it back into her bag she reflected that Catherine Turner was lucky to have found a man like Raphael. He'd grown into a fine man. But as she followed Rick down the narrow aisle, taking time to admire the movement of his body, even in the baggy trousers he wore she didn't envy the young jaguar. She'd found a man of her own, and as infuriating as Rick could be, she wouldn't trade a minute of the time they'd spent together over the past days, or the time she hoped they'd have in the future.

They stepped out of the airport into the warm afternoon sunshine. The smell of saltwater mingled in the air with the scent of car exhaust. She could hear the cry of sea birds in the distance.

The car was waiting just a few yards down the walkway, just as Raphael had promised. It was a regular four-door rental sedan, rather than a limo. Silver gray, it gleamed in the afternoon sunlight. This close to the doors she could see the plush leather interior, smell the "new car" scent that hadn't yet had the chance to fade. Lucas leaned against the front fender, arms crossed over his chest. His dark curls had more silver in them than she'd remembered, and there were definite lines of exhaustion at the corners of his hazel eyes. He was dressed casually, in a bright turquoise T-shirt over white shorts and boat shoes with no socks. Ahmad, on the other hand, was *not* dressed casually. Despite the heat, he was wearing an elegant dark gray suit expensively tailored to fit his slender frame. The white of his shirt emphasized his dark olive complexion. His eyes were hidden behind mirrored sunglasses. His expression was unreadable. In his hands was an elaborately carved box of fragrant cedar that had been polished until the wood had a reddish gold gleam. He took a step toward Josette, the box extended before him as if it was a gift.

Rick was just suddenly there, standing between them. A rumbling yowl left his lips.

To Ahmad's credit he didn't flinch or back up. The two men stood, eye-to-eye, neither giving so much as a fraction. Power built until the air between them was electric.

"Enough!" Lucas's voice cracked like a whip. "Stand down, agent. Councilman al-Narmer is on *our* side."

"I don't trust him."

Ahmad's mouth curled in a disdainful smirk. "Nor should you. All the world knows my feelings for Josette. But though you may choose not to believe me, I mean her no harm this day and the box I hold is crucial to the success of tonight's endeavor."

"Your *word?*" Rick snarled. He hadn't moved,

despite a direct order by his superior. He would probably be punished harshly for that later. But he had to extract an oath from the snake. He'd dealt with Ahmad often enough while in Charles's employ to know that his words had little value without an oath.

A pause, but then Ahmad said, "You have it."

RICK STEPPED BACK, but reluctantly. Josette knew how much Ahmad's word meant to him. He seldom gave it, but once given, he never went back on it.

She closed the distance between herself and the councilman for the snakes. Taking the box from his hands she asked, "Has the book been retrieved? Is everything ready on this end?"

"Everything but you. I went over the pertinent pages. There are cleansing rituals you'll need to perform. We must hurry."

"Um, we have one quick thing to do before we go." At least, she hoped it would be quick.

The look on the faces of all three men were exquisitely synchronized. The brows rose just before the mouths opened. She raised a hand to stop all of the questions. "If you'll get into the car, I'll explain."

Curiosity filled the air as Ahmad opened the rear door of the car for her with a small bow. She climbed in, followed closely by Rick. Lucas moved to the driver's seat and started the engine. Ahmad claimed the front passenger seat.

She cleared her throat as they drove into the Florida sunshine and she started to explain. But first a note of caution would be advisable. "Unless there are any bugs in this car, you three are about to be the only other Sazi alive, save myself, who know this information." Lucas and Ahmad exchanged glances, and Rick looked at her strangely. She took a deep breath and dropped the bomb. "There is a fourth book of power."

Rick and Lucas didn't do much more than shrug, but Ahmad's eyes widened and he turned against his belt so hard to see her face that he nearly choked himself. "You're *lying!*"

She stared him down calmly. "I'm doing no such thing. This book affects the other three to the extent that it can undo the workings inside. It holds no intrinsic power of its own, but is merely for . . . checks and balances, if you like."

"And where is this fourth book? Have you brought it with you?" Lucas flicked his eyes to meet hers in the rearview mirror.

She fidgeted with a note of chagrin. "Actually, no. It's here in Daytona, bricked up into the mosquito inlet lighthouse, back when it was built. But I might need help getting to it. I didn't really plan back in 1886 for the area to be built up so much now. It's called the Ponce de Leon lighthouse now. I saw in the travel literature on the plane that it's . . . well, it's a protected site, a national historic landmark."

Ahmad shook his head just as Lucas exploded with laughter. Rick put his forehead in his hands as she quipped, "Well, it *is* accessible, after all. And I remember right where I put it."

"If it's not gone," Rick continued.

"Or eaten by the salt air or a dozen types of marine creatures that feed on plants," Ahmad added.

Lucas finally sighed and turned onto the interstate, headed south. "Well, we might as well get it over with. We'll fix any damage later . . . somehow." After that statement, it was a quiet drive. The car hummed with tension and the suppressed magic of too many powerful Sazi in too confined a space. Josette looked up, startled. The weather was *beautiful*. With as many powerful shapeshifters as there were in the area it should be storming.

Ahmad met her eyes in the rearview mirror. Somehow he'd sensed her question without her bothering to voice it. "When we drained the seers, the weather cleared. You will, however, note that there is a very serious-looking cloud bank over the ocean to the east."

She looked to the east and grimaced. He was right. There was a storm brewing and a nasty one at that.

"It appears we may all be getting wet this evening. For I doubt you'll have the energy to do a weather working after what you're going to attempt." Ahmad's voice held none of it's usual dry amusement. Instead, he sounded . . . worried. It was unlike him, to the point that Josette looked up at him with considerable curiosity.

Again, he answered her question before she could voice it. "I have always admired Charles, and I am *very* fond of your new sister-in-law." He sighed and she could see his elegant fingers clench into fists. "I would gladly take her from Antoine. But not like this." He shook his head. "No, not like this." He turned his head to look out the window and she caught a glimpse of his expression in profile. He seemed, for lack of a better word, sad. Considering the antipathy he'd had for Josette and all her family, it was a very odd reaction.

There were convenient signs to the lighthouse, but of course, a rather inconvenient crowd milling about. She hadn't really made plans to arrive this late, nor had she brought any tools to cut through the mortar. Still, she remembered telling the handsome young bricklayer that she would need to come back for it, and he told her he would arrange for it to be accessible. She hadn't watched the final construction, but she knew it was still here. She could almost *feel* it waiting for her.

The four of them paid their admission fee and followed the line walking toward the museum that the lighthouse had become. Rather than follow most of the visitors inside, Josette slowly made her way around the base of the lighthouse, searching. Time seemed to slip away from her and she remembered seeing the building going up, knowing the fine craftsmanship that would keep it safe and sound. And then there was the running and the frantic flight from the assassins that really had been sent by Ahmad. She'd killed them, much as she'd stunned the men at the airport, with a blast of power that had rocked the ground under her. As she approached the outer wall, she gave a small gasp of delight. Could it really be this easy?

"I need everybody to not notice us. Any chance the three of you could work together on this?"

The men looked at one another and shrugged, again, nearly in perfect harmony. She felt a swell of power as a cloud of both illusion and aversion settled over the four of them. Most people would simply avoid this side of the lighthouse, and those who ventured closer would see nothing at all.

There was a crack down the entire lighthouse, just about an inch in width that seemed to permeate all the way through the brick. She could feel the power of the book just behind the brick. She slipped her fingers inside the crack. Although it had been covered over with caulking to keep out the weather, the rubbery mass was no match for her strength. There was a small space, just behind the brick, and she could feel the oilskin wrap she'd placed around the book so many years ago. She only had to pull out one brick to ease it from the hiding place, and the mortar had stayed with the brick so that when she replaced it, it fit snugly and looked whole again.

If only the rest of the trip had been this easy!

Lucas was still shaking his head in disbelief as they got in the car. "A century in an open crack in a public building, and it's still there. You live a charmed life, Aspen."

A bitter chuckle rose from her. "Not charmed, Lucas. Hardly charmed." Still, she couldn't help but smile. "Let's get out of here. We've got work to do."

The four of them returned to the car. Lucas drove with Ahmad riding in the passenger seat. Rick sat in the rear next to Josette. Only when they were on their way did Josette turn her attention to the artifacts in her possession. She knew the book, so she set it aside, and began examining the box Ahmad had provided.

It wasn't much larger than a shoebox, but it was quite heavy. The lid was a separate piece, made to fit so snugly on the base that there was barely a line to show where one ended and the other began. She ran her finger lightly over the exquisitely carved pattern of snakes, animals, lizards, and birds. Each creature was depicted in stylized detail.

"It's very beautiful." At her touch the wood warmed, and she felt power waking, stirring deep within it.

"It was my mother's dowry." Ahmad's voice and scent were empty of any emotion. "I wonder, sometimes, if that box was the only reason why my father took her as his wife. It seemed appropriate to relieve my father of it after he was killed."

There was a grim satisfaction in his voice, that she

didn't know how to answer. Apparently none of the others did either.

In silence, she turned her focus to the book. With deliberate movements she folded back the oilskin. There was power in this book, too, but it was different, a cool light breeze that tickled the hairs on her neck.

The car slowed to a stop at an elaborate metal gate set in a tall brick wall. Lucas pressed a button and the driver's side window lowered with a soft hum. With rapid strokes he tapped in a series of numbers. Slowly, ponderously, the gate rolled out of the way.

They drove up a curving brick drive that was lined with palm trees, past an elaborate fountain where naked cherubs splashed and frolicked, the water splashing musically over their stone bodies into a large reflecting pool. Fat koi swam slowly amid the lilies in that pool. Josette could smell them from her seat in the car, and her mouth began to water. Her eyes sought them out beneath the shimmering reflections on the water. She'd been denied them at the house in Nelson, but now—

"No eating." Ahmad's droll voice brought her back to the present. "It's part of the purification process."

"Ah well." Josette gave an exaggerated sigh. "I suppose they'll still be there in the morning."

"They will unless Rick eats them all first. I can smell that he wants to." Lucas pulled the car to a stop beneath a covered walkway that led from the drive to the house. Blooming vines draped from the rafters, and fat insects buzzed among the fragrant blossoms.

The house itself was longer than it was tall and made of gleaming white stucco, with a red tiled roof and large arched windows that could be left open to summer breezes. Josette could smell the chlorine of a pool, and the sound of the ocean was loud enough that she would guess there was beach access as well.

"I promise to save you at least one." Rick raised his hand in a Boy-Scout salute.

"Two at least. I'm already hungry and it's going to be a long night." She gave him an exaggeratedly plaintive look, which made him snort with laughter.

"We'll see."

The front door of the house swung open and Amber burst forward. She came to the car at a run, her hug nearly sweeping Josette off her feet before there was time to think or prepare.

"*Mon Dieu!* Thank God you're finally here." Amber stepped back, her hands still holding on to her sister's arms. She looked Josette up and down. "You are well? You look tired."

"It was a difficult trip."

"So I gathered." She let go and turned to lead them into the house.

"How are they?" Josette asked.

"They are stable at the moment." She turned, and their gazes locked. From just the look she knew that things had been very bad indeed.

"Your rooms are in back. They have French doors. We picked this place because the spell requires a covered stone courtyard." Amber ignored the men and scurried up the sidewalk ahead of her sister. It was terrible manners and very unlike her. But no one seemed to mind. They could all smell the naked fear she was trying to hide beneath her bustling manner. "There's a private bath. I took the liberty of setting it up for the cleansing ritual when I heard that your plane landed safely. It might be a little cool by now. We expected you sooner." She held open the front door. Josette stepped into an open living area with a vaulted ceiling that stretched upward. The floor was polished teak. The furnishings had obviously come with the house and been chosen by a decorator. Everything was modern, and covered in either white- or cream-colored fabric. The only colors were in the occasional throw pillow and the huge abstract painting that hung above the massive fireplace.

Still, the ocean view from the rear windows was spectacular. From here Josette could see the storm moving slowly over the water, heading this way.

"This way." Amber hustled her sister down a long hallway and through a door of dark stained teak.

It was a beautiful suite, but Josette wasn't given much time to look at it. Her sister shut the door to the hall behind her with a brisk slam and ordered. "Strip. We don't have much time. I didn't want to say anything in front of Lucas, but Nana is fading fast and so is Charles." When Josette didn't appear to be moving quickly enough to suit her Amber hissed in irritation, grabbed the book and box from her hands and tossed them on the bed.

"I said *strip,* damn you," Amber shouted, her voice cracking with strain. She started to tug at the button on her slacks.

Josette didn't argue. She kicked off her thongs, grabbed the bottom of her sweatshirt and pulled it over her head, letting it drop to the floor. It was the work of seconds to peel off her pants and underwear and follow the other woman into an elegant bathroom of white marble with gold veining and gold-plated fixtures.

White pillar candles had been scattered throughout the room. The tub had been filled with what smelled suspiciously like *goat's* milk. How they had managed to get an entire sunken tub's worth on short notice would be worth asking about . . . after the ceremony.

Moving with frantic haste, Amber moved over to the counter where there was a golden bowl filled with incense. She lit the powder before grabbing an ancient book from the counter and shoving it into Josette's hands. "I'll light the candles. The page with the cleansing spell is marked with a red ribbon." Josette took a few seconds to breathe deeply and steady her nerves before opening to the indicated page. Amber, meanwhile, was flitting from candle to candle with a press-button lighter. The room began to take on a warm glow, the white marble reflecting the golden candle-light, the veining in the marble sparkling.

The words were in an ancient tongue. Josette had done her best to master it all those years ago when Grandmère Helene had given the book to her, but it was always difficult for her to force her lips to form the harsh syllables. Still each word seemed to echo in the air of the bathroom, falling into the silence like a drop of water into a pool. With each word, each phrase, the power built, until the air hummed with energy. Josette took the lighter from her sister's trembling hand. Setting the book aside, she padded barefoot to stand in front of the second book. It was the work of a moment to light the incense. The smoke blew through the room on a sudden breeze that was wet with the promise of rain and the smell of salt. The second book opened of its own accord, to the proper page, she presumed.

There was a rumble of thunder in the distance, and the room outside the door had grown shadowed. Josette was not surprised. The power she was raising was more than the air could hold. Of course it would affect the weather. How could it not?

She set the book on the bed next to the other. She turned to give her sister a comforting smile when Amber jumped at the strength of the thunder. She would have liked to say something, but didn't dare lest it disrupt her control of the spell.

Three short steps took her to the edge of the sunken

tub. Lightning crashed overhead as she walked downward, the milk lapping at her feet, then calves. But it was as she lowered her head and body below the surface that the storm broke, and the rain began hammering at the windows in blinding sheets, the wind wailing like a banshee, stripping limbs and leaves from the trees.

Josette rose from the tub. Milk poured in rivulets down her body. She brushed her sodden hair from her eyes stepping carefully out onto a pure white bath mat. Amber had left towels within reach. Both were new, and the color of new fallen snow.

Drying herself quickly, she went to the bed. It was awkward carrying both books, the box, and a lighted candle, but she managed.

The door to the courtyard was open. Outside, the sky was near black, the roiling clouds revealed their majesty by flickering bolts of lightning. A cold wind, laden with salt, blew harsh against Josette's still-damp body. The candle flickered, but continued to burn.

They were waiting outside. In the shadowed dark she could make out the huddled shapes of the injured seers and the others who had gathered to aid them. Josette passed through the open door. She walked to the center of the courtyard. Setting down her burdens, she knelt and tilted the candle so that a few drops of hot wax fell onto the hard gray stone before sticking the candle into the hardening wax.

Still on her knees, she laid out the things she would

need for the ceremony: red, yellow, and blue powders, each in a leather bag dyed that color, and finally, wrapped in a cloth of black silk, a hand-carved dagger made from one solid piece of polished obsidian.

Carefully, she opened the first book again and turned to the correct page. Slowly, she began a chant in a long-dead language. Taking the yellow pouch in her hand she rose to her feet in one smooth movement. Her voice never faltered as she began walking a large circle with the candle at its focus, all the while letting the yellow powder trickle slowly from its bag. She stopped, just short of completing the last inch of the circle. At her curt nod the others moved forward.

Suddenly, she could feel Rick's presence, above all the others . . . but she didn't know why. Still, she didn't have time to analyze it. There was little enough time to finish before the moon crested.

Nana, unconscious, was carried to the circle by Lucas. He laid her gently in her place, standing behind and above her, grimly holding the candle she was too weak to grasp.

Tatiana supported the Duchess; her arm around the old woman's waist seemed to be the only thing holding her upright. But when she reached the circle she stood on her own, swaying, but determined—her candle grasped tight in age-spotted hands.

Antoine came next, under his own power, but with Tahira at his side. She kissed him gently before stepping back. The look she gave Josette held a desperation that wrenched at her heart.

Still chanting, Josette walked an equilateral triangle, each of the three points touching the circle, dusting the circle with fine red powder. The dusts combined, pulling themselves magically together to become a single orange line that grew in size until it circled the room.

Rick led the Ruhsal of the Hyalet Kabile to her spot. Amber half-carried Charles to the last remaining opening.

Each seer who could held a candle. For those who could not, one was placed on the stones in front of them, within the line of the circle. When, at last, everyone had taken their places Josette let the last of the powder trickle through her hands.

The circle closed with an audible pop. The sheets of rain continued to fall, but they hit the invisible barrier of power and bounced off. Outside the circle, the storm raged. Inside, there was only silence except for the steady hum of magic.

She padded softly to the center of the circle. The chant changed now, as she moved to the second book. Squatting down, she gathered up the blue bag and walked a square, trailing blue dust between the spots on the circle where four of the injured stood.

Power sprang up through the shape, the darkness of the storm driven back by flickering flames of every conceivable color: the blues of the summer sky and of the deepest midnight without moon or stars; the reds and browns of mother earth, the flickering colors of golden flame; greens of every shade ever imagined, all this and more, enough to blind the eye and dazzle the mind. Josette closed her eyes, forcing her mind to focus. Taking a cleansing breath of incense-laden air she walked to the center and retrieved the red bag. Chanting the new words she walked the second triangle, the tip of this one breaking through the base of the first, forming a six-pointed star. Each seer stood at one point, leaving the sixth empty. This spot was reserved for the essence of the person who had blocked their gifts. The ceremony would pull on his or her power, then tighten like a noose until the spell broke and the identity of the caster was revealed.

As the second triangle closed the candles in front of each of seer flared to blazing life, their light reflecting off of solid walls of shimmering power.

She was almost done now, and it was a good thing. Because her body was starting to weaken. Even as a shadowy form began to take shape on the final point of the star, Josette felt her opponent fighting with every ounce of her strength.

Exhaustion made her tongue thick, and she struggled with the complicated cadence of the chant. She had to reach the center of the circle of power to move to the next stage of the spell and complete the working, but each step was harder than the last. Her body trembled with exhaustion; it was an effort of will to simply raise her foot from the ground. Two more steps were all that stood between her and her goal, but she could not force her aching body forward. Fear lanced through her then, sharp and immediate. What if she wasn't strong enough? What if she failed? She stumbled, falling to her knees with bruising force. She closed her eyes, searching for the strength to keep moving and found Rick. He dropped his shields, silently offering her his courage, his strength, just as he'd done on the airplane. She pulled the power of his emotions inside her, used his encouragement as a crutch to stagger to her feet with the dagger in her hand. In one swift stroke she cut a deep line along her forearm, watching as the blood welled upward, looking almost black against the white of her skin in the oddly shifting light. The pain was intense, and her breath escaped through her teeth in a soft hiss.

Blood ran freely down Josette's arm, and she knew that this cut would heal human slow. The magic of the knife would see to that. Blood trailed across the stones as she moved clockwise. Beginning with Charles she walked the circle, smudging each forehead with her blood. In Nana's place she smudged both Lucas and the woman he protected.

With each step, each smudge of blood, the colors flared and the air within the circle seemed to thicken, until she moved against an unseen wind and her lungs struggled to draw breath.

Stars danced before her vision as she forced her way back to the center. Still Rick fed her power, but he was now on his knees, his shining eyes growing weaker. She lowered herself clumsily to the ground, kneeling in front of the book. By the light of the candle fastened to the stones she read, forcing each word outward to control the hostile magic she'd raised and contained. As the last word passed her lips she felt her power fly outward. It hit the wall of magic with a sound like the ringing of a massive bell.

Emotions poured over her in a scalding wave as images flashed before her eyes, turning and shifting like colored shards of broken glass thrown upward into a white light bright enough to burn her eyes: A girl of eight or so with dark hair and eyes, fighting not to cry as the other children shoved and taunted her viciously in the schoolyard, but being oh so careful not to draw blood.

The same girl, a teenager now, screaming and struggling as the men raping her laughed. A red-tailed hawk, diving to attack her where she lay tied to the ground with silver chains as the men cheered and jeered.

A stylized pawprint the color of blood on a black background and a deck of cards that spoke of their commitment.

Image after image, spinning and flickering, in and out of focus until Josette felt she would go mad. As if from a distance, she heard a woman's scream of rage that turned into the eerie shriek of a bird of prey. She slapped the caster with all her strength, tried to keep her grounded and in this place of long ago, a place before dreams.

"No!" screamed the woman. "The Sazi must not learn of this. They must not know our true intent ... that we will wash the earth of the shapeshifter race ... that we will cure them all!"

But the power would not be stopped. It ate away at the caster and through her, the woman who bound her, until it was reduced to a grayish powder that fluttered to the stones to join the other colors.

Chapter Twenty-three

SHE WOKE IN a room with no light. She could hear Rick's breathing, sense him sitting on the chair beside her bed. His fear was a living thing. She drew a deep breath to speak, wondering at the feel of air moving freely into her lungs. It felt wondrous to actually have enough air. How could she ever have taken breathing for granted?

"You're awake," he whispered the words.

"Where am I? *When* am I? Did it work? Or has it even happened yet? And why does the bed smell like Raven?" Josette's voice was a rough croak. Her throat was so dry that it hurt to speak.

"One question at a time." He chided her softly. "It's been exactly a week since the ceremony. Yes, it worked. Everyone else has been up and about for days. According to that book of yours, *if* you woke up at all you were going to be having light sensitivity and ultra-sensitive hearing for the first twenty-four hours, so Amber set you up an interior room and soundproofed the walls." His hand sought hers on the bed, giving it a gentle squeeze.

"The bed smells like Raven because I sent for him. It was the only thing I could think of. We were losing you."

"*You* sent for him?"

"He's your mate, Josette. You needed him. I'd have done anything—" His voice failed him, and it was a few minutes before he could continue. "I *did* do everything in my power for you. But it wasn't enough."

She smiled at him. "Actually, it *was* enough. It was your strength that allowed me to finish. Not Raven's. You gave me courage, and unity, and . . . love. I couldn't have done it without you."

He chose not to acknowledge it. Instead, he stood there, nearly trembling with closed eyes. "You scared the hell out of us all, Josette. Everyone's been on pins and needles, snarling and snapping at one another, praying for you to wake up." He paused. "I'd say I was the worst, but I'm not sure it's the truth. Antoine has been taking his nerves out on the furniture after Raven had to break up a fight between us. I hesitate to guess how much he owes the owners of this villa right now." Relief and amusement mingled in his voice.

"Antoine?" She couldn't keep the disbelief from her voice. Her relationship with her brother had been strained for his entire life. She'd heard, and believed, that he'd pushed to have her put down as being mad. Was it already time for his attitude to begin to change?

"He's ready to work things out, Josette. He wants to talk to you about it, as soon as you're strong enough. But first Lucas would like to debrief you. Are you up to it? If not, I'll tell him no and if he insists, I'll kick his ass out like I tried to earlier."

A small smile came to her face. That *would* be a

fight worth seeing. But no, she couldn't let him do it. The things she'd seen were too important, more important than any one person. She reached over to squeeze Rick's hand, letting him know how much she appreciated the offer. "Send him in."

He rose and walked to the door. "Close your eyes."

She did as she was told. She heard him walk to the door; winced at the squeak of the hinges as it opened. She could clearly hear Amber's voice in the hall. "You have ten minutes Lucas. No more."

He didn't argue, just closed the door and padded quietly over to the bed.

"Are you awake?"

"Yes." She opened her eyes.

"I *apparently* have ten minutes. Talk fast. What are we dealing with? Do you have any clue who's behind it?"

Josette sighed. Too much had happened for her to possibly tell him everything. So much simpler to just show him. Reaching over, she touched his hand. She opened her mind to him, allowed the night to replay for him. Every vision; every event flowed to him in as much detail as she remembered, but in fast forward, so that when there was time he could review it in his own mind, as if he'd lived it himself. When she got to the end, she revealed as much as she could of the terrain, since the only people she'd seen had died. But it was the words that were important. The place could be anywhere and could move tomorrow.

Even that small use of power exhausted her. She

sagged against the mattress, her eyelids dropping closed.

Lucas rose to his feet. "Thank you. Now rest. You've earned it."

She wanted to answer, she really did, but it was just too much effort.

She didn't know how long she slept, but when she woke again, Rick was back in the chair by her bed. There was light in the room, though the dimmer had been set to its lowest level. His hand brushed her cheek as he heard her stir.

"You're awake."

"How long was I out this time?"

He smiled softly. "Only a few hours. Amber says you're doing better, that you should be able to eat something."

Josette's stomach growled audibly at the mere mention of food. It made Rick laugh, and while the sharp burst of sound hurt her ears she was happy to hear it and even happier to feel his emotions lightening to hope, love, and joy.

"If you'd like I can fetch you one of those fat koi you were admiring in the fountain. I saved you *three*." He winked and let out a small purr that rumbled his chest. "They were pretty good, too."

"That would be just about perfect."

"Whatever you want." He whispered the words as he bent down to kiss her forehead. "Anything you want. For the rest of our lives."

Smiling, she closed her eyes as he opened the door. She wasn't expecting a vision, but then, she seldom did.

The front porch swing moved lightly under her on the porch of a large white house. She was drinking iced lemonade from a tall glass. It was hot and muggy, a typical late summer day. She was smiling as she watched Rick pushing a small blond girl of about four on the tire swing hung from the branch of an old pin oak in the side yard. The girl squealed with delight. "Higher, Daddy! Higher!" she ordered.

The tire spun, giving her a good look at the child. She had Josette's round face and sturdy build. But she had her father's golden eyes, and . . . she smelled of fur.

There were tears in her eyes when Rick came back in the room. He dropped the platter to the floor with an unholy clatter when he saw her face, and a golden fish flopped onto the carpet. Ignoring the mess, he hurried to her bedside and dropped to one knee.

"Are you all right? Should I get Amber? What's wrong?"

"Nothing's wrong." She smiled through her tears, reaching for his hand. "I just need to know, do you still want children?"

Rick didn't pick up on the hint. Instead, he looked

at her with serious eyes. "I love you. I've always loved you, and I always will. The years when we were together were the best of my life. I want that again, want to be with you."

"What about children?"

"Josette, I've been sitting in this chair for days thinking about this. I probably *do* have children out there somewhere. And even if I don't, *this* is more important. *You* are more important. I know that the assassins will keep coming after you. But we can face them and whatever else life brings us together. Come back to me, Josette. Be my wife. I don't care if we have children, or if we don't."

Tears filled her eyes. She loved him so much. "All right. Just so long as you don't *mind* my having our daughter. And if it's all right with you, I'd like to name her Ellen."